CAPTAIN OF HER HEART

BARBARA DEVLIN

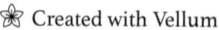 Created with Vellum

This book is dedicated to the captain of my heart, my husband Mike, although he has since promoted to battalion chief.

LADY ALEXANDRA IS
GOING AFTER HER MAN.

PROLOGUE

The Ascendants
England
The Year of Our Lord 1314

"To Aristide and Dionysia." Arucard and Demetrius sat in a dank tavern and toasted the latest nuptials to grace the Nautionnier Knights of the Brethren of the Coast. "May they enjoy the blessings of their union, as do Isolde and I."

"And as I am favored with my Lily." Demetrius winked. "Along with the little one, which grows in her belly with each new day."

"You have my sincere congratulations. And Lily is the pet name you chose in place of Athelyna?" Arucard grinned, as he recalled the drama that preceded his brother's ceremony. "The lady finds it amenable?"

"Indeed, she does." Demetrius waggled his brows. "That was the best piece of advice you ever—what in God's bones is he doing hither?"

"Who?" Arucard peered over his shoulder and started. "Aristide?"

"Good eventide, brothers." The bridegroom frowned and straddled the bench. "May I join ye?"

"Of course." Demetrius scooted to the side. "Are you all right?"

"Wherefore do you ask?" Aristide propped his elbow on the table, rested his chin in his palm, and cast a mighty scowl.

"Your forehead bleeds, as does your hand." Arucard tossed him a napkin. "Have you had an accident?"

"Is Dionysia injured?" Demetrius inquired.

"My delicate wife is most assuredly well." Aristide snorted. "And she is a red-haired hellion in hiding, which I would not wish on my worst enemy."

"What happened?" Arucard fidgeted when his fellow knight swept aside his hair, revealing a nasty, oozing gash. "Did you not heed my guidance?"

"I most certainly did, and I blame you for this." Aristide flinched as he pressed the cloth to his flesh to staunch the crimson flow. "Everything progressed nicely, until I engaged her in conversation. Really, there should be a codebook to decipher such confounding behavior."

"What did you tell her?" Searching his memory, Arucard inventoried his sage advice intended to smooth the shark-infested waters known as virgin territory. "Did I not counsel you to keep fledgling chatter elementary, before breaching her maidenhead, because it can be very traumatic?"

"For her or for me?" Aristide pounded the tabletop. "As I may never recover from this night."

"Give us the whole of it, brother." And then Demetrius

ordered an additional tankard of ale from a passing bar wench. "Start from the beginning."

"For what it is worth, because the damage is done." Aristide pinned Arucard with a lethal glare. "As you suggested, I endeavored to discern the history of my blushing bride with a few well composed queries, which I took the liberty of contriving on the eve of our union, as a prelude to the consummation of our vows."

"How romantic you make it sound, brother." Demetrius clucked his tongue. "Did I not counsel you that women require the stuff of poets to set the proper mood?"

"Yes, but in our brief meetings prior to the ceremony, Dionysia struck me as a woman of uncommonly good sense, so I saw no need to dress my language in perfume and flowers." He sneered. "She prefers honesty and forthrightness, or so she claimed, and I foolishly accommodated her request."

"That was your first mistake, because women rarely confess what they mean, and we are left to interpret their true substance." Arucard chuckled. "So what did you say to her?"

"Well, she delved into my reasons for entering the matrimonial state." Aristide scratched his cheek. "Given her professed proclivity for candor, I detailed the King's precepts, including the bequeathed earldom, which necessitated our engagement."

"Are you out of your mind?" Demetrius spewed ale. "Never do you acknowledge to your wife that the Crown forced ye to wed her. Have we taught ye naught?"

"You are lucky she did not kill you." Arucard rolled his eyes, as he suspected his friend had committed a fatal error, from which he might never rally. "Isolde would have skinned me alive, had I ever apprised her of such verity in our honeymoon period."

"Do you mean, in the years since ye married her, you have never enlightened your bride to the truth surrounding your nuptials?" Blinking, Aristide choked and sputtered, as he rubbed the back of his neck. "But how could ye avoid it? Has she never inquired?"

"Actually, Isolde is an intelligent woman, and she brought no illusions of romance to the altar, as she was fully aware of our arranged status, much to my regret. But the word 'force' never entered our bedchamber, and therein lies the difference." Arucard frowned, as he recalled his wedding night. "Brothers, you know her history, so you must understand my reluctance to cause her additional pain. We did not discuss the events preceding our vows, until she broached the subject. By the time she ventured to mention it, I had already professed my undying love and devotion, so the preface to our married life mattered not, in the grand scheme."

"Damn nasty affairs." Aristide glowered and gazed at the tabletop. "You are blessed, as she is a far better warrior than most men of my acquaintance."

"Given my impending fatherhood, I cannot fathom the level of violence to which her sire subjected his own daughter." Demetrius shook his head. "This land and its customs remain quite foreign to me."

"There is violence in every corner of the world, brother." A shiver of dread traipsed his spine, as Arucard revisited the tragic circumstances that marked the early months of his marriage. "Yet the hardships we endured strengthened our union and helped me realize how deeply I care for her, as I would give my life to save hers."

"And are you likewise afflicted?" Aristide asked Demetrius.

"Aye." Demetrius cast a ghost of a smile. "Lily holds my heart, above all else. And, much as Arucard, the path to that discovery was paved with treachery, as the matrimonial state is filled with vicious traps, none of which are marked."

"For the sake of curiosity, not that I am seriously intrigued, just how long did it take to experience said emotion?" Aristide leaned forward and cleared his throat. "And how did you know ye were in love?"

"Oh, I shudder to consider it." Demetrius pressed a clenched fist to his chest. "Love is, by far, the most confusing, excruciating, gut-wrenching, agonizing terror you will ever endure. I would equate it with Prometheus chained to the rock and the eagle's daily liver feast."

"How charming." Aristide blanched.

"Indeed, he is correct in his assertion, as it is worse than anything you might confront in battle." Arucard winced, as memories of the first pangs of love still horrified him. "And yet, once you surrender the fight and accept it, naught compares to the unutterable contentment that accompanies your wife's declaration, freely bestowed, as it is a priceless treasure."

"In that, I agree." Demetrius dragged his knuckles along his jawline. "Naught makes a husband feel more a man than his bride's requited affection, such that I cannot describe it, as there are no adequate words, and love is worth the cost it exacts. In short, it is a boon *sans pareil*."

"And if one were interested in fostering a similar commitment with his spouse, how might he attempt such lunacy?" Aristide swallowed hard and shifted his weight. "Given he has admitted, however well intended, the King forced the bridegroom to the altar?"

"Now that is a question for which I have no answer." Demetrius furrowed his brow and massaged his temple. "As even I knew better than to attempt such madness, and your transgression vastly exceeds the propitious potential of favored flowers."

"Are you not the witty knight?" Aristide moped and slumped his shoulders. "Brothers, how am I to survive the mess I have made?"

"Are you fond of Dionysia?" Arucard braced to pose the most important query, as the response would determine Aristide's future. "Do you find her attractive?"

"Her carriage is first rate, her teeth are in excellent condition, and she has a fine figure." Aristide downed his ale and signaled for a refill. "And she possesses a sense of humor and cleverness, which I find rather appealing."

"And what about the scar?" Demetrius asked. "I have heard countless jokes—"

"It bothers me not, and if you ever disparage her in my presence, I will tie ye to my rudder and drag ye back to France." Aristide yanked the collar of his tunic. "In all honesty, I scarcely notice the damn thing, as my Dion's beauty stems from an innate purity of the heart, and I delight in her company, tonight excepted."

"Dion?" Demetrius glanced at Arucard and smirked. "So you have gifted her a pet name?"

"I beg your pardon?" Clearing his throat, Aristide speared his fingers through his hair. "It is naught. Make no assumptions, which would embarrass us, brother."

"And what does the lady call you?" Arucard queried in a low voice, as he muffled his chuckle.

"That is none of your concern." Aristide opened his mouth and then closed it. "Not that she summons me with such sentimental nonsense."

Arucard and Demetrius burst into laughter, and Aristide shoved away from the table and stood.

"Hold hard, brother." After one last guffaw, Demetrius jerked Aristide to the bench. "Why run away, when we might aid your virtuous cause?"

"You have done enough." Aristide wrenched free. "I had gained precious ground with my bride, and then I listened to you and struck breakers."

"Now that is not fair." Arucard pointed for emphasis. "Never did I encourage you to apprise your lady of the conditions compelling ye to wed, as I know well the consequences of such ignorance."

"Then wherefore did you not warn me?" Aristide spat.

Arucard thrust his chin. "Perchance because I thought ye smarter than that."

"Brothers, we fight each other," Demetrius stated, with a grin. "And we are not the enemy."

"He is right." Arucard nodded once. "When it comes to the sexes, we are of like minds."

"I concur, brother." After an audible exhale, Aristide examined the injury to his knuckles. "So how am I to correct the situation?"

"Mass quantities of compensatory groveling, preferably delivered on your knees," Arucard suggested.

"And bundles of flowers, in every conceivable bloom," Demetrius urged.

"Ply her with wine." Arucard chortled. "But be careful, as too much will put her to sleep."

"And if that does not suffice?" Aristide asked.

"How is her aim?" Arucard replied.

"How do you think?" Aristide whisked the hair from his forehead and then displayed his wounded hand. "Lethal."

Demetrius grimaced. "Then you should pray—often."

"Should all else fail, it may simply be a matter of time, which requires the patience of a saint, before you and Dionysia grow as a couple." Arucard remembered the weeks, a seemingly bottomless pit of frustration, despair, and stout salutes from his mainmast, which preceded his own loss of virginity. "But if there is one glimmer of hope, you might take heart in the fact that only a husband is equipped to withstand such abuse."

CHAPTER ONE

The Descendants
Plymouth, England
January, 1813

*I*t was a well-known fact that men loved a good chase.

Whether the thrill of victory, or the possibility of defeat, lured them, the male species could always be counted on to rise to the occasion when properly baited. As far as Lady Alexandra Seymour, Alex to her friends and family, was concerned, the same could be said of the fairer sex.

Because she pursued her man.

A fortnight had passed since she had last seen her connubial conquest, Captain Jason Collingwood, and his unmistakable indifference had left her reeling. Despite hopes to the contrary, he had not attended the family holiday gathering, although she had posted a personal invitation, and had neglected to send her a present, after she had dispatched a sumptuous new coat of Bath superfine, custom-made for the captain of her heart—she would take that up with him when next they met. As the hastily hired traveling coach rocked along the road and entered Plymouth proper, she sank into the squabs and gazed out the window.

By all accounts, Jason should have tracked her, but the damn fool refused to adhere to her expectations, which she thought quite reasonable and sound. Regardless of her good intentions, gift, and profuse expressions of remorse, she surmised he remained angry, in relation to a trivial matter of no consequence, which had occurred during the previous Little Season.

But I am for Plymouth. And you may go to the devil.

All right, perhaps the situation signified more than she had realized. She cautioned herself that the words her captain had chosen to bid her farewell on the docks at Deptford were born of injured pride, nothing more. Was it not past due for him to move beyond her minor error in judgment?

"Ho-hum." With a sigh, she shook her head and frowned.

Last autumn, she had enlisted Jason's aid in a scheme of the heart. Cara Douglas, one of Alex's oldest and dearest chums, had longed to capture the attention of Lance Prescott, another of Alex's lifelong friends. Consistent with most men in similar circumstances, Lance had resisted Cara's romantic endeavors, so Alex had recruited Jason to enact a mock-courtship, in an attempt to incite Lance and inspire him to admit his love.

But Alex had omitted a few key details when she secured Jason's cooperation, such as the true identity of the suitor, in question, and the fact that Cara had rejected Lance's initial offer of marriage. In Alex's defense, there had been no nefarious motives involved, other than to bring a mulish male to his senses, as she honored Cara's request for discretion. And although Cara had deviated from their original plan, in the end, love found a way, and Lance and Cara had married in December.

Now Alex could only pray her quest to help two friends to the altar had not cost her the captain of her heart. With a violent shudder, she recalled the first time she had set eyes on the handsome naval man. In the middle of a crowded ballroom at Richmond House, she had been summoned by Lady Rebecca Wentworth, as was.

"Lady Alexandra Seymour, may I present Captain Jason Collingwood of the Royal Navy."

Standing over six feet, with guinea-gold hair and impossibly blue eyes, the man epitomized the blonde Adonis of her dreams. Festooned with braided epaulets, which marked his rank, only the exceedingly handsome male specimen surpassed the impressive regimentals. And an unfamiliar quiver blossomed in the pit of her belly, as the world pitched and rolled beneath her feet, when they locked gazes.

"My heavens, you are a captain?" Alex noted the gooseflesh shivering over her arms and extended her gloved hand. "And what ship do you command?"

"The Intrepid, and call me Jason, if I may be so bold." He bowed with a flourish, which drew several audible sighs from nearby young ladies, before squeezing her fingers and brushing a chaste kiss to her covered knuckles. "I am honored to make your acquaintance, Lady Alex. May I say that never have I seen anything so lovely as you in your red gown? Please know that both I and my vessel are at your service."

Scandalous.

Alex inhaled a sharp breath, as pulse points ignited, and she feared she might swoon.

She should have been offended.

She should have been outraged.

Instead, she found him...intriguing, a point in fact of which she suspected he was well aware, given Jason surveyed her from top to toe, as if he knew how she looked in her chemise. Slowly, very slowly, he smiled a wicked smile—matched by hers, no doubt.

"Shall we dance?"

How Alex lamented the bittersweet memory, because what had followed his elementary request had been a full-scale assault on her faculties. When Jason had slipped his arm about her waist, and he held her close, Alex had been giddy with unfamiliar but enticing excitement. Imaginary bells had sounded a carillon in her ears, delicious fire had simmered beneath her skin, and she had trembled with each successive turn about the room. To her embarrassment, she had tripped more than once, as no man had ever affected her thus.

In that moment, Alex set her cap for Jason Collingwood.

"My dear Captain, we could have such a wonderful life, if only you would do your part," she said to no one. "Must I do everything to further our relationship?"

The situation, as it stood, remained intolerable, as she had to make Jason understand they were destined for each other. And while his foul disposition, directed at her, of late, might prove useful when commanding his crew, he sometimes gave her a headache. So nagging uncertainty rested on her shoulders, as the weight of the world.

"I must be strong." In that instant, she studied her quavering fingers and emitted a plaintive cry. "Oh, Jason. I would fight Napoleon, himself, to win your love."

Determined to stay her course, Alex gave her attention to the snow-dusted landscape of the bustling seaport. Located in the county of Devon, and facing the western end of the Channel, Plymouth hosted a prominent naval base from which many expeditions launched against France, which seemed an appropriate place for her to wage a war of hearts.

And it was just around the corner, at Devonport, the main dockyard and shipbuilding facility of the British Navy, where Jason's ship, the *Intrepid*, berthed for refitting and duty under letters of marque from the Lord High Admiral. The new commission completed the well-played ruse as Jason embarked on his first solo mission for the Brethren of the Coast, a mysterious band of mariners who served the Crown in secret.

It was Jason's recent accomplishment that entrenched her belief that the hesitant captain was fated to be hers, because as a young girl Alex had often fantasized she was the wife of a knight from the famed order descended of the Templars, the warriors of the Crusades. Her father, God rest him, had once been counted among their esteemed ranks, but unlike Cara, Alex could never fathom marrying a member of the much-fabled nautionniers, because she considered them brothers. As a newcomer initiated into the order, Jason manifested the answer to her prayers.

If only he shared her perspective.

The coach came to an abrupt halt, which sent her tumbling to the floor, and she realized she had arrived at her destination. Before her breach in feminine deportment was discovered, she regained the bench and smoothed her skirts, just as the footman opened the door.

As Alex stepped to the unpaved drive, she scrutinized the little thatched cottage, which nestled amid a copse of formidable oaks. A pebbled walkway led to the entry, which had been painted a vivid green and contrasted with white-washed walls. At either side of the entrance loomed the thorny skeletons of rosebushes, which stood dormant in winter, and bare flowerbeds.

"Where should we leave your trunk, Miss Seymour?" The coachman addressed her informally, as she had not apprised him of her true identity.

"A moment, please, and I shall inquire." Without fear or hesitation, Alex marched straight up the path, grabbed the knocker, and pounded hard on the door. And then nagging doubt nipped her heels.

Painful seconds ticked past, as she considered the tenor of her welcome. Would Jason express unbridled elation or toss her on her backside? Biting her lip, she spared a quick glance at her escort, just as the latch turned with a mighty creak, and the oak panel opened to reveal a very attractive young woman.

Even as Alex sank into a dark vortex of shock and misery, she splayed her arms for balance. "I am sorry to disturb you, but I must have the wrong address."

"It is no trouble, ma'am." Dressed in a worn gown of faded print muslin, with a disheveled braid draped over her shoulder, the fair-haired beauty blinked. "Are you looking for Captain Collingwood?"

"Yes." As the world seemed to spin beyond her control, Alex thought she might revisit her breakfast. "Is this not his lodging?"

"Oh, the captain resides here, but he is at the yard." The girl wiped her hands on a threadbare apron and nodded once. "I am Molly, the cook-maid. And how may I help you?"

"I am Miss Seymour—the captain's sister." The charwoman presented a snag Alex had not foreseen, and she had to think on her feet. "Has Jason not spoken of my visit?"

"Cap'n never mentioned a sister, ma'am. But then we do

not converse much." Molly sketched a half-curtsey. "So pleased to meet you."

"I am certain my brother has more pressing matters, including the refitting of the *Intrepid*, or some such." With renewed confidence, Alex waved to the footman, who hauled her trunk toward the cottage. "Daresay it slipped his mind."

"Indeed, ma'am. I rarely see Cap'n Collingwood, as he is usually gone when I arrive, and I leave his dinner on the range before he returns. Not much time for talk." And then Molly retreated. "Will you come inside?"

Tugging at her kidskin gloves, Alex crossed the threshold and surveyed the meager surroundings. "Why, it is charming."

The main room was huge, with a high ceiling and exposed roof supports. The spartan furnishings consisted of an unmatched overstuffed chair and sofa, which were clean but frayed about the edges. Twin side tables perched at either side of the sofa, the well-worn wood floor had nary a speck of dust or dirt, and two tattered wool rugs distinguished the living area from the kitchen.

A delightful hearth occupied the middle of the side-wall, with an old black stove situated to the left. A large washbasin inhabited one corner, and a square table and chairs for two hugged a window, which overlooked the drive.

"Where shall I deposit your trunk, Miss Seymour?" The footman paused in the entryway.

"My bedchamber will be fine." Alex gazed at the charwoman. "Can you show me to my quarters, Molly?"

"I beg your pardon?" The young woman stammered, as she shuffled her feet. "Your quarters, ma'am?"

"Yes." Alex clasped her hands, as her plan progressed to

perfection. "Where do I sleep? And I should like to change from my traveling dress."

"Perhaps your brother forgot to inform you this cottage has only one bedchamber." The maid shifted her weight. "Do you suppose Cap'n intended for you to take a room at the inn?"

Alex had not anticipated that none too minor hiccup. In truth, she had not known what to expect of Jason's rented accommodations, but she had envisioned the usual palatial dwelling—a grand house, with chambers aplenty and a dependable staff. While the minuscule abode possessed unvarnished appeal, it was rather rustic for her taste, and it was a vast deal less than she required.

Facing the concerted and perplexing stares of Molly and the footman, Alex sought a suitable rejoinder, as she had to rid herself of the meddlesome interlopers before Jason returned and found her waiting, because she was not half so assured of her welcome.

"My brother is quite the gentleman, so I am positive he would want me to have privacy, and Jason will sleep on the sofa." Even as she uttered the pathetic claim, because it was obvious the piece of furniture could never support Jason's outstretched frame, Alex braced for a lightning strike.

"If you say so, ma'am." Casting a doubtful glance at the object in question, Molly walked to a rear door. "This way, please."

A decent-sized bed laden with timeworn quilts and down pillows held pride of place in the adjoining suite, if she could call it that. A single night table sat just to the left, with a small wash area to the right. Yes, her captain was a fastidious sort. Beyond an arched doorway posited a dressing room, including a chest and an armoire.

With a smile, Alex entered the closet and claimed a coat

from a wall peg. Fingering a mother-of-pearl button, she summoned heartwarming images from the past, when Jason had draped the frock over her shoulders, after she had been caught in the rain with Cara. With the wool pressed to her cheek, she closed her eyes and inhaled his signature sandalwood scent.

"Shall I unpack your trunk, Miss Seymour?" the charwoman asked in a small voice.

"Please, do so." Alex returned the garment to the peg and then peered from side to side. "Tell me, Molly, if there is only one bedchamber, where does the valet sleep?"

"The valet, ma'am?" Molly blinked.

"Indeed." Alex noted the tattered rug at the footboard and decided it would have to be replaced. "You know, Jason's manservant? Does he reside elsewhere?"

"I am sorry, Miss Seymour, but Cap'n has no valet." Molly propped open the lid on the trunk. "I believe he tends himself."

"Oh?" A chill of unease danced a merry jig down her spine. "So you are the sole servant Jason employs?"

"Yes, ma'am." Molly bent to set a pair of slippers on the floor. "Cap'n hired me to clean the cottage, wash his clothes, and prepare his evening meal. To my knowledge, he takes care of everything else."

Now that manifested another kink in her grand scheme. Given her hasty flight from London, and the deception upon which her plan relied, Alex had departed sans lady's maid. Perhaps Jason could tie and untie her laces, as that might aid her campaign to win his heart.

So as Molly smoothed the wrinkles from various gowns, Alex escorted the footman to the door and bade him farewell, with instructions to return at her written summons. And then she waved to the driver, as the coach lurched forward and eventually disappeared in a cloud of dust.

As she reassessed her bucolic accommodations, for which she had been entirely unprepared, Alex supposed she could cry. Yet she recalled her married Brethren sisters had confronted similar, if not worse, circumstances when they wagered everything for love.

In an attempt to evade the parson's noose, Caroline had stowed away aboard Dalton's ship, whereupon Trevor mistook her for a courtesan and kidnapped her. Sabrina had spent a summer transforming herself into a true English lady to win Everett. And only last year, Cara had thrown caution to the wind and seduced Lance. At long last, Alex understood their motivation, carefully inscribed in the Brethren oath.

For love and comradeship we live.

In the end, each lady had married the man of her dreams, only after they had breached the limits of polite society, and Alex resolved to follow in their successful paths. So for her, there was no going back. For good or ill, she had crossed her Rubicon.

THE SUN HAD SUNK WELL below the yardarm, when Jason steered his mount toward the single-stall stable at the rear of the cottage he had rented, while repairs to the *Intrepid* were completed. After securing the horse, he tugged off his gloves as he rounded the side of the house. It was then he noticed smoke billowing from the chimney.

"Bloody hell." Jason hastened his stride. "How many times have I told that harebrained girl not to leave a fire burning in the hearth? Does she wish to destroy my home away from home?"

And then it occurred to him that Molly might still labor at her chores, given he had amassed a mountain of mending for the efficient charwoman. At the front entrance, he tried the knob, but the bolt had been set, so he drew a key from his waistcoat pocket and unlocked the door. When he crossed the threshold, he rapped his knuckles to the oak panel.

"Molly?" He glanced left and then right. "Are you there?"

A roaring blaze warmed the room, against the chilly night air, a stewpot sat on the stove, and a tempting aroma teased his nose and his belly, as Jason shrugged from his greatcoat and tossed it over the back of a chair.

After loosening the laces at each wrist, he inched up his sleeves and walked to the washstand in the corner. As he lifted a pitcher and filled the basin, he peered over his shoulder. The house was as silent as a tomb.

"I suppose I shall have to speak with Molly." He huffed a breath, grabbed a bar of soap, worked a thick lather, and scrubbed his face. With a healthy splash of water, he rinsed away the suds and then, with eyes closed, he reached for a towel.

"Good evening, Captain of my heart."

Jason froze.

The world as he knew tilted in a violent shift, which left him reeling. Dizzy, he breathed into the cloth and told himself he had not heard what he had just heard. To gain a measure of stability, he dropped the towel and rested both hands at either side of the basin.

"Will you not welcome me to your humble abode?"

And there it was, his downfall, the sultry, throaty voice

that never failed to rouse his Jolly Roger, which woke with a vengeance just then. With his stare fixed on the wall, he swallowed hard. "Alex? Is that you?"

"You were expecting someone else?" She giggled, and his knees buckled.

Stiffening his spine, Jason marshaled his wits and turned to address his unforeseen guest. As he gazed at the woman he had spent the better part of a fortnight envisioning in his bed, pulse points fired, and his loins ignited. "What are you doing here?"

"That is not the most flattering reception I have ever received." Inclining her head, she cast him the flirty pout that always bent him to her will, and such knowledge bolstered his defenses. "I seem to recall you are far more skilled at greetings, sir. Have you not missed me? I have missed you."

Gowned in burgundy silk, his favorite color, a point of fact she knew well, with her brown locks piled high in carefree curls, Alex could rival the most skilled courtesans in England. In an act of infinite unfairness, she exuded an air of sexual prowess no woman of gentle breeding should possess, and coupled with her beauty, she was lethal. The French perfume she wore enticed his senses—well, not his senses, but another more prominent part of his anatomy.

Jason was undone.

Before he realized he had moved, he had crossed the room. In mere seconds, he drew Alex into his arms, and her soft curves melted against him. God, it felt good to hold her again. When their lips met, they ignited from the point of contact, until sumptuous heat cocooned them in their own private paradise.

With his hands, he revisited her shapely curves and pinched a pert nipple through the bodice of her dress, as he flicked and suckled her tongue. "Alex, how I have ached for you."

"And I you, Jason." And then she caressed his erection through his painfully constrictive wool breeches.

Emitting a sigh of unutterable delight, he rested his cheek to her hair, closed his eyes, and reveled in her touch. And then he wondered where his society maiden had gained such intimate knowledge, because he had never fortified her arsenal with that provocative education. In a flash, unanswered questions peppered his conscience and, thereby, deflated every inch of him.

Jason retreated, held Alex at arm's length, and scrutinized the dangerous debutante who tempted him beyond reason. Her chest heaved as she breathed in erratic pants, and she licked her kiss-swollen flesh.

"What is wrong?" She reached for him.

"Alex, just stand there, and do not move from that spot." With a few strides, he put much needed distance between them, so he could cool his blood. "I have not written, and I never apprised you of my whereabouts, so how did you find me?"

"Why are you avoiding me?" She appeared genuinely hurt. "You ignored my invitation to join us for the holidays, but I see you received my gift, and it suits you. Yet you sent me no present, in kind."

Jason opened his mouth to voice a denial but faltered.

Indeed, she was correct in her assertion, as he wore the expertly tailored garment at that very moment. It prevailed as his most favored accouterment because Alex had given it to him. And tucked in his waistcoat pocket, safe and snug, was the ring he had planned to bestow upon the woman he had intended to make his fiancée—until he learned of her deception.

"Answer my question." He rested hands on hips. "How did you find me?"

"Does it signify?" She lowered her chin. "I have traveled all the way from London, just to be with you. Are you not happy to see me?"

"I will have the truth, Alex."

"Oh, if you must." She stomped a foot. "I got your directive from Damian."

"What?" Jason scratched his temple. "Your brother knows you have journeyed unchaperoned to Plymouth?"

"Not exactly." Now she averted her gaze and garnered Jason's suspicion. "But you could allay any concerns regarding my lack of chaperone by doing the honorable by me, and I should be thrilled to accommodate you."

"Upon my word, but you are bold." And that singular characteristic was what drew him to her, as a bee to honey. "Out with it—now."

"If you must know, I obtained your address from my brother's estate ledger, when he spent the night at his bachelor lodging." She wrung her fingers. "And Damian most certainly does not know I am here, else he would heat my posterior."

"The truth, at last." And she piqued his curiosity as well as his ire. "So where does he believe you reside, at present?"

"I am sure he is not concerned." She scrutinized the hem of her sleeve.

"I will have the whole of it, Lady Alex." How could he ever trust her again?

"If you really must know, he thinks I am at Sabrina's." She huffed a breath.

"Conspiring again?" He ought to put her over his knee and spank her.

"No." She frowned. "I told Sabrina I retired to the country, with Elaine."

"And Elaine?"

"Presumes I am visiting Caroline."

"And Caroline?"

"Labors under the assumption that I chose to remain in London."

"Deceit comes easy for you." And inside him something shattered with that realization.

"Jason, please, let me explain." How sincere she sounded, yet she fooled him not. "I was motivated by good intentions, and I have apologized countless times. Will you never forgive me?"

"You claim good intentions, even as you dissemble?" He snorted. "Have we not been down this road?"

"But I only wish to set things right between us." Her shoulders slumped. "Is that not a noble cause?"

"By compounding your lies? You are mistaken if you think I am attracted to your ability to spin falsehoods." Now he found his stride. "I submit your moral compass is greatly skewed."

"When you put it that way, it sounds rather devious." Her chin quivered. "So this is my reward for all my hard work?"

"I do not mince words, Alex." Jason groaned. "And you think yourself deserving of a reward? I ought to tan your hide for this stunt."

"If it will improve our relations, then so be it." With the noble hauteur one would expect of the daughter of a duke, she stepped in his direction. "As must needs, I would gladly offer my bottom for your inspection."

"Oh, no." He sheltered behind the sofa, given her propensity to evade his defenses. "Keep away from me."

"But I only want to touch you." She favored him with a naughty grin. "You never complained before."

The inference, stark in its simplicity, brought an unfamiliar and unwelcome burn to his cheeks, as he had passed many evenings with Alex, engaging in inappropriate conduct in the gardens of some of London's most fashionable residences. And regardless of his outward demeanor, he cared for her, which is why her deception had devastated him.

At last, Jason relented. "Alex, why have you come here?"

"I already told you." She whisked a wayward tendril behind her ear. "I wish to make amends, and I shall obey your every command, if only you will give me a chance, so I might restore your good opinion."

"You never should have toyed with my favor, in the first place." How many nights he had tossed and turned, in torment, as a result of her game. "As long as I live, I will never understand how you could trifle with my affection."

"I never trifled with your affection, as I guard it with my life. But can you not comprehend loyalty, allegiance, or commitment to a longtime friend?" And then Alex had done something he hadn't foreseen. She retreated. "If you find such basic concepts foreign, if familial ties do not signify, then I should pack my trunk and summon my coach, as we do not suit, much to my displeasure and disappointment, and I have made a grave mistake."

How was it possible that the lady who had lied to Jason now made him feel a complete idiot? In truth, he should have known better than to challenge Alex. Any other woman would have cowered beneath his penetrating stare, while Alex had not the sagacity to blush.

"There is sufficient light for me to walk into the village." She turned on a heel. "I shall take a room at the inn."

"Wait." His lady halted but had not faced him, and he speared his fingers through his hair. "Are you sincere in your desire to set things right between us?"

"I am determined." She stiffened her spine. "If you will afford me the opportunity."

"And what have you to offer in your defense?" He needed to gauge her response. "How shall you entice me?"

"What would you have of me?" Alex whirled about and met his gaze, and he was shocked to spy tears in her blue eyes. "I will do anything to restore your faith in me."

Given her altered demeanor, which underscored a heretofore-nonexistent vulnerability, Jason mulled the possibilities. And then a brilliant idea shot to the fore, one that would provide a measure of recompense for his wounded pride, while exacting a well-deserved comeuppance for the inimitable but spoiled debutante.

"You may assist Molly in the household chores." Lowering his chin, he poised for her reply.

"I beg your pardon?" At first, Alex blinked, and then she sputtered. "You wish me to cook and clean, as a servant?"

"Indeed." As triumph surged in his frame, Jason smiled, because he had finally flapped the hitherto unflappable Lady Alex. "You might also aid with the mending pile, as I am rather rough on clothes."

"But I am unaccustomed to such work." The poor darling paled and appeared as if she might swoon. "And I am of noble blood."

"Then you should summon your coach, and surrender your ill-fated campaign, my dear." Not for a minute had he believed Alex would actually quit the field. "As I am no lord of the manor and hold no titles. As an ordinary man of the sea, I maintain an estate just outside London, and a home in Hampstead Heath. My properties are, no doubt, modest by your standards, thus my staff is small, as are my needs." Jason had baited the hook, and now he prepared to reel in his lady. "Perhaps you no longer fancy a union with me?"

"How dare you disparage my abilities, even as you make light of my regard?" With high dudgeon, Alex marched to stand toe to toe with him. "I can learn anything, when I set my mind to it."

He bit his tongue against laughter and shrugged. "If you say so."

"I do say." Her eyes flared. "Have no fear, as I shall meet your challenge, and you had better meet mine."

CHAPTER TWO

The hinges creaked, the door slammed shut, and Alex roused from a most pleasant but inappropriate dream, which featured her erstwhile fervent suitor in happier days. Rubbing the back of her neck, she yawned. "Jason, is that you?"

"No, ma'am." The charwoman sneezed. "It is I—Molly."

Bolting upright, Alex clutched the blanket to her chin. Just as quick, she winced, as a sharp pain in her lower back reminded her of the uncomfortable night spent on the sofa. "Good morning."

"Merciful heavens, what happened?" The petite cook-maid shuffled her feet, as she retrieved a broom. "Did Cap'n make you sleep in here?"

"Oh, no." Alex snatched her house slippers from the floor and slid them onto her feet. Then she scooted to the edge of the small sofa, dropped her legs over the side, stood, and stretched. In an instant, she flinched, as her body ached in places she never knew she could ache. "My darling brother was only too happy to surrender his bed, but I insisted he retain the use of his chamber, given his size and the fact that he must replenish his energy to oversee repairs to the *Intrepid*."

In that moment, Alex could have choked on her tongue, because nothing could have been further from the truth. The previous night, after sharing a painfully quiet meal, Jason had stormed into his quarters and slammed the door behind him. Seconds later, when he unlatched the bolt, she had allowed herself a scrap of hope, which he swamped beneath a pile of blankets and a pillow.

So the estimable captain had resolved to make the situation difficult for her, while she had anticipated otherwise. Much to her chagrin, his level of resistance, though somewhat admirable, was not normal. The stronger sex rarely refused Alex Seymour anything. With a playful bat of her lashes or a coy smile, she could bend the most stalwart man to her will. Even her brother Damian was susceptible to her tears, which she had deployed on occasions too numerous to count, for a wide variety of infractions, in order to save her posterior.

Yet Jason remained immune.

"Are you hungry?" Molly folded the blanket. "Shall I cook some breakfast, ma'am?"

"Please, do so." Alex nodded once, as she considered her predicament. "As I am famished."

"How do you prefer your eggs?" Molly stacked the bedding and pillow at one end of the sofa. "Scrambled, boiled, fried, or over easy?"

"Scrambled, please." She frowned, as she posited her next move. "And you must call me Alex."

At one time, prior to his engagement in Cara's plot to catch Lance, Jason had been Alex's most ardent pursuer. She had only to crook her little finger, and he came running. Now he seemed impervious to her powers of persuasion, so how could she reverse course?

"Would you like a slice of ham, Alex?" Molly tarried at the range.

"Yes, if it is not too much trouble." In silence, she revisited Jason's provocation.

"It will take only a minute to prepare." A hairsbreadth later, a tempting aroma filled the primary living space.

Studying the efficient cook-maid, Alex dissected Jason's words. Had he sought a wife capable of providing such basic services as cooking and cleaning? Or was his challenge a test of her mettle? Whatever the case, she would not fail. Regardless of his intent, she would prove herself worthy of his affection and a betrothal. After all, how hard could it be to complete such menial drudgery?

"Molly, I hate to be a burden, as you were hired to care for Jason, alone." Alex shrugged into her robe, belted it tight, and then strolled into the kitchen. "If you would teach me, I could assist in your duties."

"I beg your pardon?" Molly dropped her cooking utensil into the pan but quickly retrieved it. "No offense, ma'am, but you do not appear suited to charwork."

"In that I cannot argue." With a chuckle, Alex lingered at the servant's side. "But it is never too late to learn untried skills, and I pride myself in my willingness to attempt new occupations. And I should dearly love to confound my brother."

"I am not sure. You have very fine things, and I would hate to spoil one of your beautiful dresses." Molly furrowed her brow, peered at Alex, grabbed her hand, and skimmed her palm. "Just as I suspected. No calluses and soft as a baby's bottom. I would wager your beau prefers you as such."

"Perhaps we can broker an agreement, something that would benefit us both?" Alex retrieved a napkin and a fork from a drawer. "You admire my perfume. I shall make you a bargain. A bottle of France's finest scent, in exchange for your housekeeping expertise and best recipes."

"Oh, no. That is not necessary. If I help you, I will do so because I want to, not for personal gain." Molly frowned, as she seasoned the eggs and ham. "And Cap'n pays a fair wage."

"I have offended you." Alex retreated and retrenched. "I apologize, Molly, as I never meant to insult you. I had thought to reward your services, in kind."

"Have a seat at the table." Molly dished the meal. "And there is hot water in the kettle, if you wish to make tea."

"Perfect." Alex located a serviceable pot and a canister of tealeaves and then halted. "How much should I use?"

"You have never made tea?" Molly blinked. "You must live in a grand home, ma'am. And I am not certain it is proper for me to use your given name."

"Nonsense, as I am no snob." Alex picked up a spoon and opened the canister. "Now, how much tea for the pot?"

"Mother says the rule of thumb is a spoon for you and another for the pot." After conveying the plate to the table, Molly retrieved a cup and saucer from a small cupboard. "You should eat, before the food gets cold, ma'am."

"Will you not call me Alex?" She pulled out a chair and sat. "As I would dearly like us to be friends."

"Really?" Molly poured a cup of tea and passed it to Alex. "I have very few friends, as I do not socialize much, beyond my work or church on Sundays."

"How sad for you." Alex sipped the steaming brew and could have cried. "Oh, the tea is wonderful, and I made it, myself. I feel so powerful. You simply must show me everything, as I would prove to Jason that I am self-sufficient."

"All right." Molly chuckled and settled in the opposite seat. "I will make a trade, if you are willing."

"Name it, dear Molly." Alex attacked the eggs. "I am at your disposal."

"It is embarrassing to admit, but I am a strain on my parents, and I would marry before my younger brother and sister suffer." The charwoman stared at the floor. "As you seem a very fine lady, I wondered if you might help me catch a husband."

Alex choked violently.

"Is something wrong with the food?" Molly leaped to her feet, rounded the table, and smacked Alex on the back. "Are you ill?"

"Everything is delicious." Alex swallowed hard and downed a healthy gulp of tea. "You caught me by surprise."

"I am sorry." The cook-maid shifted her weight and tugged on her long braid. "Are you unfamiliar with the matter, as I know some may consider my request rather bold for a woman?"

"Oh, I am quite versed in bold behavior, Molly." If only the poor servant knew the truth. "So has a particular gentleman caught your fancy, or are you speaking in general terms?"

"There is someone special." Molly compressed her lips. "Tom Penniman, the stablemaster in Plymouth."

"How charming." Alex envisioned her sea captain and smiled. "Is he a man of character and good standing? And does he share your affection?"

"Everyone speaks well of him, and he brings me flowers every Sunday, after church." Molly refilled Alex's cup. "And thank you for your friendship. I must confess you are not what I expected when you appeared on the doorstep."

"Oh?" She recollected their initial meeting. "What did you presume?"

"I had thought you one of those London society ladies, who have no interest in maids beyond how we serve them, much less consider us people with feelings." Molly bowed her head. "I am sorry I misjudged you, as I should have known Cap'n would abide no snobbery in his kin."

"No, Jason would not." A chill shivered down Alex's spine, as Molly had provided food for thought. "So you must tell me all about your conquest, and I vow to bring him to his knees, in no time."

Molly gasped. "But I do not wish to injure him."

"I refer to a proposal, Molly." Alex giggled. "And it will not hurt your Mr. Penniman to kneel."

BY THE TIME Jason returned to the cottage that evening, he was exhausted. After securing his horse, he rounded the side of the small structure and then paused. Closing his eyes, he willed himself to resist the temptation Alex presented, but his body reacted to the mere thought of the brown-haired beauty.

Against his better judgment, he had allowed the source of his discomfit to remain at his rented lodgings, when everything inside him argued he should have sent her back to London. So why had he permitted her to stay?

Because Jason wanted Alex.

It was with that singular thought dancing in his brain that he entered his temporary residence and found the one person he desired most, sitting on the sofa, with a serious expression, and concentrating on a repair to a shirt. "Good evening, sweet lady."

"Hello, Jason—*ouch*." Wincing, she stuck her injured finger in her mouth, and all manner of naughty imaginings assailed him. "Is it possible to bleed to death from countless pinpricks? And how was your day?"

"Productive." He laughed. "And how about you? Have you assisted Molly with repairs to my clothes?"

"Actually, I completed the mending, myself, because Molly feared I might ruin one of my dresses." Alex held a shirt for his inspection. "She promised to bring a frock more suited to heavy labor, tomorrow."

"My compliments to the seamstress, as I can scarcely note the stitches." Then he slipped his hand inside the sleeve and pulled the garment taut. "Uh—Alex. We seem to have a minor problem."

"Oh?" She gazed at the lace-edged cuff. "Did I miss something? Is there another tear?"

"Not quite." With a chuckle, he held the sleeve for her scrutiny. "You sewed the end shut."

"What?" She wrenched and tugged at the fine lawn. "This cannot be possible. *Blast*."

Jason burst into laughter.

"And just what do you find so funny, Jason Colling-wood?" With an impressive scowl, she yanked the offensive item from his grasp. "After all my hard work and bloodshed."

"There, there, my dear." He surrendered to another fit of guffaws but quieted when she cast him a fiery glare. "It is only a shirt, and you are new to such work."

"Bloody hell." With a groan, she rummaged through the remainder of the mending pile, emitting one unladylike curse after another. "I repeated the same mistake on several sleeves. *Oh*—I attached the end of this collar to the other."

"Molly will help you set it right, in the morning." He patted her back. "Perhaps I should wash up, while you serve dinner."

"I will not ask Molly to correct my error, as this was my task, and I shall complete it if it takes until dawn." Crestfallen, Alex sighed. "And I did so wish to please you."

"You think me vexed?" For a scarce second, Jason pondered his next move, as he knew from past experience he could not be too careful with the delectable Lady Alex. With that in mind, he settled on a half-hug and then sought shelter at the washstand. "I am proud of your effort, love. Now dish our meal, as you should replenish your strength, if you intend to sew all night."

"You are horrible to make sport of my mishap." Alex stomped to the stove.

"Something smells delicious." Jason peered over his shoulder and winked. "Did you prepare the food?"

"No," she replied, with a precious pout, and he longed to bite her lip. "Molly cooked before she departed, but she pledged to teach me a few of her best recipes, later this week."

"Lord, save us." Jason rolled his eyes, as he could only conjure the potential for disaster. "Just try not to burn down the house."

"Blackguard, you take that back." Wielding a wooden spoon as a weapon, Alex bared her teeth. "I can do anything, if I am so inclined, and I am most definitely inclined, sir. Now not another word, or you will wear the contents of this pot."

Jason clamped his mouth shut and splayed his palms in mock surrender. And then they sat and ate in silence. How disarming Alex was as she glanced at the mending pile and furrowed her brow. And how it touched him that she cared so much for his good opinion. Perhaps there was hope for them. "Stop worrying about it."

"I can't." She drew her napkin from her lap, stood, and gathered the dirty dishes. "Once I have cleaned the kitchen, I shall redo the repairs."

"Alex, do not overtire yourself." He caught her by the wrist. "I will not have you waning, and it is enough that you tried."

"This was your idea." She snatched his plate. "And I will do it right, or I shall cede the fight."

And so Jason adjourned to his comfortable chair, lit a cigar, sipped his favorite brandy, and pretended to read the latest edition of *The Mariner's Mirror*. But Alex captured his attention to the detriment of all else.

Humming a flirty little ditty as she tarried, his not-so-pampered princess washed, rinsed, dried, and stowed the dishes and utensils. And as she toiled, she attacked, albeit unknowingly, every reason he had composed for delaying their betrothal—and of that there were many.

Never had Jason shared his concerns regarding marriage and war, as he believed the two inextricably intertwined, given his father's occupation, subsequent demise in battle, and Jason's mother's related heartbreak and death, soon after.

At the ripe old age of twelve, Jason had been orphaned. An elderly uncle had liquidated the humble estate and purchased a midshipman's commission in the navy, aboard the HMS *Perseus*, and Jason had gone to sea and never looked back.

But Lady Alexandra Seymour had changed everything from the moment he spied her in the Richmond's ballroom, bedecked in red velvet, as an enchanting seraph. Never had he seen anything so lovely, in his life, and the incomparable Lady Alex had struck a blow from which he might never recover.

"What is it about dishwater that makes my skin so dry?" With a grimace, she rubbed her hands. "And my nails may never be the same."

"Complaining already?" Jason chuckled, as he could not resist baiting her. "You may quit your campaign and return to London, at any time."

"I make an observation, you horrible man. Am I not allowed a measure of protest, given the circumstances? And I would remind you that Seymour's are made of sterner stuff." Alex sorted the clothing, assessing her various mishaps, and groaned with each new unfortunate discovery. "How could I have made so many mistakes? It will take all night to set it right."

"Shall I massage cream on your palms?" How he ached to touch her, and the mere suggestion woke the beast below his belly button.

"No, thank you." Alex plopped onto the sofa, grabbed the scissors, and attacked the stitches on a shirt. "I can take care of myself."

"My dear, I do not doubt you in the least." And then he flinched and shifted in his seat, as she ripped apart two haphazardly joined swaths of fabric with violence of which he had not presumed her capable.

With renewed focus on the quarterly maritime journal, Jason compressed his lips against laughter, as his heretofore-prissy debutante swore a blue streak that could make the crustiest sailor blush. The remainder of the evening passed in an awkward mix of uncomfortable, tension-filled silence interspersed with spontaneous invective. After a couple of hours, he yawned, stood, and stretched.

"The hour is late, and I am for bed." To his surprise, she portrayed no outward sign of acknowledgement, so he bent and placed a kiss on the crown of her head.

In an instant, Alex gasped and peered into his eyes, and what he spied in her blue depths had him reconsidering his intent to retire, as his loins erupted in flames. Tempting fate, he nudged her nose with his, and she trailed her little pink tongue along the sumptuous flesh he loved to suckle.

The walls fell away, the floor tilted beneath his feet, and the light from the fireplace and candles dimmed, as desire enveloped them. Alex glanced at his mouth and then returned her gaze to his, in an unspoken invitation. And how he longed to take what she offered—and more, without hesitation.

Warning bells pealed in his ears, and Jason retreated. "You should put down your mending and rest, as I have other shirts, thus my need is not pressing."

"I will sleep as soon as I complete my work." She frowned, and disappointment weighed heavy in her countenance, as she gave her attention to her task. "Goodnight, Captain of my heart."

And there it was, the familiar endearment he relished more than he was willing to admit. "Pleasant dreams, Alex."

With that, Jason found safe haven in his modest quarters, as he threw the bolt, not that he expected his errant society miss to accost him in the middle of the night—he should be so lucky. As a man on a mission, and he was most definitely of a singular mind, in seconds, he stripped naked, snatched a small towel from the washstand, and slipped between the sheets. Reclining amid the pillows, he draped the cloth over his crotch, blew out the candle, closed his eyes, envisioned his lady, and put four fingers and a thumb to most excellent use.

It was early the next morning when Jason, preparing to depart for the docks, entered the great room and found Alex sound asleep, sitting in the same position on the sofa. With her delicate features relaxed in repose, she could have passed for one of Botticelli's angels. But he knew better.

At her side, in a neat stack, his clothing had been sorted and folded. Without waking her, he picked up a shirt and examined her handiwork. Though he fancied himself no authority on sewing, never had he enjoyed such expert repairs, and it pleased him beyond words that his lady had taken such pride in her work. After pulling on his greatcoat, he bent, rested his palms at either side of her head, and studied the only woman who had ever inspired serious contemplation of a trip to the altar.

Her long brown hair had loosened from the severe topknot she had sported the previous night. The fine-boned, heart-shaped face, serene and sublime in slumber, often occupied his dreams. Classical features, finely arched brows, and a cute little nose had snared his interest at first sight, as had her curvaceous figure. And her mouth—now that exemplified perfection and begged for a kiss, something he had indulged on occasions too numerous to count.

But it was her blue eyes, piercing in their potency and fringed with the thickest black lashes, which had never failed to set him on his heels. With a single glance, regardless of intent, Alex could turn the most stalwart of men into a blithering idiot, and she quite took his breath away.

It was, perhaps, his uncontrollable reaction to the chestnut-haired beauty that had fascinated him from the moment they met. At the age of one and thirty, he had thought himself immune to feminine wiles. Given Jason had spent the greater portion of his youth at sea, his education in the sexual arts had taken place in dockside taverns, in the arms of some of the most hardened doxies in London and Jamaica.

As he amassed a sizable fortune in prize money, which he had invested with care, he purchased the favors of more refined courtesans. But the attachments never extended beyond expensive brandy, fine cigars, raw lust, and sordid acts no gently bred virgin would provide in her lifetime.

Or so he thought.

Alex had not simply altered his views but had blown his preconceived notions of society maidens out of the water. She pursued him with an unrivaled aggression and openness many men would kill to possess. And she would be his bride, but not yet.

Moved by a power impossible to deny, Jason pressed his lips to her forehead. "I am so proud of you, Alex."

As he retreated, he paused. Asleep, his lady appeared so innocent—so helpless. Temptation beckoned, even as he reminded himself no gentleman would take advantage of her oblivion. But he held no title, as he was a man of the sea.

So he bent and stole a kiss.

~

"OH, THIS IS TERRIBLE." Alex rubbed the back of her neck and winced. "I ache everywhere."

"You poor thing." Molly perused the various garments.

"Your work is very fine, but why did you not wait for me to help you?"

"Because I wanted to do it." And so she had, completing the repairs in the wee hours of the morning. But Alex would not complain, as the ensuing short rest included a most vivid dream, which featured Jason and a delicious kiss that gave her shivers whenever she thought of it. "Besides, given your extensive list of chores, I loathe compounding your tasks."

"Nonsense, as it is no bother, and this is my light day." The charwoman carried Jason's clothing into the dressing room. "I have only to wash the linens, scrub the floors, haul firewood into the bedchamber and kitchen, replenish the preserves, carry in fresh water for your bath—"

"That is quite enough." Alex stretched and yawned. "I should clean the floors, if you will teach me how to use a mop, and then I will assist in all your chores. And if I have overlooked anything, you must tell me, as I intend to assume my fair share of the labor, for the length of my stay. What's more, this afternoon, I shall fetch the water for my much-deserved bath."

"Do you think that wise, Alex?" The maid put away the last of Jason's garments. "You are new to housework, and you may not be able to move, tomorrow."

"Fear not, fair Molly." Alex lifted her chin. "I am stronger than I look." Of course, she had no idea what joy awaited her, as she commenced her toils.

First on her agenda was a date with a broom, and she swept a good dust storm in the small cottage, while the cook-maid boiled preserves. By the time Alex wrestled with the mop, blisters had formed on her palms, and twice she stepped into the bucket of water.

"Oh, and I have always considered myself a graceful

sort." Alex wrung the hem of her morning dress. "And I fear I have ruined my slippers."

"That is why I remove my boots, before I clean." Molly stowed the preserves and rested hands on hips. "And we need only put your slippers at the hearth to dry them."

"Will they not stain?" She could not wear soiled slippers.

"I know not." The charwoman shrugged. "Does it matter, as they are still serviceable?"

For the umpteenth time, Alex checked her opinion. Was it possible? Could it be true? Was she a snob? "I suppose not."

"And you brought several pairs, so you should designate these as your housecleaning slippers." With that, Molly slapped her thighs. "Now we should strip the bed, and wash the linens."

Once again, Alex plunged into the seemingly endless, dark vortex of misery and pain polite society had the nerve to call domestic work. After laboring over a large basin and a rather strange board contraption, which rendered her knuckles raw and her lower back a bottomless pit of hellfire and torment, Alex and Molly hung the sheets on a line to dry. Then the efficient maid explained how to make preserves, trim the wicks on candles to reduce smoke, and clean the windows.

"May I ask a question?" Weighted with a third load of logs, Alex huffed and puffed, as her arms screamed in protest from such foreign drudgery.

"Of course." Molly kept a brutal pace and whistled as she tarried.

"Why does Jason not collect his own firewood?" The man had better sing her praises, given her efforts.

"Cap'n usually does for himself." The charwoman all

but bounced with energy, as they rounded the side of the house. "But the stores are quite low, and it is my duty to maintain the cottage."

"I know not how you manage it." Alex checked her footing, as she almost tripped on an exposed root. "As God is my witness, when I return home, I shall give every member of my staff a raise in pay and a full day of rest, per week. And never again will I take them for granted."

Molly laughed and kicked the front door, which she had left ajar, and walked into the bedchamber to deposit her load. Following in her wake, Alex bent to relieve herself of her burden. When she stood, she snagged and then tore the hem of her dress on the wood.

"Oh, no." The cook-maid smacked her forehead. "How could I be so forgetful?"

"No worries." Alex inspected the damage. "After mending Jason's clothes, I can repair this, myself."

"That is not what I meant." With a frown, Molly disappeared into the great room. When she returned, she carried a garment. "I brought you one of my frocks, which I intended to give you before we commenced our chores. You are a bit thinner than I, so it should suffice."

"Then I should put it on, after my bath." Alex wiped her brow and sighed. "So, what is next?"

"We need only to replenish the kitchen barrel, boil some water, and fill the tub. Once you have enjoyed a good soak, which you have more than earned, I will braid your hair and teach you a recipe, as we cook dinner." With a mischievous grin, Molly asked, "So, are you familiar with a shoulder yoke?"

Alex gulped.

The odd looking contraption consisted of a wooden plank, which spanned the width of her shoulders, and buckets suspended from ropes at either side. Weighted with water drawn from the well, Alex engaged in a wicked waltz with what she would describe as a rudimentary torture device.

"The trick is in the timing and balance." Molly retreated but maintained close proximity, as if teaching Alex to walk. "Go slow."

"All right." Alex stepped gingerly, but the yoke was heavy and clumsy. She weaved left and then right, and then she surged forward. In an attempt to stabilize the contraption, she lurched. One bucket swung behind her, knocking her backward, and she landed hard on her bottom, just as the other pail soared, tipped upside down, and covered her head.

"My goodness." Molly freed Alex from the vicious contrivance. "Are you injured?"

"Just my pride." Alex squeezed the water from her hair and assessed the damage. "Well I may not require a bath, after my impromptu shower. Really, I am soaked."

The charwoman reached for the yoke. "Let me—"

"No." Holding the plank, Alex stood. "I made you a promise, and I intend to keep my word. Now, shall we try again?"

"As you wish." The cook-maid clucked her tongue. "My, but you are stubborn."

"Molly, you have no idea."

The second time proved the charm, as Alex navigated the deuced yoke with success, although she almost crashed at the doorstep. But the third rotation she navigated with nary a glitch, and at last the chores were completed.

When Alex sank into the tub, she could have cried, as the heretofore-simple pleasure had never felt so good. Enveloped in soothing warmth, she closed her eyes and conjured fanciful visions of her life as the wife of Captain Jason Collingwood. But she comforted herself in the knowledge that the blisters and muscle aches would be worth it, in the end, when she looked back on her adventure into housekeeping hell and what she had done for love. Wiggling her toes, she giggled. "I wonder where we will live?"

"I beg your pardon?" Molly inquired.

"Sorry." The fantasy Alex had woven with such care had vanished, in an instant, when she opened her eyes. "I did not know you were there."

"I hate to disturb you, but you must come out, now." Molly retrieved a towel. "That is, if you still hope to prepare Cap'n's dinner, under my direction."

"Oh, I do so wish to cook for Jason." Alex stood and stepped from the bath. "And I shall impart sage advice on how to attract a man."

"Do tell, dear Alex." The charwoman all but bounced.

After donning the well-worn printed muslin dress Molly had brought, Alex sat at the end of the bed and braided her hair in the maid's usual fashion. Later, she assumed an altogether foreign position before the stove and stirred delicious smelling gravy, which she had produced with valuable guidance.

"All right." Alex bent to check the bread in the oven. "So how shall you approach your Mr. Penniman, when next you meet?"

"I should incline my head, ever so gently, dip my chin, and gaze at Tom through my lashes." Molly demonstrated her newfound prowess. "How was that?"

"Perfect." Alex wiped her hands on her apron. "Such tactics have served me well, as I have often rendered Jas—I mean, gentlemen incapable of forming a coherent sentence."

Once Molly had departed for the day, with a gifted gown from Alex's belongings, Alex collected dishes and utensils from the cupboard and set the table. "Jason had better sing my praise for the effort I have expended today."

And no sooner had she uttered the statement than the man in question strode through the door.

"Good evening, Alex." Jason shrugged from his great-coat and hung it on a wall peg. "How was your day?"

"Very enlightening." Not to mention painful, but her travails were worth their weight in gold in anticipation of his commendation regarding her hard work.

"Upon my word." He surveyed the surroundings. "Everything looks shipshape. Molly outdid herself."

Alex could have strangled him.

CHAPTER THREE

*H*ow was it possible for a woman to possess provocative toes? As Jason entered the little cottage he shared with Alex, he found her standing, barefooted, before the stove.

Wearing one of Molly's old dresses, a modest frock with a frayed lace collar, and with brown locks woven in a single braid and draped over her shoulder, Alex could have passed for a servant to the undiscriminating eye. Until she cast a charming glance and favored him with a coy smile, which underscored her patrician features and never failed to set his heart racing.

"Good evening, Captain of my heart." How he loved her welcome, delivered in the sultry tone that ignited a raging inferno in his loins. "Are you hungry?"

Oh, yes.

But not for food.

The well-honed control he had spent Sunday afternoon fortifying with the best ale at the Blood and Swash tavern fled him in a scarce second. Gazing heavenward, he doffed his greatcoat and prayed she would not notice his animated

Jolly Roger, as it was dangerously jolly and only too ready to lay siege to her virgin field.

Six days had passed since the inimitable Lady Alex had arrived on his stoop, and he had yet to bed her. Either his halo shimmered, or he had lost his mind, as both were possible, given the circumstances.

Temptation personified, he considered Alex a prime piece, bedecked in the latest fashions money could buy. With her hair coiffed atop her head or in a fountain of care-free curls, and an expensive gown accentuating her generous curves, the society maiden's attire served as a potent reminder of her status and kept the beast at bay.

But the new Alex, the provincial ragamuffin, tested the limits of his sanity and his breeches, as he found her unutterably irresistible. Had she paraded about the ton's ball-rooms in such garb, she would incite a riot. The thick braid evoked images of his Alex, sans clothing, engaged in a tanta-lizing impersonation of Lady Godiva, and he vowed, right then and there, to one day enjoy that fantasy, in truth.

"You should wash for dinner."

Jason blinked. "I beg your pardon."

"Our meal is ready." The object of his affection and the source of his discomfit carried two plates to the table. "Do you not intend to wash before we dine?"

At that moment, there was only one thing he desired, and it had nothing to do with the meal. Bolstering his defenses, Jason walked to his lady, rested a hand at the small of her back, and stared into her blue eyes. When Alex trailed her tongue across her rosy lips, he stopped short of his destination, as it was a ploy for which he had fallen on occasions his pride had not allowed him to count.

"Dinner smells delicious." Given her duplicity, he ques-tioned everything about her, so he dropped his hand to his side and cleared his throat. "Did you cook this, all by yourself?"

"Indeed." How sincere she seemed, as she gushed beneath his meager praise. "After you departed this morning, I trapped and skinned the rabbits, just as Molly taught me. And I followed her recipe for hare stew, to the letter."

"Ah, my favorite." No doubt the astute Lady Alex had seized upon that information and hoped to capitalize on his favor. Jason poured water into the corner basin and scrubbed his hands and face. "By the by, have you misplaced your slippers, or have you started a new trend?"

"Oh, that?" She shrugged. "Molly prefers to complete her chores without shoes, and I must profess equal fondness for the habit."

"You are comfortable?" He pulled out her chair and then settled himself in the opposite seat. "Are you not cold?"

"Not in the least." She draped her napkin across her lap and then paused. "Tarrying over a hot stove keeps me plenty warm."

Then Alex leaned forward and compressed her lips, and he realized she waited for him to sample her fare. So with heightened expectancy, Jason picked up his fork and speared a generous bite. To relish the experience, he held the sample in his mouth—and almost gagged. The temperature singed the tip of his tongue but not so much to temper the stomach-churning taste.

In a flash, he bent and spat the repulsive morsel to the plate. To mitigate the foul flavor, he grasped a pint of ale and gulped half the contents.

"What is wrong?" With shock investing her expression, Alex gasped. "Do you not like it?"

"Bloody hell." Shuddering, Jason set down his fork and

took another swill of ale to erase the persistent hint of the offensive concoction. "Alex, just how much sugar did the recipe suggest you put in this stew?"

"Sugar?" His society miss wrinkled her nose and snickered. "Silly man, you do not put—*oh*. Please, do not tell me I mistook the sugar for salt."

"Do not fret, love." He snorted and then burst into laughter. "I am sure it could happen to anyone, as they are both white."

"Perhaps I can set it right? It may only require the addition of salt to counteract the sweetness." Her mouth fell agape, when he snatched her plate from the table and stood. "Wait—what are you doing?"

"This fare is fit for neither man nor beast." Jason dumped their portions into the pot, which he then carried outside. With a hearty heave-ho, he tossed the food to the ground. "Woe the poor creature that stumbles upon your odious feast."

"You are horrible to make fun of me." Alex folded her arms and loitered in the doorway.

"No, your stew is horrible, and I am honor-bound to save us from it." He halted at the edge of the stoop, as their respective positions brought them almost eye-to-eye. In a single swift move, he twined her braid in his hand and gently tugged. "But I am proud of you, love."

"Proud of what? Regardless of my hard work, I produced an inedible meal unworthy of praise." She mustered a precious pout and lowered her chin in defeat, and he claimed a whisper of a kiss. "And I did so wish to please you."

"Darling Alex." Jason pulled her closer and rubbed his nose to hers. "What matters is that you tried."

And then in defiance of his instincts, he freed her braid,

wrapped an arm about her waist, claimed her mouth in a sumptuous assault, carried her into the house, and kicked the door shut behind him, without ever breaking contact. After dropping the empty pot to the table, Jason unleashed his hands, resting a palm to her delectable derriere and the other at the nape of her neck. When he rocked his hips into hers, Alex favored him with a sultry moan, as their tongues dueled.

The erotic heat of his society maiden, coupled with her succulent lips, far more tempting than the sweetest confection, well nigh drove him insane. And when she wound her arms about his shoulders, and speared her fingers into his hair, he shifted his attention to her modest but accommodating dress.

In seconds, he perched in a chair, situated his lady in his lap, untied the ribbon at her bodice and chemise, and then bared one breast. At that point, he halted, only to discover Alex watched him. Why was he not surprised? So he pressed on her pliant flesh caresses intended to incite—to arouse. And he recalled the first time he had touched her thus, albeit through a heavy gown.

In the drawing room at Seymour House, in London, just prior to enlisting his aid in Cara's plan to catch Lance, Alex had caught his wrist and set his palm to her bosom. To his chagrin, he had assumed her silent plea indicative of a healthy desire for him. Now he wondered if her bold behavior had been nothing more than means to an end.

Holding her gaze, Jason licked her pert nipple, and his lady gave vent to a plaintive cry. Her cheeks flushed a lovely pink, yet she belied no hint of shyness, trepidation, or fear. So he repeated the decadent maneuver, but he lingered and suckled, as she bucked and wiggled, and his thighs erupted in flames.

To her credit, Alex never averted her stare, even as he teased her soft skin with gentle nips of his teeth, and in that moment he realized she wanted him. That knowledge worked on him in ways he could not have foreseen, and he turned it to his advantage. "Why did you not tell me the truth about Lance and Cara?"

"What?" She inhaled a shivery breath, as he sucked hard on her nipple. "*Jason.*"

"I want to know, Alex." Wielding his tongue as a weapon, he lured her into his trap. "I will have the whole of it."

"Because Cara begged me not to betray her confidence." She wrenched her head from side to side and then bit the fleshy part of her hand.

"And you value her affinity more than mine?" Again and again, he plied her with a licentious massage.

"No." With something between a sob and a sigh, she arched her back. "Jason—*please.*"

"Why did you lie?" With a flick of his wrist, he hiked her skirt and then walked his fingers to the honey harbor at the center of her core. When he found her warm and wet, he groaned and shifted his weight. "Out with it."

"I promised Cara, and I could not break my word." And then she emitted an achingly sweet cry. "I have known her since birth and you not half so long."

"So you acted out of loyalty?" Summoning the expertise of a lifetime, Jason played a masterful accompaniment with his hand and mouth. "And what of us? Am I nothing to you?"

"You are the captain of my heart." She twisted and turned to a heady mix of half-screams, moans, and sighs. "Had we an arrangement, I should have allied myself with you. But we have no understanding, so Cara claims my allegiance."

Even in the throes of passion, Lady Alex had made a convincing argument, and he could not dispute her logic, given her strong familial ties. The burden he had carried since discovering her betrayal seemed to vanish, and his thoughts seized on an altogether nobler goal. "Do you remember that afternoon we spent in the drawing room of your home?"

"Yes," she responded on a shivery exhale.

"Why did you encourage me?" He played an arresting drumbeat between her thighs, urging her ever higher, as he clenched his jaw and fought the beast in his breeches. "Were you curious?"

"Lance did it to Cara." Alex whimpered and yanked his hair. "I wanted to know you, in that way."

"Why?" Now her confession was a gem not to be missed. "Am I so special?"

"Because you make me feel—*oh*, I know not how to describe it." Her breath hitched, when he grazed his chin to her nipple. "My belly flutters, as if I have swallowed a swarm of butterflies, and I am warm inside, from head to toe, even when there is no fire in the hearth. And I ache, but it is not painful. It is a hunger, one I can neither explain nor comprehend, but I want more."

"And has anyone else affected you, thus?" As he uttered the query, Jason braced for her reply.

"Only you, Captain of my heart. That is why I had to find you." She rattled the roof with an ear-splitting shriek, and he suspected she neared completion. "I wanted to make amends, as you are everything to me."

"Then consider the matter closed, dearest Alex." With that, he manipulated the succulent flesh between her legs, faster and faster, increasing the intensity, as he covered her mouth with his. Telltale rigidity heralded her release, even as she bit his lip, and her spectacular contractions tempted him beyond reason. Without warning, the fully loaded cannon in his crotch fired a violent fusillade, and his gut clenched repeatedly from the force of his climax.

For a long while, Jason simply held Alex, and she hugged him, in turn. Apologies and explanations swirled in his brain, when it dawned on him that he had just accosted a highborn woman of character, but as he attempted to retreat, she squeezed him.

"No." She nuzzled him "Please, do not leave me, as I would savor our glorious intimacy."

"Enjoyed yourself, did you?" He chuckled.

"Yes." With a flirty giggle, she placed a chaste but inexpressibly tender kiss on his cheek. "Reality is much better than my dreams or the hints and innuendos from the Brethren wives."

"I beg your pardon?" Ah, it was good to have his Alex back. "You dream of me?"

"Oh, yes." She nodded. "Every night, without fail, you visit my bed."

"Really?" And there was the characteristic aggression he relished. "What do we do in your dreams?"

"We kiss." Resting her head to his chest, she grabbed his wrist and resettled his palm to her bare breast. "And you touch me, like now. Sometimes, you run away, but I chase you."

"Do I ever chase you?" The woman could steal candy from a babe.

"There is no need, as I am yours, Captain of my heart." Alex framed his face and drew him to her, but he pulled up short when he spied tears in her blue eyes. "And I am so sorry I disappointed you. I offer you my solemn vow, as a lady, that I will never again keep secrets from you."

"I believe you, love." Comforting warmth soothed his nerves and his pride, as Jason nipped her nose. "And I owe you an apology, as I should not have been so cross."

"Then I am truly forgiven?" she inquired in a small voice.

"It is blood under the bridge, sweetheart." Jason peered at the stain manifesting the proof of his desire and the limits to which Lady Alex had pushed him, and he had yet to bed her. Had he thought her dangerous? "Now I should ride into town and fetch our dinner."

And perhaps the cool evening air would chill his other appetite, which had grown by epic proportions and had nothing to do with food.

MONDAY MORNING, Alex idled at the stoop, humming a frisky little ditty and tapping her foot in rhythm, and fixed her gaze on the end of the gravel drive, as she awaited Molly's arrival with baited breath. How she wished she could share the truth of her situation, as Alex was bursting with joy.

The captain of her heart had departed for the shipyard, after she had cooked a delicious and substantial breakfast with nary a mishap. And to her inexpressible delight, her knight had lauded her efforts with a soul-stealing kiss that warmed her to her toes. At last, their troubles seemed behind them, and now she wished to celebrate another victory.

Given her extensive lessons on attracting the stronger but not so astute sex, and subsequent success with Jason, Alex envisioned all manner of possibilities for Molly's future with Mr. Penniman. "Perhaps we should plan a double wedding?"

Closing the door, she assessed the cottage. After washing, drying, and stowing the dishes, Alex wiped the stove and table clean. Had she checked the barrel? When she noted the depleted supply, she dusted her hands and exited the house.

At the single stall stable, she collected the shoulder yoke and two buckets. In minutes, she pumped water from the well into the pails, attached them to the ropes, bent and shrugged into the yoke, and slowly returned to the cottage. It required an awkward use of her dancing skills to negotiate the front entry without spilling a drop, but she managed, much to her relief.

Once she had filled the barrel, Alex returned the yoke to the stable and then gathered wood. When she opened the door, she discovered the charwoman standing in the great room.

"Molly, I am so glad you have, at last, arrived." Alex stacked the logs beside the hearth. "Do tell, how did it go with your beau?"

"I never should have burdened you with my troubles." The cook-maid doffed her coat, bonnet, gloves, and boots and stored them by the front door. "And Cap'n does not pay me to engage in gossip."

"My dear friend, are you all right?" As Molly turned, Alex gasped. "Oh, no. What happened?"

"Nothing of consequence." She shrugged. "And I should complete my chores for the day."

"Molly, I know well the face you sport, as I have spent the past month behind a similar expression, so I recognize the signs of disappointment and heartbreak." Trepidation traipsed her spine, as Alex escorted the charwoman to the table and pulled out a chair. "Sit, and spare no detail, as I should make a pot of tea."

"But my work—"

"—Can wait." Alex lit the stove, poured water into the kettle and set it on the range, and then scooped two spoons of tealeaves into the chipped porcelain teapot. "Did your Mr. Penniman visit you on Sunday?"

Molly nodded once.

"Did you follow my advice, to the letter?" Alex resituated the empty chair so she could perch beside her friend. "And did you wear the gown I gave you?"

Molly dipped her chin.

She searched her mind for the hiccup in her plan. Given the inherent naïveté of the backwater population, Alex's strategy should have landed the stablemaster with little if any difficulty, as he was no match for a lady of means and education. "Then what went wrong?"

"Oh, Alex." Molly emitted a half-sob. "It was horrible." And then she burst into tears.

The water in the kettle boiled, and Alex stood and retrieved a towel. After filling the teapot, she closed the lid. Then she drew two cups from the open shelf, along with two napkins from a drawer, grabbed the teapot, and carried everything to the table. As Molly wept, Alex set the table and poured the tea.

"Feeling better?" With a napkin, she daubed Molly's cheeks. "Perhaps you should start at the beginning."

"Well, nothing went as planned, even though I adhered to your instructions." Molly made a startling blare, when she blew her nose on the napkin. "According to my Tom, men do not marry loose women, as he called me. He said my behavior was shameful, the gown was indecent, and he accused me of cavorting with unscrupulous ladies."

"I beg your pardon?" In that instant, Alex wondered whether or not Jason kept a bottle of brandy in the cottage, as she needed a drink. "He dared call me an unscrupulous lady?"

"Not exactly." Molly sniffed. "Tom does not know you."

"That may be, but he insulted me, however indirectly." Alex folded her arms and humphed. "I am offended, just the same. And that dress is all the rage in London."

"But we live in Plymouth, not London." Sporting a pained expression, the charwoman bit her lip and sighed. "And I am no grand lady, as are you. When I loved him with my eyes, as you showed me, he thought I suffered some sort of seizure. I am a simple country girl, and perhaps that is what Tom wants. Never should I have tried to be someone I am not."

Molly's words struck Alex as a bucket of water in the face, as the maid's predicament mirrored Alex's situation. Had Jason not reminded her on occasions too numerous to count that he was not to the manor born? Other than his recent commission and knighthood with the Brethren, he held no titles, and never had he referred to himself as Sir Collingwood. What if he preferred a bride of similar station? Was that why he had not proposed?

"Oh, Molly. I fear I have erred grossly on two fronts, and I will never forgive myself if I have cost you the attentions of Mr. Penniman." Alex mulled her position and the possibilities. "And I should summon the coach and depart for the city, at once."

"I do not follow." Molly blinked. "And why should you leave? Have I done something wrong?"

"No. But I have done you wrong, and I vow to make amends." Alex clasped hands with Molly. "Forget everything I told you, as you are a charming young woman, in your own right. And never should you mask your true nature to attract a man, as you cannot build a future on a foundation of lies. But I want you to keep the gown, as it suits you."

"But what of you and Cap'n?" Molly squeezed Alex's fingers. "I know you are not siblings."

"Excuse me?" Alex averted her stare, as it unnerved her that Molly had guessed the truth. "I know not—"

"I swear I will never tell a soul." With another gentle wrench of Alex's fingers, Molly said, "I confided in you. Will you not vouchsafe the same?"

For several seconds, Alex pondered Molly's request. How she wished her sisters were within reach, as she needed their wise counsel. Given she had not apprised them of her destination, it was too late to divulge her secrets, and she desperately needed to talk to someone.

"You are correct, in that I am not what I have claimed." In minutes, Alex disclosed her identity, the length of Jason's courtship, the plot involving Lance and Cara, and the ensuing disagreement with her captain, which had led to the spontaneous journey to Plymouth. "I must face the fact that I may not be the woman Jason desires. If I must alter my character to garner a proposal, then I am not the wife for Jason, as much as it pains me to admit it."

"That is so unfair, in light of your efforts, which I think so very brave." Molly frowned and sipped her tea. "By the way, this is delicious, but you should no longer assist with my chores, as you are a fine lady of rank, and I am far beneath your station."

"No small thanks to you, as you taught me to brew tea." Alex reclined in her chair and drained her cup. "And I deem your acquaintance priceless, dear friend, as you have made me a better person. Caroline once said that polite society is anything but polite, and I did not quite comprehend her meaning, at the time. But one of the perks of being the daughter of a duke is I can bend the dictates of feminine decorum, to a degree, without serious repercussions, and no one determines my alliances, so hell will freeze before I cede your fellowship."

"Then promise you will not leave, at least, not yet." Molly refilled their cups. "As I have so enjoyed your visit. And I believe Cap'n cares for you. Would you give up your fight before the battle is won?"

"No, as I am no coward." In silence, Alex calculated the days, as she would not risk discovery and a forced marriage, which she deemed a fate worse than death. "All right. I will stay a few more days—a sennight, at most. But then I must return home."

"WHAT A DEUCED DILEMMA." Alex stood before the stove, stirring something in a pot. "However am I to make sense of this mess?"

Jason closed the door quietly and tiptoed until his lady was within striking distance. Without warning, he slipped his arm about her waist, rotated her to face him, and kissed her hard and fast. "Perhaps I can be of service?"

"Oh, you horrible man." Her pitiful attempt at reproach fooled him not, in light of her arresting smile and glowing countenance. "You startled me."

"That was the plan, love." He nipped her nose and then set her at arm's length, as he untied his cravat. "So what troubles you?"

"Well, if you are sincere in your request, I tried to help Molly with her beau, but nothing went as planned." She returned her attention to the pot, as he shrugged from his greatcoat and frock. "Now I am unsure how to correct the damage in her relationship with Mr. Penniman."

At the washstand, he flinched. "Alex, stay out of Molly's affairs."

"But I have to make things right, after—"

"No." He tossed the towel into the basin and rested hands on hips. "Given your last disastrous turn at matchmaking, I will not allow you to meddle in my maid's concerns, as I rely on her to run this house."

"But—"

"I said no, and I meant it." The mere thought of his lady working her magic on the country boys gave Jason collywobbles. "If you interfere in her dealings with Tom, I will put you over my knee and heat your posterior, so not another word about it. Now, I am starved, so what is for dinner, as it smells delicious?"

"Filet of turbot with lobster sauce, boiled carrots, and fresh Bath buns." Alex pouted, and he longed to suckle her bottom lip. "Have a seat at the table, and I will serve you."

"I like the sound of that." When his society miss settled his plate before him, he scrutinized the fare. In the interest of self-preservation, after her initial catastrophic gastric concoction, he approached every successive meal with a healthy does of caution. To his utter amazement, Alex had managed to surprise him again. "This is superb, darling. You have outdone yourself."

"I am glad you like it," she murmured, as she shuffled a carrot in circles.

Wait a minute. He paid his pampered miss a compliment, and she scarcely noted it. No gloating, innuendos, or double-entendres? "So did you have a pleasant day?"

"Mmm hmm."

"And you cleaned my shirts?"

"Mmm hmm."

"Might I splay you on the sideboard?"

"Mmm hmm."

"As I should much prefer to feast on the bounty between your legs."

"Mmm hmm."

"*Alex.*" Jason pounded his fist on the table.

"What?" She blinked and dropped her fork. "Is something wrong?"

"May I have a glass of ale?" he inquired, with a smile.

"Of course." She jumped to her feet. "How could I have been so forgetful, as I know you take ale with your dinner?"

It touched him that she showed genuine concern for his welfare. And when he challenged her to assume partial responsibility for Molly's chores, never had he presumed she would fulfill her part of the bargain with such gusto. In her own way, she had won him all over again.

Yet he could not wed her.

At her young age, if he made Alex a war widow, she would be destined to spend her life as a plaything for the rich, passed about as a favored toy. London society fretted not for her rank and connections, when it came to a failed marriage, regardless of the circumstances. And he cared for Lady Alex too much to condemn her to an empty existence as another man's mistress, subject to the *ton's* derision and censure for the capriciousness of fate.

"Jason, might I ask you a question?" Alex handed him the glass of ale and returned to her seat.

"Anything, love." But he wondered if they could enter into an arrangement, which would enable her to continue her life sans the stigma of widowhood, should he meet his demise at sea, while binding them, should he survive.

"Do most men not appreciate bold women?" she inquired in a small voice.

"In what capacity?" He surmised her query had everything to do with Molly and the stablemaster.

"I am uncertain." Alex shrugged. "As a wife, I suppose."

"In truth, no." On the few occasions he had dealt with Penniman, Jason presumed the lad would prefer Molly's quiet, unassuming disposition. "I would wager most men seek not a spirited bride, rather, they prefer the opposite."

Of course, he neglected to mention that he tended toward the latter, when it came to her.

"Oh." Was it his imagination, or had she appeared crestfallen?

In deafening silence they dined, until Jason pushed back his chair, stood, and stretched. "That turbot was inspiring, my lady. Believe I shall read the newest edition of the *Mariner's Mirror*."

"Would you mind doing so in your bedchamber, as I wish to complete my kitchen chores and retire early." Alex collected and stacked the dirty dishes. "And Molly wishes to teach me how to jar preserves, tomorrow."

"By your leave." For a minute, Jason fingered the ring in his waistcoat pocket. Should he propose? "Good night, Alex."

CHAPTER FOUR

*T*hree days later, Alex still fought uncharacteristic and unwelcome tears. Exhausted, she had spent the past few nights tossing and turning, after Jason's unspecified but implied preference for demure women. Emitting a plaintive sob, she washed the breakfast dishes and cleaned the kitchen, as she awaited Molly's arrival.

A dull ache had taken residence deep in her chest, and she struggled to breathe. At one point, she feared she might swoon, so she sat by the window, after stowing the last of the plates. Resting her elbows atop the table, Alex cupped her chin in her palms and sighed. "I will not cry."

Now she understood Cara's reticence regarding Lance's first prosaic proposal, and why the elder Douglas sibling had refused his offer of marriage. It was not until Lance had convinced Cara of his love that she had accepted him. Likewise, as Jason owned Alex's heart, she would settle for no less than the same commitment, on his part.

"Alex, are you unwell?" Molly asked, as she stood in the doorway. "I called to you, but you did not answer."

"Good morning, dear friend. And I am fine." She wiped

a wayward tear and mustered a smile, even as inside her something fractured. "What is our schedule for today?"

"We must clean the cottage from top to bottom." Molly hung her outerwear on the wall peg and then retrieved the broom, mop, and bucket from the pantry, where she kept her supplies. "Although that is not so monumental a task, as you might think, given your maintenance in my absence. Should you ever require an occupation, you would make a fine charwoman."

"I consider that high praise, coming from you." At last, her dark spirits eased, and Alex giggled. "Shall we commence the work? And you might mop his bedchamber, while I tend the great room, as I swept his quarters after he departed for the yard."

"Alex, you really must not take so much upon yourself, else I will have to ask Cap'n to cut my pay in half. And I brought you a bottle of my vanilla water, as you may favor it." Molly shrieked. "You folded and put away his clothes, too?"

"Yes. And thank you for the thoughtful gesture, but now you must accept my perfume, in fair trade." Alex picked up both rugs and relocated the furniture, so she could complete a thorough job. "And have you spoken with Tom?"

"Oh, I almost forgot." Molly abandoned her mop and charged into the great room. "Put down the broom, as I require your full attention."

"What happened?" Alex ceased her drudgery and plopped on the sofa. "You must tell me everything."

"Yesterday, as I walked home, I passed Tom on the road. At first, I bowed my head in shame." Molly bounced beside Alex. "But then I recalled your advice, and how we can't leave everything to chance, which I weighed with your suggestion to be myself, so I greeted him in my usual tone."

"And?" Alex wound tight as a clock spring.

"He acknowledged my presence but said nothing." Molly clasped Alex's hands. "And then I thought to myself, 'What would Alex do?'"

"Yes—and?" Alex squeezed the cook-maid's fingers.

"So I asked him how he fared, and he inquired after the same." The charwoman inhaled and then blurted, "I apologized for my disagreeable behavior, and he asked permission to visit me on Sunday. Is that not wonderful news? I am so hopeful."

"It is indeed cause for celebration, and hope is always a good thing." And now Alex could retreat to London and nurse her injured pride. "Perhaps you can show me how to make a batch of Shrewsbury cakes, and we can have tea, as an impromptu feast."

"That is an excellent idea." Molly bit her lip and inclined her head. "And what of you and Cap'n? Has he proposed?"

"No."

"Oh."

"As that was my primary purpose in traveling to Plymouth, I have failed." Alex stood and dusted her dress. "But I cannot regret the journey, as I met you, and I have learned so many new things. And you must promise to write, as I will bring you to London, as my guest."

"You sound as if you have surrendered." The cook-maid clutched her hands to her chest. "But you must not yield, as I have seen how Cap'n looks at you, which is how I knew you were not related, as my brother never admires me in that way. Cap'n holds you in great esteem."

"While I believe Jason is fond of me, I am no longer assured of his regard. My sisters were correct, in that I should not have rushed the situation, but I love him, so I must follow my heart." She retrieved the broom and sought consolation in her chore. "But if I must pretend to be something other than myself in order to win him, then he is not for me."

And so Alex gave herself to her toils, laboring in concert with Molly, and found refuge therein. That afternoon, she learned how to cook and jar preserves. And then she baked four pans of Shrewsbury cakes, which the charwoman proclaimed the finest she had ever tasted. With a small portion of bundled cakes, Molly departed for home. Only then had Alex filled the tub, which persisted as her favorite task, as it signaled the end of her work, and she would soon after sink into a hot bath.

Later, she sat on the sofa and braided her hair, which she had just finished when Jason strolled into the cottage. "Good evening, Captain of my heart."

"Lady Alex, you are a sight for sore eyes." He tossed his greatcoat over the chair and then stopped to kiss the top of her head. "How was your day?"

"Productive." The ease with which they usually conversed seemed strained to her, and she searched for a saucy response to rouse his humor. Instead, cold emptiness pervaded her senses, so she stood and sidestepped the object of her affection. "Are you hungry?"

"Famished." He frowned. "Are you all right?"

"Everything is fine." As had become their routine, while she served dinner, Jason steered for the washstand, and they met at the table. "I made a lovely ragout of beef, with a side of macaroni and cheese, and for dessert I baked Shrewsbury cakes."

"My compliments to the chef." As he shoveled an impressive mouthful, he hummed his appreciation. "May I admit something, without fear of reprisal?"

"Of course." Alex bolstered her defenses, as she prepared for rejection. Had he, at last, mustered sufficient courage to admit the truth? Biting her tongue, she prayed for strength and vowed not to embarrass herself. "What did you wish to impart?"

"When you showed up at my doorstep, and I issued my challenge, never had I thought you capable of the task." Grasping her hand, Jason pressed his lips to her knuckles, and she shivered. "You would think I should have learned not to underestimate you, by now, love."

"Praise, indeed." Prior to their disagreement, such words would have brought her inexpressible elation, but Alex celebrated no victory.

The remainder of their meal passed in uncomfortable silence. Once her captain had cleaned his plate and wolfed down three cakes, he stretched his arms over his head. As she collected the dishes, she leaned to retrieve his napkin, and Jason caught her about the waist.

He sniffed the air. "What is that smell?"

"I beg your pardon?" Puzzled, she dropped the cloth. "Can you describe it?"

"What a sweet aroma." In the wake of a deep inhale, he wrenched her close and thrust his nose into the curve of her neck, and she gasped. "Hmm. It is you."

"Oh, that." She swallowed hard, as he nuzzled her, and despite her reservations, a sparkle of hope glimmered. "Molly gifted me a bottle of her vanilla water. It is quite different from my usual scent."

"It suits you." When he licked her throat, her knees buckled, and he drew her into his lap. "And you taste good, too."

"Jason, I do not think we should—" In a flash, he bent his head and covered her mouth with his, and her mind blanked. Without thought or care for the consequences, Alex twined her fingers in his hair and joined the fray, as she ached to kiss her captain.

The world as she knew it tilted on end, and the little cottage yielded to a fantastical illusion, featuring a flirty chorus of mystical fairies and arrow-throwing chubby cherubs. Molten heat poured through her veins, and desire simmered beneath her flesh. As though he had read her thoughts, her captain kneaded her breast, and she moaned in pleasure.

Was it possible that her conclusions were hastily drawn? Had she leapt to unsupported deductions woven from whole cloth? Could it be possible Jason intended to propose, else why would he seduce her?

In that instant, armed with passion, Alex charged the fore. When Jason shifted to loosen her bodice, she walked her fingers to his crotch and delighted in his arousal. How she yearned to examine what she had only caressed through his breeches, as that particular aspect of his anatomy quite fascinated her.

Driven by the now familiar hunger, which had long since ceased frightening her, she broke their kiss, arched her back, and shoved his head to the one place she most wanted his attention. For a couple of seconds, Jason suckled hard on her nipple, and Alex relaxed and sighed.

But when he halted and met her gaze, she flinched. "Is something wrong?"

"No." For a while, he simply stared at her. Then he furrowed his brow and asked, "Do you wish to know me, as I know you?"

"Yes," she replied without hesitation, though she knew not what his proposition entailed.

"If you change your mind, you need only indicate your

preference, and I will abide your choice." Jason fumbled with the hooks at his waist, clutched her wrist, and slipped her hand inside his breeches. At her first touch of his miracle of flesh, he groaned and rested his forehead to hers. "You have no idea how many nights I have dreamed of you, like this."

"You dream of me?" In that moment, her heart sang.

"Aye." He closed his eyes when she squeezed him. "I have worshipped you for an eternity, it seems."

"Have I hurt you?" Alex stilled. "I know not what to do for you."

"No, love." Baring his teeth, he hissed. "I suffer the same hunger that plagues you."

"Will you show me how to please you?" She nibbled playfully on his bottom lip and thrilled when his fingers closed over hers, and he schooled her in an urgent rhythm. Tension built, spiraling ever higher, the shot fired, and Alex bolted.

As their tongues met and dueled, Jason hiked her skirt, inched his palm along the sensitive inner side of her thigh, and she dropped her knees wide in unspoken welcome. To her unutterable delight mixed with relief, he accepted her summons.

"Ah, my Alex is wet for me." And then her captain launched a full-scale assault on her faculties, as he took the helm and steered her into heretofore-unknown erotic seas, and she would never complain.

Moving in concert, she stroked his length in time with the sweet havoc he wreaked at the apex of her thighs. With a sensuous symphony comprised of her pants and moans, interspersed with his grunts and groans, she floated on a cloud of resplendent euphoria. Until decadent spasms carried her into delicious oblivion, which was rudely interrupted when Jason dropped back his head, contorted his face, which well nigh scared her to death, vented an inhuman growl, and a hot, glutinous substance spattered her hand as she worked him.

"Jason?" Shocked by the unknown, Alex sat still and recalled a peculiar conversation with the Brethren wives, in regard to their respective spouses and their naughty habits.

The man howls, mid-coitus, as a wolf bays at the moon.

Trevor calls to his maker, again and again, with unrestrained fervor.

Dirk roars like a lion.

It was comforting to know Jason's enthusiastic bellow manifested his appreciation of her new ability, but no one had mentioned the rather startling explosion from the particular male protuberance Brie commonly referred to as the Jolly Roger. "Is that normal, or did I break something of great importance?"

"Oh, Alex." At first, her captain chuckled, but then he shook with boisterous mirth. "No, you did not injure me, but I submit there was nothing normal about that."

"So I pleased you?" How she detested her little girl voice, which belied her confidence.

"What do you think?" The smile he bestowed upon her melted her heart, but then he faltered. "You truly do not understand what just happened, do you?"

"No," she whispered. "My mother died when I was young, as I already told you. My knowledge of the sexes is confined primarily to Damian's collection of Rowlandson's etchings. And while the Brethren wives have shared some of their marital adventures, this I would have remembered."

"But you are quite popular in the ton's ballrooms." Jason removed his fingers from between her legs and pulled down her skirt. "Have you never explored the possibilities with another man?"

"How dare you ask such a thing." Alex scooted and sat upright. "Never have I touched a man thus, and it is unforgivable of you to suggest otherwise. I ought to—"

"I apologize, Alex. But, upon my word, you are the boldest woman of my acquaintance." Jason trailed a finger along the curve of her cheek. "What I meant to say is you could have your choice of a hundred men, at least, and many with titles. Why am I, a most unworthy beneficiary, the most fortunate recipient of such indulgence?"

"Because you are the only estimable man to ever capture my interest." Though she lamented freeing him, she snatched his napkin and cleaned her hand. "You commanded me from the moment we met."

"How I savor the memory of you, standing in the Richmond's ballroom, bedecked in your red gown." He kissed her temple. "Do you recall when I declared that both I and my vessel were at your service?"

"Yes." And she cherished that reminiscence.

"I have a confession to make." Jason narrowed his stare and grinned. "When I mentioned my vessel, I was not referring to the *Intrepid*."

"Then I should impart that was no secret." Alex giggled. "Yet I could not be angry with you, as no one had ever spoken to me in such audacious terms, and how handsome you were in your regimentals, which proved a powerful combination."

"So the other night, when I ravished you, that was your first completion?" He drew invisible circles across her décolletage.

"That is what you call the sensation?" She shrugged. "Never have I experienced anything like it."

"In Shakespeare, it is known as the 'little death,' but there are various names." Jason caught the crest of her ear with his teeth. "Release, climax, but heaven on earth is more apropos, when it comes to you."

"My, but you say the sweetest things." Myriad thoughts swirled in her brain, as curiosity snared her attention. Ever since she was a young girl, Alex could resist anything but temptation, and Jason personified temptation. So she peered between their bodies and drew back the waistband of his breeches, but she paused. "May I?"

Arching a brow, he dipped his chin. "Be my guest."

Were it anyone else, she would never venture into such dangerous territory, but Jason was the captain of her heart, so she feared him not. Taking a deep breath, at last, she opened the front closure and glimpsed what she had stroked in her palm.

"It is not what I had imagined." Surrounded by a nest of blonde curls, the length of his Jolly Roger boasted a plum-shaped tip, and a rather strange pouch, of sorts, sat at the base. As she fondled the peculiar but potently male aspect of his anatomy, she marveled at the oddity. "The skin reminds me of a turkey neck, which I sampled after Damian brought several fowl from America for Christmas dinner."

"Bloody hell, Alex." To her surprise, her captain burst into laughter, even as his most fascinating protuberance grew in her grasp. But then he quieted and covered her hand with his. "You rouse me again, Lady Alex."

"I am sorry." Alex half-turned and pressed her lips to his neck. If only he would propose marriage, so she could accept.

"Never apologize for that, love." Cupping her chin, Jason brought her gaze level, and then he covered her mouth with his. As he had taught her, she resumed the gentle but decadent massage, and he once again flicked up her skirt.

A piercing clap of thunder rumbled over the cottage and rattled the windows. Much to her chagrin, her captain halted his play, and she followed suit.

"What is the matter?" She rested her head on his shoulder, and when he withdrew his fingers, she frowned.

"I have taken liberties to which I have no right." Grasping her at the waist, Jason lifted her from his lap. "I apologize, Alex. My only excuse is I find it difficult to deny you, but I suppose I should be thankful I did not claim your bride's prize."

Knife to the heart with lethal precision.

"Would that be so bad?" She folded her arms and shivered. And then it occurred to her that she might have misconstrued the situation. "And I did nothing against my will, should you concern yourself with such worries."

"You know, I believe I have finally identified what I find so appealing in you, dearest Alex." Jason stood, fastened his breeches, and speared his fingers through his hair. "You give of yourself without reservation or inhibition. Rather, you possess a generosity of spirit that is unrivaled by any other woman I have known. Given what you risked for Cara, how you have assumed a vast deal of Molly's chores, the way you extended friendship to a cook-maid, and your willingness to share your body with me, you are, perhaps, the most munificent lady of my acquaintance."

Something in his tone disturbed her, as she gathered the dirty plates and conveyed them to the basin. After filling the kettle with water to boil for washing the dishes, she considered her next move. It was now or never, so she cast her lot on love.

"By the by, I neglected to mention that I have decided to

send for my coach. If you will post my missive, on your way to work, tomorrow, the hired rig should arrive in the evening." The future she desperately desired played a series of magical vignettes, and she stiffened her back. "After all, I came here to set things right, and I have achieved my goal, so it is time I return to London."

Silence blanketed the cottage, interrupted by the occasional echoing thunder. Conscious of nothing save the beat of her heart, as she awaited Jason's response, Alex prayed for a betrothal. With her most fervent dreams hanging in the balance, she wrung a drying cloth.

"A storm approaches." Jason strolled toward his chamber, and her hopes dwindled with each successive step. At last, he turned and faced her. "I should be happy to dispatch your correspondence. Goodnight, Alex."

Inside her, something fractured. She would cry, but not until he closed his door and set the bolt. "Goodnight, Captain of my heart."

A BRILLIANT FLASH of lightning brought Jason alert from a deep sleep, and he sat upright at the ensuing thunderous roar. Rubbing his tired eyes, he yawned. The wind howled, and rain beat a rapid salvo on the window. He rolled on his side and envisioned Alex, bucking in his lap, and her effuse cries of release filled his ears in licentious accompaniment.

"Bloody everlasting hell." In the dark, he shot from his bed, walked to the washstand, poured water into the basin, and splashed his face. But nothing could soothe the ache that burned in his chest, as he pondered Lady Alex's departure. How he longed for her to stay, yet she never should have journeyed to Plymouth, and he never should have permitted her to share the cottage, so he would suffer her absence in silence.

The room had grown cold, so he added a couple of logs to the fire and stoked the blaze. At the footboard, he grabbed the extra blanket and unfolded it. Just as he was about to slip between the covers, he noted a thread of gold light emanating from beneath the door.

"Alex, are you awake?" He shrugged into his robe and cinched the belt at his waist. "Are you all right, love?"

No response.

After unlocking the bolt, he set the oak panel wide and shuddered, as the great room was bone-chilling cold. A single taper illuminated the living space, as the fire had long since extinguished. But what troubled him was the empty sofa.

"Alex." Could she have gone outside, in the torrential downpour, for some unfathomable reason? Jason crossed the floor in a handful of strides, twisted the key at the front entry, pulled open the door, and peered into the gale. "*Alex.*"

Sheets of rain pounded the earth, and the mighty oaks twisted and turned in the wind, amid the staccato flashes of nature's tempest, and he fought to close the portal. Convinced she had not ventured into the vicious winter storm, he scanned the immediate vicinity.

The modest frock she had worn at dinner, and as she had sat in his lap as a most sumptuous dessert, had been draped over the large chair. And then it occurred to Jason that he had yet to glimpse his lady in her nightgown. If only he could find her.

"Alex?" And then he heard it, a whisper of breath followed by a ghost of a whimper. He held high the candle and turned. "Answer me, now."

"I am here." She sobbed.

"Where are you?" He glanced to the left. In the dining area, he squatted, searched beneath the table, and his gut seized. "Darling Alex, what happened?"

Huddled against the wall, with legs bent, arms wrapped about her shins, and her forehead pressed to her knees, Alex shivered. Jason reached and touched her, and her flesh was clammy. He had to warm her before she caught her death.

Setting the candlestick on the floor, he first attempted to join her under the small table, as if his six-foot frame would fit. Cursing himself a fool, he stood and wrenched the small piece of furniture away from the window. Then he retrieved and blew out the taper.

In one fail swoop, he scooped Alex into his arms, carried her into his chamber, kicked the door shut behind him, and settled her on the mattress. After tucking the blankets about her, he tended the fire. When Jason returned to his lady, it dawned on him that the one woman he most wanted to find warming his sheets sat, albeit weeping, in the middle of the bed.

While a gentleman would offer support and comfort, he doubted his ability to resist the irresistible debutante, as she wore nothing more than a diaphanous silk confection, which had caught the attention of the cannon in his crotch. Primed for a voluptuous battle, and restrained only by his flimsy satin robe, Jason swallowed hard, stared at the ceiling, and prayed for strength.

"Alex, please, talk to me." He shook her shoulder and retreated to a safe distance. "Why are you crying, love?"

"You left me." She emitted a plaintive wail.

"What?" Without thought of the hazard, he sat on the edge of the bed.

"I could not find you." She peered at him, and terror invested her lovely features.

"Nonsense, darling." He caressed the gentle curve of her cheek. "I am right here."

"You were gone." And then his society miss once again behaved completely out of character for a gently bred virgin. Before he could stop her, she climbed into his lap, slipped her arms about his waist, and hugged him as if her life depended on him. "And I was alone."

"It must have been a dream, sweetheart, as I have never abandoned you." Jason gritted his teeth when she wiggled her hips, and her bottom teased his wickedly exuberant Jolly Roger, which ached to weigh anchor in her harbor. Summoning unimpassioned thoughts, he focused on the flickering flames in the hearth, which reminded him of the fire raging below his belly button. "Would you not be more comfortable—"

"Hold me, please." She rubbed her nose to his neck, framed his face with her delicate hands, and covered his mouth with hers.

Now that was his dream—Alex loving him, initiating the seduction, yet it was no illusion. When the truth struck Jason as the icy waters of the Baltic, molten heat poured through his veins and pooled in his loins. Grasping at the last vestiges of self-control, he tried to set her apart from him, but Lady Alex evaded his maneuvers and seized the advantage. Dropping her knees to either side of his thighs, she straddled him and scooted close, until she nudged the swell of his healthy erection.

"*Oh.*" Gazing into his eyes, she inclined her head and suckled his lower lip.

Everything inside him roared at once, as he was ravenous for her. Would his lady laugh at him, if he apprised her of the fact that he had been with no other woman since the night they met? Would she mock his devotion? Would it frighten her to know that he desired her, above all else, given he was no nobleman and adhered not to the strictures governing the peerage?

"Alex, we should stop, as you know not what danger you court." Despite warnings to the contrary, he slipped his hands inside the slits of her nightgown, rested his palms to the twin swells of her succulent bottom, and schooled her in an erotic massage. "I am a man, not a saint."

She moaned low in her throat and thrust her hips.

And Jason was undone.

In a flash of lightning, which portended the ruination of her maidenhead, he toppled Alex on her back and covered her. Yes, there would be hell to pay, and he would gladly compensate the ferryman—tomorrow.

Because tonight, consequences be damned, he would take Lady Alex.

CHAPTER FIVE

*a*s the storm waged war beyond the walls, a tempest of an altogether different sort raged within the tiny cottage. Safe, warm, and stretched long in Jason's bed, Alex admired her sea captain, as he hovered above her. In the dim light from the fireplace, his haunting countenance grew far more intoxicating with each successive flash of lightning. And when he doffed his robe, she feared she might melt into the down mattress, as there was nothing so magnificent or fascinating as his naked form.

Then he skimmed her thighs, inched her nightgown to her waist, and she shifted, until he whisked the silk garment over her head. The gossamer material seemed to float in the air, as a corporeal remnant of maidenhood, which she longed to relinquish to her knight.

"You are beautiful, Alex." Jason circled each breast with his finger, before resting his palm to her belly. "Never could my fantasies have conjured the magnitude of your splendor."

"Jason." Bared for his delectation, a society miss should have been embarrassed, yet Alex could muster no shame.

Instead, she cupped his cheek and traced his lower lip with her thumb. "Make me yours."

"My lady, your wish is my command." In that instant, he gave her his full weight, as he nudged her legs wide and settled his hips to hers. "But you are already mine."

And then he covered her mouth with his, and the race commenced. With his tongue as a decadent lure, he licked and suckled, tempted and taunted, as nothing escaped his attention, and she answered his call.

In a naughty maneuver she would never have foreseen, he kissed and nibbled a path to her navel, then moved lower, and his head bobbed and weaved between her thighs. "What sweet curls you have, darling."

When he turned her on her stomach, and spared nary an inch of her bottom, pressing on her licentious caresses that defied the limits of polite society, she almost swooned. And then he flipped her onto her back and retraced his decadent path.

"Captain of my heart, please." Molten heat smoldered beneath her skin, excitement and anticipation charged every nerve, and her muscles flexed with some unknown but altogether tortuous desire. She squeezed his shoulders and squirmed. "I can take no more."

"All right, sweet Alex." Propped on an elbow, Jason chuckled and grasped her thigh. "Lift your heels for me, love."

Following his direction, she abided his request, and he rewarded her with a far more intimate connection than she ever thought possible. A blush burned in her cheeks, as he probed her, and she closed her eyes when he slipped inside her.

Strange sensations assailed her faculties, and she clung to reality, even as the dizzy heights of passion beckoned.

Foreign tension built at her core, as he pressed on her a tender invasion, which evoked happy tears. *Être aux anges*, she soared to a heretofore-inexpressible precipice of bliss—until excruciating pain threatened to split her in two, and Alex screamed.

"*Stop.*" Gasping in shock, she pounded his back with her fists. "You are hurting me."

"Alex, hold still." Jason planted her wrists at either side of her head. "Calm down, darling. It will pass."

"I am calm." She winced. "And I am still."

"You most certainly are not." He rested his forehead to hers. "Virgin's discomfit, which occurs only once, is unavoidable and brief, and it will ease when you relax."

"I am relaxed." With a deep breath, she gazed at her captain and adjusted her legs.

"Only you would argue with me, mid-coitus. Yet, had I done my job properly, you should not retain the ability to think, much less speak. So I may have failed you, in my haste to have you, sweetheart." With his teeth he nipped her nose. "Allow me to rectify said deficiency. Kiss me."

Again, Alex applied herself in obeisance of his request, and when Jason flexed his spine, withdrew from her, and then reversed course, she braced for the agony, until he seated his flesh deep within hers. To her amazement, a new, pleasant, and overpowering enticement captured her senses.

To her unutterable delight, Jason repeated the succulent slip and slide, carrying her to a place where she existed as something more than herself, often altering his cadence to grind his hips to hers in maddening, illicit rotations. The incomparable voluptuous attachment, more emotional than physical, and far more arresting than she could have fathomed, left her reeling, and Alex surrendered to the all-encompassing sensual tide.

But she wrenched to the mortal plane, as panic danced a jig down her spine, when her knight reared up, hooked his arms behind her knees, and lifted her legs into the air. Exposed and vulnerable, she stared at her conqueror, and he winked. For a scarce second, she smiled, and then he thrust. Oh, what she felt, as she no longer knew where she ended and he began. She screamed his name, but it came to her in an echo, as if from afar.

Just as Alex thought she could bear no more, everything inside her twisted and turned to accommodate her captain. Then the world tilted, and the now familiar delicious spasms provoked another shriek of exultation. And there it was—that mystical realm where she separated from her corporal self and drifted on an imaginary cloud of ecstasy.

IN THE FAINT light that signaled the dawn of a new day, in more ways than one, Jason slipped from Alex's side, much to his regret. At the washstand, he splashed cold water on his face, shaved, and then cleaned his teeth. As he brushed his hair, he paused, leaned on the edge of the basin, gazed at his reflection in the mirror, and frowned. "Collingwood, what have you done?"

With her hair in a tangled mess, the woman of his dreams slept the sleep of the sated. In a flash, he closed his eyes and revisited cherished memories of the stormy night and his questionable endeavors, which had resulted in the salacious education and utter debauchery of the highborn daughter of a duke.

In the closet, he stepped into a pair of buckskin breeches, shrugged into a lawn shirt and a grey waistcoat, and then tugged on his Hessians. As he tied his cravat in a precise mathematical, a lilting tapestry of feminine sighs and achingly sweet cries echoed in his ears, along with a bold request he would treasure until he died: *May we do it again, Jason?*

To his credit, he had given her what she wanted—thrice.

With a chuckle, he shook his head. The brazen wench, with a body made for sin and a voluptuous appetite to rival his own, had kept pace and loved him well into the wee hours. Indeed, for a barely ex-virgin, his Alex manifested irresistible temptation that could make a grown man weep and drive him mad as a March hare for want of her.

After retrieving his coat from a peg, he returned to admire the inimitable society miss. Heaven on earth rested beneath wrinkled sheets and a mountain of blankets, which presented a far cry from the woman who had woken him with a bawdy massage of his oh-so-reliable morning erection and then proceeded to feed his hunger with his most favored fare. With her cheek cupped in her palm, she evoked a familiar comparison to Botticelli's angels. Given the events of last night, Aphrodite better suited Alex.

The fire had guttered, and the room had grown cold, so he situated three logs in the rack and tended the hearth, until he had stoked a roaring blaze. Cradling his head in his hands, he groaned. "Enough of this insanity."

Invested with unswerving determination, by which she might have been intimidated were she *compos mentis*, he stalked his vulnerable, incognizant lady. At bedside, he leaned over her and pressed his lips to her forehead. "I have wronged you, Alex. And I pray that, some day, you will forgive me."

Despite mental warnings to the contrary, Jason claimed a kiss from his sleeping siren. If not for his duties to the Crown, he would forgo the shipyard and spend a sennight in her arms. Yet more pressing matters held his attention and calmed his Jolly Roger.

In slumber, Alex gave vent to a sultry moan, cast a feminine smile, and shifted, baring a creamy shoulder. Had he thought her temptation personified? The woman was downright lethal.

"Rest well, sweetheart. God knows you earned it." Averting his gaze, he stood and drew the blanket to her chin. "I should not have taken you, as we cannot marry amid war, so I vow never to weigh anchor in your harbor again."

Given their nocturnal activities, she had not written the summons for her coach, and he would encourage her to compose that missive tonight, as he had to send her home. Donning his coat, he walked to the door. With his hand on the knob, he stopped and glanced at his lady. Without doubt, he would break his newly sworn oath the second he returned to the cottage.

WITH A HEALTHY YAWN and a robust stretch, Alex flinched, as she ached in places she had not known she could ache. Cocooned in warm blankets, which were supplemented by a roaring blaze in the fireplace, she rubbed her eyes and sniffed. It took her a few minutes to discern where she had slept and, more importantly, with whom she had shared a bed. As recognition dawned, a virile melody of male grunts and groans serenaded her, salacious images from the glorious tryst with Jason danced in her brain, and she bolted upright, hugged herself, and squealed in delight. "*Hallelujah.*"

Clutching the covers to her chest, Alex scanned her

immediate vicinity, wiggled her toes, and giggled. Had she known her chivalrous knight would find a nightmare so inspiring, she would have conjured all manner of nocturnal demons, a long time ago. At last, she had got her captain to pounce and, oh, had he pounced. Of course, he had licked, suckled, nibbled, and caressed every inch of her body, as well, and she had no complaints.

Now if only he would propose.

With that thought weighing heavy on her heart and mind, she flung back the blankets, leaped from the bed, and snatched from the floor the lawn shirt Jason had worn yesterday. When she donned the simple garment, her nautionnier knight's signature sandalwood scent wreathed her.

"Hello." At the long mirror, she studied her reflection and smiled. "My name is Alexandra Collingwood, wife of Jason Collingwood, captain of the *Intrepid*."

A fanciful illusion sprung to life, the sidewalks of London magically appeared in the tiny cottage in Plymouth, and Alex enacted her own private promenade. With a curtsey, she nodded an acknowledgement to an imaginary visitor. "Good afternoon, I am Mrs. Collingwood. Do you know my husband? He is the bravest, handsomest sailor in the Royal Navy."

Whirling in circles, as a giddy young girl with a new dress, she laughed aloud—and then came to an abrupt halt at the footboard. A vivid crimson stain marred the pristine white sheet. Had Caroline not warned that most women bled upon the loss of their maidenhead? Alex had always presumed that a lie to encourage chastity, as the prospect had certainly frightened her.

Grasping a fistful of linen, she hauled the covers from the mattress. Despite her budding friendship with Molly,

Alex could not share the particulars of something so personal, with the charwoman. Yet she would kill to confide in one of her lifelong friends. And now she understood Cara's reticence after the elder Douglas had seduced Lance.

Had Alex thought she loved Jason? In the wake of their torrid night of passion, what she now harbored for her captain far exceeded the depth of affection she had coveted upon her arrival at the humble abode, so she would speak of it not as a whimsical crush or fancy.

In mere minutes, she added a log to the fire in the bedchamber and then lit another blaze in the great room. After boiling sufficient water for the tub and the large wash-basin, she soaked the soiled sheets as she bathed.

Later, dressed in one of Molly's modest frocks, and with her hair braided, Alex scrubbed the stain. She had just rinsed away the evidence of her affair when the cook-maid strolled through the door.

"Alex, what are you doing?" The charwoman untied and removed her bonnet and then shrugged from her coat. "This is my light day, and you have already completed one of my primary tasks."

"I thought if I made an early start on our chores, you might consent to join me for brunch." Alex stood upright, stretched her back, and wiped her brow. "And will you help me wring the linens?"

"Of course." Molly halted opposite Alex and smiled. "And I should love to have brunch with you, but you need not have gone to so much trouble, as the housework remains my duty."

"Nonsense. You are never a bother." Alex twisted one way, and Molly rotated the fabric in the other direction. "I quite enjoy the work, as it keeps me honest."

A SENNIGHT LATER, as Alex looked back on the days subsequent to the consummation of her relationship with Jason, her delightful memories coupled with dreams for their future. And although her knight had yet to broach the question foremost on her mind, she anticipated a proposal with baited breath.

On Wednesday, when he returned from the docks, she had hoped for a betrothal agreement. Instead, Jason had stormed through the door like a bull in a china shop, charged her without reservation, tossed her over his shoulder, and carried her to their bed.

Hours had passed before they dined.

Thursday featured a devilish repeat performance. As she had nursed a pot of stew, she innocently inquired whether or not her captain had an appetite, to wit he replied, "I am starved." With that, he had scooped her into his arms and conveyed her to their bed.

Hours had passed before they dined.

Friday, ah, Friday, now that was a truly memorable evening. After donning his silk robe, she had met her lusty knight at the door and made a bold declaration. "Tonight, I wish to ride you, and you must teach me." And with his prurient pedagogy, her rogue sailor more than fulfilled her challenge.

Hours had passed before they dined.

Saturday and Sunday, they scarcely moved beyond their chamber, except when Alex prepared their meals. But what she had not expected was Jason's sneak attack after lunch. Just as she had dried and put away the dishes, he spread her across the little table and made love to her until she screamed. She would never look at the kitchen the same, again.

And that brought her to Monday evening. As Molly had departed, Alex awaited her rakish sea captain's return, wearing nothing but a smile and one of his lawn shirts, which she left open, to invigorate her man. How she loved rousing her knight.

A familiar clip clop snared her attention, and she doused the fire in the oven, so the braised beef would not burn. After a quick check of the cottage, she stood beside the hearth, hoping the bright blaze would provide a flattering and fortuitous backdrop.

Jason trod into the great room, cast a glance in her direction, and came to an abrupt halt. "My lady, you are a vision."

"Good evening, Captain of my heart." She toyed with her single braid. "I missed you today."

"I never would have guessed as much." As was his fashion, he lowered his chin and made straight for her. "And I thought of you every second, of every minute we were apart."

Contrary to his previous enthusiastic onslaughts, he framed her face with his hands and bestowed upon her an inexpressibly tender kiss, and in that moment Alex fell in love with him, all over again. Then Jason bent, swept her off her feet, and conveyed her to their shared quarters, and she took advantage of her position to untie his cravat.

"You wear too many clothes." After flinging the yard-length of linen to the floor, she unhooked his collar and shrieked when he flung her to the mattress.

"Take off the shirt, sweetheart." In a flash, he stripped to the waist. Then he sat on the edge of the bed, dropped his boots, stood, and unfastened and shed his breeches. Naked and aroused, he dragged the long mirror to the footboard and situated it, so she could gaze at her reflection.

"Why do we need that?" Perched at the end of the mattress, Alex gulped.

"The shirt, love. Else I will rip it from your beautiful body and add to the mending pile." Jason positioned behind her. "And I want to admire your face, as I take you."

"Oh, all right." Struck with sudden and unwelcome shyness, she shrugged from his garment, and he tossed it to the floor.

"Now, on your knees, Lady Alex." With a firm grip on her hips, he knelt between her legs. "Lean forward and clutch the footboard for support."

In an instant, the diminutive chamber grew unseasonably hot, and she compressed her lips and abided his request. "Like this?"

"Perfect." And then he bent his head and licked and nibbled her derriere. But when he spread her backside and trailed his tongue along the cleft, in a concupiscent maneuver of which she never would have conceived, her gut clenched.

"*Jason.*" In the mirror, she met his heated stare, as he pressed on her an illicit massage. "What are you doing?"

"Shh." With a devilish smile, her captain inched close, curled about her body, and penetrated her bottom hole. "Do not fear, sweetheart. Trust me, I will not hurt you."

"But—is this allowed?" When he pushed deeper still, unfamiliar but pleasurable tension coiled in the pit of her belly, as he stretched and filled her, and she moaned. "Never have I heard of or seen—*oh*—anything of the sort."

"I would have been surprised if you had, because I learned this particular orientation on a trip to India, and I have longed to share it with you." When Jason seated himself inside her, he groaned, and she marveled at the power she unwittingly wielded over him. "Relax, and open your mind, Alex. There is nothing wrong with what we do, given we are consenting parties, but if you wish me to stop, you need only say so, and I shall obey."

Emboldened by his expression of pure ecstasy, she found pleasure in the pleasure she gave him. "You may continue, Captain of my heart."

With a primal grunt, he slumped and nipped the back of her neck, as he played havoc in the aperture at her core, with his fingers. At first, he thrust slowly, but when he sank his teeth into her shoulder, he quickened his pace. The lascivious bump and grind, unlike anything she had ever known, scorched Alex to the marrow, and coupled with his naughty fondling, she soon teetered on the precipice of sweet completion. Just as she reached for that oh-so-sumptuous pinnacle of their erotic waltz, Jason withdrew from her rear channel, rolled her onto her back, and rejoined with her in a single fluid flex of his spine.

"I want your honey harbor, love." Hooking an arm behind her knee, he lifted high one leg and recommenced the decadent dance. "There is no one like you, Alex. You fascinate me as has no other woman."

How she wished she could form a response, but his declaration, although lacking the much-hoped-for proposal and the four-letter word she ached to hear, rendered her speechless, all the same. So she surrendered to the tantalizing tide, which ebbed and flowed, as Jason navigated her to the very edge of hedonistic oblivion, where she clawed at the blissful crest, before he tempered his movements in maddening undulations.

Wavering on the brink of insanity, she dug her nails into his forearms. At last, he gave her his weight, claimed her mouth, and drove her relentlessly, pumping hard and fast, to the decadent finish, where she slipped the bonds of reality and yielded to fiery passion with a vast deal more than healthy scream.

When next Alex resurfaced, she discovered her knight gone, sat upright, and frowned. "Jason?"

"Coming, darling." With a steaming bucket in each hand, and wearing only his silk robe, he entered the chamber. "I thought, perhaps, you would fancy a bath."

"How very kind of you." The tub hugged the side wall, and he dumped the hot water, as she stood. "Will you scrub my back?"

"My lady, after that remarkable performance, I will wash whatever you wish." He waggled his brows and sketched a bow. "Now, your humble servant awaits to fulfill your bidding."

"Jason, are you not the charmer?" She giggled and sank into the bath. Soon she would assume her new social status as Mrs. Collingwood, and they would enjoy countless such revered occasions. "Oh, I am quite sore in a rather unusual spot."

"Sorry, love." With a wink and a boyish grin, he retrieved the soap, worked a rich lather, and tended her as though she were a most invaluable treasure. "But you make it impossible to restrain myself, when you are so accommodating."

And then some unknown interloper pounded on the front door and interrupted their interlude.

"Who in bloody hell could that be at this hour?" Swearing a string of invective that left the sear of a blush in her cheeks, he dried his hands. "Remain where you are, as I shall return, posthaste."

The lull of muffled voices almost rocked her to sleep,

and when Alex dipped her chin beneath the surface of the water, she jerked alert. The fire in the hearth dwindled, and the room had grown cool, so she swiped the towel from the washstand, dried herself, slipped into her robe, and threw two logs on the blaze.

Myriad approaches swirled in her brain, as she considered how best to introduce the topic of marriage. Given their less than appropriate activities, of late, she had to steer her sailor for the altar. But she doubted his steadfastness not for a minute.

"Well this is deuced lousy timing." With a heavy sigh, Jason reappeared, holding a curious missive. "I just received orders from the Lord High Admiral."

"When do you depart?" A twinge of concern shivered over her flesh. "And how long will you be gone?"

"Given the completed refitting of the *Intrepid*, I am to rendezvous with the Brethren at the North Forelands in three days." Jason speared his fingers through his hair and scowled. "And I am to patrol the North Atlantic for up to six months."

"Six months?" Since she was a little girl, Alex had always dreamed of a church wedding, with London society in attendance. But her future husband's occupation necessitated altered plans. "Then we should speak to the local parson, as soon as possible. And I should send a missive to Damian, that he might procure a special license. In the interest of expedience, I shall use a local vendor for my dress, and I would dearly love to have Molly stand with me, if you do not object."

"I cannot marry you, sweetheart."

"Of course, you can, as it is just a matter of securing the requisite papers." In haste, she ticked off items from a mental list, as was her habit. "We might hold a small reception at the inn in Plymouth. Oh, we will be the talk of the Season and the most marvelous couple in London."

"No."

"I beg your pardon?" The poor man looked to be on the verge of an apoplectic fit. "If proper etiquette concerns you, I promise, I do not expect you to kneel. But I can see us, now. We shall attend all the balls and dance every dance. And we will make the most beautiful babes and spend summers in the country."

"Will you not listen?" Jason huffed a breath. "We are at war, Alex. And I am to cast off on an extended tour of duty, knowing not when or if I shall ever see you again. This is no time to wed, when the future is uncertain."

"But you claimed my virtue." She swallowed hard. "No nobleman would treat me, the daughter of a duke, thus."

"Need I remind you that I am no nobleman?" He arched a brow.

"Then are you bereft of honor?" How could she impress upon him the urgency of their predicament? "Because without you, I am ruined."

"Since you gave yourself to me, of your own free will, with no spoken vows." He shifted his weight. "I could ask the same of you."

"How dare you." She bared her teeth.

"Why did you come here?" He folded his arms. "Was it to trap me into marriage?"

"*Trap*?" Knife to the chest with lethal accuracy. "You are the worst sort of blackguard, sir. My brother could secure any number of men who would kill to have me. I favored you with my bride's prize because—"

"Because—what?" He lashed out with an arm.

"Because I love you." And then she anticipated his reply. White as a sheet, Jason retreated and then collapsed on the mattress. Alex had expected him to drop to his knee, not the bed. Excruciating minutes ticked past, and her dream died a slow, agonizing death, counted by the steady beat of her heart, as it broke. "Oh, I see. You do not share my devotion."

"Hell and the Reaper." He cradled his head in his hands. "I know not what to say."

"I believe if the obvious does not strike you, then it may be best to hold your tongue." Devastated by his rejection, she would die before she ever apprised him of her distress.

"I wish you had never journeyed here." Another brutal cut.

"In that we agree, yet I cannot regret my actions, because it is better to know the truth, and I owe you an apology." A spontaneous plan shot to the fore, and she marched into the closet, opened her trunk, and collected her traveling gown. "Had I known you did not return my affection, I never would have trespassed on your hospitality. And now I have only to be ashamed of my actions."

The horse in the stable provided fortuitous transportation, and she could take a room at the inn, until her coach arrived. After securing her garters and stockings, she stepped into her kid half boots. As Molly had taught Alex, she pulled her chemise over her head, followed by her heavy twill dress, and tied the laces, herself, which proved a tad tricky.

"Alex, please do not be angry, because I do this for your own good. I refuse to make you a young widow, because you deserve better. My mother was destroyed when my father died in battle, and she passed shortly thereafter. I will not do that to you, because you have your whole life ahead of you. If the worst happens, you will survive, without me."

"Such endearing sentiment." As she tugged on her

gloves, she strolled into the chamber. "Given I come from a family of mariners, with a proud tradition of service to His Majesty, I would have you know I am made of sterner stuff. You truly know me not, and you are a stranger to me."

"What are you doing?" His gaze swept her from head to foot. "Why are you dressed?"

"Do you expect me to remain here, with you, given what has transpired between us?" She scoffed. "I hope that someday we renew our acquaintance as friends, but I shall require time before that comes to pass. I am sure you understand my position."

"Alex—"

"Do not address me so informally, sir." Fueled by high dudgeon, she lifted her chin and stiffened her spine. "I am Lady Alexandra Seymour, and you are nothing more than a lowborn sailor."

"Perhaps." He narrowed his stare. "But I was man enough to satisfy you, this evening."

"You are vile—"

"Please, sweetheart. I do not wish to fight with you." He extended an arm and flicked his fingers. "Come let us talk things through. Perhaps we can broker an agreement?"

"I beg your pardon? I gift you my heart, and you would make me your whore?" How could she have been so wrong about him? "You must think me despicable, that I would settle for such terms. Had I known you cared so little for me, I never would have offered you more than that first waltz."

"Be that as it may, you cannot intend to leave, now." Jason lurked large in the doorway. "I will sleep on the sofa, and you can send for your coach, at first light."

"Do not worry about me, Captain Collingwood, because I can take care of myself." With a quick sidestep, she stormed into the great room and fetched her coat. "And I shall send for my things, so you need not concern yourself with them."

"Where will you go?" Garbed only in his robe, he drew up short. "You lied to your friends."

At the front door, Alex freed the bolt and then peered over her shoulder. "But I am for London, and *you* may go to the devil."

CHAPTER SIX

*I*t had been six months since Jason had seen Lady Alexandra Seymour. Six months since he had held her in his arms. Six months since he had made love to her. Six months since that fateful evening in Plymouth, when she had stormed from his rented cottage. Six months to change his mind where the delectable, brown-haired hellion was concerned.

As he manned the helm on the quarterdeck, a chill of dread coursed his spine. The warm July wind rustled through his hair, as the *Intrepid* sailed into the docks at Deptford, and the familiar scent of musky river water and brine weighed heavy in the air. The crew sang dirty little shanties and scrambled into the ratlines and across the decks, in a flurry of activity expected of a ship returning to port.

How many tormented nights he had spent at sea, reliving that horrid ending with his lady, and she was his lady—though she knew it not. He had all but torn apart Plymouth in search of his errant debutante, prior to his departure, but Alex had vanished without a trace. Then again, preparation for his journey had consumed much of his time and forestalled his efforts to locate his future wife.

The innkeeper had explained that no woman of quality had patronized his humble establishment, and neither had anyone fitting Lady Alex's description taken the stage to London, thus he had cast off without discerning her whereabouts, which had left him imagining all manner of tragic possibilities.

"Drop anchor." Jason checked their position at berth and gathered his charts. "Mr. Hemmings, have my trunks delivered to the docks."

"Aye, sir." The second in command dipped his chin.

As Jason descended the gangplank, he braced for the impending confrontation with Alex. However he dressed it, he had treated her abominably in January, and if he had to crawl on his knees to secure her forgiveness, he had prepared for such prospects. Now if only he could persuade her to marry him.

How odd it was that their positions had reversed. Then again, the sheer brutality of war had a peculiar way of defining life in the simplest terms. In short, he had realized, however late, that his Alex was an uncommonly strong and fiercely independent woman—so unlike his mother, God rest her. In the event of his untimely demise, his society miss would survive, manage the household, and rear their children, come what may. With Alex as his bride, he could sail into battle with an easy conscience. Indeed, she fit every single rational item on his rather long list of matrimonial requirements, including some irrational ones he refused to examine.

"Step lively, brother." Dirk Randolph, a fellow knight of the Brethren, elbowed Jason and then charged the field. "My Becca awaits."

"My love." Rebecca took a flying leap into Dirk's outstretched arms and bestowed upon her husband an amazingly thorough kiss.

"Out of the way, Collingwood." Trevor Marshall, the other recent entrant into the famed order descended of the Templars, almost trampled Jason. "I see my sweet Caroline."

As Trevor and his countess enacted a similar scene, with a heated clinch that invoked the burn of a blush in Jason's cheeks, he chuckled.

"*Ahoy*, Collingwood." Lance Prescott, with his new bride Cara at his side, waved a greeting. "That was a devil of a maneuver on the Channel. Thought that French corvette had caught you unaware."

"Stop ribbing him." Cara smiled. "How are you, Jason?"

"I am quite well, thank you. And I am never unaware, at sea." Jason narrowed his stare and stuck his tongue in his cheek. "Because I have no distraction below decks."

"Scandalous, Captain Collingwood." Cara cast a pout, but it lasted all of two seconds before she giggled and gazed at Lance. "I do so love sailing with my husband. Perhaps, someday, you might take Alex on a mission."

At the mere mention of his lady's name, he sought her face among the small crowd that had gathered to welcome home the Brethren of the Coast. There were ten in the original group of close-knit friends, but their number had grown as each had charted their course for love.

The first to wed, Caroline had been mistaken for a courtesan and kidnapped by Trevor. Then fate brought Dirk a wife, when he was tasked with the beautiful former spy for the Counterintelligence Corps, in a plot to catch a traitor. Sabrina, Cara's brash younger sister, landed next in the parson's noose, when Lord Everett Markham decided she was the bride for him.

But Cupid's arrow had spared Blake Elliott, duke of Rylan, his partner in all conquests of the fairer sex, Damian Seymour, duke of Weston and Alex's elder brother, and Dalton Randolph, nicknamed the Lucky One for his way with the ladies and familiar habit of tossing a coin. Lady Elaine Prescott, Lance's young cousin, presented the only unattached Brethren woman.

And that brought Jason to his curiously absent Alex.

"Welcome home, Captain Collingwood." Admiral Mark Douglas, the legendary naval man and head of the Nautionnier Knights, slapped Jason on the back. "How was your journey?"

"Long, sir." He scanned the immediate vicinity. "I was wondering—"

"Where is Alex?" Damian inquired.

"At Penhurst Castle." Although Admiral Douglas spoke to Damian, he stared at Jason and frowned. "She removed to the country in April, where she has remained."

"How unusual." Damian scratched his temple. "Is she ill?"

The Brethren women gathered near, and they favored Jason with a discomposing array of harsh expressions, which left him tugging at his cravat.

"No, she is not ill, per se." Admiral Douglas shuffled his feet and cleared his throat. "But you should depart for East Sussex, at once. Given the urgency of her situation, I have taken the liberty of summoning your traveling coach, and you may forgo tonight's debriefing."

"Thank you, sir." Damian groaned. "Please, don't tell me her accounts are in arrears again."

"You could say something is in arrears." Sabrina scowled, and Jason gulped.

"Hush, my lady wife. Not another word." Everett wagged a finger at his bride and then leaned close to whisper to Jason, "Brother, were I you, I should sail for the East Indies, as you will never escape the mess you have made."

For some unknown reason, Jason shuddered. "I beg your pardon—"

"But I am for the country." Damian bowed.

"Weston, wait." Jason glanced at the admiral. "Sir, if I may eschew our meeting, I should prefer to journey with Damian, as we have business to discuss."

Admiral Douglas nodded once. "Of course—"

"As well you should." Caroline humphed.

"Darling, why so angry?" Trevor bent, as his wife cupped her hand to his ear. Then his eyes grew wide, and his mouth fell agape. "*Bloody hell.*"

In that instant, Jason surmised Alex had shared the details of her ill-fated trip to Plymouth and his subsequent rejection. But had she taken drastic measures in the wake of his refusal to marry her? The second such nonsense formed in his brain, he quashed the idea. "Are you amenable to such proposition, Weston?"

"I should be glad of the company." Damian smiled and arched a brow. "I gather our business involves my sister?"

"It does, indeed." To his men, he said, "Deliver my trunks to the Duke of Weston's coach."

And thus Jason's course was set.

~

THE FOLLOWING EVENING, as they passed the little village of Penhurst, and neared the Weston ancestral pile, Jason assessed his appearance and then glanced out the window. The coach veered from the main road and traversed a route along the English coast. Soon the escarpment yielded spectacular vistas of the Channel.

"Nervous, Collingwood?" Damian grinned.

"Would you expect otherwise, were you in my position?" In reality, Jason had no idea what waited at Penhurst Castle, given his last disastrous meeting with Alex. At least, he had secured her brother's permission to wed.

"To be honest, I cannot even fathom what you must suffer, as of this moment." Truer words were never spoken. All of a sudden, Damian burst into laughter. "Upon my word, but I must send Blake a message."

"Why?" Confused, Jason rubbed the back of his neck. "What has he to do with my situation?"

"Nothing, really." Damian slapped his thighs. "But I gave him a ration of angst when he forced Caroline and Trevor to the altar, and he wished me similar difficulty with Alex. Just wait until I deliver the news that I have managed my willful sister's nuptials with nary a headache. And I have you to thank for such happy developments."

"Well, let us not place the cart before the horse." Jason shifted in the squabs and recalled Alex's parting words, last January: *But I am for London, and you may go to the devil.* "She has yet to accept me."

"What is this—do you anticipate complications?" That was putting it mildly. Damian compressed his lips and averted his gaze. "As I, for one, doubt not her fondness for you."

Jason came alert. "Has she spoken of me?"

"On occasions too numerous to count." Damian rolled

his eyes. "And I have witnessed, firsthand, evidence of her regard."

"I beg your pardon?" Jason crossed and then uncrossed his legs. "I know not—"

"Give me some credit, brother." Damian folded his arms. "I know a well-ravished woman when I see one, but fear not, as I have no plans to schedule a dawn appointment at Paddington Green. But had my sister objected to your...compliments, and had I any indication your rendezvous had progressed beyond a few illicit kisses, you would, even now, stare down the unfriendly end of my best flintlock pistol."

Facing the man known by his friends as the voice of reason, Jason gulped, as the coach passed between two massive stone gateposts, bearing the eight-pointed wind-star insignia of the Brethren of the Coast. After traveling a trail that hugged the cliff tops, a huge silhouette rose in the distance.

Penhurst Castle manifested the ancestral seat of the Weston dukedom, and Jason knew well its history, as Alex had often spoken of the grand estate. Gifted to the first duke of Weston, along with the title, in the fourteenth century for services rendered to the Crown, his lady had described it as a monumental structure of mystical qualities, which often provoked visions of medieval knights in armor. As the sun sat well below the yardarm, he could note nothing more than a few stone turrets and frieze carved parapets.

When the coach entered the forecourt, Jason glimpsed the impressive residence in which Alex had been reared. Lanterns cast a saffron glow over the front access, and double doors of polished mahogany had been set wide, as the driver drew the horses to a halt.

Standing in the foyer, just visible, with her back to him,

Alex directed the staff, and comforting warmth pervaded his chest as he gazed upon her. Every adroit entreaty failed him, and the well-honed diplomacy of a lifetime abandoned him when he needed it most, as he pondered a greeting.

"Ready to meet your doom?" Damian chuckled and descended the coach.

"Welcome home, Your Grace." A very proper butler bowed.

While Damian conversed with the servants gathered at the steps, Jason studied his lady. When she whirled about, a radiant smile lit her expression.

Their eyes met and held.

Her countenance of joy faded, in a flash.

Jason teetered on the brink of unconsciousness, when he fixed his gaze on her belly, which had grown fat with what he had every reason to suspect was his heir. And his goose was well and truly cooked.

"WHAT IS *HE* DOING HERE?" Nestled in a high back chair, Alex folded her arms and made a point to avoid his stare.

Jason perched on a daybed and attempted to blend into the background. To say that he was shocked by recent revelations was too pale a description.

"You are not to ask questions." Damian grabbed a crystal decanter of brandy and drank directly from the container. "You are to answer questions—specifically, what manner of blackguard got you with child before wedding you?"

Alex thrust her nose high and sniffed. "That is none of your affair."

"I beg to differ, my dear sister." Damian slammed the

cut glass bottle on the blotter. "As head of this family, *you bloody well are my affair*."

Now Jason understood the chilly receptions with which the Brethren wives had welcomed him at Deptford. And Everett's warning made perfect sense, as well as Trevor's reaction to Caroline's whispered comments. But what puzzled him were Alex's actions.

To what purpose would she hide the truth of parentage?

Had she not pushed for their union? Had she not followed him to Plymouth in said endeavor? Their impending delivery aided her campaign and left him no quarter. For good or ill, he had to marry her.

So why had she not played her advantage?

"Alex, I insist you reveal the identity of the scoundrel that fathered your babe and abandoned his commitment." Damian pounded his fist to the desktop. "You will tell me, now."

In the line of fire, and given the consequences of his bad behavior, Jason withered, as *he* was the scoundrel Damian sought.

"I will not." His lady remained steadfast, and then and there she gained newfound respect.

She could have handed Jason to her furious elder sibling and loomed large at dawn, as he fell to Damian's shot. Instead, she protected Jason. And as Alex guarded their secret, he availed himself of the opportunity to appraise her profile.

While the face mirrored that which haunted his dreams, without fail, her body had undergone some rather pronounced changes. Even though she was clothed, he noted her breasts had grown considerably, and he was quite pleased with that prospect. But her protruding belly gave him cause for concern.

Jason had seen myriad increasing women in his lifetime, and he could not recall a single pregnant female that presented so...huge. It was only last autumn that Everett had teased Sabrina, in regard to her girth, suggesting she had eaten a whole pumpkin. Alex appeared to have swallowed an entire patch, as her lap had all but vanished beneath her burden. Yet, to him, she had never been lovelier.

"Damian, for the love of Christ stop shouting—"

"The child is mine." Jason had spoken before he realized he had uttered a single word.

The study grew silent as a tomb.

Alex blinked and then mouthed, *No.*

The center of attention, he sighed and tugged at his cravat, which was a nervous habit he had acquired as a midshipman, while serving a captain who had insisted every crewmember wear the neck cloth.

"What did you say?" Damian narrowed his stare.

Jason squared his shoulders and braced himself. "Alex carries my child."

"Are you telling me you claimed my sister's maidenhood without first taking the vows?" Damian rested hands on hips. "Form your response carefully, as it may be your last."

"Yes, I own her bride's prize." Jason speared his fingers through his hair, which was another norm he had tried but failed to break. "And I am prepared to do the honorable by her."

"No, you will not." Alex stood and hugged her belly. "Because I refuse to marry you."

Now that was the one declaration Jason had fully expected upon arrival at Penhurst. "Alex, we must—"

"Lady Alex, to you." Her notorious temper resurfaced

with a vengeance and alleviated his concern for her health, to some degree.

"We have long since moved beyond formalities, love." How he wished he could have spared her the shame and humiliation of her circumstances. No wonder she had retired to the country.

"I am well aware of our past affiliation, Captain Collingwood, as I bear the proof of your fickle fancy." Then she smiled, which had not fooled him for a second. "While I thank you for the offer, I have no wish to wed anyone —ever."

"Are you out of your mind?" Damian bounded around the desk and stood toe-to-toe with his sister. "As you chose him, you will marry him."

"Damian, please, calm down." Alex inhaled a shaky breath. "Perhaps Captain Collingwood and I can negotiate an arrangement."

She could not have hurt him more had she struck him. How ironic it was that their positions had reversed since that fateful day in Plymouth, when she had sought a betrothal, and he had suggested an arrangement. And now he comprehended the justification for her ire.

"Calm?" Damian snorted. "You want calm?"

"Now see here, Weston—" In that instant, Damian grabbed a fistful of Jason's cravat and hauled him to his feet.

"Good God, man, and I use the term loosely, what were you thinking?" Damian bared his teeth. "Brethren do not defile and debauch our women. We preserve their honor, as we revere their bodies. We protect our ladies—we do not ruin them and sail into the sunset, leaving them to face the consequences, alone. You are unworthy of the Nautionnier Knight's badge, but you leave me little choice, so you will restore her reputation, or you will die."

"Damian, stop this nonsense, at once." Inching to the edge of her seat, Alex frowned and then stood. "Captain Collingwood is blameless, so you must release him."

Confronted with such potent anger, many a hired sailor would have withered beneath Damian's glare, but Alex had not so much as flinched when she defended Jason.

"Evidence to the contrary precedes you, dear sister." Damian wrenched hard and set Jason on his heels. "She is but nine and ten, and you?"

"One and thirty." Jason blanched, as the difference in their ages highlighted his copious culpability. "And I—"

"It was not his fault," Alex said in a small voice. "Because I seduced him."

Once again, uncomfortable silence settled on the study.

Poor Damian paled, stumbled backwards, perched on the edge of his desk, peered from side to side, located the decanter of brandy, and downed a healthy swill of the amber intoxicant. With a hand pressed to his chest, he huffed a breath. "Pray, explain yourself."

"Forgive me for what I am about to impart, as I am ashamed of my behavior." Alex stiffened her spine, and Jason, leery of another attack, adopted an offensive posture. "In January, when you made a supply run to Belgium, I obtained Captain Collingwood's address from your ledger, followed him to Plymouth, and made untoward advances on his person, until he succumbed to my feminine wiles."

That she protected Jason only heaped more shame on his miserable hide. "Alex—"

"It is true." How he cherished her fiery spirit.

Damian bobbled as a newborn babe. "But I thought you visited Sabrina?"

"I lied." She bit her lip.

"You lied *to me*?" To Jason's surprise, Damian extended

his arms and flicked his fingers. "If you were so resolute in your decision, why did you not talk to me? Collingwood and I could have negotiated the terms of your marriage."

"I am so sorry, brother." Alex stepped into his embrace, and sighed. "But I made a horrible mistake, and I—"

Flinching, she closed her eyes, scrunched her face, and gasped.

"What is it? Is something wrong?" Damian offered support. "Are you unwell? Is it the baby?"

"Are you in pain?" Concern shot to the fore, as Jason rested a hand to the small of her back. "Are there complications?"

"Do not touch me, sir." She shoved him hard, and he retreated. "It is nothing."

"Are you certain you are all right?" he inquired.

"Why do you ask?" she replied, with an acid tongue.

"Because...well...you are rather rotund, even for an expectant mother." The steely expression with which she impaled Jason bloody well scared him to death. "Of course, I could be mistaken."

"Not that it is any of your business, but Dr. Meade informed me at my last appointment that he detected two distinct heartbeats." Her chin quivered, and he had a hunch that if she cried, Damian would kill Jason.

"I do not follow." He scratched his cheek. "Two heartbeats?"

"The doctor deduced I carry twins, you ignorant ass." Now she pouted. "My size is appropriate to my condition, and I will thank you not to make further comments, which I find quite inconsiderate."

"*Twins*?" The world shifted beneath his feet, and he swayed. Just as fast, Damian passed the decanter, and Jason gulped about a third of the contents, before wiping his mouth on his coat sleeve. "As in more than one babe?"

"What troubles you, Captain?" Alex asked, her query dripping sarcasm. "Wish me merry, as they concern you not, for I have no intention of standing as your blushing bride."

"I beg to disagree, Alex." Jason consumed another generous swig of brandy and returned the bottle to Damian. "As those babes are mine, you belong to me. My claim is irrefutable."

"I rebuke your claim, on my children and I, Captain Collingwood." It irritated him that she refused to address him informally, as if they had shared nothing more than polite conversation. "We have had no need of you these past six months, so I will not wed, and you cannot force me. There ends the matter."

With that, Alex turned and quit the room.

Stung by her rejection, Jason searched for counterarguments, anything to alter her perspective—until a solid blow to the chin sent him to the floor. Rubbing his jaw, he glared at Damian. "What was that for?"

"The honor punch." Damian offered a hand, which Jason accepted with a prodigious dose of skepticism. "Now that we have dispensed with the noblemen's justice, which you abided with commendable affability, we must plan your wedding."

"You can't be serious." As he dusted his coat and adjusted his cravat, Jason grimaced. "Did you not witness what I just witnessed? She refused me. You will have to hold a pistol to her back, else she will never consent."

"Do you or do you not wish to live to see the morn?" With indefatigable equanimity, which Jason found indefatigably exasperating, Damian drew a sheet of parchment from a drawer and snatched his pen from the inkstand. "And what my sister wishes is of no consequence, at this point."

"Damian, you know, very well, that I journeyed here with the expressed intent of proposing to Alex." Resolved to correct the situation, and determined to make her his wife, Jason stretched to his full height and folded his arms. "We spoke of nothing else, during our drive."

"Indeed, that is the only reason you retain the ability to draw breath." The duke sketched a missive without missing a beat. "By the by, how does tomorrow strike you, for a wedding day?"

CHAPTER SEVEN

*R*eclining on the *chaise* in her sitting room, Alex rubbed her belly and smiled. Pronounced movement, which increased with each passing day, portended rambunctious children—so like their father. That singular thought evoked images of her sea captain and awakened all the associated emotions she had tucked deep in her heart, where she was always honest with herself, the cold day in February when Dr. Handley had confirmed her pregnancy.

Which of her friends had betrayed her confidence and apprised Jason of his impending, two-fold bundle of joy? After throwing her over in January, when she had all but begged him to marry her, the damn fool man had the audacity to believe he could make an offer that she would accept?

"You have some nerve, Jason Collingwood." The minute she uttered his name, she gave vent to a plaintive cry. "Oh, Jason. Why are you here? I gave myself to you, and you wanted me not. How can I ever trust you again?"

And yet, when she closed her eyes, he magically materialized, as a captivating illusion. From his guinea-gold locks spilling wildly over his shoulders, to his polished Hessians, his attire bespoke a well-heeled English gentleman. In Damian's study, her new nemesis had sported an ivory cravat, a navy waistcoat, and a brown coat. Fawn-colored breeches encased his muscular thighs and lean hips, which she recalled with frightening detail, given it had been six months since she had shared his bed.

In a licentious fusillade, memories of the time she had spent in his rented cottage assailed her, as had his rejection.

I will not marry you, Alex.

"Blast." The tears fell, much to her chagrin. Energetic kicks roused her from the momentary pity party, and she hugged her belly. "Sweet angels, he is not worth my devotion, but you merit mine."

Propped on her elbows, Alex shimmied to the edge of the *chaise*, in what had become an embarrassingly frequent exercise in lunacy to escape reclining positions, and stood. Resting palms to hips, she stretched her back and moaned. The bellpull seemed miles away, though it required mere steps to reach it, and she yanked with all her might to summon her meal. What troubled her was that her once graceful walk had devolved to an awkward waddle, beneath her temporary but precious cargo.

In her bedchamber, she studied her reflection in the long mirror and practiced a carefree stroll. When her first endeavor produced something more akin to a cow with its hooves stuck in the mud, she completed three additional rotations about her quarters.

"Sabrina is right. Pregnancy is grossly unfair, as women must suffer the morning malaise, the weight gain, the swollen feet, and the birthing process, while men get their jollies and an heir." Studying the intricate lace situated at what had been her waistline, the thin strip of Alençon only emphasized her girth. Rotund, indeed. A knock at the door snared her attention. "Who goes there?"

"It is Conrad, your ladyship."

"I am not receiving, Conrad."

"Yes, my lady, I am aware of that." Then why had the butler disturbed her? "However, if I may, I beg an audience with your ladyship, because it is a matter of utmost importance, else I never would have disregarded your orders and intruded on your privacy."

"Is my brother with you?" Suspicion nipped at her heels, as she shuffled to the door. "I warn you, I shall brook no tricks."

"No, my lady." The doorknob rattled, and she retreated a step. "But I am here on His Grace's behalf, though he does not know it, because his behavior is cause for great concern."

"What is wrong with Damian?" She hugged the oak panel and bit her lip. "Is he ill?"

"Please, my lady." Palpable anxiety invested Conrad's tone, and Alex fretted for Damian. Had her ruin pushed him beyond the brink of despair? Had he taken desperate action and harmed himself? "Grant me an interview."

Despite her reservations, Alex unlocked the door. "Are you alone?"

"Yes, my lady." The silver-haired butler nodded.

In a peculiar defensive tactic, she surveyed the hall, and then she retreated to permit him entry. "Hurry."

"I am reluctant to disturb you, my lady." The stodgy manservant stood at attention. "But I do so under the gravest of circumstances."

After securing the bolt, she exhaled in relief. "What is this about Damian?"

"His Grace is distraught, my lady." With a pained expression, Conrad gazed at the floor. "The staff have tried everything to reach him, with no success."

"I do not understand." The weight of the world settled on her shoulders, as never had she intended Damian to suffer her shame. "What has my brother done to warrant your interest or consternation?"

"His Grace has barricaded himself in the drawing room, and he refuses to take sustenance. As far as I know, His Grace has had no sleep, since his arrival." And then Conrad leaned close, cupped his hand to his mouth, and whispered, "I believe His Grace has overindulged in spirits, your ladyship."

"Damian—foxed?" Alex gasped in horror, as never, to her knowledge, had he drank to excess, because he refused to cede control to that extent. "You must be mistaken."

"Would that I were, your ladyship." A tic above Conrad's right eye underscored his discomfit and heightened the tension investing her frame.

"Oh, dear. I must go to Damian, now." Alex tottered to the door and twisted the key. "Where is Captain Collingwood?"

"Captain Collingwood departed an hour ago, to fetch Mr. Catchpole, at my request." Conrad followed her into the hall.

"Do you think it necessary to summon the vicar?" She swallowed hard, as never could she live with herself had Damian taken drastic measures to cope with her shame.

"Unfortunately, I think it imperative, your ladyship."

In the gallery, Alex glanced at her sire's portrait and dipped her chin in blithe salute. At the landing, she veered right and descended the grand staircase. In the foyer, she turned left and halted before the double doors that led to the drawing room. With her hand on the knob, she pressed her ear to the oak panel and prayed for the slightest signal that Damian remained hale and whole, and Conrad had worried for naught.

"His Grace has locked the door, my lady." The butler frowned.

"Damian will never refuse to receive me." In that instant, she rapped her knuckles to the wood.

"*Who goes there?*" At Damian's terse reply, she jumped.

"I do not know, your ladyship." Conrad compressed his lips and clasped his hands behind his back. "His Grace does not sound too welcoming."

"It is Alex, my dear brother." She tried the knob, but it yielded not. "Open the door, Damian, because I must speak with you."

Silence spoke volumes.

"My lady, if I may." Conrad produced a key from his coat pocket. "I thought it best to wait for your intervention before revealing our advantage."

"Marvelous." Her heart pounded a rapid salvo in her chest, and she prepared to confront the single most reliable source of support and comfort during her formative years. Now, it was her turn to comfort Damian, and she resolved to succeed. "I want you to unlock the door. When I step inside, secure the bolt behind me."

"As you wish, my lady." Conrad furrowed his brow.

A soft click pierced the solemnity, and she sidled into the drawing room. She turned and winked at the butler. "Wish me luck."

"My lady." Conrad drew a handkerchief from his coat pocket and patted his temples. "I hope that, some day, you might forgive me."

And then he slammed shut the door and reset the bolt.

Confused by Conrad's curious statement, Alex peered into the darkness. Well-appointed, the drawing room at Penhurst Castle boasted a massive stone fireplace, emerald velvet draperies, and Italian embroideries. Of all the chambers in the imposing seat of the Weston dukedom, the drawing room was her favorite.

"Damian, are you there?" She took two tentative steps.

"Aye." The morose timbre tugged at her heartstrings. "Come in, my dear."

"Will you pull the drapes, brother?" Although she could navigate her home with her eyes blindfolded, she would not risk injuring her babes in an unexpected tumble. "I can have Cook prepare your favorite breakfast, and we can enjoy our morning meal, together. Will that not be lovely?"

All of a sudden, the drapes parted, and shimmering light flooded the room. With a hand, she shielded her gaze from the glare, until her sight adjusted, and then she spied three silhouettes.

Gooseflesh covered her arms, a wicked shiver traipsed her spine, and overpowering dread licked at her nerves. Alex struggled to catch her breath, but terror clawed at her throat, and a vicious cramp ravaged her gut.

The trio of men gathered before the mullioned windows made no attempt to disguise the fact that they waited for her. At left, Damian loomed as the specter of doom. At right, her downfall, Jason boasted the meticulous coat of gray Bath superfine she had gifted him for Christmas. But it was the imposing figure at center, Mr. Catchpole—the vicar —who captured her attention to the detriment of all else.

"*No.*" Quick as a flash, Alex rotated and scurried for the exit. The cool metal knob chilled her fevered palm, as she searched for the key, which should have rested in the lock. Then the meaning of the butler's parting remark dawned, and she resorted to pounding the oak panel. "Conrad, let me out!"

"Stop your nonsense, Alex." Damian caught her by the waist and steered her toward her fate. "Do not make this difficult."

"Brother, no." She dug her heels into the thick Aubusson carpet, to no avail. Regardless of her protests, he ushered her to the makeshift altar. "Please, do not do this to me. Our parents will roll over in their graves, if you force me to wed."

"You have left me no choice." He shoved her forward.

Jason fast approached, and she had to act, so she cast the only lifeline that remained at her disposal. "If you do this, I will never speak to you again."

Damian halted.

Alex sighed in relief.

"Do you mean that?" He toyed with a thick lock of her hair and grimaced. "You would punish me for doing my duty by you?"

"Damian, I have no quarrel with you, and I would rather die than hurt you, but I am no disinterested spectator here." She clutched his hand and squeezed his fingers, as she had to make him understand her position. "This scene has a predictable ending, so I must object."

"Am I to suffer your transgressions gladly?" How she ached for her brother, as he bore the stress of her mistakes as a morbid mask. "You would ask me to ignore the repercussions of your decision? And what of your babes? Would you make them bastards, for society to ridicule and scorn?"

"I have thought of that, and it matters not, because I shall protect them." In truth, her dreams for her children's future involved fanciful birthday celebrations, play dates with the next Brethren generation, and joyous holidays.

"But I would have you do nothing, given Jason does not want me."

"What he wants is irrelevant, and I have done nothing, because I merely hold you to the bargain you made with Collingwood, when you went to his bed." Damian tucked a stray tendril behind her ear. "For good or ill, you made your choice, which I am compelled to honor. Were it possible, were there some measure of recompense or legal remedy, know that I would employ it, but you have left me no quarter. He is your only option, Alex. Given the babes you carry are his, Collingwood maintains all rights. You belong to him, now."

"So I am to be forced?" Grasping at the scarcest scrap of hope, she played her last card. "I am to be shackled in the drawing room with you and the vicar as witnesses, with no family, friends, well-wishers, or church? Is this the wedding you want for me?"

"No. The ceremony I envisioned for you was the stuff of fairy tales, the realm of make-believe. I pictured you gowned as befits a queen, with a tiara of diamonds crowning your head, and ensconced in our town carriage, pulled by my best team." It was then she spied tears in her brother's eyes. "I dreamed of the day I would escort you down the aisle at St. George's and stand with pride when you spoke your vows. At your wedding breakfast, I would have toasted to your eternal happiness and prosperity. To know that will never happen, I am more sorry than I can say."

"But it does not have to be this way." Alex glanced at Jason and rued the moment they had met. "Damian, I need never return to London. I can remain here, for the rest of my life."

"That is not possible, sister." Damian shook his head.

"Why not?" Control of her destiny stretched beyond her

grasp, and she sobbed without restraint. "Please, I can serve as chatelaine, as I have acted as such for years. Why should that change?"

"Because you were not meant to live alone." Damian produced a handkerchief from his coat pocket and dried her cheeks. "That is a fate worse than death, and I will not allow it."

"But I will never be alone, because I have you and my babes," she replied, with a whisper of optimism.

"My darling girl, I will take a wife, when I find a suitable candidate, given I have long desired a family." Once again, he nudged her into the breach. "My future duchess will serve as chatelaine for my properties, thus relegating you to the shadows."

"Perhaps you could secure a cottage." If Alex had squandered her brother's support, then she was truly lost. Adrift in a sea of uncertainty, she clung to the last vestiges of hope. "I would be happy—"

"You have made your decision." Damian paused and cupped her cheek. "Now you will uphold it."

"But Captain Collingwood and I have no understanding." She covered his hand with her own. "I have given him nothing."

"You gave him your body." With a countenance of unutterable gloom, he compressed his lips. "Now you will give him your oath."

"This is a travesty." When Damian positioned her beside Jason, Alex folded her arms. "I am dead to you, brother."

"As you wish." At his terse reply, she almost swooned.

"Lady Alexandra, it is a pleasure to see you again." Mr. Catchpole offered a somewhat unsteady smile. "Despite the inauspicious occasion."

"Good day, Mr. Catchpole." She dipped her chin. "I have no wish to wed, given there is no cause."

"All evidence to the contrary." The vicar glanced at her belly, and then he removed his spectacles and rubbed the bridge of his nose. "I have known you since I christened you, so if you tell me this man is not the father of your babes, I will not compel you to marry, and His Grace will have to find another to do his bidding."

A lie danced at the tip of her tongue, along with vehement repudiations and sharp disavowals, which she suspected would condemn her to the bowels of hell had she voiced them. "He is the father, Mr. Catchpole."

The vicar resituated his spectacles on his nose, lifted a leather-bound tome, and opened to a marked page. "Please, join hands."

Jason reached for her, and Alex wrenched free. "We have joined enough."

With a wide-eyed expression of shock, the vicar cleared his throat. "Dearly beloved, we are gathered here today…"

Lady Alexandra Collingwood.

As the daughter of a duke, she retained her title and rank, along with a few select terms that aptly described the angry beauty.

Wife.

Expectant mother.

Jason shuddered.

Of course, he could think of other more appropriate appellations, which no lady of character would dare articulate: Hellion, virago, termagant, harridan, and she-wolf…oh, the list was endless.

The occasional ping of silver meeting china punctuated the silence, and despite claims otherwise, his brother-in-law had offered no felicitous toast. As he sat beside his bride in the cavernous dining hall at Penhurst, which seemed to emphasize the sparse wedding party consisting of Damian, Alex, and Jason, he mulled the day's events.

While Jason had answered each petition Mr. Catchpole had posed, Alex had stood tight-lipped and taciturn, which spoke volumes as to her mood, and Damian had responded in her stead. And although the good vicar had announced their union official, in the eyes of God and the law, they had shared no kiss to seal their vows, which was fine with him, as he feared she might bite off his head—or another, more estimable protuberance, given her dour spirits.

It was her unforeseen ire that had rendered him befuddled. After all, had she not wanted to marry him? Had she not declared her love? Had she not bucked propriety and shed her societal façade, along with her clothes, and taken to his bed as a practiced seductress in her endeavors? Aside from her pregnancy and body, what had changed?

"May I be excused?" Alex inquired in a small voice.

"You have not—"

"But you have—" Jason glanced at Damian.

"Sorry, Collingwood. Old habits die hard." Her brother frowned and averted his stare. "I defer to your authority."

"You have consumed almost nothing." How could he reach his errant wife? "Think of our children."

"I enjoyed a large breakfast, sir." It bothered him that she refused to look at him. "So I am not hungry."

"Perhaps I can tempt you with lighter fare?" Recalling Alex's fondness for sweets, he altered his tack with his sullen spouse. As he drew a platter of desserts to her place setting, he said, "Do you see anything to your liking?"

"Please, sir. I am rather exhausted, as it has been a trying day, to say the least." While Jason had anticipated all manner of curses heaped on his soul, in the wake of his forced wedding, he had not prepared for the new version of Alex, blanketed in a dense mixture of reticence and disconsolation. "May I retire?"

"All right, my lady wife." He pushed his chair from the table, stood, and dismissed the approaching footman, as Jason preferred to assist his bride. "You may go to your room."

Again, Alex stunned him with her dejected countenance, as she bowed her head and slumped her shoulders, and he could tolerate her conduct no further. With a finger, he tipped her chin and brought her gaze to his. The wrenching anguish he spied in her blue eyes struck him as a vicious punch to the gut.

"Rest well, sweetheart." He was not sure why he had done it, but he pressed on her a gentle kiss. "We journey to our country home, tomorrow."

"Yes, sir." She half-curtseyed and waddled from the dining room.

"Collingwood." Damian tossed his napkin on his plate.

What now? "Aye?"

Damian shifted his weight and grimaced. "I have taken the liberty of installing your personal belongings in my sister's chambers."

"For the love of all creation—*why*?" Jason had reached the end of his tether. "In case it has escaped your notice, Alex detests me, and you would drive me into her bed?"

"It is your wedding night." Damian shrugged. "It made sense, at the time."

"Trust me, I am well aware of my marital state, but Alex increases." A fact Jason could not ignore. "In deference to her condition, I would not take her without her encouragement and consent."

Damian focused on the floor. "But you must consummate your vows, else the union is not legal or binding."

"I hate to point out the obvious, but Alex and I consummated our vows in January, and the proof of our success grows in her belly." Jason snorted. "I would assert I am irrevocably bound to your sister."

"Quite right." Damian stood. "I have lost my appetite. Would you care to join me for a brandy?"

"Brother, at this moment, I could use a bottle." Jason chuckled and slapped Damian on the back. "How in bloody hell am I going to correct the mess I have made of my situation?"

"There you have me, as my experience tends toward courtesans, not wives." Damian snickered, as they crossed the foyer. "And I apologize for my heavy-handed tactics, as it was not my intent to meddle in your personal affairs. But my sister possesses a certain obstinacy of spirit, and you would do well not to discount it."

"Ah, yes. Her notorious stubborn streak." Jason whistled in monotone. "We have met."

"Oh, Collingwood." In that instant, Damian laughed, and the tension nagging Jason's shoulders dissipated. "I do not envy the road ahead for you and my sister. And on that note, you have yet to sign the marriage contract."

In the study, Jason came to an abrupt halt. "Why does it feel as though I am returning to the scene of the crime?"

"Perhaps because Alex looked on you as a sword-wielding executioner?" Again, Damian surrendered to uncharacteristic mirth. "I still cannot believe she ambushed you in Plymouth, and I wish you had sent her home, posthaste. Why did you delay, when you might have spared yourself your current predicament?"

"Damian, I mean no disrespect, but I have never met anyone half so bold as Alex, and I could never resist her." And then Jason dropped into a high back chair, propped his elbows to his knees, and rested his chin in his palms. "But the short answer is I care for her."

"Well said, brother, and I am delighted to hear it." Damian retrieved a folder and set out two documents. "Have you apprised my sister of your engaged affection? It might go a long way to smooth ruffled feathers."

"Do I look like a brainless nincompoop?" That singular question posed the heart of Jason's dilemma, given Alex had declared her love, and he had rejected her. "Under the circumstances, I doubt she would believe me, and I have no idea how to convince her of my sincerity."

"Have you considered asking the Brethren husbands for advice, as all four gave less than stellar performances in the marriage mart and should have learned something from their misadventures?" Damian filled two brandy balloons and passed a glass to Jason. "They must have some sage wisdom to impart, and what could it hurt?"

"Damian, you are indeed the voice of reason, as the thought had not occurred to me." Had Lance not sought such counsel in his attempt to bring Cara to the altar? "I shall compose a series of letters upon our arrival at Stratfield Manor."

"Then you need only sign the contract, and our business is concluded." Damian wrote Alex's name, then affixed his initials, and Jason scribbled his endorsement.

"I suppose that does it." Jason downed his brandy. "But I am for Bedfordshire. In light of the change in my accommodations, will you direct me to my wife's quarters?"

"Of course, and you must promise to write me, from time to time, and tell of my sister and your heirs, as I fear she may never forgive me." Damian walked Jason to the door. "At the top of the stairs, turn left. On the other side of the gallery is a long hallway. Alex's apartments are the third entry on the right."

"Brother, I shall dispatch regular correspondence, and once I repair the damage to our relationship, I will encourage her to contact you, too." They shook hands. "And thank you, for hearing my side."

"Well, I could not kill you, as I would have orphaned my future niece, nephew, or both." Damian grinned. "I wish you luck, as you will need it."

In mere minutes, Jason navigated the chasmal residence and loitered at the portal of Alex's quarters. Nervous as a green lad with his first whore, he thought he might knock. Then again, it seemed unwise to provide his spitfire bride warning of his presence. Cursing uncharacteristic indecision, he at last turned the knob and set wide the oak panel.

A fire in the hearth warmed and illuminated the sitting room, which featured a large wingback chair and a daybed piled high with pillows. But he had no interest in the furnishings.

An entry to the left opened to another, much larger chamber. An impressive four-poster, the most massive he had ever seen in a woman's quarters, held pride of place at the center of the back wall. To his surprise, the bed was empty. A fireplace bathed the room in soft light, and just then he located the object of his affection, standing before the only window with the drapes still tied.

Moonlight cocooned her in a silvery glow, which rendered all but invisible the silk creation she wore. Similar to the attire with which she had taunted him in Plymouth, the diaphanous gauze only emphasized the tempting cleft of her bottom. In a flash, Jason recalled what he had done to her luscious derriere in vivid detail, and he gritted his teeth against a groan.

When Alex inclined her head and hugged her pronounced belly, something inside him seized, and his gut clenched. Had he thought her beautiful? The term seemed insufficient, as he found her breathtaking. Focused, determined to right the wrongs of the past, he crossed the floor, slipped his hand beneath her long locks, closed his fingers about the hair at the nape of her neck, tipped back her head, rested a palm to her belly, and kissed her.

CHAPTER EIGHT

*I*n soft, subtle sashays, Jason loved Alex with his mouth, and she could have cried. It was so wonderful to taste her captain again, and then his rejection intruded on their delicious interlude, haunting and taunting, and she withdrew.

"Why are you here?" She tottered to the mantel and gazed into the blaze. "And why did you kiss me?"

"Just correcting your oversight, love." His rich baritone melted over her, like honey on a hot scone, and left nothing untouched.

And, oh, what she felt.

"I do not follow." How often she had dreamed of their wedding night, yet her fantasy had never included a forced marriage and an unplanned pregnancy. "What have I neglected?"

"I believe it customary to seal the marital vows with a kiss, or would you argue otherwise?" Was her husband flirting with her?

"Well now you have had your kiss." And Alex wished she had donned a more conservative robe. "So you may take your leave, and I shall see you in the morning. I wish you a pleasant rest, sir."

"Not so fast, my fetching bride." Jason chuckled, in that sensual rumble that sent delicious shivers over her flesh. "As my personal belongings have been moved here, compliments of your brother, I will sleep here."

She gasped in horror at the prospect, because she could resist so many things, but randy Jason—oh, no. "But—you can't mean to take me in this condition."

"Would you like me to try?" He grinned, and the ice encasing her heart fractured.

"Of course, not." She lied, as her body never failed to respond to his flirty summons.

"Are you sure, because you do not sound very certain of yourself?" Her naughty husband trailed a finger along the curve of her cheek, her jawline, her neck, and then he traced imaginary circles on her décolletage. "And I am most definitely at your service, my dear wife."

"Yet you love me not." She grasped at a lifeline, to forestall his lusty assault, because if he touched her in that place at the apex of her thighs, he would have her.

"Perhaps, not." With a mighty frown, he dropped his hand to his side. "But I desire you."

And there it was, the source of her torment and shame, plainly spoken. "That was never enough for me."

"What is that supposed to mean?" Jason inclined his head.

"You are a wise man, though you have done your best to convince me otherwise, so figure it out for yourself, sir." Shielded in anger mixed with despair, Alex unfastened the lone button of her robe. "I should warn you that I sleep in the nude, as I find nightgowns altogether confining and uncomfortable, at this stage in my pregnancy, so you should avert your gaze, given my *rotundness* offends you."

"I beg your pardon?" He settled hands on hips and shifted his weight. "When did I ever make such a callous statement?"

"Did you or did you not comment on my size, when you first arrived?" With a deep breath, she steeled herself for his derision and dropped her robe to the floor. Then she drew back the blankets, fluffed a mountain of pillows, and enacted the wonky exercise required to recline in bed.

"Alex, I admit I am, at times, an ignorant arse, and I regret my thoughtless comment, but I plead temporary insanity, as your condition was a deuced shock." After doffing his coat and waistcoat, he untied his cravat and flung the linen swath across the back of a chair. Then Jason sat and tugged off his boots. When he unhooked his breeches, she closed her eyes. "All right, where is the rapier retort? What happened to my fiery society miss? You know, the brazen spitfire who followed me to Plymouth?"

"You destroyed her." The mattress dipped, dislodging her pillow supports, and she rolled to the side, into Jason's arms. Hovering close, with their noses mere inches apart, he hugged her. "I am all that remains, sir."

"Will you stop addressing me so formally?" As she tried to resituate herself, he held her firm. "And what are you about, with the pile of cushions, as you cannot be comfortable? Is this your way of erecting additional barriers between us?"

"I need not add to our troubles, sir. But my elevated position is the only posture that affords a measure of relief that I may sleep, as our babes are restless." It was then she realized her husband had deliberately baited her. "And I show you that deference which is owed to a husband, as I have been bred to obey."

"How many times must I remind you I was not to the manor born?" Jason brushed his lips to hers. "As you so correctly pointed out in Plymouth, I am but a low-born sailor. I never attended Eton or university, thus my education took place above and below decks, courtesy of the Royal Navy, and I am quite proud of my history, as I have no use for titles or such foppery."

"Are you finished?" She moaned, as he kissed her again.

"No." With a fistful of covers, he drew the sheet to her chin. "How can I help you, love? There must be a more relaxed station. Will you not lean on me?"

"I would, but then I could not rest when you leave me— and you will leave me." How Alex needed his strength, but she had trusted him once, and he had disappointed her. "And I would not inconvenience you."

"Darling, you are never an inconvenience, and I have no intention of leaving your side, unless duty calls." He splayed a hand protectively over her belly. The babes kicked, and his eyes grew wide. "Is that what I think it is?"

"Yes. Your children are most active at night." She smiled at his countenance of inexpressible wonder. "But I thought you would return to London, after installing me at Stratfield Manor."

"*Installing you*?" Jason blanched, and she could not help but giggle. "Sweetheart, you are my wife, not some contracted heir maker. Bloody hell, but the peerage infests your mind with such revolting notions."

"Then you intend to reside with me?" All right, she was a vast deal more than relieved that he would not abandon her to the country, yet Alex knew not what to expect of her husband.

"You really think the worst of me, do you not?" How wounded he appeared, as he slipped his arm about her shoulders. "And who could blame you, given my abominable treatment. My lovely bride, I know I hurt you. If I could go back in time, to that awful day in Plymouth, know that the outcome would have been quite the opposite, as I should have married you. But now we are wed, and your honor is restored. Let go your anger and make the best of our situation."

"Are you serious? Is that all you have to say for yourself?" She had almost fallen for him—almost. "It will take more than pretty words and easy manners to resolve our problems, sir."

"I do not suppose we can straighten out our difficulties in a single conversation, dearest." Jason shuffled the pillows and encouraged her to recline on her side, with her belly nestled in a cushion he had placed with efficiency and her head resting on his shoulder. "I ask for a chance, Alex. Give me the opportunity to redeem myself, nothing more."

"But you ask so much." She pressed her palm to his muscled chest. "And I know not if I can survive another disappointment. I must consider my babes—"

"*Our* babes." As was his way, he raked his fingers through her hair and massaged her scalp.

Memories, bits of the past flooded her consciousness, and Alex sniffed, as she revisited cherished moments from their courtship and her time in Plymouth. Soon, the tears flowed, as she mourned the fanciful dreams she had coveted since they met two years ago.

"Do not cry, darling." He cradled her head, and she sobbed without restraint.

"I weep not for you." In truth, Alex lamented the man

she had thought Jason had been, and it had almost killed her to discover he was not her knight in shining armor.

"Of course not." Still, he held her.

"I grieve what might have been." And what grand aspirations she had envisioned.

"Alex, I know we begin our life under inauspicious circumstances, and I understand that I failed you." He could not possibly comprehend what he had done to her. "Please, do not turn me away."

For several seconds, she pondered his request, as his heartbeat lulled her into a relaxed state. Although she would deny it should her husband inquire, she desperately needed him—the man of honor she had pursued to Plymouth, not the blackguard who left her alone, unwed, and pregnant. And while she had heaped a boatload of hellfire and brimstone on his imaginary head during those six months he was at sea, part of her celebrated his return, as he owned her heart, body, and soul, much to her chagrin.

"Are you sincere in your desire to set things right between us?" It was a question he had posed, the day she had arrived at the small rented cottage.

"I will do anything to restore your faith in me." Another mirror response, and it cut like the sharpest knife, as she longed to believe him. "Tell me what you would have of me, and you shall have it."

"You must earn the chance you seek, but I know not what I require, as I hardly know myself, any more." In that moment, she dried her eyes and peered at him. "I am lost, Jason."

"Beautiful Alex, allow me to help you find yourself again." And then he tipped her chin and covered her mouth with his.

~

"I WILL ALWAYS BE HERE, Alex. While I know you remain angry with me, you must understand that I acted in the best interest of your children. I am still your brother, and I love you." Damian sighed, in a mournful exhalation she felt all the way to her marrow. "If you ever need me, you know how to reach me."

Alex stiffened her spine and faced forward, as she refused to look at Damian. Yes, she was furious with him for forcing her to wed, because she considered his action a bitter betrayal, but she feared she would collapse into a fit of tears if she met his gaze, as he had been her staunchest defender for as long as she could remember. How much heartbreak could one woman withstand?

"Are you ready, my dear?" Jason handed her into the traveling coach. "We have a full day ahead of us."

"For the last time, must we journey to Stratfield now?" As she glanced at the graceful equipage, Alex blanched. "My stomach is rather fragile, and—"

"If you have your way, we will never leave Penhurst, so what is the difference, whether now or later?" When she settled her skirts and sank into the squabs in the middle of the bench, he frowned. "Will you scoot to one side, please?"

"You wish to share a seat?" Alex gulped at the prospect, because the morning malaise might necessitate a quick exit. "Jason, you should not—"

"Never mind." Without ceremony, her husband plopped beside her, turned, and drew her into his lap. "There. Surely we shall pass a far more enjoyable trip so comfortably situated."

"Do you intend to force your attentions on my person for

the duration of our travels?" Alex wiggled her hips and then froze, when her errant knight hissed.

"Easy, love, as you tempt me beyond reason." With a flirty nip of her ear, he chuckled and squeezed her thigh. "And in response to your question, the answer is no. I intend to force my attentions on your person for the duration of our marriage, as I count that state-sanctioned right chief among the perks of my newfound status as your lord and master."

"Lord and master, indeed." And then she noted the telltale bulge of his erection, and it dawned on her that he spoke the truth. He wanted her. That seemingly insignificant bit of information worked on Alex in a manner she could not have anticipated, and she involuntarily clenched the muscles between her legs. "Jason, I swear I am not trying to be difficult. My last carriage ride did not end so well, and I would spare you the unpleasantness."

"My dear wife, I manage a boatload of surly sailors for a living." Jason kissed her forehead. "I promise, whatever you throw at me, I can handle it."

Famous last words.

And so Alex rested her head on his shoulder and wept softly, as they passed through the gates of Penhurst Castle, leaving behind all that was familiar and comforting for—what, she knew not. Resolved to persevere, she closed her eyes and drifted into dreamland.

The sun was low in the western sky when Alex woke, hours later, cursed with the most prominent malady in her cadre of pregnancy plagues. At some point, Jason had shifted and propped in the corner, but he held her close in his lap. He dozed peacefully, unaware of the danger lurking in his midst, and she reconsidered disturbing him—just as a tidal wave of nausea struck her. As bile rose in her throat, the world spun out of control.

"Jason, wake up." With a violent shake, she roused him. "Hurry."

"What is it, darling?" He yawned and stretched.

"Stop the coach, as I fear I am going to—" To her utter mortification, Alex revisited the large breakfast she had enjoyed at Penhurst, on his coat.

"Good God, my wife erupts." Jason lowered the window, just as she surrendered to another wicked paroxysm. Then he pounded a fist to the ceiling. "*Hoi*! Hold Hard. Mrs. Collingwood is ill."

The coach came to an abrupt halt, and she would have fallen to the floor, had her husband not held her firmly in his grip. Jason lifted her in his arms and kicked open the door. As soon as her feet hit the ground, Alex collapsed on her hands and knees and heaved. Again and again, she retched, and to her inexpressible amazement, her fledgling spouse provided unshakeable support, for which she was grateful, as she needed his kindness just then.

When pins slipped from her coiffure, threatening to place her long locks in the line of fire, her captain knelt beside her and pulled back her hair. "Let me help you, love. Just rest against me, relax, and do not fight it."

"I think it has passed—" And then she vomited, with the driver and footmen as witnesses, in a repeat performance of monumental embarrassment.

"Take your time, sweetheart." Jason rubbed her shoulders and along her spine. "We are in no hurry."

"Captain Collingwood, would her ladyship like a drink of water?" The driver offered a military-styled canteen. "We have plenty, and we are happy to share."

"Thank you." After helping Alex stand upright, her

husband shrugged from his spoiled coat and fetched the canteen. "How is your constitution, darling?"

"Better." She swayed, and Jason rose to the rescue.

"Easy, Alex." He wet a handkerchief, wiped her face, and then pressed the linen to the back of her neck. "There is no rush, and we will continue our trip when you are ready."

"Oh, that feels delightful." How she longed for her comfortable bed and an uninterrupted, rejuvenating nap. "But I do not think I can go much further, as I am exhausted."

"No worries, love." He held the canteen to her lips. "Here, drink some water, but take small sips, else it will come up as fast as you swallow it."

"How do you know so much about morning sickness?" Of course, her particular brand of the ailment paid no heed to the hour of the day, as the queasiness struck her without prejudice.

"It is not so dissimilar from the illness that strikes most landlubbers during their maiden sea voyage." In a flash, Jason bent and swept her into his arms. "The footmen cleaned the coach, so we are good to resume our travels." To the coachman, her captain said, "Keep your team at a trot, and stop at the first inn, as we shall take a room and break our journey for the night."

"Aye, sir." The driver nodded. "And I will steer toward the verge, for the smoothest ride possible, given the lane has large ruts."

Reclining in the squabs, Alex smoothed her skirts and sighed, as her fragile belly had quieted. But just as she balanced on the bench, her curious spouse lifted her to his lap. "Jason, I am quite capable of sitting on my own."

"I am well aware of your independent streak, sweetheart, as we have met on occasions too numerous to count." He favored her with a sweet kiss, which she deemed far too brief. "But I missed you terribly, these past six months, so indulge me. I wish to hold you."

"You thought of me?" Alex cursed herself in silence, as she sounded bloody interested.

"Every minute we were apart." Cupping her cheek, he frowned. "And as I explained last night, I know I hurt you. While our problems will not resolve themselves in a mere sennight, I ask only for a chance to make amends, that you might believe in me, again."

"You promised not to pressure me, yet you already break your vow." And Jason terrified her, because he possessed the power to destroy what little remained of her. "Do you not comprehend that the chance you seek requires a measure of hope for success, on my part?"

"And you are afraid to invest the minutest amount of faith in me?" Why had he appeared the injured party, when he had wronged her? "Am I not worth the risk?"

"I asked the same of you, in some fashion, last January, in Plymouth." Alex sniffed and peered out the window. "We both know how that turned out."

"So you refuse me?" Jason replied in a morbid tone.

"On the contrary, sir." With all the determination she could muster, and that was not saying much, in light of her near-complete devastation, she met his stare. "The chance is yours to win or lose, with no guarantee of cooperation or success, as you have no right to make such demands."

"May I inquire why my honorable request is met with such unfriendly terms?" In that moment, he pressed his palm to her belly.

"When I ventured to Plymouth, I did so with a noble purpose, a sincere desire to set things right between us, with no assurances." For the umpteenth time, visions of those most happy days spent in the cottage evoked a plaintive cry. "You posed your challenge, conditions you devised as a means of punishment for my sin of omission, and I think it safe to say I surpassed your requisites. And you know how you rewarded my efforts."

"And it is your turn to mete retribution?" He arched a brow.

"No, as I harbor no such spurious motives." Alex wiped a stray tear. "I act in the interest of self-preservation and nothing more. What you ask, given our history, I simply cannot give you, at least, not now. My children take priority."

"All right. It will not be my first voyage into unfamiliar and unwelcome waters." Then Jason grasped the hair at the nape of her neck and kissed her hard. "Mark my words, I will win you back."

CHAPTER NINE

"*D*arling, wake up." Jason nuzzled Alex's temple, as she slept in his lap. "We are home, sweetheart."

Studying her in deep slumber had fast become one of his most treasured pastimes, as he could pretend, if only for a moment, that their situation was as it had once existed between them. In light of the conditions by which he pursued reconciliation, he had lingered in a chasm of desolation in the wee hours of the morning, until a brilliant plan formed in his brain.

How he longed for *his* Alex, the brazen young debutante who had flirted with him, propriety be damned, the seductive sylph who had lured him to bed with come-hither stares and take-me smiles, and the shameless siren who had lusted after him every bit as much as he had her. Yet he could not turn back the clock.

But what naval man possessed a bounty of knowledge regarding pregnant, scorned women? And then he recalled Damian's advice, which Jason had actually discounted, and it had occurred to him that his newfound family featured incomparable resources. Trevor, Everett, and Dirk were fathers, and each had stumbled on their path to the altar.

"Wake up, my lady wife." With a renewed sense of purpose, he nudged her nose with his, as the coach halted at the entrance to his humble estate. "Alex, we have arrived."

At last, she stirred. With a healthy stretch and a yawn, she blinked. "Are we at Stratfield, already?"

"You dozed for the past four hours, love." The footman opened the door, and Jason handed her to the graveled drive. "How fares your belly?"

"Much better, thank you. The dry toast worked wonders." And then she gazed on their country home. "So this is Stratfield Manor? How many bedrooms are there?"

"Indeed, it is our primary residence," Jason stated with pride. "And it has sixteen private chambers, rather small by your usual standards."

Made of red brick, with mullioned windows across the face, the building boasted the modest vernacular-Baroque tradition. The grand structure, the largest and most sumptuous he had ever owned, situated amid a copse of oaks trees. The edifice featured an upturned frieze beneath an inviting double-door entrance pediment, all of which Jason had favored the moment he had seen it.

"I never said that." Alex peered left and then right. "How many servants do you employ, and why are they not assembled to welcome us?"

"Oh, they are gathered, as there are just the two—"

"*Just the two?*" She emitted something between a sob and a sigh. "Are you out of your mind?"

"What?" Confused, he scratched his cheek. "I am one man. My needs are simple, as am I. Must I remind you that I was not born with a silver spoon in my mouth?"

"And do you lack a brain, as well?" And there it was, a

flash of his fiery Alex, and he could have cried. "Damn silly fool, you might have given me some warning. I can't manage a household this size with only two servants. Are you trying to kill me? If you care not for me, have you no concern for our children?"

"Of course I care, but my mother cooked and cleaned, on her own." How he loved baiting his society bride. "Are you telling me—"

"And did she run a sixteen-room manor?" Alex folded her arms and tapped her foot in an impatient rhythm he remembered with fondness.

"My childhood home more closely resembled the cottage in Plymouth." A charming flush colored the apples of her cheeks, and he could scarcely resist stealing a kiss. "Now, allow me to introduce our staff."

"Are you the butler?" Alex stepped to the fore.

"Ah—well, I suppose so." The tall and lanky codger, with salt and pepper hair, winked at Jason. "I do open the door, from time to time."

"My lady Alex, meet Gertie and Arnold." He dipped his chin and chuckled. "They have been friends of mine for years."

"Gertie?" His wife opened her mouth and then closed it.

"It is short for Gertrude, ma'am. But no one has called me that since I was a wee babe." The diminutive and chubby maid bowed like a man. "Welcome to Stratfield Manor. May I call you Alex?"

"Gertrude, forgive my forwardness, but may I inquire after your full name?" From the set of Alex's shoulders, Jason realized he was in trouble.

"Gertrude Mathilda Phipps." Poor Gertie shuffled her feet. "I beg your pardon, ma'am. I meant no offense."

"It is all right." His bride smoothed her skirts and sighed. "Are you the housekeeper, Mrs. Phipps?"

"It is Miss Phipps, ma'am. I never married." Gertie elbowed Arnold. "We are brother and sister. And as to whether or not I am the housekeeper, I do not rightly know."

"Mr. Phipps, Miss Phipps, I am so pleased to make your acquaintance. In a proper English residence, 'your ladyship' or 'my lady' is the appropriate form of address for an individual with my rank, and I shall call you as is appropriate and respectful of your station. To permit otherwise would risk subjecting you to ridicule or censure by our future guests, and I would spare you such embarrassment. And as chatelaine of Stratfield Manor, all decisions involving the estate house management fall to me." Then Alex walked up the entrance stairs. "Miss Phipps, let us have tea tomorrow, and we will discuss my requirements for an efficient and organized staff. And why are there no flowers in the beds?"

"Do I look like a gardener?" Jason caught the wary glances Gertie and Arnold exchanged. "And I have been at sea these six months."

"So I must hire gardening staff, as well, given the grounds are in a state of utter disrepair." Alex came to an abrupt halt in the foyer. "Why are there buckets on the floor?"

"The roof leaks, my lady." Arnold laughed. "If we forget to put out the buckets, or we are caught unaware, the house will flood."

"Phipps, show the footmen to the master suite, so they may deposit her ladyship's trunks." So the first impression was not the best. No doubt Alex would have the estate in order within a fortnight.

"Right away, Jas—er, what should I call you?" Phipps rubbed the back of his neck and narrowed his stare.

"Captain Collingwood will suffice," Alex responded. "And Miss Phipps, kindly unpack my trunks, and I shall join you shortly to supervise." Then his bride pinned him with a heated glare. "May I see you in the study, Jason?"

"As you wish, your ladyship." He sketched a mockery of a bow and then stood as escort. "May I show you the way?"

"The threadbare carpets must be replaced, along with the worn wallpaper." Alex wrinkled her nose as he steered her down the hall to the left. "There are cobwebs and dust covering every painting. And I can't even fathom what it will take to restore the shine to the floors, as they look as if they have not had a good cleaning in the last one hundred years."

"I am sure you can manage it." That should provoke the full-fledged return of his spitfire. "And here we have my private domain."

"Oh, dear. I had hoped for a small measure of improvement." She sat in a high back chair near the hearth, and a cloud of dust enveloped her. Coughing and sputtering, Alex stood. "Has none of the furniture been covered?"

"Did you expect me to take care of such tedium?" Jason shrugged.

"Then everything is ruined." Much to his dismay, she cradled her head in her hands and sobbed. "What in the world possessed you to bring me here? I am grateful our babes are yet unborn, as the dangers this broken down shack you call a manor presents to their health and welfare are too disconcerting to contemplate."

"What is this? Are you afraid of a little dirt and grime?" He had expected a hailstorm of curses, not tears. "Where is my brave Alex?"

For a few seconds, she simply stared at him. And then something caught her attention. She walked to the side wall, drew a handkerchief from her dress pocket, and wiped the white film from an oval mirror. "Do you know what I see when I gaze at my reflection?"

"My beautiful wife?" Although he chuckled, he sensed he had crossed some imaginary line in the sand, and there was no retreat.

"I glimpse a stranger, someone altogether foreign. Her eyes are bereft of spirit, and her face is a blank canvas. A cold, empty shell encompasses and stifles the fire that once burned within Lady Alexandra Seymour, but she is no more." She hugged her belly, as tears streamed her cheeks. "Unwanted and unloved, she yielded to fate for the sake of her babes. Forced into marriage, a death sentence in her humble estimation, she surrendered her dreams and abandoned everything she thought she knew about herself. The Alex you seek no longer exists. In her place remains a lifeless being, and she is lost, alone, sad, and very frightened."

Jason's blood ran cold. "Alex, I had no idea—"

"Have I not tried to tell you?" She inhaled a shaky breath and dried her face. "I offered you everything, and you left me nothing. Shall I describe my shame and humiliation, when I informed Admiral Douglas of my pregnancy? Damian was at sea, I needed help, and the usual channels were barred to me, as an unmarried woman with child, lest I scandalize my family name."

"I am so sorry, sweetheart." Without thought, he drew her into his arms, albeit from the side, in order to accommodate her belly. "And you need never be afraid, as I will let no harm befall you."

"Oh, Jason, *you* scare me. And I worry we may never recover." As the magnitude of her heartbreak dawned on him, he held her tighter. "And now I have this wreck of a home to salvage, which I shudder to consider, as everything needs either remodeling or replacing. There is so much work, and I near the end of my pregnancy."

"Perhaps I should hire someone to oversee the estate, in your stead." Cupping her cheek, he kissed her forehead. "Would that ease your mind?"

"No." She sniffed and then burrowed in his chest. "I was bred for just this situation, and I will not fail you, but I should warn you that the restoration will be very expensive."

"Spend whatever you wish, darling." Now that was a phrase he had never before uttered. "Make Stratfield a loving environment in which to raise our children."

"I shall remember you said that." And then she inched from his grasp. "Now, if you will excuse me, I should instruct Miss Phipps on the proper method for unpacking and airing clothes."

"Just a minute." Jason was not sure why he had done it, but he caught his lady, framed her face, and pressed on her a gentle kiss of which he had not thought himself capable. "Never fear me, Alex, as I would sooner take my life than hurt you again. And I know it is difficult for you to believe me, so I accept your challenge, with no promises on your part."

"You do?" The surprise in her tone cut him to the core, as she had so little faith in him, yet he could blame no one but himself.

"Aye." An unfamiliar pain weighed heavy in his chest. "And you should discuss dinner plans with Gertie, as we have no cook, and her kitchen skills are, well, horrible."

"Do we have any rabbit traps?" She tapped a finger to her chin. "As I could make your favorite stew, the partiality of which your babes share, as I crave it constantly."

"Sounds delicious." If it were the last thing he could achieve, he would restore the spark to her eyes. "And I will have Arnold put out the traps, at once."

"Thank you." Alex opened the door and then peered over her shoulder. "Can you give me directions to my chambers?"

"Of course." Wait until she discovered Stratfield Manor had only one master suite. It was that feature, alone, which had persuaded him to buy the rundown estate, along with its decrepit furnishings. "At the landing of the grand staircase, turn right. The master suite is at the end of the hall."

"Then I will see you at dinner." She mustered a half-hearted smile that had not fooled him for a second.

As soon as Alex closed the door, Jason rounded his desk and sat in the large chair. When his posterior connected with the cushion, a cloud of dust overtook him, and he suffered a vicious coughing fit. After a couple of violent sneezes, he opened the top drawer and located serviceable stationary, because he had letters to write.

FOUR DAYS LATER, a courier delivered two much-anticipated responses to Jason's correspondence. Hugging the envelopes to his chest, he checked the foyer for any signs of his bride before adjourning to his study. Ensconced in the sanctity of his private domain, he locked the door and strode to his desk. Just as he plopped to his seat, he cursed, as the now familiar cloud of dust incited a wicked coughing fit.

Given Trevor's tenure as a father, and his bawdy proclamation that the production of his third offspring ranked as chief among his concerns, Jason opened Lockwood's letter first. The dramatic script, typical of Caroline's husband, contrasted with the elementary information and counsel the missive contained.

"I am to rub her feet?" Jason grimaced. "That is the great secret to wedded bliss?"

Without thought, he slumped in his seat, and another nasty fog engulfed him. Using the parchment as a fan, of sorts, he choked, sputtered, and pondered Trevor's advice.

So he was to express a sudden affinity for her ankles, heels, and toes—and pretend to enjoy the experience? Why could he not just caress her breasts, as they looked quite swollen? Perhaps Alex would prefer he soothe her hips, her succulent thighs, the luscious undersides of her knees...

Of course, that line of thinking was exactly how he ended up in his current predicament. And he could not fault his friend's logic, as feet presented safe territory, compared to other more delectable parts.

Then he gave his attention to the second letter, swiped it from the blotter, and ripped open the envelope. To his absolute befuddlement, Everett dispensed identical sage advice. Yet Woverton also expounded on the virtues of back massages, with particular care paid to the lower region, near the base of Alex's spine, and her shoulders. According to Everett, Sabrina often rewarded his efforts with most passionate appreciation.

"*Passionate* appreciation?" Jason snorted, propped an elbow on the armrest, and cupped his chin in his palm. "What on earth could Everett mean, as Alex has permitted nothing more than a few pleasurable kisses? I may have destroyed her confidence, but pregnancy killed her licentious appetite, and I would restore both."

And then he digested the remaining contents of the dispatch. The last recommendation involved hiring a nanny. While Sabrina had suffered the worst symptoms of her condition, Everett had conducted interviews, had arranged for the prospective candidate to meet with his wife, and had settled the contract and wages. In turn, Sabrina had declared Everett the most thoughtful husband and had been generous in her thanks.

"What in bloody hell do I know of nannies?" Then again, he hired sailors to staff the *Intrepid*, so he considered himself highly qualified to employ household personnel. "All right, I will do it."

With the best of intentions swirling in his brain, he tugged open the top right drawer, and the bottom fell to the floor. Muttering a slew of invective, he knelt and retrieved the spilt contents. After stacking his stationary atop the desk, Jason dropped into his chair, and the maddening dust cloud provoked another blistering string of expletives.

"My lady, you should rest before the next applicant arrives." Gertie's shrill tone sounded in the hall. "You have been on your feet all morning."

"Could you make a pot of tea, Miss Phipps?" Alex moaned. "And I shall take a short nap in the back parlor."

"I will see to it, at once, your ladyship," the housekeeper replied.

In less than twenty-four hours, Alex had earned Gertie and Arnold's everlasting devotion via their stomachs. And in true Alex fashion, she had charmed a group of local dandies to transport four wagonloads of new furnishings to the house, after a painfully slow coach ride into town, on their first full day in residence.

Yet with Jason she remained blanketed in uncharacteristic reticence and melancholia. No matter how hard he tried to make amends, she kept him at arm's length, and an underlying hesitance marked her every move. And his heart bled for her.

With a smile, he pushed from his desk and all but ran into the hall. It was time to test the solicited advice, as his bride had taken a break from her busy schedule. Unsure of his welcome, he second-guessed his tack. But he had vowed to win her back, by any means necessary, so he turned the knob and opened the door.

The freshly hung drapes had been drawn, and Alex reclined, dozing on a new *chaise*, with her feet propped on a pillow. Trevor and Everett, god bless them, had been correct. Moving slow and steady, Jason tiptoed—yes, he deuced tiptoed, on the pristine carpet, but a floorboard creaked and betrayed his presence.

In a flash, Alex jumped. "*Oh*, Jason. You startled me."

"Relax, love." He halted, until she closed her eyes. Just then, Gertie, carrying a tray laden with a teapot, cups, and a plate of biscuits, entered the parlor. "Shh. My wife sleeps."

"Poor dear." The housekeeper dipped her chin, as she set the tray on the table. "She will wear herself out, sir. And that is not good for the babes."

"I will caution her," Jason replied, in *sotto voce*. "You may come for her when the next applicant arrives."

"Yes, Captain." The housekeeper smiled. "If I may say so, Lady Alex is a very fine woman."

"Yes, she is quite simply magnificent." And in a moment of temporary insanity, he had refused to marry her and, in so doing, had destroyed the best thing that had ever happened to him. "But I thank you, just the same."

Alone, at last, he lifted his bride's feet, tossed the pillow to the floor, and shuffled to the end of the *chaise*. After a gentle shift to his left, he positioned Alex's heels in his lap and removed her slippers. When she sniffed and rolled her head to one side, he froze, lest he disturb her. As her breaths returned to a steady rhythm, he commenced his task.

According to Trevor, the arches required the most attention, so Jason used the pads of his thumbs, tracing small circles in the subtle indentations, and Alex lauded his efforts with a lusty moan that harked back to those sumptuous days in Plymouth. Then he massaged the outer edges of her soles, and she let forth a robust cry of pleasure that summoned the trusty old Jolly Roger, too long neglected, into action.

Soon, a heady chorus of *oohs* and *ahs* brought Jason to the brink of ecstasy, and as he kneaded his magic on her provocative little toes, he lowered her feet and thrust his hips in time with his handiwork, engaging in a naughty caress of his stubborn erection. How he savored her touch, however unintended.

"What are you doing?" Alex inquired in a high-pitched voice.

With a violent flinch, he opened his eyes, gazed at his wife, and cleared his throat. "I am massaging your feet, sweetheart."

"Indeed?" She arched a brow and frowned. "Because it appears you use my feet to rub your—are you aroused?"

"Do you really have to ask?" He chuckled.

"But—why?" Sporting a charming blush, she licked her lips. "I mean...that is to say, given my condition, what could have stimulated you?"

"You think yourself unattractive, my dear?" Stunned by her question, because it presented another confusing character deviation he had not foreseen, she could have knocked him over with a feather. "Alex, you are pregnant, not dead, and you have never been lovelier."

"But you think me fat." And now she pouted, which he could never resist.

"Now I know very well I never said that." Jason rolled his eyes. "I may be many things, but I am neither daft nor forgetful."

"Then it appears you suffer selective memory syndrome." She lifted her chin, and for the briefest second, he glimpsed his Alex, but she retreated beneath her shroud of sadness. "Does *rotund* ring a bell?"

"You have a mind like a steel trap." Resuming his massage, he teased her soles with a feathery caress and rubbed his finger between her toes in a repetitive, illicit rhythm. Then he stuck his tongue in his cheek and winked. "Remind you of anything?"

"Jason Collingwood." Her mouth fell agape. "You are incorrigible."

"I am your husband, and I want you." He walked his fingers to her calves. "What is incorrigible about that?"

Their eyes met, held, and the promise of passion ignited, just as it had all those months ago. And so he rode that much prayed for but absent of late tide and inched his palms to her knees. She inhaled a shaky breath and bit her lip, and he damn near spilt his seed in his breeches.

And then a knock at the door interrupted what had been a pleasant interlude.

"Oh." The disappointment in Alex's expression gave him fledgling hope, until she drew her feet from his lap, dropped her legs over the edge of the *chaise*, and smoothed her skirts. "Come."

"Your ladyship, I beg your pardon for the intrusion."

Miss Phipps peered inside and smiled. "The next potential candidate for employment awaits you in the drawing room."

"A gardener, I believe." Alex glanced left and then right. "Is it Mr. Hardy?"

"Yes, ma'am." The housekeeper nodded once. "And I have provided tea and fresh biscuits, my lady."

"You are a fast learner and a treasure, Miss Phipps." Alex giggled, and pride swelled in his chest, as his wife performed her duties with flawless perfection and her customary enthusiasm. In fact, when dealing with the staff, her generosity of spirit, which had attracted him from the first, had resurfaced—with everyone but Jason. "I shall have to take excellent care that you never leave me, as you are quite indispensable."

"Humph. That will never happen." And then Gertie glanced at him. "Captain Collingwood, a Mr. Henson is here to discuss repairs to the roof, and he is in the foyer." With that, Gertrude half-curtseyed and exited the parlor.

"Alex, I must applaud your efforts, as never has Gertie addressed me with such refined manners." He chuckled. "How did you manage it?"

"It is simple, really." She shrugged. "I merely explained that our guests bring certain expectations to the employer and servant relationship. Should she or Mr. Phipps deviate from that course, prospective visitors might take it upon themselves to upbraid our staff, and then I would embarrass myself with a vast deal more than vigorous defense of my personnel. Never would I allow anyone, regardless of affiliation, to mistreat our domestics, as they are, in a sense, our extended family."

"Well said, sweetheart." Had he once thought Alex a snob? Jason could not have been more wrong. Just then, she leaned forward and almost fell to the floor. "Weigh your anchor, love. What are you about?"

"I can't find my slippers." She teetered, and he caught her in the nick of time.

"Easy, darling, else you risk injury to yourself and our babes." In an instant, he knelt before her. "Your shoes are right here, but I gather you cannot see them over your belly. Allow me to assist you."

As Jason lifted her foot, it occurred to him that he had overlooked the power of seduction in his quest to restore his fiery Alex. While most society maidens tempered their desires, his bride had presented something altogether to the contrary. In short, she was the most passionate woman he had ever known.

With a flick of his wrists, he hiked her skirts, bent his head, and trailed his lips up her calves to her knees, where he licked and suckled her flesh. Holding her gaze, he moved from one leg to the other and repeated the decadent maneuver. When she closed her eyes, gasped, and then emitted the softest, sweetest moan, he could have danced a jig.

Again and again, he pressed on her caresses meant to entice and arouse, and she speared her fingers through his hair. And just as he gained his bawdy stride, the cannon in his crotch fired a violent fusillade, and he rested his forehead to her knee and groaned, as wave upon wave of delicious release wreathed and ensorcelled him.

When next Jason surfaced, he discovered Alex scrutinizing him. "Did you just—"

"Yes, I did." Mortified, he sat on his heels and peered at the telltale stain penetrating his breeches. "Now I must change clothes."

"So it is true." It was a statement, not a question. "You desire me."

"When have I not?" He pulled down her skirts and eased her slippers to her feet. "Will you not let me have you? I promise, I will be gentle, but I burn for you, Alex."

"Jason." She uttered his name in a bare whisper, as she had when they made love, and cupped his cheek. "I wish I could give you what you want, but I can't. I am sorry, but I can't."

"All right, I will not pressure you." He mustered a grin, though inside he ached for her. Standing, he clasped her hands, drew her from the *chaise*, wrapped his arm about her waist, and kissed her hard and fast. "Now you must away, else I might break my vow, but I would caution you to take care, as I would not have you waning."

"Yes, sir." Alex made to withdraw but reversed course without warning, and she ever so briefly brushed her lips to his, much to his surprise. "I bid you a good afternoon, Jason."

As his wife fled the parlor, without so much as a backward glance, he smiled. Oh, it was a very good afternoon.

A FORTNIGHT LATER, Alex groaned and pressed a hand to the small of her back, as she climbed the grand staircase. After another full day of interviews, during which she broke only to supervise a thorough cleaning of the kitchen, she was exhausted. To her abiding delight, the floors had been resurfaced to perfection, and she admired the lustrous wood grain of the balustrade and individual steps.

Tomorrow, the roofers should complete their repairs, and

the last five chambers would be repainted. And high on her list of priorities were appointments with one furniture maker, two landscapers, three interior designers, and four local merchants.

Yes, in only a couple of weeks, she had brought a shine to the grand estate home, with which she had fallen in love from the moment she first gazed beyond the coach window at Stratfield Manor. At the landing, she halted, peered into the gallery, and examined the navy distemper wall coverings, in the Dossie tradition, which she favored, framed in rich mahogany. Well, the huge open space would serve as a gallery, once she commissioned a few portraits, given the large open hall remained bereft of a single painting. But such niceties yielded to more important items.

Monday next, an army of carpenters and plasterers would repair the exterior edifice, and then Alex could focus her energies on decorations and furnishings, excepting what she had already obtained for the drawing room, the back parlor, the dining room, and the master suite.

When she waddled through the double doors leading to the sitting room she shared with her husband, she yawned. As she entered the octagonal-shaped bedchamber, which she adored the moment she first arrived to unpack her belongings, she scrutinized the opulent velvet drapes, elegant wall coverings trimmed in mahogany, and bedclothes, all boasting the sumptuous navy blue her husband preferred. Why she persisted in futile attempts to win Jason's love she neither knew nor cared, yet she clung to the barest thread of hope that he might someday gift her his heart.

"Ho-hum." She covered her mouth and then stretched.

Given Alex had yet to hire a lady's maid, she had relied on the skills Molly had imparted to dress herself. But in recent days, she had struggled to tie her laces. After a few awkward twists and turns, accompanied by grunts and groans of frustration, she glanced at the bellpull and rued calling Miss Phipps at the late hour.

So Alex sat at her vanity, kicked off her slippers, reached behind her, shifted left and then right, and ceded the fight. Despite her better judgment, she studied her reflection in the mirror and frowned. An empty shell stared back at her, and she wondered how long she would survive the daunting despair that underscored her every waking hour. Leaning forward, she folded her arms atop the vanity, rested her head, and closed her eyes.

An abrupt jolt brought her alert countless minutes later.

"You fell asleep, love." Jason carried her to the bed and eased her to the mattress. "I have loosened your laces, and I will help you undress."

"Thank you, as I can no longer manage on my own." Yet she had not wanted him to see her nude. "And I have not hired a lady's maid, as it has been difficult to find a suitable candidate."

"Why did you not summon Gertie?" After flicking up her skirts, he unfastened her garters and rolled down her stockings. "She would have been only too happy to provide assistance."

"Because it is late, and she has retired." Alex leaned to one side, as Jason bunched her gown at her hips, before whisking the garment over her head. Wearing only her chemise, she crossed her arms to cover her breasts. How unfair it was that she still craved his body and his touch, every bit as much as she craved peach jam pudding with sardines. "Will you fetch my nightgown?"

"Do you truly need one, as it is a warm night?" To her surprise, her husband knelt and massaged her feet. When he pressed his thumbs to her arches, she moaned, and he chuckled. "Feel good?"

"Oh, Jason." Alex dropped back her head and sighed. "It is divine."

As he rubbed her toes, kneaded her heels and ankles, and stroked the tops of her feet, she hummed an accompaniment of sheer delight. Little by little, as he worked his magic, the day's weariness and tension slipped from her shoulders. Lost in a euphoric haze, she had not noticed he had changed positions until the mattress dipped, and he sat beside her.

Once again, her knight tempted her with gentle but well placed caresses to her spine, paying particular attention to her lower back. When Jason encouraged her to lean on him, she resisted not, because she needed his strength, yet she was too afraid to tell him.

"How is that?" It was then he untied her chemise, drew it to her waist, and kissed her temple.

"Wonderful." But she gulped as he walked a naughty path to her bosom with his fingers. "What are you doing?"

"Shh." As he caught the crest of her ear with his teeth, he traced flirty circles about her nipples. And then he ruined the pleasant interlude, when he squeezed her breasts.

"*Ouch*." She winced and grabbed his wrists. "Please, do not do that, as I am so swollen and tender. It is quite painful."

"Sorry, Alex." Jason withdrew and cursed under his breath. "Had I known I would hurt you, I never would have touched you there."

"Oh, I would expect you to know everything about pregnancy." The poor man appeared so contrite she could not resist teasing him. "I mean, the day we arrived at Stratfield, you had nary a scrap of food in the kitchen stores, yet you have enough brandy to see you through winter for the next ten years, I imagine."

"Point taken." He grinned. "May I ask a favor?"

"Of course." She studied the chiseled muscles of his torso, as he stripped. "This is, after all, your home."

"Our home." Naked, he blew out the candles and then joined her in bed. As he situated the pillow, as she liked it, she turned on her side and rested her head on his shoulder. "Allow me to attend your needs until you hire a lady's maid."

"What?" In the dark, she flinched. "You cannot be serious."

"On the contrary, I am deadly serious."

"But—why?" The prospect bloody well terrified her. "I mean a lady's maid does more than dress me. She helps me bath and styles my hair, among other things."

"Excepting your coiffure, I would be happy to do whatever you require, as I am your husband." As always, he ran his fingers through her hair and then rubbed her scalp. "Give me a chance, sweetheart. I promise, I will not fail you. And we could use the opportunity to foster intimacy, as a newlywed couple."

Fear resurfaced with a vengeance, as Alex considered his simple but profound proposal. How lonely she had been when she left Plymouth. And those six long months without him had been absolute misery mixed with terror, given the daunting prospect of her ruin and her children's bastardy. But Jason had compensated for her deficiencies. Had he not earned a measure of reprieve?

Even as she considered the possibilities, she could not stifle a shiver of unease. "All right, Jason. You may act as my lady's maid."

CHAPTER TEN

"*J*ason, stop." With arms outstretched and fingers flicking, Alex giggled. "What are you about?"

"It is a surprise." Standing behind his wife, covering her eyes with his palms, he kissed her temple and nodded to Phipps. "Are you ready?"

"Oh, yes." She all but bounced on her heels. "I am uncontrollably excited."

A fortnight had passed since he had launched his voluptuous attack of his erstwhile-spirited bride, and he had tarried with due diligence to achieve a particular milestone in the battle to win her heart. The nighttime massages had gained him some, but not enough, ground to induce her to share her body, and he had developed some serious callouses while tending his own needs. If he were lucky, his gift might prove a crowning finish—the *coup de grâce* in their private war.

"All right, no peeking." With a hearty chuckle, he stepped to the side, as he wanted to gauge Alex's reaction when she spied the new nanny, for the first time. The manservant opened the door and granted entry to the woman Jason had hired to nurse the babes. "You are not to look until I permit it."

"Please, hurry." Hugging her belly, she shuffled her feet. "Neither I nor your children can bear the suspense."

"Then you may open your eyes." A swell of pride filled his chest, as he anticipated the litany of ways his wife might express her gratitude. "For you, darling."

"I beg your pardon?" For some odd reason, Alex winced, blinked, and her smile faltered. "Is this your idea of a joke, as I do not understand your meaning?"

"My lady Alex, allow me to introduce Miss Goodbody." Perhaps his bride would, at last, admit him to weigh anchor in her harbor, as he had been adrift for far too long. "She is to care for my heirs."

"So pleased to meet your ladyship." The nursemaid offered a less than elegant curtsey. "And although I have never been a nanny, I promise to do my best to attend to your babes."

A strangled cry permeated the quiet, as Alex bared her teeth. So his wife had thought him incompetent? Well, it appeared Jason had managed to confound her, and he had composed a lengthy list of circumstances by which he would show his affection, as he quite enjoyed the moment.

"Miss Goodbody, would you mind waiting in the drawing room?" With a clenched fist pressed to her bosom, Alex inhaled a shaky breath. "I need to speak with Captain Collingwood, in private."

"Of course, ma'am." The nursemaid bowed and exited the study.

Without hesitation, Alex waddled to the door, turned

the key in the lock, and Jason came alert in a flash. Passion kindled beneath his flesh, and fire erupted in his loins, as he foresaw a few licentious kisses, at least. Or had his bride intended a full-scale seduction? Yes, that was his thought—until she marched to stand toe to toe with him and slapped his face.

"You bastard." Then his firebrand grabbed the lapels of his jacket. "How dare you bring your whore into my home. Where did you find her—the docks?"

"Alex, I—"

"And pigs will fly before I allow her anywhere near my children." Then she grimaced and gasped. With a couple of steps in retreat, she again hugged her belly. "Never would I have believed you capable of such cruelty, but if you plan to install your mistress in this house, then you had better bid farewell to your most male member. As God is my witness, I will cut it off, slice it as bread, roast it in the oven, and serve it to you for dinner. Then I shall return to Penhurst, even if I have to walk the entire distance. And if you attempt to stay me, there will be a fine wake in this residence."

Stunned by the impressive display of fury, Jason remained stock-still, as Alex stomped from the study. At first, ire raged, given her churlish response to his generosity.

How dare he?

How dare she.

After all his hard work, after all his good intentions, how could his wife refuse his gift? And what was he to make of her scathing accusation? How had he ignored her desires, given pregnancy limited his opportunities to provide assistance? Once their children were born, he could assume a more active role in her schedule, as she enjoyed little time for herself. Trevor and Everett had advised their spouses benefited from such support.

So where had Jason erred?

For several minutes, he replayed Alex's outburst—and then a new realization dawned. Slowly, he smiled. Indeed, his present may not have produced the expected response, but her remarkable display of temper had him laughing. Now that was *his* Alex, the heretofore-brazen hellion, so absent of late, he dearly missed. To his infinite relief, the woman of his dreams persisted somewhere beneath the downcast façade and timid demeanor, and he had only to resurrect her. While he may have crushed her spirit, he had not destroyed it.

But how could he revive his much-cherished vixen sans anger?

The answer, when it came to him, seemed so pedestrian. In what had become a familiar, if not exasperating, routine, Jason rounded his desk, plopped into his chair, and grimaced as the usual nettlesome cloud of dust engulfed him. "Bloody everlasting hell."

Why was it Alex had bought furniture for almost every room in their house but had yet to purchase a new chair or desk for his domain? Once the smoke cleared, he retrieved a wooden box, withdrew a stack of notes, and counted an ample sum. Bills in hand, he trod to the bellpull and yanked hard.

Seconds later, Phipps entered the study. "Yes, sir?"

"Give this money to Miss Goodbody." When he returned to his desk, he sat with care. "Tell her there has been a mistake, and we have no need of her services, thus we wish to compensate her for her trouble. That will be all, Phipps."

"As you wish, sir." Arnie snickered, and Jason would have taken exception to the concurrent smirk had he not more important matters on his mind.

The gaping hole from the broken drawer all but mocked him, as he recalled where he had stored his stationary, and he shifted to the left. When the aged knob broke off in his hand, Jason swore a slew of invective and used a letter opener to pry the panel loose. With parchment in grasp, he wrenched the pen from the inkstand. It was time to enlist the full compliment of the Brethren husbands.

WHAT DOES SHE LOOK LIKE? S.

It was a curious question.

Three days after the nefarious nursemaid fiasco, Jason sat in his study and rubbed his chin, as he pondered the letter he had received by special messenger. The correspondence relayed Everett's response to the disastrous hiring, and subsequent firing, of Miss Goodbody.

To Jason's dismay, Everett seemed just as perplexed by Alex's ferocious reaction to the potential nanny, because Sabrina had acted quite the opposite. As Jason read and reread the missive, disappointment invested his frame and chilled his marrow, until he noted the singular sentence, written in telltale feminine script, at the bottom of the stationary.

But what did Sabrina mean?

When he had penned the advertisement for *The Times*, which announced the search for a nursemaid, the qualifications focused not on appearances, as that had not signified from his perspective. Instead, Jason had centered his concerns on the prospective candidate's ability to supervise his children. Still, as he had solicited the advice, common sense suggested he should consider Sabrina and Everett's opinion.

If memory served, Miss Goodbody was young, had blonde hair, blue eyes, a trim figure, and, oh yes, very large —Jason almost fell out of his chair. "Hell and the Reaper."

Could the solution have been so obvious? Was the answer so simple? While Alex had always struck him as a complex coquette, when it came to matters of the heart she viewed the world in such elementary concepts as black and white. And she possessed a jealous streak that had set him on his heels the night he had dared ask a particular widow to dance. "It is no small wonder she did not kill me."

With recharged confidence, he jumped from his seat, marched to the door, and set wide the oak panel. In the foyer, Phipps bowed, and Jason halted. "Where is my wife?"

"In the back parlor, Captain." Arnie smiled. "The new cook burned the afternoon refreshments."

"That does not bode well for dinner." Or his difficult bride's mood. As he entered the back parlor, Alex rested hands on hips.

"You must be firm with your staff, Gertie. Else they may take advantage of you." Alex inclined her head. "If the tea is too cold and the biscuits too hard, return the tray to the kitchen. If you reject mediocrity at the outset, it will never persist in this household."

"Yes, my lady." Miss Phipps curtseyed. "I promise to do better."

"Do not fret, dear friend. With patience and understanding, we will get it right." Just then, Alex peered at him, and Jason could only pray she would offer him similar courtesy, given she had said almost nothing to him since the incident with Miss Goodbody. "That will be all, Gertie."

The housekeeper cast him an expression of sympathy, as he held open the door for her. Once alone with his perplexing spouse, he folded his arms, and she turned and gazed out the window. "I wish to speak with you."

"Indeed?" She stiffened, and he stalked her. "Make an appointment, as my schedule is full for today."

"I think not, as we are married, thus all prior engagements must perforce yield to mine." Ignoring her frown, he escorted her to the *chaise*. "Have a seat, my lovely wife. There is something I wish to discuss, which remains unsettled between us."

"Oh? Am I remiss in my duties?" Reclining amid the pillows, she refused to meet his stare, even when he perched beside her, drew her feet into his lap, and removed her slippers. "What did I forget?"

"A matter of significance." Braced for a lightning strike, Jason caressed her ankles. "Miss Goodbody."

"Humph." Alex's scowl would have made the most experienced sailor quiver in his boots. "I refuse to confer about that woman."

"Excellent. Then you may listen to me." Considering his words, he mulled the precious ground he had lost in his attempt to make strides with his wife. "My lady, I admit I made a mistake in hiring Miss Goodbody, as I should have consulted with you, regarding your requirements for the position. What I do not understand is your presumption regarding her commitments as a member of this household. Would you please explain to me what you found so offensive in her person?"

"Aside from the fact that she was to act as your mistress?" Alex sniffed.

"I beg your pardon?" Befuddled, an annoying state to which he had become accustomed, of late, Jason scratched his cheek. "What on earth ever gave you such a ridiculous notion?"

"The woman was unsuitable." She lifted her chin and frowned.

"Based on what criteria?" Again, he reviewed his prerequisites for employment.

"You can't be serious." Alex snorted. "The only thing Miss Goodbody is fit to serve is ale in a dockside tavern—and I would wager that would not be the lone offering on her menu."

"And you know this—how?" What had he missed? What critical piece of the puzzle eluded him?

"Her hair was strewn about her shoulders, not in the respectable top-knot one would expect of an individual in her profession. Her attire was immodest, in contrast to the usual decorous uniform of a nanny. And she is too young. Were she a lady of character, she would still require a governess." Then Alex quieted, and she furrowed her brow. "And her...bosom is enormous."

"But I thought that made her perfect for the job." Jason studied the pattern on the rug. "Should not all nannies possess such ample endowments?"

"*What*?" His bride appeared on the verge of an apoplectic fit.

He gulped. "Forget I said that."

"Not a chance." Had he thought her fierce? "Expound on your assumption—now."

"I figured her breasts would prove useful—"

She shrieked. "In what manner?"

"In the event you chose to use her as a wet nurse for the babes." So much for improving their relations. "Given we anticipate twins, she would have produced plenty of milk for our children."

For a protracted pause, Alex stammered, choked, and blinked. Then, to his utter dismay, she burst into laughter.

Just when it seemed she would calm herself, his confounding wife collapsed into another unrestrained fit of hilarity. In a state of unrest, Jason shifted and rolled his shoulders.

"Oh, dear." Pale, she swallowed hard, giggled, and wiped a stray tear. "Do you really believe large breasts equate more milk?"

Unsure how to respond, he shrugged.

"Jason Collingwood." At last, she smiled, and he sighed in relief. "Never have I heard anything so preposterous."

"Well, it seemed logical, at the time." And he had rushed the interview, in his haste to please Alex. "I was only trying to help, as you have been occupied with the new staff and the renovations."

"How thoughtful, silly man." She wiggled her toes, and he teased the soles of her feet with his fingers, eliciting a glorious yelp. "Whatever am I to do with you?"

"Why, whatever you wish, my lady wife. So is it safe to presume my innocent, if incorrect, assumption incited your anger?" Now he stroked her shapely calves. "Did you truly believe I intended to avail myself of Miss Goodbody's...body?"

"Yes." The poor darling appeared so remorseful he could not summon a rebuke. "I am ashamed to admit I did, but in my defense, that is customary behavior for men of the *ton*."

"My dear, I wish—very much—that you had voiced your objection to Miss Goodbody before weaving unsustainable conclusions from whole cloth. You could have spared us needless suffering." Of course, Jason recalled the difficulties surrounding their marriage, and her supposition was not unreasonable. "And while I am familiar with the shenanigans characteristic of so-called noblemen, I must again stress the fact that I am a simple sailor. In front of your brother and Mr. Catchpole, I vowed to keep myself only unto you, and I meant it. There will be no mistresses between us, not now, not ever."

"Then I owe you an apology." As Alex adopted a charming pout, he fought the urge to nibble on her delectable little chin. "I see now that you were, in your way, trying to be of use. And it would be nice to have a reliable nanny, but I would hire someone I know, as I will not place our children in the custody of a stranger. I suppose I over-reacted."

"It is all right. This marriage business is like navigating unfamiliar waters, so we are bound to strike breakers. And I am soon to be a father, something about which I know nothing." In play, he tapped a finger to the tip of her cute nose and then cupped her cheek. "In future, might I suggest you tell me when I have offended you? It would make life simpler, as I cannot read your mind."

"I will do my best." With a smoldering, sexy stare reminiscent of happier days, Alex turned into his palm and set her lips to his heated flesh.

Jason went up in smoke.

How long had it been since they had made love? Judging from his reaction to a kiss that had not involved his mouth, it had been far too long. Without thought, he drew her near, leaned forward, and kissed her.

And she kissed him.

When Alex twined her fingers in his hair and held him to her, he groaned, as he had primed for another wicked slap on the cheek. So when she prodded him with her tongue, licked and suckled his, he could have cried like a baby.

"Jason." With a breathy sigh, she scored her nails at the

nape of his neck.

"Alex." How he had missed her.

Then she flinched and retreated. "Oh, Jason."

"Oh, Alex." He closed the distance.

"The bowl." She flicked her fingers. "Hurry."

A porcelain dish, bearing painted rosebuds, sat atop the table, and he snatched the delicate container. "You mean this?"

With nary a word of warning, his wife bent and disgorged the contents of her belly. Well *that* killed the mood. Had his hedonistic skills deteriorated to the point that the only response he could summon from his bride was a violent round of retching?

"I am so sorry." Beads of perspiration dotted her forehead, as Alex again heaved hard.

"No worries, love." In that instant, Jason realized she rued the interruption, too. When she teetered, he wrapped his arm about her and offered support, which she accepted with an unmistakable countenance of pure gratitude. And although she had not conveyed such sentiment, he apprehended that she required his assistance. In that moment, everything changed.

While he had focused exclusively on material expressions of affection, intended to foster marital accord and some semblance of trust, he had ignored his greatest advantage. In short, Alex needed his strength, his comfort—him. How could he have been so blind?

As she grew weak, she swayed, so he lifted her into his lap, as he balanced the bowl. For a brief second, he thought she might resist his care. Instead, his wife closed her eyes and collapsed against him. "Better?"

"Yes." She sighed, as he wiped her brow with his handkerchief.

"Is this normal, sweetheart?" He tucked a dangling tendril behind her ear. "Does the sickness always last so long, or are there complications?"

"According to Dr. Handley, it varies. Some women suffer nausea until they give birth. Perhaps you should—*oh*." He retrieved the bowl in the nick of time, as she suffered another blow to her constitution.

"Hush, darling. Do not try to speak." As she wrenched and convulsed, he held her. "Poor little thing. You have had a terrible go of it."

After a few minutes, Alex relaxed in his arms and gasped for air. For a long while, Jason held his bride and marveled when their babes moved in her belly. With each successive motion, something within him stirred. It was a foreign sensation, neither sensual nor companionable, but nonetheless powerful.

It sparked as a weight in his chest and spread, as comforting warmth, throughout his limbs. Then the odd awareness charged every nerve, and he gave Alex a gentle squeeze. While countless women had ventured into his lap during his naval tenure, none had been his wife, heavy with his heirs. That remarkable fact, alone, made the experience with his bride far more arresting.

The door opened, and Alex started.

"Pardon my intrusion." Gertie halted. "Is her ladyship unwell?"

"Indeed, and I would appreciate it if you would return the bowl to the kitchen." Jason cradled Alex's head. "And would you bring us a ewer of cool water and a clean cloth?"

"Of course, sir." Gertie dipped her chin.

"But I am quite recovered." His wife shifted.

"Nonsense, my dear." He nuzzled her temple. "You are as green as a toad. Allow me to dote upon you, please. I find, to my surprise, I rather fancy this aspect of married life."

"You do?" He could not ignore the shock in her tone.

"Indubitably." Jason grinned. "It beats arguing. By the by, is it safe to presume you are no longer angry with me?"

Before Alex could respond, Gertie entered the back parlor.

"And here is the water, along with a fresh pot of chamomile tea and some dry toast." After depositing the tray on the table, the housekeeper excused herself.

Jason wet the cloth and daubed Alex's face. "How is that, sweetheart?"

"Pure heaven," she replied in a bare whisper.

"And how do you take your tea?" He poured a cup of the steaming brew.

"Black with one sugar." She smiled and resituated herself in his embrace. When he held the cup to her lips, she took a sip and hummed in appreciation. "Delicious. And it is much sweeter when you make it."

Ah, she flirted with him. "Imagine that."

"And in regard to Miss Goodbody, you are forgiven."

ALEX, *I have a surprise for you.*

The man must harbor a death wish.

Propped against the back of the new sofa in the drawing room, she traced the pattern on the navy damask, as Jason explained why he had again usurped her authority and hired another nanny for their children. As she stared at her feet, which she could view because the standing, bent position that relieved the weight of the babes afforded her a clear vantage, she pondered how many various ways she could kill her husband and escape justice.

There was the ancient halberd in his study. The nasty battle-ax would, no doubt, split his thick skull with incomparable ease. Perhaps then Jason would learn not to meddle in the employment of servants, given that was her charge.

"Are you ill, sweetheart?" The polished toes of his top boots presented a tempting target, as he ventured within striking distance. "Shall I fetch a basin?"

"No." Damn fool man. He would do better to don the ancient suit of chain-mail armor that occupied a prominent corner of the foyer and served as primary dust collector for the household. As she stretched upright, she rubbed the small of her back. "Give me a minute to digest your latest development."

"Now do not be angry—"

"I am not angry," she snapped.

"Evidence to the contrary." Jason snickered, and she met his gaze. "Keep an open mind, darling. I promise, you will love this candidate."

Keep an open mind? Had she done any less since his last disastrous turn at chatelaine? Had she not been magnanimous, accepted his amends, along with his tempting kisses? Oh, why had her husband been so damned agreeable? It would have been much easier to remain vexed with an ill-tempered grouch or an insufferable boor.

No, she had married a blonde Adonis in skintight breeches, which left little to the imagination, and her naughty thoughts had run amok. How could she defend herself against his licentious advances when she could not align her mind and body in a common cause?

"Come with me, love." Jason took her hand in his. "Let us not dally."

"Your new charge can wait till hell freezes, for all I care." Alex dragged her feet.

"Are you going to form an opinion before you even meet the poor woman?" Her errant husband chuckled and gave her a gentle nudge. "Let us away, my lady wife."

"I require no such formalities to know she will not suit." As he steered her into the hall, she mustered a mighty scowl. "I still recall your last hire."

"You wound me, Alex." He cast her an inexpressibly disarming pout, and her knees buckled. "Have you so little faith in me?"

"It is not a question of faith. The truth is I know you too well." She snorted. "Let me guess, this one is a redhead."

"Now I resent that, Alex." Now he laughed. "Really, I do."

"I fret not for your feelings." How could he betray her, after she had invested the minutest amount of trust in him?

"You are going to regret that, when you meet her." The door to his study fast approached, as he relented not.

"I doubt it." She wrenched hard, yet he gave her no quarter. "Jason Marston George Collingwood, she had better not be another local beauty, or so help me—"

"So help me—what?" He stopped dead in his tracks and cornered Alex against the wall. "Ah, I love it when you employ that *governessy* tone, and I savor this side of you, as you are rather feisty when jealous. I find you quite arousing."

"You do?" Then she shook her head. "That is to say, I am not jealous." How pathetic and interested she sounded.

"Are you sure?" With the devil in his visage, her shameless captain grinned and slipped his finger, in an illicit rhythm, into her cleavage. "Do you remember the afternoon you brought me to completion with your breasts?"

"Yes." She swallowed hard, as delicious memories revisited her in staccato flashes. "How could I forget?"

"I treasure that reminiscence, as it saw me through my lengthy mission." Jason bent his head and trailed his tongue across her lips. "And I feared I might go mad from wanting you."

"Yet you rejected me." Alex had uttered the assertion before she realized she had spoken, and that elementary statement brought his licentious behavior to a halt, much to her disappointment. But for the first time in her marriage, she wished she could rescind her declaration.

"You have not forgiven me, and I cannot blame you." Her captain rubbed his nose to hers. "But allow me a measure of acknowledgement, as I am trying to restore your good opinion. Will you do that, for me?"

How earnest he appeared, as she mulled his request. Despite the fear nipping at her heels, Alex decided, then and there, that she needed to believe in her husband. And she required his heart, to survive. So she found herself perched on the banks of another Rubicon. On her last outing, she had drowned in a sea of rejection. If he failed her again, he would kill her.

"All right. I will not fight you." In that second, Jason rewarded her with a breathtaking smile. "But I would prefer you consult with me on employment matters, as I am chatelaine of Stratfield."

"Alex, you may have whatever you wish, as you have made me very happy." And then he bestowed upon her a searing kiss, which left her dizzy. "Now, for your surprise, which I vow shall please you."

With that, Jason opened the door to the back parlor, as she smoothed her skirts. When she glanced at the candidate for nursemaid, Alex was...elated. "*Molly*."

CHAPTER ELEVEN

"*I* arrived yesterday afternoon." Molly poured two cups of tea. "Cap'n installed me below stairs and bade me keep out of sight, until he could surprise you, this morning. I hope you are pleased."

"Dear friend, I am overjoyed, but I had no idea you wished to be a nanny." After fluffing a pillow, Alex reclined on the *chaise* in the back parlor. "I thought you intended to continue in service as a charwoman."

"Well, that was my original plan." The onetime house-maid averted her gaze and picked at her sleeve. "I had hoped Mr. Penniman and I would take employment in a grand household and work for a single family, for the remains of our days."

"And what of Mr. Penniman?" A pang of guilt settled on her shoulders, as Alex recalled her advice doomed her friend. "You had renewed your acquaintance prior to my departure from Plymouth. Did you never resolve your differences?"

"We spent some lovely Sunday evenings, just talking." With a wistful expression, Molly emitted something between a sob and a sigh. "But he wanted the girl he once knew, the Molly who existed before I met you. And I find it impossible to revert to that person, as you changed me."

"What have I done?" Not only had Alex ruined her life, but also she had wrecked Molly's future. "I was wrong to meddle in your affairs, as you were content with your situation, until I spoiled it."

"No. You are mistaken, as you were right about me." With tear-filled eyes, Molly smiled and shrugged. "I was too naïve and trusting, and I had no confidence. But I like the way I am now. Yes, it cost me Mr. Penniman, but I have hope that I might enjoy a marriage with a strong man who adores me, as Cap'n does you."

"Do not emulate me, as I am a poor role model." Alex offered her handkerchief. "Your nose is running."

"Thank you." After a healthy blare, Molly giggled. "Captain Collingwood is a prime catch. And when I think of what you did to land him, well, I do so admire your courage."

"Your admiration is seriously misplaced." If only she could travel back in time and undo her actions. She would not have ventured to Plymouth. She would not have seduced Jason. But then she would have no babes growing in her belly, and that she would never regret.

"Now why do you blush?" Molly chuckled. "I wish I had your courage, given what you enjoy. Cap'n loves you just as you are, else why would he have married you?"

Because he got me with child, and my brother would have killed him, otherwise.

"Jason required a chatelaine to manage his properties, and we are compatible." As she summarized the truth of her relationship with her husband, her heart fractured, and

Alex wanted to cry. "And my family's connections are impeccable."

"And now you have a blessed event to anticipate." Molly squeezed Alex's fingers. "You have it all, brave Alex. A perfect existence. What more could anyone want?"

"Indeed, I am very fortunate." She could have swallowed her tongue. "Molly, I must ask you never to speak of what happened in Plymouth. What I did—"

"My lady, I would never do so." The former charwoman compressed her lips. "You may rely on me, as your faithful confidant and servant. And when the babes arrive, I will guard them with my life."

"Then it appears I have a nanny, for as long as you wish to fill the position, dear friend." And Alex was grateful for the support, as she cherished Molly's companionship. "So are you comfortable in your quarters?"

"Yes, indeed." Bouncing in her seat, Molly nodded with unabashed enthusiasm. "Miss Phipps gave me a lovely room just off the kitchen. This morning, I woke to the aroma of fresh-baked scones."

"Then perhaps you might assist me in decorating the nursery, given the designer arrives today." Alex checked items on her imaginary to-do list, a habit crucial to her ruthless organization. "And we should assess the room next door, as it adjoins the nursery, and I would prefer you reside there, once the children are born."

"Of course." The nanny inclined her head. "I am at your disposal, and—"

A knock at the door interrupted Molly, and Miss Phipps entered the back parlor. "Excuse me, your ladyship. A gentleman has arrived about a position."

"That must be the designer." Alex tapped a finger to her chin and then scooted to the edge of the *chaise*. "Show him to the drawing room, and I shall be right there. Molly, please refresh the tray, and join us, as I would appreciate your opinion regarding fabrics and paint colors."

"Yes, ma'am." The nursemaid collected the tray.

With her usual rocking motion, Alex waddled down the hall. When she strolled into the drawing room, she was nonplussed to discover a somewhat rugged, but altogether quite handsome, young man waiting.

Blessed with unruly black hair, green eyes, and chiseled cheek bones, he would have set many a heart aflutter in the *ton's* ballrooms, if not for his dusty, well-worn overcoat. No, he had not fit her expectations of one of London's most prominent and popular designers. And he carried no portfolio. Instead, an old trunk, which had seen better days, rested just inside the door.

"Mr. Harper, I presume?" She extended her hand. "I am Mrs. Collingwood."

"I beg your pardon?" He retreated a step.

"You are Mr. Harper, the designer I employed to decorate the nursery?" Alex inquired.

"No, ma'am." He shook his head and shuffled his feet. "I am here about the listing for a stablemaster."

"My mistake, as I expect someone else." She laughed. "But the stable is my husband's responsibility, so you must speak with Captain Collingwood. If you would follow me, I will show you to the study."

"What about my things?" He shifted his weight and blushed.

"You may leave them here." And then she whirled about and made for Jason's study, with the curious applicant, in tow. At the door to her captain's domain, she rapped her knuckles on the oak panel and then entered. "I apologize for the intrusion, but there is someone here to see you. He wishes to interview—"

"Tom?" Recognition dawned in his expression, as Jason stood, rounded his desk, sidestepped her, and exchanged a vigorous handshake with the young man. "What in bloody hell are you doing here?"

"Jason, my friend." The interesting stranger rocked on his heels. "I understand you need a stablemaster."

"You know each other?" she asked, given their informal exchange.

"We do," her husband replied. To Tom, Jason said, "Are you serious? I thought you intended to remain in Plymouth."

"I did, but my plans changed, which is why I am here." The prospective stablemaster rubbed the back of his neck. "Must I explain?"

"No." Jason chuckled. "I believe I get your meaning, and the job is yours, as I count myself fortunate to have you."

"I am grateful." Tom grinned, when Jason chucked the stablemaster's shoulder.

And then Jason faced her. "Darling, allow me to introduce Tom—"

"Beg your pardon, Captain Collingwood, but her ladyship requested the nursemaid deliver refreshments for the interview." Phipps set the oak panel wide and bowed.

Carrying the tray loaded with a teapot and a plate of sweets, Molly entered the study. When she glanced at Tom, the nanny sobbed and dropped the tray.

"Molly, what is wrong?" Alex stumbled to avoid the hot tea.

"What is *he* doing here?" A look of sheer horror marred her lovely features.

"He is the new stablemaster." Alex attempted to comfort her friend, but Molly wrenched free.

"No." The nursemaid crossed and uncrossed her arms. "Not him. Anyone but him."

"But—why?" Puzzled, Alex glanced at Jason, then Tom, and then Molly. "For heaven's sake, what is the matter?"

As Molly wept, she trembled. "You have hired my Mr. Penniman."

"He must go. I insist upon it."

"Absolutely not."

"I will not have him in my home."

"Tom resides not in our home. He lives in the stable house, with the other hands."

"Jason."

"Alex." He mocked her sigh.

"But I fear Molly will not stay, if we keep Mr. Penniman." Alex gave Jason her back, while he untied her laces. "It is far more important to have a nanny we trust than a reliable stablemaster to tend the horses."

"My dear, I am not going to fire Tom, to make the nursemaid happy, as Molly does not dictate the terms of employment on this estate. And I will find no one more qualified for the position, so I refuse to surrender him." Jason drew the bodice of her gown to her waist, steadied her with his arm, and she stepped from the garment. "You must speak with Molly. By the by, how does she fare?"

"Terrible." Alex frowned, sat on the edge of the bed, and lifted each foot, in turn, as he removed her stockings and garters. "She locked herself in her room and refused dinner. And she will not talk to me."

As Jason helped her undress, it occurred to Alex that the odd ritual had fostered a new level of intimacy between them. Despite the underlying sting of rejection and heartbreak, and the fact that they had yet to consummate their vows, they had grown together, as a couple.

"How is Mr. Penniman?" She tugged the ribbon of her chemise. "I thought the poor man would swoon, after Molly ran from the study."

"In shock." Jason deposited her clothes on a chair and shrugged from his coat and waistcoat. "He had anticipated a warmer reception."

"So it is true?" Given she slept naked, she scooted from the mattress, grasped the edges of her slip, and attempted to pull it over her head, but she became entangled in the linen. "He came here to renew their acquaintance?"

"Aye." He unknotted his cravat. "Tom loves the chit, and he intends to marry her."

"He told you as much?" The sheer material bunched at her shoulders, and she twisted and turned, to no avail. "Did he use those precise words?"

"Yes." Jason doffed his shirt, glanced in her direction, and chuckled. "Careful, darling. Let me help you. Lift your arms."

"Then why did he reject her in Plymouth?" She obeyed his request, and he set her free, before claiming a kiss. In that instant, it occurred to her that the same could have been said of Alex and Jason. Had her husband noted the similar circumstances? "He could have had Molly, without argument, as she wanted to marry him."

"I know not the private details of their relationship." Sitting in a chair, he hauled off his boots. "I suppose he made a mistake."

That was the grand explanation?

He made a mistake?

And upon such clumsy revelations, minus compensatory groveling, all wrongs were righted, thus erasing the pain and humiliation? She must overlook countless spent tears and sleepless nights? What of her disappointment and shattered dreams? Had he honestly believed he could wipe the slate with a single prosaic sentence? Oh, no. It would take more than that to resolve their differences.

But then Alex recalled they discussed the nanny and the stablemaster. And Molly enjoyed an unparalleled advantage: Tom's love. As declarations were not won and lost on an everyday basis, a fact Alex knew only too well, then it remained in Molly's best interest to accept Tom.

Yet Mr. Penniman seemed an intelligent sort. Had he said what he expected Molly wanted to hear, in an effort to woo her? Had not Jason done the same, upon his return to England? On their wedding night, he had not promised her love, only a desire to wed her. Would that he had done so sooner.

"I fear the matter has ended, in Molly's estimation." Alex returned to the four-poster she shared with her husband. "And he has no one to blame but himself."

"I beg to differ, my beautiful wife." After stripping from his breeches, her captain approached the bed, naked and aroused. "The situation is not concluded, and I see not how she could pretend otherwise, given her reaction. Had Molly not cared for Tom, he could not have hurt her."

"I do not follow." She perched at the edge of the down mattress, as Jason reclined, situated a pillow, and then reached for her. "Tom dismissed Molly."

"He acted in haste, Alex." He held the cushion in place, as she rolled to her side and rested her head on his shoulder. "Is Molly so perfect? Has she never erred? Has she never committed deeds she later regretted?"

"She is hurt." *As am I.* "It requires time to heal such wounds."

"Well I suggest she reconsider her tack, before it is too late." As was his way, Jason rubbed her scalp. "Grudges will not keep her warm at night."

"Perhaps if he were not so insistent, she might have been more amenable to reconciliation." Alex snuggled close, with her palm on his magnificent chest, as he tucked the covers beneath her chin. "Mr. Penniman should not have expected to show up on our doorstep and demand forgiveness."

"What a curious statement." Her husband tipped her head and covered her lips with his, and then he nipped her nose. "As I treasure fond memories of a charming young noblewoman who did just that, and I could not resist her."

In the dim light from a single candle, which sat atop the bedside table, she studied her husband. To her chagrin, she could not refute his assertion, because he was correct in his estimation. She had intentionally deceived Jason, in regard to Lance and Cara's romance, and then she had journeyed to Plymouth in search of absolution.

But that was in the past, as was his rejection.

So Alex nestled amid the sheets and closed her eyes, but sleep came not for her. Myriad thoughts commanded her attention, as she weighed the significance and finer points of their discussion. At last, she sighed and drifted to the fringe of dreamland, until a repetitive motion brought her alert. Without moving, she peeked at her husband.

The blanket rose and fell, at the location of his crotch, and he clamped his eyes shut, gritted his teeth, and shifted his hips. While it had been seven months since those glorious days in Plymouth, Alex recalled, in sumptuous detail, his voluptuous methods and motives.

Long absent hunger unfurled, flourished, and swelled within her, and heat pooled in that neglected place between her thighs. An arresting choral comprised of his grunts and groans lured her, as a lodestone. Slow and steady, she walked her fingers below his belly button and grasped a towel.

"Alex?" At that moment, Jason flinched. "What are you doing?"

"May I?" She skimmed her hand beneath the cloth and found him hot and hard.

He narrowed his stare. "You wish to pleasure me?"

"Yes." She licked her lips. "More than you know."

For several seconds, her husband studied her. "Might I ask a favor?"

"Of course." She commenced the decadent maneuver, just as he liked it.

"Will you grant me the same privilege with your body?" He hissed, as she fondled the pouch at the base of his erection. "I need to touch you, Alex."

A host of refusals traipsed the tip of her tongue. "All right."

With a wicked grin, her captain pulled her closer, set his lips to hers, parted her legs, and instigated a full-scale assault on her most intimate flesh. And the ice encasing her heart melted.

AUGUST HAD SEEN the end to the Battle of the Pyrenees, after the reinforced British Fourth Division, under the leadership of Arthur Wellesley, Marquess of Wellington, forced Soult and two French corps to retreat into France. Such action summoned the full compliment of the Brethren of the Coast into combat, much to Jason's frustration.

When he received official correspondence from Admiral Douglas, Jason had lamented the timing, because he had, at last, breached his wife's defenses. Ever since that first amazing night, when Alex had stunned him with a brilliant flanking maneuver and assumed command of his Jolly Roger, he had lauded her naughty finger work with a stout, one-gun salute, every successive dusk and dawn. And she never failed to fire his cannon, although she still refused to make love to him.

And he had yet to gain significant ground beyond their bedchamber, so the rift in their relationship consumed his thoughts, to the detriment of all else. The goal was not the issue, as Jason knew precisely what he wanted from his wife, yet he knew not how to obtain what he desired, given he had rejected her offer in Plymouth.

Again and again, her declaration haunted his dreams. In an embarrassing instance of everlasting shame he might never live down, he had accused her of attempting to trap him into marriage and then questioned her motives. Alex's reply, completely unforeseen, had rendered him speechless and dizzy, and it echoed in his ears, even now.

Because I love you.

And in a moment of unmitigated stupidity, he had refused to wed her. Were his present pain half so great as hers, she had suffered cruelly at his hands. In happier times, she had called him the captain of her heart, and he ached to occupy such a prominent position in her life.

"Jason, are you ready?" Alex stood in the entryway of his study. "Your trunks are packed and loaded, and I ordered the cook to prepare a substantial meal for your journey."

"You know me so well." With his maps and charts secured, he gazed at his bride and her disarming gown of pale yellow, which boasted a lace-trimmed bodice that accentuated her generous bosom. "Come here."

"Should I close the door?" She cast him a shy smile. "Do you intend to make inappropriate advances?"

"Yes." He winked. "But I submit it is impossible for me to make *inappropriate* advances, as I am your husband and, therefore, licensed to sail your harbor, at will."

"Reprobate." Her giggle belied the insult.

"Have I ever pretended otherwise?" As he drew her into his embrace, she blushed. "You were unutterably captivating this morning, sweetheart."

"Something to remember me by." How Jason longed for that glow with which Alex had always greeted him, but she remained locked in a dense, ever-present cocoon of reserve tinged with melancholia, which pervaded their every interaction. "And what will you do aboard ship, without my busy hands?"

"Redevelop callouses." Because the chair behind his desk would envelop them in a cloud of dust, and might not support their combined weight, he steered her toward the old sofa. He assumed a comfortable position and then slapped his thighs. "Have a seat, love."

"But the staff awaits, and—"

"Please, darling." He patted her bottom. "Allow me to bestow upon you an equally sweet recollection, that you may think of me, with fondness, while I am at sea."

Palpable hesitation invested her frame, and then she sidestepped his legs and settled into his lap. "Be quick, as you must depart before noon."

"You do know how to undermine a man's confidence, Alex." Still, Jason flicked up her skirts and initiated some naughty finger work, of his own. Of course, he had lied, in part, regarding the purposive nature of their interlude, as he sought to commit her awe-inspiring audial accompaniment to memory, which he would replay in his bunk aboard the *Intrepid*.

A chorus of breathy sighs and half-smothered shrieks lauded his efforts, as he held Alex. And Jason longed to kiss his wife, but he refused to stifle her sultry moans, which he coveted as a priceless treasure. All too soon, she twined her fingers in his hair, yanked his head, and gave her scream of completion into his mouth. Hers was the most resplendent release he had ever witnessed.

"May I make a confession without fear of reprisal?" His bride rested against his chest.

"Of course." He caressed her cheek with his thumb.

"I had worried we could hurt the babes with our questionable behavior." She nuzzled him.

"That is a sound, sensible conclusion, sweetheart." He pulled down her skirt.

Alex sat upright. "Then why are you laughing?"

"Because I find you absolutely arresting." With that, he scooted to the edge of the sofa. "Now, I must away."

"Have you any idea what your mission entails?" Alex stood, and he followed suit. "Did the admiral's missive give you any expectation of the tenure?"

"No, love." Jason collected his belongings and offered his escort. "Now, see me to the coach."

Together, they navigated the hall, turned right at the foyer, and stepped into the sunlight from a cloudless sky. The staff formed a line, and he bade farewell to Gertie and Arnold. In the forecourt, he turned and slipped an arm about Alex.

"Take care of yourself and my heirs." He cupped her cheek. "I will not have my wife waning."

"Yes, sir." She cast him a timid smile. "And you do the same."

"I will." Conscious of the crowd gathered, Jason claimed a brief kiss and hopped into the coach. "Drive on."

The traveling equipage lurched forward, and he reclined in the squabs. The servants filed into the house, but his bride waved and remained on the graveled drive. The team picked up speed, after they completed the curve. For some reason he could not explain, he kept his gaze fixed on his lady. As the horses steered into the straightaway, he stuck his head out the window, just as Alex buried her face in her hands.

"*Hoi*, hold hard." Jason flung open the door before the coach came to a halt, and he leaped from the moving gig. Running at a full pace, he crossed the yard in mere seconds. "*Alex*."

She jerked, glanced at him, and held her arms wide. "Jason."

"Darling." With care for the babes, he turned her to the side and hugged her tight. "Why the tears, love?"

"Because you are leaving, and I know not when I shall see you again." She wept and sobbed without restraint. "I am afraid."

"What do you mean, as I shall return, as soon as I complete my mission." With his handkerchief, he dried her cheeks. "What have you to fear?"

"I had thought you might prefer to remain in London." Alex shivered and inhaled a shaky breath. "And the prospect of childbirth scares me."

"What could have possibly given you such a ridiculous notion?" He daubed her cute little nose.

"Because you never stated otherwise." A fresh spate of tears coursed her creamy complexion. "And most men of the *ton* abandon their pregnant wives to the country, while they seek divertissements elsewhere."

"Alex, look at me." He tipped her chin and pinned her stare. "I am no man of the *ton*. And I plan to attend the birth of our babes, if I have to move heaven and earth to be here. I promise, I will be with you. Now tell me you believe me, love, as I need to hear it."

"I believe you." She hiccuped.

"Do you?" He pressed his lips to her temple. "Because I give you my word, as a nautionnier knight, I will come home, to you."

"All right." And then his lady favored him with a glimpse of the old Alex, as she cast a smile that shimmered as sunlight on the ocean. Just as quick, she furrowed her brow, and the glow faded. "I miss you already."

"Oh, love." Even though the coach had turned and reappeared in the forecourt, Jason cared not for propriety or prudence. Right then and there, he kissed his bride as a man just returned from an extended voyage. "I miss you, too."

"I have made you late." Yet Alex clutched the lapels of his coat.

"You may delay me, any time." He claimed another soul-stealing kiss. "Are you recovered?"

She simply nodded.

It should have been easy to depart, as duty called. But something within him stirred, and Jason languished in bone-gnawing agony. No matter how hard he tried, he could not surrender his wife. For several minutes, he held her, until she sniffed and retreated.

"I am sorry, Jason." She shrugged. "The babes have made me a water pot."

"No apologies necessary, darling." Retracing his earlier steps, he paused at the coach, brought her knuckles to his lips, stole one more kiss, and then patted her bottom. "Now go inside, my girl."

"Yes, sir." She sketched a mock salute. "Please, be careful."

"Your wish is my command." When she entered the house and closed the door, he returned to the coach and resumed his journey. But he noted a telltale silhouette in the drawing room window and could not help but chuckle. A strange weight blossomed in his chest, warmth suffused his muscles, and Jason grinned, as a revelation dawned. "Oh, Alex. You still care for me."

CHAPTER TWELVE

"Thank you so much for rescheduling our appointment, Mr. Harper." Alex smiled at the designer, as she opened the door to Jason's domain. "This is my husband's study, and I will pay double your usual fee if you can work your magic in a fortnight, and transform this disaster into a dream for my captain."

"I should be too happy to—" Mr. Harper blanched and readjusted his monocle. "Upon my word, but never have I seen the likes of this décor."

"Yes, it is a tad antiquated." Wreck was more appropriate, as it was the last neglected chamber of the grand home, and not by accident. "The furnishings came with the estate."

"Do you mean to say Captain Collingwood actually purchased these items? They belong in a museum, as well as the refuse." The decorator turned his nose to the centerpiece of the room. "Why is there a hole in the desk?"

"The drawer collapsed. Oh, no. Do not—" Alex winced, as the poor man made the mistake of sitting in the chair, and a dust storm engulfed him. That particular trap she had reserved for Jason. "I am so sorry, Mr. Harper."

Alex tottered to his aid, as the designer shot to his feet, coughed, and wheezed. She brushed off his coat, and he blew his nose. Then he retrieved a small notepad from his pocket and borrowed the pen from the inkstand.

"We must replace everything, your ladyship." He sneezed, as he jotted a list. "What have you in mind?"

"I wish to continue the mahogany trim and navy wall coverings, as that is Captain Collingwood's favorite wood and color." She tapped her finger to her chin and contemplated her change of heart, spurred by Jason's promise. The improvements manifested an olive branch, of sorts. "And the desk must be hand-tooled and fit for a king, with a matching throne, in the Sheraton tradition, as I shall accept nothing less. And I should think two Hepplewhite chairs, facing the desk."

"What about a rendering of the Collingwood family coat of arms, which should hang over the fireplace?" Mr. Harper scratched his temple. "Have you an example?"

"Yes." Alex produced an old journal. "I found a drawing, when my staff removed my husband's personal affects, in preparation for the renovation."

"This is perfect." He scrutinized the sketch. "I know a local artist, and he is very skilled. If we offer him a bonus, he may be able to compose a suitable painting, in your time frame."

"Wonderful." And then she bit her lip, as she pondered her next request, because she knew not how Jason would react to a certain item. "Perhaps you can recommend someone to create a small portrait, very tiny, on short notice. I am available for private sittings, as my husband is at sea."

"Indeed, Mr. Appleton will suffice. And what of the shelving?" The decorator grazed a ledge with his finger, the plank collapsed, knocking three additional boards to the floor, and he jumped. "We require four new bookcases."

"Can you include two special, wall-mounted displays, with glass doors?" Alex walked to an old trunk and lifted the lid. "My husband's pride and joy is a collection of ancient spy glasses and compasses, which I would feature, as they are quite fascinating."

"And unusual." He squatted and assessed the various items. "You know, we might acquire a Harrison chronometer, at auction, as a nice addition, given Captain Collingwood's predilection for seafaring tools."

"I rely on you." She nodded once and recalled Jason's farewell, which brought telltale warmth to her cheeks, even now. "And I would exchange the sofa for a daybed, something substantial, as my husband possesses a robust stature."

"Very good, your ladyship. And what is the budget for the chronometer?" He arched a brow. "I should warn you, a Harrison could fetch a substantial sum."

"Spare no expense." Alex folded her arms, as she nurtured the small amount of faith she had invested in her captain. "And I believe we are done, here. Shall we adjourn to the nursery, as I have an entirely different set of requirements for that room?"

"Of course, your ladyship." At the door, Mr. Harper paused, gave the study a final appraisal, and shuddered. "And I had thought I had seen it all."

"I understand." Alex chuckled. "So when can you start?"

"Given the magnitude of the transformation, I shall dispatch my men to begin the demolition, this afternoon."

The designer wiped his brow. "Then we should commence the reconstruction, first thing in the morning, with your approval."

"Please, do so." As she climbed the stairs, she gazed at her bare hand and frowned. Jason had yet to gift her a wedding ring, and she had not mustered the nerve to broach the topic, but that was before her husband's departure, when he had jumped from a moving coach to console her. And though she would never admit it aloud, Alex coveted hope. "As for the nursery, I would like everything done in blue and yellow."

"Would you not prefer a more neutral palette, in the event you carry a girl?" Mr. Harper furrowed his brow. "We can always add gender-specific tones, at a later date."

"No." She shook her head. "Without doubt, I bear boys, as they are far too rambunctious."

"As you wish, your ladyship." The decorator laughed. "I know better than to argue with a woman in your condition, as my wife accurately predicted the sex of our three children, so blue and yellow is our theme."

When they entered the nursery, Alex was surprised to discover Molly, standing before the window, drying her eyes. The nanny attempted to conceal her tremulous state behind a rigid smile that had not fooled Alex, for a second.

"Molly, are you all right?" She surveyed the surroundings, as if expecting to find Mr. Penniman.

"Yes, your ladyship." Molly sniffed. "I fear I may be catching a cold, nothing more."

"Mr. Harper, this is Miss Duckett, my nursemaid." Alex eased into the large, overstuffed chair in the back corner. "Shall we discuss the décor?"

As the designer comprised another list of purchases, Alex studied her nanny, as she suspected Molly was not ill.

After another hour-long consultation, during which she selected fabrics for draperies and bed linens, she bade farewell to Mr. Harper.

"Alex, despite my promise, I am no longer certain I can remain at Stratfield Manor." Molly averted her stare and shuffled her feet. "Since Tom arrived, I find it difficult to tolerate his presence."

"But I thought you had no interest in Mr. Penniman?" Alex rested her heels on the ottoman. "And we rarely see him, as he resides with the stable hands."

"And yet he tempts me," Molly whispered. "Do you understand my distress?"

"More than you know." Alex could have written a book on temptation, as her captain had enticed her, beyond reason. "But I cannot lose you, so tell me what I can do to alleviate your discomfit, as I will not relinquish you without a fight."

"Tom is smart, my lady." Molly vented a plaintive cry. "No matter what I try, he wiggles his way into my heart and renders me a pile of mush. You must help me resist him."

"Are you sure that is what you want?" Alex revisited the most cherished memory of Jason, running to console her. It was his noble action that had inspired a kernel of faith, which she hoarded as a priceless gem. "You were very fond of Mr. Penniman, when you lived in Plymouth. Are you positive you do not welcome his attention?"

"Tom can go to the devil." Molly gasped and covered her mouth. "I beg your pardon, my lady."

"No worries, dear friend." Once again, Alex and Jason's relationship seemed inexplicably intertwined with that of the nanny and the stablemaster. "But I must caution you not to act in haste, as such decisions may not be so easily undone."

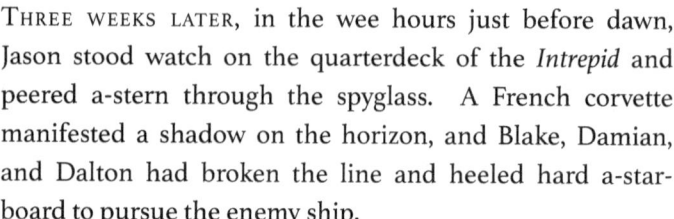

THREE WEEKS LATER, in the wee hours just before dawn, Jason stood watch on the quarterdeck of the *Intrepid* and peered a-stern through the spyglass. A French corvette manifested a shadow on the horizon, and Blake, Damian, and Dalton had broken the line and heeled hard a-starboard to pursue the enemy ship.

"Shall we join the fun, Cap'n?" Mr. Edgerton, the first lieutenant, inquired. "Should we beat to quarters?"

In that moment, Jason envisioned his wife, recalled her fears, remembered her tears, and he ached to hold her. "No, as a fourth share is hardly worth the effort. Maintain course and heading."

"Aye, sir." The first lieutenant dipped his chin.

In the distance, off the bow, the North Foreland posited a warm welcome to the Thames Estuary, which brought him closer to home and his Alex. And much like the Brethren husbands, Jason kept the canvas hardened in, to catch the wind.

Almost five hours had passed, when the *Intrepid* sailed into the docks at Deptford, and he all but ran for his coach, sidestepping the heartfelt reunions that inspired nothing more than deep-seated desire for Alex. As he sank into the squabs, in preparation for the drive to London, Jason retrieved from his waistcoat pocket the wedding ring he had yet to give his bride.

Fashioned of old gold, the jewelry boasted a large oval sapphire surrounded by diamonds, the latter he had added for his lady. The family heirloom had belonged to his mother, and he had planned to place it on Alex's finger, but she had refused to join hands at their wedding ceremony. He had carried the bauble on him, ever since.

When he arrived at his London residence, he unlocked the door and waited as the driver unloaded Jason's trunks. Alone in his bachelor's lair, he stood in the foyer, as a disconcerting shiver of unease traipsed his spine. Gazing into the drawing room, he discovered nothing amiss, yet a strange emptiness permeated his being, and he suffered Alex's absence as a vicious blow.

The palatial townhouse, bereft of fresh flowers, sumptuous rugs, comfortable pillows, and all manner of useless knickknacks, lacked the warmth of their country estate. It lacked Alex's touch. In short, she had made their grand house a home. Had he no previous engagement, he would ride hell-bent for leather into her arms, but duty called. As customary, Admiral Douglas had summoned the Brethren to the usual meeting room at White's to debrief the mission.

"Good afternoon, Captain Collingwood." Haynes, Jason's factotum, strolled into the foyer. "I knew not when to expect you. Shall I unpack your trunks?"

"No." Jason rested hands on hips. "I shall return to the country, tomorrow. Prepare a bath, as I have an appointment, this evening."

"Yes, sir." Haynes bowed.

So Jason passed the next few hours savoring a fine cigar and soaking in the tub. At the agreed upon time, he skipped down the stairs, navigated the alleyway, entered the mews, saddled his horse, and made for the gentlemen's club. To his surprise, the full compliment of the Brethren husbands had already gathered.

"Jason, we saved you a seat." The admiral smiled and signaled for a drink. "As your brother knights have made their report, I need only inquire whether or not you have anything of significance to add?"

"No, sir." Jason reclined and stretched his booted feet.

"As per orders, I rendezvoused with the *Surprise* northwest of the Bay of Biscay and transferred communiqués, supplies, and reinforcements. Beyond that, the mission was unremarkable."

"Delighted to hear it." Admiral Douglas lowered his chin and gazed at the floor. "How is Alex?"

"Heavily pregnant, but doing well, when I left her at Stratfield." He shifted his weight and tugged his cravat. "Admiral, I never had the chance to thank you for the assistance you provided my wife, during difficult circumstances."

"Son, I claim no special insight into the games people play, but yours was bad form—*very* bad form." The admiral downed his brandy, stood, and straightened his coat. "But that is the last you will hear of it, from me. Felicitations, on your nuptials. I hope you find as much happiness in your marriage as mine has brought me. Knights, I bid you a pleasant evening."

Everett whistled in monotone and shattered the tense silence, once the admiral had exited the room. "Brother, I am glad you were at sea when all hell broke loose, as my wife and my father-in-law wanted to kill you."

"As did Caroline." Trevor rolled his eyes. "And you are still *persona non grata* in our home, until Alex declares otherwise."

"And Rebecca wanted to string you up from the highest yardarm. I have not seen her that mad since—" Dirk drained the contents of his glass, swallowed hard, and grimaced. "Never have I seen her that mad."

"And what of Cara?" Jason glanced at Lance. "Does she wish to skewer me, too?"

"No, brother." Lance propped his elbow on an armrest. "Cara and I know there is more to the story, and we owe you a debt we can never repay. And I would not cast stones, given I took Cara before we spoke the vows."

"You are right." Trevor frowned. "Who are we to judge, as I kidnapped and claimed Caroline, prior to a proper ceremony."

"My Becca seduced me, in advance of our wedding." Dirk grinned. "She was quite intent on meeting her fate, so I have no complaints."

"Well I like that." Everett clucked his tongue. "Am I the only one who did the honorable by my bride?"

"So it appears." Trevor snickered. "And then she jumped from a moving coach to escape the deflowering."

In concert, save Jason, the Brethren husbands burst into laughter.

"Very funny." Everett flagged a waiter for another round of drinks. "Brothers, I wish, very much, that one of our bachelor knights might learn from our mistakes, as it has become quite painful to watch another man run aground, especially when he does so in such spectacular fashion."

"I am so glad to provide sport for your amusement." Jason slumped forward. "My friends, I have beached my campaign and am in dire need of your expertise in marital affairs."

"That is the understatement of the year." Trevor rubbed the back of his neck. "What were you thinking could happen, when you took her?"

"Was that chief among your concerns when you first bedded Caroline?" Jason inquired, with disgust.

"Point taken." Trevor frowned. "Pray, continue."

"Put yourself in my boots." Jason recalled the days in Plymouth. "What would you have done, had the woman of your dreams showed up on your doorstep, sans chaperone, and offered herself on the proverbial silver platter?"

"I get your meaning." Everett compressed his lips. "Then why did you refuse to marry her, given you had claimed her bride's prize?"

Jason arched a brow.

"Alex told Sabrina the whole of it," Everett explained. "And my Brie keeps no secrets from me."

"Because I am an ignorant arse." Jason slapped his thigh.

"In that I will not argue, and you are lucky to be alive, Jolly Roger intact, as I spoke with Damian prior to our departure." Dirk huffed a breath. "So answer the question."

"We are at war, and there are no guaranteed tomorrows." In a painful flashback, Jason relived the heated contretemps with Alex. "And you know how society treats young widows. I do not want that for her, should I meet my demise in battle."

"Yet you made her your whore." Dirk pinned Jason with a lethal stare. "Was that somehow better than widowhood?"

"Watch it, brother." Jason bared his teeth. "I made her my wife, as I had always planned, and no one knows more than I that I erred."

"Except, perhaps, Alex. And therein lies the crux of your dilemma." Lance checked his timepiece and stood. "I beg your pardon. While I loathe interrupting our festivities, Dr. Handley is to examine Cara, and I should be there when he arrives."

"Commiserations." Jason came alert. "Is she ill?"

"Aye." Lance appeared concerned, as he shuffled his feet. "She is exhausted, and her belly has been downright fragile, for the past few weeks, at sea. Must confess I am worried."

"I do not think she is ill, Lance." Trevor chuckled and peered at Everett, who snorted.

"Sounds as if she is pregnant," Jason blurted.

"You know, you are smarter than you look." Everett folded his arms and glowered.

"Bloody hell, Collingwood." Dirk smacked Jason on the shoulder. "Did you think it necessary to ruin the surprise? Cara may now want your head."

"You believe my wife is with child?" Visibly pale, Lance swayed, toppled over the chair, and fell to the floor. "But she said nothing to me."

"Whoa, brother." Trevor bent and hauled Lance to his feet. "And that is their way."

"Easy." Dirk perched at Lance's right. "Take it slow, as there is no rush."

"Now there is nothing to worry about, as Dr. Handley is a deuced fine physician. He delivered my son with nary a mishap." Everett straightened Lance's cravat, dusted the lapels of his coat, and then smacked him gently on the cheek. "Snap to it, man. Here is what you must do, on your way home. First, stop by Howell's, purchase the largest tin of chamomile tea they have in stock, and place a recurring order for the next nine months. Then visit the hothouse and procure a bouquet of Cara's favorite flowers."

"I am to be a father." It was a statement, not a question. Again, Lance teetered, and the Brethren husbands reached for him. With a tear-filled gaze, he grinned. "Tea and flowers. I can do that."

Then Lance turned on a heel and exited the room. On his second step, he broke into a full sprint.

"Poor bastard." Dirk guffawed. "Has no idea what lies in store for him."

As the atmosphere calmed, the nautionnier knights relaxed, and Jason pondered his predicament.

"By the by, I meant to ask you something. Mind you, I

would never pry into your personal affairs, but curiosity gnaws at my gut." Fidgeting, Trevor glanced at Everett. "Is it true that you removed the beds from Sabrina's private apartments?"

Everett growled and thrust his chin. "I did."

"But—why?" Dirk blinked.

"Need I remind you that my lovely but misguided bride left me, when she labored under the harebrained notion that I loved her not?" Everett shuddered. "Scared ten years off my life, and I still have not recovered. So I ensured I would never again come home to an empty four-poster. And I had the walls separating our chambers torn down. Now my Brie and I share a single, large room, whether we reside in the city or the country, and I highly recommend it."

"What happens when you quarrel?" Dirk queried. "Not that I am familiar with such difficulties."

"On the rare occasion we argue, my countess takes it out on me, between the sheets." Everett waggled his brows. "Best idea I ever had, and I sometimes seek excuses to rile her."

"You are a bloody genius." Trevor narrowed his stare. "What company did you use to execute the renovations?"

"Ooh, I love it when you say that." Everett smirked. "And Benson and Sons completed the remodel at our Park Lane home and Beaumaris."

"And Sabrina voiced no complaints?" Dirk leaned forward and inclined his head. "She was amenable to the refurbishment?"

"I gave her no opportunity to protest." Everett shrugged. "I did what any sane husband would do and simply waited until we ventured to London, to have the work done in the country. Then, when we journeyed to Beaumaris, the crew demolished our apartments in the city.

Even had she disagreed with my decision, it was too late when she discovered the alterations. But my most unlikely lady expressed nothing but delight and showed her appreciation in the coin I favor."

"I wonder how Rebecca would react to such developments." Dirk peered at the ceiling. "It would be worth the risk."

"Gentlemen, given I share a single apartment with my bride, as I hold no titles, can we refocus the discussion, as I am in a terrible fix." Jason toyed with the ring in his waistcoat pocket. "How may I steer my marriage into calm seas?"

"To begin with, I must correct your assertion." Dirk pointed for emphasis. "For good or ill, you are Sir Collingwood. Whether or not you wish it, you are a member of society, further distinguished by your wedding to the daughter of a duke. As such, you must abide the precepts by which we have lived, since birth."

"Bloody hell." Jason speared his hair. "Whatever am I to do now, as I am entirely out of my element?"

"The answer is altogether pedestrian." Trevor lit a cigar and took a long draw. "In the privacy of your residence or your traveling coach, with the shades down, of course, you may indulge your every desire with your bride. In public, polite behavior runs contrary to male instincts."

"But there are ways to subvert society." Everett winked. "My Brie is partial to libraries, and I have made love to her in some of London's most palatial mansions."

"Oh, I say." Trevor scoffed. "Tell me you have not waylaid her in our—"

"I have." Everett clucked his tongue. "Twice."

"That is nothing." Dirk crossed his legs and drummed his fingers on his thigh. "Becca prefers studies and desktops, in particular."

"*No.*" Everett gulped. "Not my desk."

To wit Dirk cast a lazy grin and held up three fingers.

"I must remember to replace my blotter." Everett scowled.

"Enough, as you have made your point." Jason had reached the end of his tether. "You enjoy blissful unions, so how do you propose to help me achieve the same happy results?"

"Have you told her you love her?" Everett asked, in a soft tone.

"Must you always cast that line?" Trevor sneered. "Mark my words, one of these days you will get us killed."

"Will you cease your prattle?" Everett groused. "You know as well as I that Alex needs his declaration."

"So have you or have you not pledged your troth?" Dirk folded his arms. "Tell us the truth, Collingwood. Are you in love with Alex?"

"I am unsure." Jason adjusted the lace trim of his sleeve and rested his hands in his lap. Then he propped his elbows on his knees. "Just how does one know when one is thus afflicted?"

Dirk glanced at Trevor, who peered at Everett, and Jason feared he might vomit.

"Well that is our first clue." Everett chuckled.

"I do not follow." Jason's ears rang with panic.

"That you equate affairs of the heart with distress, trouble, or the cause of suffering is noteworthy." Dirk reclined in his chair and met Jason's gaze. "Describe something for me. When you reflect on your situation with Alex, how do you feel?"

"As though someone ran a ramrod up my arse. As if I have swallowed lead shot." He bit back the bile rising in his throat. "I would equate it with Prometheus chained to the rock and the eagle's daily liver feast."

In unison, Dirk, Everett, and Trevor said, "You are in love."

"Hell and the Reaper." Yet the revelation was no real surprise, as Jason had suspected his attraction to Alex had long since passed a predilection of the fleshly sort. "Brothers, I am in love with my wife."

"Well I am impressed, as the first time I accepted that remarkable fact, in regard to Caroline, I almost jumped overboard." Trevor raised his glass in toast. "To Jason and Alex."

"Hear, hear," Dirk and Everett replied, in concert.

"Can we save the celebration, as I remain at odds with my bride?" Despite an urge to the contrary, Jason knew he had to confide in his co-conspirators, if he had any hope of winning Alex back. To his unutterable embarrassment, he detailed the events, as they had occurred, in Plymouth, excepting the physical relations. But the last confrontation again rendered him dizzy. "Gentlemen, I may have made a fatal mistake. In haste, and to my inexpressible shame, I accused Alex of attempting to trap me into marriage."

"Are you out of your mind?" Everett choked on his brandy. "Does Damian know that?"

"I would wager not, as Collingwood lives." Dirk winced. "Yet I am speechless."

"But that is not the worst part." Jason sighed.

"There is more?" Trevor's eyes grew wide as saucers.

"Aye." Jason braced for the shock. "When I inquired after Alex's reasons for giving herself to me, without a promise of matrimony, she claimed she did so because she loved me. And then I rejected her."

Trevor's mouth fell agape.

Everett smacked his forehead.

Dirk closed his eyes, lowered his chin, and groaned.

"Well I am at a loss, and I need another drink." Everett flagged a waiter. "Upon my word, but you swept the pool, when it comes to self-made disasters."

"What if I have squandered my chance?" How Jason wished he could travel back in time and undo the damage. "What if I have lost her?"

"Not by a long chalk." Dirk propped his chin in his hand. "Because when it comes to their heart, women are not so fickle."

"But Alex fears me." Deep-seated dispiritedness nestled in his breast, and Jason shook his head. "She has said as much, on more than one occasion."

"It is because she loves you," Everett expounded.

"That makes no sense," Jason replied.

"Yes, it does." Perched on the edge of his seat, Trevor sat upright. "As you hold your wife's heart, you posses the power to destroy her. In light of your rejection, that is what frightens her."

"So how am I to win her?" Jason remained clueless.

"Brother, you must embark on the courtship to end all courtships." Everett quivered. "And I do not envy you."

"And you must make your declaration." Dirk smacked a fist to a palm. "As she needs that."

"Is there not another way?" No man relished such maudlin sentiments. "What if she rejects me?"

"Perhaps you should rehearse your pronouncement," Trevor suggested. "As my wife once promised me, quite accurately, I might add, it gets easier the more you utter the singular statement."

"I will practice, as I can do it." Jason nodded once and inhaled. "Alex, I love you."

"Well, that was not too bad." With a strange expression, Trevor averted his stare. "For an amateur."

"Who do you think you are fooling?" Everett rolled his eyes. "That was terrible."

"Indeed." Dirk blanched. "Can you manage it without the green face?"

"I do not think so." Jason cradled his head in his hands. "Bloody hell."

"There, there, brother." Dirk slapped Jason on the back. "You must not lose faith. All you need is a little polish and refinement."

"Plus a boatload of blind luck." Everett shot Trevor a side-glance, and they collapsed in a fit of convulsive hilarity.

And so it was, with that vote of confidence, Jason returned to his townhouse, just as the sun had set. Again standing in the foyer, he handed his coat, hat, and gloves to Haynes and lamented another night without Alex, relaxed in slumber, at his side.

Then Jason started and reversed course. "Send for the coach, and have my trunks loaded, posthaste. I depart for the country in half an hour."

CHAPTER THIRTEEN

*T*he coach lurched to a halt, and Jason roused from a light sleep to discover he had arrived at Stratfield Manor. Given the breakneck pace with which the coachman had driven the team, they had cut an hour off the usual journey and landed at the doorstep at the crack of dawn.

Pulling on his coat, Arnie appeared in the entry. "Captain Collingwood, welcome home."

"Thank you, Phipps." Jason stretched his back and yawned. "Has my wife risen?"

"No, sir." The butler brushed his bangs from his face. "Her ladyship sleeps late into the morning, as she is in her last month of pregnancy and requires additional rest."

"Is she unwell?" He clenched his gut at the prospect. "Are there complications?"

"No, sir." Arnie smiled, as he directed the footmen. "Dr. Studly advises her ladyship's condition is quite normal, for the final weeks of her term. And as the renovations to the house are complete, she enjoys more idle time."

"Then I shall join her, in our chamber, after I deposit

these ledgers in the study, as it was a long ride." Jason skipped up the stairs.

"Captain—wait." Phipps followed in Jason's wake. "Sir, please, I can convey your effects. In light of your trip, you must be exhausted."

"I am quite hale and hearty, old friend." Jason steered down the hall to the left and then strolled into his domain. "And I need to—"

For a second, confusion fogged his brain, and Jason came to an abrupt halt. In a flash, he retraced his steps, glanced from side to side, checked his bearing, and re-entered his study.

"It was her ladyship's doing." Arnie cleared his throat. "She personally directed the renovation, selected every scrap of furniture, and spared no expense."

"Thank you, Phipps." Jason swallowed hard, as he digested the alterations to his sanctuary, which touched him more than he was willing to admit, to himself or anyone else. "That will be all."

The wall coverings of navy blue, trimmed in mahogany, his favorite color combination, continued the theme from the rest of the grand house. Draperies of lush velvet framed the window and highlighted a massive, hand-tooled desk, which held pride of place and bespoke categorical power and prestige. Running his finger in the grooves of the delicate carvings, he examined the most impressive furnishing he had ever owned.

It was then Jason noticed the small portrait of his bride. With a sigh, he smiled, and uncharacteristic tears blurred his vision. "Exquisite, darling."

As he returned to stand at the center of the room, he gazed upon a magnificent rendering of the Collingwood coat of arms, hanging above the fireplace. On the mantel rested a unique maritime clock, and upon further inspection he discovered the timepiece was, in fact, a rare Harrison. "Superb, sweetheart."

Matching bookcases filled the right wall, and on the opposite side, two large displays featured his collection of spyglasses and compasses, including the family heirloom his father had used. Jason rotated and absorbed the majesty and intimacy of his sanctuary and wiped the moisture from the corner of his eyes.

Without thought, he ran from the study and ascended the stairs, two at a time. In the gallery, he skidded to a stop, as resplendent works of art filled the cavernous hall. But what snared his attention was the large, full-length portrait of his bride, hugging her swollen belly.

After untying his cravat, Jason doffed his coat and waistcoat, and trod down the corridor, which led to the octagon-shaped chamber he shared with the woman of his dreams. In the sitting room, he deposited the clothing on a chair and then eased open the interior door.

The apartment remained dark, and Alex slept, propped on a mountain of pillows. He stifled a chuckle, as he stripped from his shirt, boots, and breeches. The bedroom was chilly on that cool September morning, so he relit and stoked a blaze in the hearth. Naked and aroused, so what else was new, he slipped between the sheets.

As soon as he drew a cushion to his side, his wife rolled into him, snuggled close, rested a hand to his chest and her head to his shoulder, sighed, and smiled a feminine smile. He tucked the blankets beneath her chin and exhaled in unutterable contentment. And Jason vowed that, somehow, some way, he would declare his love.

～

THE SUN PEAKED through the heavy drapes, as Alex yawned and nestled closer to Jason's warmth. Then she flinched and opened her eyes. Had she conjured a lifelike dream? If so, it was a most cherished fantasy, which had graced her waking hours every day, without fail, since her captain's departure.

The subtle rush of his breath gave her gooseflesh, and she caressed his glorious chest. But that vision and sensation had summoned her from peaceful slumber only yesterday, so she skimmed her fingers lower and squeezed his oh-so-reliable erection, which her reveries had neglected to replicate with any semblance of accuracy. "You are home."

Jason started and woke. "Hello, beautiful."

"*Oh.*" Alex shrieked and hugged him tight. "How I missed you, as it has been difficult to sleep without you at my side."

"I missed you, too. And I apologize for interrupting your routine." With a chuckle, he winked and kissed her forehead. "You warned that might happen."

"You are forgiven, as you kept your promise and returned to me." Then, to her embarrassment, she wept.

"Sweetheart, please do not cry." Her knight cupped her cheek and teased her lips with his thumb. "I drove all night to be with you, and I can bear anything but your tears."

"I am sorry." How Alex wanted to tell him the truth, as while she had decorated his study, surrounded by his personal items, he had captured her, all over again. But once before she had proclaimed her love, and Jason had rejected her. In her current vulnerable state, she could not withstand another disappointment, so she raised her defenses. "I have a surprise for you, which I would show you after breakfast."

"Well I have a surprise for you." He cast her a lopsided grin. "I may have ruined your surprise."

"You have seen it?" Crestfallen, she pouted.

"If you reference my study, yes, I have, and it is...never have I...you should not...*bloody hell*." Jason gritted his teeth and groaned. "Alex, you have outdone yourself. When I purchased Stratfield, I had imagined a serviceable country estate to raise a family. What you have managed, in so little time, humbles me, as you have exceeded my expectations, and I am so proud of you."

"Praise, indeed." And she could have danced a jig, were she not eight months pregnant, but ever-present doubt nagged at her consciousness. "So you are not vexed that I commandeered your private space, in your absence?"

"On the contrary, everything is beyond compare, and I cannot believe you procured a Harrison. Really, darling, you are amazing." And then Jason furrowed his brow and frowned. "But I do have one complaint."

"Oh?" Alex had celebrated her victory too soon. "There is something not to your taste?"

"Yes." He tapped a finger to her nose. "Your picture on my desk—"

"We can remove it." Knife to the heart with lethal accuracy. "It was just an afterthought—my little joke."

"Hold hard, love, as this is no joke, to me." Jason toyed with her nipple, and she gasped. "My issue is not with your portrait, as I should prefer nothing more than to gaze on your stunning face, but with the size, as the current rendering is too small. With your permission, I would take the miniature with me, aboard the *Intrepid*, as it is perfect for travel. And we can commission a larger work for my desk."

"You wish to carry my image with you, to sea?" In that moment, her heart sang.

"Have I made you happy?" Now Jason gently stroked her breast. "You glow, my dear."

"Yes." Emboldened by his request, she again searched out his erection. "And I would wager I can inspire a bit of euphoria in you, too."

"Wait." Jason peered at the bedside table. "Where is the cloth, as we will need it?"

"In the top drawer." As he came to life in her hand, her confidence soared, and she worked him, hard and rough, just as he liked it.

"I am a poor substitute for your naughty finger work, darling." He hissed, and moisture seeped from the plum-shaped tip. "I had better situate the towel, as this will not take long."

Truer words were never spoken, because no sooner had her captain put in place their odd protection than he opened his mouth in a silent scream and let fly a wicked volley. Over and over, he grunted and thrust his hips, and his completion seemed never-ending.

At last, Jason relaxed and laughed, in his booming baritone. "Oh, Alex, how I needed that."

"So I gather." She giggled. "And you made a mess. Should I discard the cloth?"

"That is your fault." Suddenly, her husband glanced at her, narrowed his stare, and shifted until he hovered above her. Rubbing his nose to hers, he slipped his fingers between her thighs. "You tempt me beyond the limits of sanity and self-control, and leave the towel, as we are not finished."

"Do I?" She shivered, as he teased her most intimate flesh, and their interlude harked back to treasured memories of those carefree days in Plymouth.

"Yes, but I think you know that." He growled when she

moaned. "How I savor your pleasure song. Sing for me, sweetheart."

Alex went up in flames.

❧

"ALEX, I LOVE YOU." The world shifted beneath his boots, and Jason teetered and collapsed into the chair, in his study. For a few minutes, he gasped for air, and nausea clawed at his throat. As the room seemed to spin out of control, and his ears rang, he bent forward, rested his head between his knees, inhaled, exhaled, inhaled, and exhaled. "This is deuced humiliating, Collingwood. Your sire must be rolling over in his grave."

Without thought or care, he stood, and the room tilted left and then right, and he dropped to his seat, sans the old infuriating dust cloud, to his relief, thanks to his wife's procurement of the new, high-back leather masterpiece that currently supported his miserable arse. Focused on the ceiling, he growled in frustration, speared his fingers through his hair, slowly rose to his feet, and leaned on his desk for stability.

The miniature of his bride, the chief source of his discomfit, seemed to mock him. "Darling, I swear I will get this right and make my declaration without vomiting."

Dirk, Trevor, and Everett had been right. Uttering that simple but nonetheless powerful phrase constituted the most terrifying prospect of his existence. Then again, perhaps he approached the situation in reverse. Instead of centering his efforts on the declaration, he should commence the courtship.

Now that posed a daunting task, as never had Alex required such formalities, and whores demanded only money, thus he had no experience with such triviality. From the first waltz, his bride had made no secret that she wanted him. How ironic it was that Jason had accused her of deceit, when the reality was his wife wore her heart on her sleeve. In his ignorance, he had trounced her generous spirit, to his everlasting regret.

"I know what I can do for her." He snapped his fingers. "My bride adores roses, and, thanks to her efforts, I have a rose garden."

So with his constitution quite recovered, he strolled to the door, unlocked the bolt, and strode into the hall. Taking a shortcut through the house, he navigated the back parlor and then exited via the terrace. As he rounded a large hedge, a sharp rebuke had him ducking for cover.

"You soiled my dress." Carrying a basket of cut flowers, the nursemaid stomped her foot and thrust her nose in the air, and Jason stifled a snort of laughter. "Get out of my way."

"But—apples are your favorite fruit." The bungling Mr. Penniman retreated, and his shoulders slumped. "I had thought we could slice it in half and eat it beneath the oak tree, near the creek. It boasts a lovely view of the countryside."

"I have no time for such nonsense." Molly sidestepped the clumsy suitor and pranced toward the manor. "My mistress requires my assistance."

It was the nanny's newfound confidence and haughty demeanor that drew Jason up short and distracted him from his mission. As his former cook-maid dressed down the stablemaster, she garnered a measure of respect.

There was something vaguely familiar in her condescending tone and aloofness. With an expression of utter confusion and dispiritedness, Tom scratched his chin.

Suspicion nipped at Jason's heels, and he returned to his study.

The household accounts occupied him until lunch, given Alex's spending spree, so it was only when his stomach grumbled that Jason realized he was hungry enough to eat his toenails. When he entered the dining room, he halted, as the nursemaid huddled beside Alex, who occupied her usual place at his left.

"Just do as I told you," his darling bride said, in a low voice. "Show him no mercy, and everything will be fine."

In that instant, Molly spied Jason and jumped. "Good afternoon, Cap'n."

"Oh, Jason." With a hand pressed to her temple, Alex cleared her throat. "I am so glad you could join me, as I am quite starved. That will be all, Molly."

"Then it appears my timing is excellent." As he perched at the head of the table, he draped a napkin in his lap. "So what did I interrupt, as you two looked thick as thieves?"

"How you do exaggerate." Her nervous laughter further piqued his curiosity and suspicion. "We discussed additions to the nursery, as I remain unhappy with the overall renovation."

"Good afternoon, Cap'n and your ladyship." Miss Phipps conveyed two steaming bowls. "We have your favorite, sir. Lady Alex requested hare stew to welcome you home."

"Smells delicious." So it appeared his charming bride had recovered another facet of her long absent personality, yet he would have preferred to leave her matchmaking skills in the past.

"How was that, Lady Alex?" Gertie compressed her lips. "Did I get it right, this time?"

"Perfect." His wife beamed, as a proud parent, and again

he glimpsed the old Alex. "And fret not, as I scheduled interviews with prospective footmen and kitchen maids, and I intend to hire additional servants, in the coming weeks. We should be at full staff, soon. And I would rather you limit your activities to that of primary housekeeper."

"Very good, ma'am." Miss Phipps half-curtseyed.

As he speared a morsel, Jason glanced at his glass of water and frowned. "I believe I would prefer ale with my meal."

"Right away, Cap'n," Miss Phipps replied.

"Stand fast, Gertie." After pushing from the table, he stood. "I remain unaccustomed to such service and would fetch my own drink."

When he entered the kitchen, he located a mug and a pitcher of ale.

"Look at you." Molly humphed. "You are covered in dust and smell like an animal."

Jason peered out the window and discovered the erstwhile sweethearts engaged in another heated battle.

"What do you expect?" Tom folded his arms. "I am a stable hand."

"Then I suggest you confine yourself to the yard." The nursemaid turned on her heel, but the stablemaster stayed her.

"Will you never forgive me?" Tom clutched Molly's fingers. "Is there no second chance for us?"

"I begged you to marry me, in Plymouth." She sniffed. "And you refused."

"I made a mistake, Molly." Tom brought her knuckles to his lips. "Have you never done anything you regretted?"

A strange sense of *déjà vu* traipsed Jason's spine.

The nanny and the stablemaster navigated stormy seas almost identical to that of Alex and Jason. How had he missed the similarity? And Molly's new attitude mirrored that of his once fiery wife.

Had Alex intervened on behalf of her close friend? Had his bride provided intimate advice? If so, then all was not lost, as his vivacious society maiden persisted beyond the walls of their bedchamber. He exhaled in relief. And then a grand idea formed in his brain. Perhaps in reuniting the servants, he could reconcile with Alex.

But he had to ascertain whether or not his wife supported the nursemaid, before he plotted his course. When he regained his seat, he noted his pregnant better half had devoured most of her portion. "You have some appetite, darling. Been busy, since our lazy morning, in bed?"

"You should always be so lazy, Jason." She averted her stare and blushed. "And Molly and I are refining the final furnishings in the nursery, as I want everything to be perfect for our babes."

"My lady, I shall forgo my morning ride and linger with you, amid the sheets, to your heart's content." He waggled his brows, and she giggled, a lilting sound that kissed his flesh. "Your attention to detail is commendable."

"Thank you." It had not escaped his notice that she had shed another layer of reserve and blossomed beneath his praise. "Molly is indispensable, and I am grateful that you brought her to Stratfield."

"Then we are most fortunate she has decided to remain in our employ." Alex's cherubic ebullience well nigh stole his breath. "It seems the stablemaster's presence no longer distresses our nanny."

As she had just consumed a healthy mouthful of stew, Alex choked violently.

"Careful, love." He patted her back. "You should not bite off more than you can chew."

"Remember, I eat for three." How innocent she appeared, as she fluttered her lashes, a tactic she had used in London.

"Have some milk, sweetheart." He slid her glass within reach. "By the by, I overheard a heated row between Molly and Tom. My heretofore-shy charwoman has grown quite bold." He counted to three. "In fact, she reminds me of you."

Alex spat milk across the table.

In that moment, Jason required no further proof of his wife's involvement in the romantic affairs of the nanny and the stablemaster. And he relished her pitiful attempts to disguise her involvement, as she could never hide anything from him.

"Oh, dear." She wiped her face and swallowed hard. "I know not what came over me."

"Are you all right?" He tamped a guffaw. "Have a care for yourself and our babes, darling."

"Of course, I am fine." She shifted in her seat. "But I have a request, if you are not too busy, today."

"My lady, I am always at your service." And that was an understatement. "What would you have of me?"

"I wondered if you might have a word with Mr. Penniman." As Alex inclined her head, she cast him a doe-eyed glance and worried her bottom lip. "If it is not too much trouble."

"It is no trouble, at all." For a minute, he thought she intended him to act as her *aide-de-camp*. Together, they would conspire to bring together the nanny and the stablemaster, and that might inspire a second reconciliation. "What is your problem with Tom?"

"His manners." As she toyed with the last bite in her bowl, she frowned. "And his demeanor toward me."

"What?" Now Jason bristled with anger, as he would brook no mistreatment of his wife. "Has something happened between you two, since my departure?"

"Yes." Alex furrowed her brow. "Mr. Penniman has been rude to me, on occasion, and I know not why. But it is rather disconcerting, as I have tried to welcome him, in accordance with your wishes. I even bade Mr. Harper renovate the stable house, yet the stablemaster expressed no acknowledgement or thanks."

"I will speak with Tom, after lunch." He drained his mug of ale and pounded a fist to the table. "If he cannot show you proper respect, he can return to Plymouth."

"Oh—no." Alex grabbed his wrist and then recoiled, as if he had burned her. "I am sure it is nothing more than a simple misunderstanding. You must not terminate him, as you, yourself, commented, we are fortunate to have Mr. Penniman in our employ."

"So you would have me counsel him?" Jason checked his ire and clutched her hand. "To what purpose?"

"Advise him of his place in our household." When he massaged her palm with his thumb, she shivered, and how he loved flustering her. "Mr. Penniman conducts himself above his station, nothing more. But I shudder to think how Blake or Damian would respond to such behavior, and I would preserve the stablemaster's head on his shoulders, for Molly's sake."

"Then say no more, darling." From his perspective, Tom required a visit to the tailor and the barber. Then Jason would instruct his young charge on the finer points of personal grooming and shaving. Given the nicks and cuts on Tom's chin and throat, the lad had been graced with an easy approach to horses yet persisted at serious risk of bleeding to death. "As your every happiness is my fondest desire."

Alex's mouth fell agape, and then she blinked. "Is that so?"

"Indeed." With a chuckle, he deposited his napkin on the bowl, pushed from his chair, stood upright, and bent to kiss her. "Are you intending to nap, today?"

"Yes." Alex gazed at him, with a misty-eyed, dreamy expression he had not seen since Plymouth. "Dr. Studly advises it, for the health of our children."

"When?" He licked the curve of her neck. "As I would join you."

"In about an hour, I suppose." Her breath hitched, when he plunged his tongue into the cleft of her cleavage. "Jason, I am to sleep, during that time."

"My naughty bride, I mean to hold you, nothing more." He chuckled, as he again tasted her lips. "But I like the way you think, and, if memory serves, release relaxes you, as nothing else."

"You are correct, in your estimation." She giggled. "And you are insatiable."

"Always, where you are concerned." Yes, his bride was ripe for courtship. How had he missed the obvious signs? "Then I shall meet you in our chamber, in an hour."

"I look forward to it." As he made to retreat, Alex stayed him, with a palm to his cheek. Holding his stare, she emitted the softest whimper, before she covered his mouth with hers. It was at once a sultry summons, impossible to deny, and the promise of a sensuous assignation unlike any they had enjoyed since January. "Until then, lady mine."

～

"AND DO NOT BE TOO hard on Mr. Penniman." Alex studied her husband, as he adjusted his cravat, and she marveled at the change in his demeanor. Had the sea air affected his brain? "I believe he is new to estate work."

"I shall try to contain myself." Jason smiled his mischievous smile, as he exited the dining room, and her heart melted.

Now she had executed her plan much easier than she had anticipated. And how accommodating was her husband, as if he welcomed the opportunity to provide assistance. In light of her captain's obliging nature, she had almost revealed her part in the tragedy that was Molly's affair. In the nick of time, she had recalled her husband's edict forbidding such machinations, delivered during a heated discussion, at the cottage in Plymouth. So she had acted otherwise.

Then again, he had not inquired after the nanny. Had Jason questioned Alex's involvement, she would have admitted everything, sparing no detail. Long ago, she had learned her lesson, and never again would she lie to her husband, but she had altogether altruistic motives for instructing Molly.

For some reason she could not fathom, the nanny and the stablemaster gave Alex hope for her and Jason. If she could manage to reconcile her staff members, then she just might win a much prayed for reunion with her captain.

Perhaps that ambition had led her to kiss Jason. It was the first she had initiated, since that dark day in January, when he had crushed her dreams and rejected her love. But something inside her had rekindled beneath his praise, and Alex seemed powerless to resist the lure her husband manifested, so she resolved to ride the crest of desire and see where it landed her. Yet she coveted an abundance of caution, as another disappointment would destroy her, forever.

"Thank heavens he is not providing equal advice to Mr. Penniman." Sharp movement in her belly had her sucking a breath, and she shook her head. "Now don't you two start with me. Miss Duckett will be just fine, as long as your father is none the wiser."

CHAPTER FOURTEEN

*T*o forgive or not to forgive?

Now that was the primary question Alex pondered, as she gazed at the toes of her slippers and breathed deeply to relax. Bent forward, she rested her hands on the back of the sofa, in the drawing room. The odd position, which would have looked awkward to the casual observer, relieved the pressure of the babes in her belly, and she had identified every serviceable scrap of furniture, of requisite height, in the house, to indulge in an impromptu respite.

As the graceless pose soothed her physical aches, it spawned mental torment. Wrestling with indecision and the double-damned fear that paralyzed her, she considered whether or not to let bygones be bygones, in regard to her husband and his original refusal to wed her, given the situation between the nanny and the stablemaster had improved.

At first, Molly had been quite cavalier with Mr. Penniman. The nursemaid had been brash and, in some circumstances, condescending, as she upbraided her less than elegant suitor. But of late the former cook-maid rarely mentioned Tom's name. No longer had she blushed in his presence, and she had not flinched at the sound of his voice. Perhaps the two young lovers had, at last, reconciled.

A cluster of vibrant pink roses appeared, as if from nowhere.

"Oh." She started and lifted her head. "Jason?"

"Good afternoon, my lovely bride." Grinning from ear to ear, he rocked on his heels. "It is our usual nap time, is it not?"

As if on cue, the mantel clock chimed the hour."

"Yes." For the last three days, he had joined her, in bed. "The bouquet is for me?"

"Of course." He sketched an elegant bow. "I raided our garden, as it is the end of the season."

"But—why?" Confused, she blinked.

"Do I require a reason?" He arched a brow.

"No." The babes moved, and she winced. "But you have never given me flowers. In fact, you never gave me anything, when in London."

"I know that." With a heavy sigh, he shuffled his feet. "Mine was a sorry excuse for a courtship, love."

"Were you courting me then, as I hadn't noticed?" In retrospect, he had gifted her nothing, not even a miniature of the *Intrepid*, as was customary of sea captains, when wooing prospective brides, during the two years she had pursued him. In contrast, she had given him everything.

"Alex, I have not done right by you, in so many ways. In effect, I took you for granted, and I would rectify that slight and never again repeat that mistake." Jason trailed a finger along her cheek. "May I court you, now?"

"What is the point?" She shrugged, even as she almost choked on her enthusiasm. "We are married."

"Better late than never." He wiggled his brows, and she could not help but laugh. "What have you to fear?"

Complete and utter devastation, the likes from which I will never recover. "If that is your wish, who am I to stop you?"

"Then let us begin anew, darling." He handed her the simple but charming arrangement and then swept her into his arms. "Right now, I should guard your slumber."

"Jason, be careful." Worried he might drop her, she clung to him, but he carried her upstairs as though she weighed nothing more than she had without the babes. "Do not injure your back."

"Alex, I do not break so easily." After entering their sitting room, he kicked the door shut and repeated the action, when he conveyed her to the bedchamber, and then set her on her feet.

As always, he untied her laces, removed her dress, and knelt to take off her slippers, garters, and stockings. He drew the chemise over her head, before lifting her to the four-poster. And then it was time for the main event.

Jason doffed his boots, cravat, coat, waistcoat, and shirt. Wearing only his skintight breeches, which tempted her even in her condition, he climbed onto the mattress, fluffed the pillows, and situated the cushion on which she rested her belly, at his side. When she had assumed her favorite position, he cradled her head and kissed her hair.

Without warning, she burst into tears.

"Why are you crying, darling?" He scratched her scalp, as he hugged her. "Are you uncomfortable? Are you in pain?"

"It is not what you think." She sobbed. "Oh, Jason. I saw us like this, last year, when I dreamed of our future. I had envisioned such grand plans for us, and then every-thing fell apart. In those six months you were gone, I had thought it would never happen, and I surrendered my fantasies, but here we are, together." She wept without shame.

"Alex, I must confess I remained ignorant of the seriousness of the misery I caused you, until now—until this very second." He gave her a gentle squeeze. "And I have repeatedly broken my promise not to pressure you into reconciliation, when I vowed otherwise. While I will never stop trying to restore your faith in me, know that I will never leave you, so there is no rush. Take all the time you need, love."

"Do you mean that?" She shifted to look him in the eyes. "Truly?"

"Yes." He frowned. "And I cannot apologize enough, for hurting you, for abandoning you, when you needed me most. I understand you are afraid, and that is your due. But I hope, very much, that you can find it within you to trust me, again."

In that moment, the imaginary but nonetheless vicious chains shackling her heart loosened, and Alex sighed in relief. Invisible walls, so long imprisoning her in a miserable tomb of melancholy and fear, crumbled in a flash. He could not have known it, but Jason had just freed her from the powerful bonds of disappointment, devastation, and despair.

"Shall I pleasure you, so you might have your nap?" He tucked the blankets snug about her. "Tell me what you wish, and you will have it."

"Will you hold me?" She nuzzled his chest. "I do so love sleeping in your arms."

"Of course." With a finger, Jason tipped her chin and bestowed upon her an achingly tender kiss. "Rest, angel. I will be here, when you wake."

The realm of fanciful reveries danced at the fringe of her

consciousness, and Alex smiled as she drifted. No longer would she fight her husband. No longer would she resist his overtures. No longer would she erect barriers between them. She would retrench. She would hope. And, with a little luck, she might find herself, again.

$\approx$

"Ouch." Alex secured the needle and thread and sucked the end of her injured finger. Had any lady ever met her fate from countless pinpricks?

"Did you hurt yourself, your ladyship?" Molly leveled her gaze on the embroidery and grinned. "You are not concentrating, as your stitches are uneven."

"Dear friend, how many times must I remind you that, in private, I wish you would call me by name?" Alex dropped her hoop to her lap. "And I am distracted."

Of course, that was the understatement of the decade, as she had thought of nothing but her captain's liberating proclamation, delivered during her nap, three days ago. The morning that followed, when the new day dawned, brought with it the tepid return of Lady Alexandra Seymour, as was, and Mrs. Jason Collingwood had yet to fully reconcile the two.

"I sympathize with your affliction." With a deep-seated frown, the nursemaid halted her work. "It is strange, how we think we want one thing, when we desire quite the opposite."

"Has something happened between you and—" A knock at the door interrupted Alex. "Come."

"I beg your pardon, your ladyship." Mr. Penniman, bearing an armload of firewood, entered the room. "Captain Collingwood bade me stock the hearth, as the staff remains short of footmen."

"Thank you, Mr. Penniman." Alex smiled, although he had not spared her a glance. But what struck her was the change in his appearance.

The chocolate brown coat and fawn colored breeches he wore fit as if they had been made expressly for the stablemaster. Someone had taught him to tie a proper mathematical, as his pristine cravat complimented a burgundy waistcoat, and a pair of polished top boots completed his impressive ensemble. Had the stableman employed the services of a tailor? But his attire was not the only aspect that had undergone a miraculous transformation.

His raven black hair had been cropped into the latest fashion, emphasizing a strong forehead and chiseled cheekbones. And his face was clean-shaven and bereft of a single smudge of dirt or grime. Had she thought him handsome? In truth, Tom Penniman would incite a riot, in the ballrooms of the *ton*.

"My apologies, for the disruption, your ladyship." He sketched an elegant bow. "With your permission, I will leave you, now."

"Mr. Penniman, will you not acknowledge Miss Duckett?" It struck Alex as odd that he ignored Molly. "Is the nanny not lovely, in her pink dress?"

"Forgive my oversight." With his stare firmly fixed to the floor, Mr. Penniman inclined his head. "I beg your pardon. Good afternoon, Miss Duckett."

"The same to you, Tom—I mean, Mr. Penniman." The nursemaid leaned over the armrest of her chair and gushed, as would an eager pup, yearning for a pat of approval from its master. "It is a beautiful day."

"Indeed, we enjoy very fine weather," Mr. Penniman

replied, in monotone, and compressed his lips. "Will that be all, your ladyship?"

"Yes, Mr. Penniman." Stunned by his cold demeanor toward Molly, Alex gulped, as her well-intended advice may have sunk the nanny's ship. "You are excused."

As soon as Mr. Penniman quit the room, Molly burst into tears.

"Oh, dear." Alex offered her handkerchief. "What happened? What went wrong?"

The nanny wailed louder.

"He made no attempts on your person, did he?" Alex wiped the nursemaid's cheeks. "He has not accosted you."

"I should be so lucky." Molly sniffed. "Oh, Alex. I am in a terrible state. Tom no longer wants me. He only has eyes for the upstairs maid."

"Colleen?" Alex tapped a finger to her chin and envisioned the new servant. "But I just hired her, and she is very young. The chit laughs at everything."

"And now my Tom loves her." Burying her face in her hands, Molly sobbed.

"Dear friend." Alex wrapped her arm about the nursemaid's shoulders. "Tell me the truth. When you asked me to help you resist Mr. Penniman, you really wanted my counsel on attracting him." It was a statement, not a question.

"How did you know?" The nanny's chin trembled, as she gazed at Alex. "What gave me away?"

"You and I have more in common than you realize." Alex pondered her predicament. "That is why my advice was designed to garner his attention."

"What?" With an expression of utter horror, Molly shuddered. "Do you mean that your instruction was intended to lure Tom?"

"Yes." With a smile, Alex gave Molly a gentle nudge. "I suspected you had not abandoned your campaign."

"Oh, *no*." To Alex's dismay, the nanny slumped forward, in a heap of misery.

"Molly, what have you not told me?" A chill of unease shivered down Alex's spine. "Please, talk to me."

"I have made a terrible mistake." The nursemaid hiccuped. "Because I was not honest with you, I am to blame for what has happened."

"You speak in riddles, and I am confused." Yet Alex suspected she had committed a grievous error. "And I have an awful feeling."

"Do not worry about me, my lady." With a plaintive sob, Molly clutched Alex's hand. "You are not at fault, as my plan failed because I misread your sage guidance."

"But I thought my directions quite clear." In a flash, Alex catalogued her suggestions and could find no flaws. "Where did I steer you amiss?"

With her arms wrapped about herself, Molly stood and walked to the window. "You are innocent, Alex."

Despite attempts to the contrary, Alex blanched and braced for a lightning strike. "I would not say that."

"But you are, as I twisted your recommendations to suit my purpose." Molly vented a self-mocking snort. "My mother once told me that manipulating men was quite simple, as one need only pretend to favor the opposite of the desired objective. So I tailored my behavior to countermand your counsel, thinking I might win Tom."

"Oh, Molly." Shifting from side to side, Alex scooted from the sofa and joined her friend. "Would that you had confided in me, as I would have aided you, whatever your endeavor."

"It is all right." The nursemaid dried her tears on the

sleeve of her plain frock. "I brought this on myself, as I envied your marriage, and I thought Tom was my match, as Captain is yours. Perhaps I was not meant for that sort of happiness, and I should settle for the blessings of a secure occupation and a comfortable residence."

Hideous laughter, haunting and taunting, filled Alex's ears, and she swayed. A series of rejoinders, rebukes, and rejections echoed, and she shook her head. Grasping the shield-shaped back of a Hepplewhite chair, she clutched a fist to her chest.

"Do not despair, Molly. It is never too late." The declaration, freely made, worked as a balm, soothing frazzled nerves, but something she had not foreseen happened, just then. A surge of confidence invested Alex, spreading from her heart, inch by inch, until it suffused every muscle with a burst of derring-do, leaving her no choice but to act. "The cook baked some fresh Bath buns, this morning, and I know they are your favorite. Why don't you enjoy an early tea, and will you send in Phipps, as you make for the kitchen?"

"That sounds lovely." The nanny sniffed. "Thank you, your ladyship."

Alone, Alex paced before the window. Wringing her fingers, she peered beyond the glass, at the manicured lawn and boxed hedges. As she had cared for the grounds of the manor, she had to nurture her staff, as they were her responsibility.

"You wished to see me, your ladyship?" Artie entered the drawing room, and Alex marveled at his elegant appearance and refined manners.

"Yes." Nagging self-doubt reared its ugly head, but Alex quashed it. "Will you ask Gertie to deliver a pot of tea, some Bath buns, and black butter to the back parlor? And send for Mr. Penniman to join me, posthaste."

"Very good, your ladyship." Phipps bowed.

With hope as a shield, Alex tottered to the oval mirror and assessed her appearance. Molly had arranged Alex's brown hair in loose curls, with a single thick lock draped at her neck. Turning left, she scrutinized her silhouette, which lacked the refinement of her pre-pregnancy figure, but the pale blue morning dress accented her creamy complexion, to perfection.

And then she studied her reflection. Trailing her knuckles along her cheek and throat, she inhaled a shaky breath and smiled. How long had it been since she had spared a second glance at her attire? Marking another triumph, however small, Alex charged into the fray.

"You wished to speak with me, your ladyship?" Tom Penniman bowed, with polished refinement, which piqued Alex's suspicion.

"Indeed." Reclining on the *chaise* in the back parlor, she sized up her prey. "Will you light the fire, as I am chilled? And I wondered if you might join me for tea, as we have yet to become better acquainted."

"As you command, your ladyship." Despite his calm response, he moved with a stiff and awkward gait, as he approached the hearth, squatted, and nursed a blaze.

"Have a seat, Mr. Penniman." Unpracticed and suffering from months of inactivity, she devised an impromptu attack, yet it felt so good to stretch her independent wings. "And may I call you Tom?"

"You may refer to me however you wish, your ladyship." The stablemaster perched on the edge of an overstuffed chair. Again, Alex marveled at his miraculous metamorphosis, as the young man was altogether quite handsome.

"You do not approve of me, do you, Tom?" In anticipation of his answer, she held her breath.

His cheeks flushed a charming red, and he shifted his weight. "It matters not how I—"

"I know I am not your favorite person, but I would like to know why?" In advance of what some might consider an unforgivable slight, she raised her defenses, lest she overreact. "You have my permission to speak freely, without fear of reprisal."

In a flash, Mr. Penniman came alert, pinned her with a harsh stare, and whispered, "You killed my love."

"I beg your pardon?" Confused, Alex set down her cup of tea, which jostled, as she trembled with shock. "Please, explain your accusation, as I have done no such thing."

"Perhaps I have exaggerated, as Molly lives." He scowled. "But she is no longer my girl, because you poisoned her head with fancy notions."

"I do not follow." Yes, she had encouraged Molly to try new things, but how had that harmed the nursemaid? "Miss Duckett is impressionable, but that should have changed nothing between you."

"You changed everything, your ladyship." Tom crammed his hands into his coat pockets. "From the first, I have loved Molly, as she was a simple maiden, bereft of guile or pretentious airs. For years, I brought her daisies, after church on Sundays. Now she wants roses, which I cannot afford to purchase on my salary."

"We have a rose garden, and you may select an arrangement, when the blooms are in season." Alex twined her fingers in her lap, as the solution seemed quite elementary. "That should resolve your difficulty."

"There is more, my lady." The stablemaster sighed. "We had planned to purchase a small parcel of land, and I had intended to build a cabin, for our family. We are but poor country folk, so we could not manage much, but I would have constructed a comfortable home to raise our children. Now she wants to live on an estate. Do I look like landed gentry?"

"No." Little by little, Alex's renewed confidence flagged, as the enormity of her disastrous matchmaking skills weighed heavy. "Pray, continue."

"My heart holds me captive to the dreams Molly and I once shared, and I am her prisoner." When Tom met her gaze, she recognized his pain and torment. "I gave her all I had to offer, and she rejected me. Have you any idea, can you even begin to fathom the depth of my agony?"

"Actually, I can sympathize with your dilemma, more than you realize." But then a particular point occurred to Alex. "If you feel that way, why did you spurn her, in Plymouth?"

"Because I knew not what to make of her altered state." Tom pushed from the sofa and paced. "Molly has always been sweet and honest. Then she came at me, gowned in a style I found utterly foreign and indecent, with her face painted, batting her lashes as some cheap doxie, and she scared me. I preferred her as she was, without useless ornamentation."

"I am so sorry, Tom." Alex searched her mind for a solution.

"But I cannot blame you, entirely." Mr. Penniman paused and compressed his lips. "In my ignorance and confusion, I shunned her. Then I heard gossip, in town, and talk of a noblewoman residing with Captain Collingwood. When Captain enlisted my aid to secure the cottage, I found the dress Molly had worn and confronted him. Cap'n told me about you and your friendship with my Molly."

"You have my word, as a lady, I never meant to harm your relationship." At that moment, Alex rued the day she had meddled in the nanny and the stablemaster's affair. "And all is not lost."

"How I wish that were so, your ladyship." With shoulders slumped, Tom shuffled his feet. "I apologized, but Molly refused to forgive me. I declared myself, but it meant nothing. In the end, she rejected me as I had foolishly rejected her. Have you any idea how it hurts to have your devotion mocked and refused?"

"Yes, I believe I do, Mr. Penniman." Alex nodded, as reality struck her as a punch to the face.

Molly Duckett, simple country girl, had found herself a good man, and Alex had spoiled everything, with her horrible but well-intended counsel. She should have known better than to interfere, after the Lance and Cara fiasco. But never let it be said that Alex could not learn from her mistakes. Hell would freeze before she stuck her nose where it had not belonged. Yes, her days of playing cupid had ceased.

Just as soon as she set things right between the nanny and the stablemaster.

"My lady, I never meant to make you cry." Tom knelt at her feet, drew a handkerchief from his coat pocket, and dried her cheeks. "Forgive me."

"There is nothing to forgive, as I owe you an apology." Alex extended her hand, which he clutched in his. "And I vow to repair the damage I have caused, and I swear you shall have Molly."

"Will you help me?" the stablemaster inquired, with an expression of hope.

"Yes." She dipped her chin, and he placed a chaste kiss on her knuckles.

It was to her misfortune that, at that precise moment, Jason barged into the back parlor.

Her husband glanced at Alex, Mr. Penniman, and to Alex. Then Jason narrowed his stare and stretched to his full height. "What in bloody hell is going on here?"

"Jason, I can explain." Withering beneath her spouse's ire, she peered at Tom. "You are dismissed, Mr. Penniman."

The stablemaster winced and ran from the room, with his neck intact.

"Alex, did you put your lovely little nose in Tom and Molly's affairs?" Her captain arched a brow and grimaced. "Answer me, now. And do not insult me by pretending an oblivion we both know you harbor not."

In an effort to form a suitable response, one that would save her posterior, she studied the pattern on the upholstery of the *chaise*. In most English country houses, the back parlor ranked of relative insignificance. The primary function of the diminutive living space was to provide a quiet place for the mistress of the manor to enjoy afternoon tea, meet with servants, or—

"*Alex.*"

"Yes, sir?" She snapped to attention.

"Did you, or did you not, insert yourself into Tom and Molly's relationship?" He folded his arms, hugged a parcel to his chest, and thrust his chin. "After I forbid such shenanigans, back in Plymouth."

Brave and unafraid, Alex scooted to the end of the *chaise* and stood. "Yes."

Jason blinked. "You admit your involvement?"

"I do, as I have nothing to hide, and my motive is honorable." She squared her shoulders. "And I promised I would never deceive you again."

"Your honesty spikes my guns, sweetheart." He huffed a breath and shook his head. "And I must extend equal candor, as you are not alone in your matchmaking machinations, because I taught Tom the finer points of grooming, gentlemanly behavior, and procured new togs for the lad."

"You did that, for them?" When he nodded, Alex stepped in his direction. "But—why?"

"Because they belong together, as do you and I." Jason mirrored her move and closed the distance between them. "If Molly and Tom can resolve their differences, then there must be hope for us."

"Really? I believe that, too." Riding a wave of conviction, unlike any she had known since Plymouth, Alex smiled. "What is in the box?"

"You shimmer, love. How I cherish this side of you." To her surprise, her captain clicked his heels and presented the beribboned package for her inspection. "A gift, which is long overdue. I ordered it, prior to my departure from Deptford, on my mission, and it was delivered, this morning."

"Ah, yes." Alex giggled, as the desire to flirt with her husband, nonexistent of late, returned with a vengeance. "The belated courtship."

"Shall I convey this to the sofa, so you may open it?" Jason extended his arm, and she rested her palm in the crook of his elbow. "And how beautiful you look, in your blue dress."

"Why Captain Collingwood, are you trifling with me?" Gooseflesh covered her from head to foot, as he eased her to the cushions. After untying the navy satin bow, she lifted the lid, parted the paper, and gasped. Inside, nestled in a bed of cotton, was a miniature replica, complete with masts and sails, of the *Intrepid*. "Oh, Jason. I used to pray you would gift me a model of your ship. How did you know I always wanted one?"

"I did not—until now, as I am an ignorant arse." With a mighty glower, he groaned. "But, in the seafaring ranks, this makes you my woman."

"Blast." To her infinite frustration, she wept. "I am so tired of crying, but mine are happy tears."

"Darling, Alex." Her husband moved the box to the table and lifted her to his lap. "I owe you an ocean of apologies, as I neglected you sorely in London, and I wonder why you pursued me. But I vow never again to forget you, if you will give me a chance to prove myself."

She was not sure why she had done it, but Alex framed his face and kissed her captain with all she had and for all she was worth. Fire erupted from their point of contact, searing their lips as their tongues twined, and cloistered them in blazing heat. Undeniable hunger blossomed in her belly, and she angled her head, drawing him deeper into the intimate connection. When, at last, they parted, Jason rested his forehead to hers.

"Is it wishful thinking, or was that an affirmative?" He claimed another quick kiss.

"Yes." Even as he favored her with a boyish grin, she shivered. "If you are sincere in your courtship, I will not fight you. While I am still scared of the possibilities, should you fail me, no longer will I allow fear to rule my life. But you will rue my wrath, Jason Collingwood, if you disappoint me again."

"No worries, love." He chuckled. "As you shall soon discover your distress is unwarranted."

"Do not make sport of my apprehension, as my trepidation is well founded and much deserved." Alex sat upright.

"Has no one ever leveled your world, shattered your dreams, and destroyed the person you thought you were, in a single catastrophic blow?"

"Actually, yes." Jason held her close and cradled her head. "When my parents died, leaving me an orphan, and my uncle bought my commission. But I found my way, and so will we."

"Consider your heartbreak and devastation, and then add an unwed pregnant member of the peerage to the mix." Recalling her promise, she relaxed in his embrace. "Polite society is anything but, and had you not returned and married me, my life would have ended, and our babes would have been forever branded bastards. But you could have sailed the seas, with nary a concern, and never looked back. For those six months you were gone, that was the reality I contemplated, and part of me died to tolerate it."

"No, sweetheart. You are still very much alive." Jason shifted, tipped her chin, and met her gaze. "Together, we will find what has gone astray, and I will fulfill the dreams and grant you the future you thought lost, if I must labor in that endeavor until my last breath."

"I believe you will try." The mantel clock sounded the noon hour, and she slid from his lap. "I should check our lunch."

"Alex, wait." Her captain stood and clutched her hands in his. "There is something I wanted to tell you. I...that is to say...for a long while—"

"Jason, are you ill?" She reached up and pressed her palm to his forehead. "You are pale."

"It is nothing." He released her and dropped to the sofa. "I look forward to our nap."

CHAPTER FIFTEEN

wo days later, Jason stood before the mirror in his study, practicing what had become an exercise in lunacy. After adjusting his cravat, he tugged on the lapels of his coat, smoothed his hair, and cleared his throat. Then he shifted his weight and stared at his reflection.

"My darling wife, for a long time I have wanted to tell you—no, that is no good." With a sneer that would have reduced the saltiest tar to a puddle, he narrowed his stare. "Most beautiful Alex, from the moment I first spied you, in the Richmond's ballroom, I knew you were the girl for me and—she is no girl, you addled arse."

Grasping his hands behind his back, he paced. Given his tenure in the Navy, Jason had no prior experience with perfume and poetry, so he ventured into unfamiliar waters. Searching his limited knowledge of courtship, he composed another oratory. "Dearest and loveliest Alex, your body is—"

A knock at the door brought him to a halt.

After unlocking the bolt, Jason opened the oak panel. "Tom? What can I do for you?"

"I beg your pardon, Captain Collingwood, but might I have a minute of your time?" Mr. Penniman shuffled his feet. "It is a matter of utmost importance."

"Of course." Jason granted the stablemaster entry and then reclined in the new chair, behind the massive desk he so favored. "Have a seat and tell me what concerns you."

"First, let me say that I would never encroach on your generosity were it not absolutely necessary." Tom inched forward, tugged on his cravat, and then smoothed the sleeves of his coat. "I wonder if I might secure a loan or an advance on my salary?"

"Is everything all right?" Intrigued, Jason stretched upright. "Are you in some sort of trouble?"

"No, sir." Then the lad shifted and frowned. "Well, you might call it trouble, as I wish to court Molly."

"I beg your pardon?" He almost fell to the floor.

"Sorry, Cap'n." The expression of utter helplessness investing the stablemaster's face invoked a tidal wave of sympathy. "I intend to woo Molly, with flowers and such."

"Indeed?" Jason rubbed the back of his neck. "And such frippery costs money, does it not?"

"More than I could have anticipated, sir." Tom rolled his eyes. "Ladies covet perfume, roses, fine chocolates, lace handkerchiefs, and the like. Daisies no longer satisfy my girl, as she has developed a taste for Lady Alex's Belgian truffles, along with your wife's French fragrance. Do you comprehend my dilemma, Cap'n?"

"More than you know." But Jason had an epiphany, in that moment. The stablemaster could not have known it, but he had just inspired a brilliant idea.

Alex had a brash, bold disposition—well, she had before Jason destroyed her. But the very things that Tom high-lighted bespoke the return of the fiery society maiden.

Probing his memory, he made several mental notations and scoffed.

In his desire to court Alex, Jason had solicited advice from everyone who knew her, but none knew Mrs. Collingwood half so well as her husband. While her friends had responded with sage counsel, recommending sweet little gestures, the former Lady Alex Seymour had lived large.

It was her zest for life, and all its niceties, that had attracted him to her, at the onset. And for a newlywed couple, such finery posed opportunities to win his bride's heart.

"Captain Collingwood, I shall be happy to assume additional duties, to compensate you for the loan." Tom wiped his brow. "I will do anything to marry Molly."

"That is not necessary, as we are, in many respects, unlikely allies." Jason drew a key from his pocket, unlocked the top drawer of his desk, retrieved a wooden box, and counted a generous sum of notes. "You may consider this an early wedding present, and I believe you and I can strike a blow for bungling suitors, if we pool our efforts."

"Cap'n, this is a vast deal more than I can repay, in my lifetime." The stablemaster scratched his cheek. "But if you have any insight into wooing the fairer sex, I am your most ardent pupil."

"Well, I gathered a bouquet for my wife, and she was most grateful, so I would wager I might score a far grander victory with a full arrangement and, perhaps, a bit of original poetry." Bolstered with renewed purpose, Jason grabbed a stack of parchment from a drawer and snatched the pen from the inkstand. "Let us scribble a few thoughts."

"Oh, I say." Poor Tom blanched. "I am uneducated, Cap'n."

"There is nothing to it, as you need only rhyme." Jason

composed a few ideas. "How difficult is that?"

"I must trust your judgment, as I am, most definitely, out of my element, Cap'n." Tom stood. "But I can fetch a couple of vases from the kitchen."

"Tell Phipps I want the finest crystal." Jason listed several words he discerned conveyed the appropriate sentiment, as he wanted his lady in no doubt of his ardor. "And fill them with water, so we may present our women with the arrangements, this afternoon."

"Aye, sir." The stablemaster ran into the oak panel.

"Tom, you must open the door, before you may exit." Jason couldn't help but laugh.

"Yes, Cap'n." The lad shrugged and then charged forth from the study.

After a few minutes, Jason read his fledgling attempt at the stuff of poets and groaned. Without ceremony, he crumpled the stationary into a ball, tossed it into the wastebasket, and began again. Concentrating, he mulled the sentiments he ached to impart.

The second effort comprised a pitiful improvement on the first, so he sent the drivel into the trash and resolved to succeed with the third endeavor. Scratching out various passages, he mixed half of one sentence with another and struck syrupy, maudlin gold.

So Jason transposed the poem to a clean sheet of parchment and admired his accomplishment. "This is not so tricky as I had guessed, and I possess a talent that had been unknown to me."

In that second, Tom returned, bearing two cut-glass vases. "Miss Phipps said Lady Alex will have our heads if we break these."

"Sit them on my desk, and let us storm the garden, in search of flowers." He folded the missive, slipped it into an envelope, and inscribed his bride's name on the front. "When we complete our arrangements, you may compose your love verse."

"I dread it, sir." The stablemaster clutched his hands to his stomach. "As I am no bard."

"Nonsense." Jason chucked Tom's shoulder. "And I shall help you, as it turns out I am quite the sonneteer."

MY MOST BEAUTIFUL ALEX,

> *Your body is like a well-stocked larder;*
> *How I love to weigh anchor in your honey harbor.*
> *Your breasts like cannonballs make my Jolly Roger stout;*
> *How your naughty finger work inspires me to shout.*

—Jason

Alex read and reread the card, which accompanied a rather unusual display, if she could call it such, of flowers, and burst into laughter. Gasping for air, she swallowed hard and attempted to calm herself, but she surrendered to another fit of giggles. At last, she wiped a tear from her eye, pressed a hand to her swollen belly, and examined what had to have been the most unique floral presentation she had ever received.

An elegant crystal vase, containing bits of leaves and twigs floating in muddy water, had been crammed, for lack of a better term, full of roses, to the extent that some blooms had broken and hung askew. But the bundle also featured what appeared to be small branches from the hedgerow, to her inexpressible confusion and amusement.

"Merciful heavens, what is that mess?" Miss Phipps stood, hands on hips, in the back parlor and frowned. "I should reprimand the maid—"

"You will do no such thing, as they are a gift from Captain Collingwood." Sitting at her escritoire, Alex gazed at the arrangement, yes, that description was far too generous, and smiled. No words could convey the heights of her delight. "And never have I enjoyed lovelier roses."

Then she glanced at Miss Phipps. In unison, they collapsed in unrestrained mirth.

"Oh, dear." Gertie neared. "Should I resituate the blooms and change the water, your ladyship?"

"No." In truth, Alex had not the heart to change one aspect of Jason's gift, which she cherished as priceless artwork. "I would not, for the life of me, diminish my husband's overture."

"But the roses will not survive more than a day or two, at most, in that muck." The housekeeper snickered. "I should instruct him, else he will strip the bushes bare, with minimal reward."

"You will say nothing, as I can always plant more." So her captain courted her, as promised. Had she thought she loved Jason? In that instant, her capacity for said emotion grew in epic proportions, filling her chest with heretofore-unimagined bliss, and confidence charged the field. "Miss Phipps, I should like to change the dessert menu, for tonight."

"Have you a craving, my lady?" Gertie queried, with a grin. "I shall have cook prepare whatever you wish."

"Indeed, I do." A sweet recollection jolted her memory, and Alex contemplated the logistics. If she caught her husband in the right place, at the right time, she could pleasure him, on her knees, with her lips, given a fortuitously placed pillow. With his hedonistic tutelage, had she not licked a favorite sweet from his most prized protuberance, in Plymouth? "I should like cherry compote, with shortbread and mascarpone."

Perhaps it was time for Alex to woo her captain.

"A PLEASANT AFTERNOON, Molly. Sorry, I am late, but the pantry ledger did not balance, and it took me almost an hour to reconcile the amounts." Alex strolled through the sitting room and into the bedchamber. "And then there was a minor emergency in the kitchen."

The household remained short of staff, and she had yet to hire a lady's maid, because she found it difficult to replace Lily, her servant from Penhurst. Lady's maids were like extended family, and she counted Lily a friend, so Alex struggled to employ a successor. So she compensated the nanny to perform the duties Jason had not assumed.

"I am ready for my bath, and I am in dire need of a long soak, so you may be excused, after you help me undress." Alex kicked off her slippers and stopped short.

The tub had been situated by the fireplace, and rose petals floated atop the water's surface. Pedestals, bearing huge floral arrangements, occupied almost every corner of the octagonal-shaped room. As Alex rotated, she discovered her husband.

"I wager it is going to be a very pleasant afternoon, indeed, my lady wife." With a broad smile, Jason strutted from behind an oriental screen. "And I owe you a boon, given your naughty tongue work, last night, which was quite spectacular."

"And here I thought it was the cherry compote that

inspired your raucous approbation." She gave him her back, and he loosened her laces. "The roses are stunning. Thank you, Jason."

"The compote was nice, too." As he inched the dress to her waist, he pressed his lips to her temple and then cupped her breasts. "And the roses are roses. You are stunning. How are your knees, today?"

"A little sore." Alex stepped free from her gown. "Where is Molly?"

"I arranged a distraction for her, as well as you, so I might spring my surprise." Jason squatted to unhook her garters and remove her stockings. "Oh, love. You are bruised."

"I shall select a thicker cushion, next time." When she wobbled, she grasped a handful of his hair. "Wait a minute. Did you start the fire?"

"What fire?" Jason stood and drew her chemise over her head. "As I lit the oven, but it was a ruse to divert you. I used a little wood and added paper, so it would smoke, for dramatic effect."

"A little wood?" Alex snorted, as he led her to the bath. How strange it was that her nudity no longer embarrassed her. "I could have built a ship with the amount of timber you used, and you never burn paper in the oven, as the blaze is too hot. Really, Jason, you could have brought the house down, about us. As it stands, I might have to purchase a new oven."

"Hell and the Reaper." Her captain adjusted a pillow behind her neck, as she reclined and sank into the fragrant water. "Should I check the situation?"

"No, as I took care of it." Alex sighed and closed her eyes, but she stole a peek at her beautiful husband, as he stripped to his breeches and shirt. "When I could not locate the lord of the manor, I summoned Mr. Penniman and Phipps, and they organized an impromptu fire brigade from the stable hands. Everything is all right, though you scared ten years off Gertie's life. But the kitchen requires repainting."

"Well, as no harm is done, let us enjoy your bath, sweetheart." As Jason rolled up the sleeves of his shirt, he glanced at her and winked. "And the next time I am in London, I shall search out a tub large enough to accommodate two, for our townhouse and Stratfield."

"Do you intend to wash me?" she inquired, when he picked up the bar of soap and worked a generous lather with a cloth. "If so, you should take off your shirt."

"As you wish." She bit her lip and shivered, when he shed the fine lawn from his impressive frame. Then he snatched the soap and cloth from the floor. "Are you chilled, love? Is the water not warm enough? Now, where were we?"

"Everything is perfect. Jason, while I appreciate the roses and the poetry—why are you doing this?" She shrieked, as he scrubbed the soles of her feet. "We are married, and never did I anticipate such care."

"Because you are my wife, and I am courting you." She bent forward, so he could bathe her back and shoulders. "And I enjoy attending your needs, more than I thought I would."

"Do you?" She giggled, as he rubbed her belly, but the babes kicked, and she winced. "Oh, our children are rowdy sorts, just like their father."

"Does it hurt?" With an expression of reverence, Jason stilled and pressed his palm over her navel.

"Sometimes." She sucked in a breath, as her precious cargo seemed to dance a jig.

"You are amazing, Alex." Jason rinsed the suds, bent, and kissed her girth. "I am in awe of you."

Once again, beneath his praise, she blossomed. There was so much she wanted to tell her captain, but she lacked the courage. Yet his belated courtship bolstered her nerve, and she vowed to declare herself, again.

"Thank you for my poem and the flowers." She giggled, as she recalled the verse. "It was a very romantic gesture."

"They are Collingwood originals, my dear." After depositing the soap in a basin, he collected a towel and lifted her from the tub. As he dried her, he waggled his brows. "Bet you never would have suspected I wrote such sentiments, had I not signed the note."

"Oh, I believe I would have guessed." She clucked her tongue, as he blotted her cheeks. "Now, it is time for our nap."

As was his way, Jason swept her off her feet and carried her to the bed. After situating the covers, he arranged the pillows.

"Wait." Alex caught his stare and drummed her fingers on the mattress. "Remove your breeches."

To wit her captain cast her a slow, sensual smile. "Darling, while I am rather fond of your busy hands, what I most treasure is the glimpse of *my* Alex, when you touch me."

"But I seem to recall you once sang an altogether different tune." She rolled on her side, assumed her usual position, and sought his self-professed stout Jolly Roger. "Do you not remember your pledge to change me, when we were in London? You said Damian coddled me to excess, and you would tame my fiery independence. I had thought you might prefer my more fearful, sedate side."

"I was never so wrong in my life, Alex." Cradling her head, he kissed her hair. "Because you were perfect."

CHAPTER SIXTEEN

*T*here was pleasure in the morning, pleasure in the afternoon, and pleasure with the evening sun. And if Jason could have coaxed his charming bride from her shell, or enticed her to permit him entry into hers, there would have been pleasure all throughout the night. Alas, Alex refused to let him make love to her.

The rosewater bath had failed in its ambition, the chocolates he fed her as they lounged in the new gazebo had given him false hope, and so he had resorted to a desperate pursuit akin to that of a randy sailor just returned from a long voyage. Still, his uncharacteristically shy bride had not relented. Release had been claimed in the palm of her hand, and once in her succulent mouth, but not in her honey harbor.

"I beg your pardon, Cap'n." Carrying a small table, Phipps halted in the sitting room. "Have you a preferable location?"

"Near the hearth, as the evenings are chilly." Although Jason enjoyed the tender interludes with his bride, and her naughty finger work, each subsequent climax intensified his desire for true intimacy. Because the old Alex was a passionate creature, he believed he could resurrect his fire-brand, once and for all, if they joined their bodies. And that was his primary objective. "Does my wife suspect anything?"

"No, sir." The butler grinned. "The staff has worked hard to keep your secret. And the stable hands are carrying up the chairs, using the back stairs, to avoid her ladyship."

"Excellent." Untying his cravat, Jason strolled into his changing room. "Hold the dinner bell for an extra five minutes, as I would dress for the occasion, and I prefer to be ready, when Alex enters our chamber."

"Very good, Cap'n." Arnold cleared his throat. "We are prepared."

So what should a sea captain wear to seduce a gently bred noblewoman? Never had Jason given much thought to his attire, as he had spent his formative years in a uniform. When it came to sex, he opted for nudity, unless he had been at sea and could not have been bothered to undress beyond that necessary to achieve completion.

"Captain Collingwood?" Gertie called. "Are you there, sir?"

"Yes, Miss Phipps?" While Alex adored him in black formalwear, Jason selected a simple satin robe and matching trousers. Both garments belted at the waist, so he could strip naked, jump in bed, deploy the Jolly Roger, and ravish his bride, in a matter of seconds. Humming a bawdy shanty of seduction on the high seas, he assessed his reflection in the long mirror. "Not bad, Collingwood."

"I set the table, Cap'n." Gertie smiled, as he strutted into the bedchamber. "Shall I deliver the entrees?"

"Have everything portioned into covered dishes." He

combed and smoothed his hair. "I intend to serve my wife, myself."

"Yes, sir." She snickered. "I hope you prove a better server than flower arranger."

"Very funny, Gertie." At the washstand, he scrubbed his face and then applied a liberal amount of sandalwood, as Alex once confessed the scent drove her to the limits of self-control.

The new maid, a giggly silly girl, rolled a trolley, loaded with various silver salvers, into the room. With Miss Phipps supervising, they completed the preparations.

The butler dipped his chin. "Sir, we are ready."

With one last check of his appearance, Jason rested hands on hips. "Then signal my wife."

A peaceful calm fell over the octagonal-shaped suite, as he twiddled his thumbs and paced the floor. He embarked on a grand tour of the chamber, stopping at each bouquet of roses and sampling their scent. Then he scratched his head, as he wondered whether or not he had lit too many candles.

The dinner bell pealed.

For some unfathomable reason, Jason panicked. He glanced left and then right and jumped on the bed. Reconsidering his pose, he leaped from the mattress and sank into the overstuffed chair, which boasted a superb view of the gardens. Plagued by uncharacteristic indecision, he charted a course for the end of the four-poster, but as he neared, he stubbed his toe on the footboard. *"Bloody everlasting hell."*

Hopping like a deuced rabbit, he grabbed his offended appendage and swore a slew of expletives that would have made his sire proud—just as Alex entered their suite.

"Jason, what happened?" She tottered to stand before him. "Are you all right?"

"I am fine, darling." In actuality, he was a damned lubberly nincompoop. "And how are you, this evening?"

"A bit tired." She wrinkled her nose and stretched her back. "Miss Phipps struggles with entries to the pantry account, and the ledger is a disaster, as I have yet to balance the numbers. In the morning, I shall teach her to calculate the proper supply totals and—"

It was at that precise instant she noted the fantasy he had created just for her. With mouth agape, her expression softened, and she rotated, inch-by-inch.

"Surprise, darling." In welcome, he splayed his arms wide.

"Oh, Jason." To his satisfaction, she waddled straight into his embrace. "While I know you woo me with ulterior motives, I do so love being spoiled, and everything is beautiful."

"I had hoped to please you." He kissed the crown of her head and smiled. "May I have the honor of your estimable company for a private dinner, my cherished wife?"

"How could I decline such a gracious offer?" Once again, she beamed with joy, as she met his stare, and he decided, right then and there, that he would court her for the rest of her life. "Will you help me slip into something more comfortable?"

"Sweetheart, undressing you is a treat not to be missed." He growled. "And I possess a particular talent for stripping you bare."

"Yes, you do, and I rather enjoy your saucy brand of ravishment." She gave him her back, and he tugged the laces. "Second only to your poetry, as your talent for oration is unrivaled."

"Then I shall endeavor to compose an ode." He snickered. "Is that why you pursued me, in London?"

"No." Grasping his shoulder for balance, she stepped from the garment. "What drew me was your strength, which tempted me from that first waltz. And the way you spoke to me gave me delicious shivers, as no one had ever approached me thus. But there is something more that lured me, which I found impossible to resist."

"And that would be—what?" While conversation had not ranked high on Jason's list of priorities, for an evening of seduction, her spontaneous confession fascinated him.

"Given I was raised in full view of society, and could never escape my connections, I have long desired something genuine amid the false smiles, excessively polite manners, and fancy gentleman's garb." After doffing her chemise, Alex eased into one of his large robes, as it accommodated her belly. "You gave me hope for something real, something true among the fabricated, polished facades of the *ton*."

"You pay me a compliment I do not believe I deserve, love." And she shamed him, given his ultimate aim for the night. "I would have thought my demeanor and associations too rough for the daughter of a duke."

"Oh, no." She giggled, as he led her to the table. "I fell in—that is to say, I adored you."

The chamber grew silent as a tomb.

The mood had turned, and gone was the light-hearted ambience, as he held her chair. Jason glanced at his seat, which had been positioned opposite his lady, and frowned. He yanked the piece of furniture, situated it beside Alex, and then shuffled his place setting.

"That is better." He lifted the first cover from an oval dish and picked up a serving spoon. "Are you hungry?"

"All three of us are starved." It troubled Jason that her ebullience had faded, and he vowed to restore her buoyancy. "So you have never told me what you found attractive about me."

"Aside from your voluptuous body in that memorable red dress, it was the fire in your eyes that captivated me." Downcast, Alex averted her gaze, and it was too late when he realized his mistake. "But to leave you with the impression that it was your appearance, alone, that enchanted me would be a gross inaccuracy and an insult to your considerable qualities."

"And that would be—what?" She mocked him with his earlier challenge, as she fiddled with her napkin.

How he wished he possessed sufficient courage to profess his love, but he had only managed not to puke, during his afternoon practice. But there were other ways to make his declaration. He scooted back his chair and slapped his thighs. "Come here."

Frowning, she furrowed her brow. "Jason—"

"Come here." Clutching her wrist, he lowered his chin and narrowed his stare. "Now, Alex."

"All right, but it is your fault if I faint, as I am famished." She sidestepped his legs and perched in his lap.

"Then allow me to rectify that problem." After stacking his plate atop hers, he uncovered the various entrees, picked up a fork, and speared a carrot, which he fed his bride. Then he teased her with a healthy taste of turbot with lobster sauce, until she laughed. Bite by bite, interspersed with flirty kisses, his haughty society maiden emerged from the dour comportment of the woman he had devastated in Plymouth. In her good humor, he found pleasure unlike any he had ever known and something he never would have foreseen.

As he cared for his wife, Jason struggled with powerful possessiveness. The urge to protect her and his children overwhelmed him and might have moved him to tears, had she not rewarded his efforts with an arresting smile. In that instant, Alex's happiness had become of paramount importance.

"Darling, what bewitched me, from the start, was your generous nature, which I did not fully understand, in London." He caressed her belly. "It was in Plymouth, when you befriended Molly, a charwoman, and later, here, at Stratfield Manor, when you took Gertie and Arnold under your munificent tutelage, that the depth of your benevolent spirit struck me, and the contrast is quite startling. Whereas then you concealed nothing from me, now you hide from me, and it is a rare and cherished moment that I glimpse *my* Alex."

"Then why did you refuse to marry me?" She cupped his cheek. "I need to reconcile the past with the present, so I might move forward."

Oh, his bold society miss had just made a spectacular return.

"I told you, back in Plymouth. Never would I have made you a young widow." He trailed a finger along the curve of her jawline. "But the truth is there are no justifiable reasons for my actions, darling. I wronged you, and I shall go to my grave with that singular regret, as I ache for my Alex."

"I know, and I am trying to find her." To his surprise, she pressed her lips to his. "And I do so long to believe in you, again."

"Do you?" Hell, he would write her an anthology full of sappy poetry, if it helped him regain her good opinion.

"Yes," she replied in a whisper. "And I should apologize to you, as now we must both settle for less than what might have been."

"*Settle*?" Jason scoffed. "How so?"

"You, because it is obvious I am not your choice, else you would have done the honorable by me." She rested her hand to his chest. "And I because I yearned for so much more, yet I must accept what I have, when I might have had it all, had I been patient."

Repudiations and rebuttals traipsed the tip of his tongue, yet he responded not. For a long while, Jason simply held her, and Alex clung to him. Tension hung in the air, thick as London fog, as they were two lost souls, each seeking to find their way back to a place they had gone, before.

"Are you partial to dessert, sweetheart?" That was not what she needed to hear from him, but coward that he was he reached for a lifeline. Jason uncovered the last untouched dish to reveal a bowl of luscious strawberries. "As I recall, these are your favorite."

"Indeed, you are correct." With a charming blush, Alex dipped her chin. "And you do tempt me, sir."

"Then let us adjourn to our bed." He waggled his brows. "Where I shall feed you, with my own hands."

"That sounds like the perfect ending to a wonderful meal." She eased from his lap, walked to the four-poster they shared, doffed her robe, and slid beneath the covers. "Coming, darling?"

"Oh, I hope so." He swaggered to the edge of the mattress, untied both belts at his waist, dropped his clothes, and joined her amid the sheets. Though he tried to resist the lure of her naked body, he marveled at the changes. Boasting crimson nipples, her breasts were huge, and he burned to make love to them, as he once had in the little cottage.

Alex emitted a plaintive sob, clamped her eyes shut, and

winced. Then she exhaled and peered at him. "The babes are restless."

So was Jason.

Yet, in that instant, he envisioned his children, bobbing and weaving, as they attempted to dodge the fearsome Jolly Roger, and he blanched. "Is it bad?"

"No worse than usual." Gritting her teeth, she hissed and hugged her most prominent protrusion.

It was then he noted the tiny belly button he had once filled with his seed had mutated into a webbed mass of jutting flesh, with tiny tracings of purple veins, just beneath the surface of her skin. "May I touch you?"

"Of course." Alex gave vent to something between a sob and a sigh.

As Jason set his palm to the crest of her abdomen, a sharp movement startled him. The proof of life, the result of their union, manifested a humbling experience, and no poetic phrase could express the magnitude of his joy.

Instead of enacting the seduction he had planned, he simply fed his wife strawberries, as they spoke of dreams for their future, and that of their children. And for the first time since arriving at Stratfield, his Alex surfaced sans intimate activity, and he counted the occasion a most precious boon. So he resolved not to make love to his bride—that night.

ALEX WANTED nothing more than to make love to her husband, given his tender care and thoughtful gesture, so she walked her fingers to his erection and was shocked to discover him not so erect.

"Not tonight, sweetheart." Grasping her wrist, Jason

kissed her knuckles, and then settled her hand on her belly. "You need rest, love."

"But I am not so tired, as you might think." To her frustration, she tried but failed to stifle a yawn.

"Evidence to the contrary." As he set the bowl of strawberries on the bedside table, he chuckled. "Snuggle close, sweetheart. It is cool tonight, and I would not have you catch a chill."

"But I am never cold when you are near." And now she was hungry—but not for food. Oh, where was her naughty sea captain, when she needed him? "Jason, I am not averse to pleasure, and we are married, as you always remind me."

"Go to sleep, Alex." As was his way, he tucked the blankets to her chin and rubbed her scalp.

But she wanted her husband.

That was the last coherent thought she had that night.

PEEVED WAS TOO TAME a word for Alex's disposition, as she had longed to make love to Jason, and her husband had put her to sleep. To add insult to injury, he had breakfasted without her and departed for a ride, before she had shown a leg.

"*Ouch.*" A speck of blood formed on her fingertip, where she had pricked herself with a needle, and she frowned at her embroidery, because her stitches were crooked and loose. "What a deuced mess."

"My lady, are you all right?" Molly grinned. "You seem a tad out of sorts, today."

Well that was an understatement. "I am fine, and thank you, for asking. But I am quite well."

"Then may I confide in you?" The nanny bounced and

tossed aside her silks. "It is about Mr. Penniman, and I am dying to talk to someone."

"Of course, you may rely on me." How Alex wished one of her friends were available, that she might impart her secrets. As Molly worked for Jason, Alex could not share such personal information with a staff member. "I am the personification of judiciousness."

"Oh, Alex." The nursemaid peered over her shoulder and then leaned forward to whisper, "Tom has been so attentive, of late."

"Indeed?" Alex giggled, when Molly nodded with enthusiasm. "And you may speak up, as the door is closed, so no one can hear you."

"I hardly know where to begin, as there are so many developments to report." With a squeal of delight, the nanny clutched a fist to her bosom. "Never had I dreamed any man, much less my Tom, could be so thoughtful—or inventive."

"How wonderful for you." Alex pondered all the considerate expressions of affection, including the bawdy poetry, Jason had bestowed upon her. "And I am the first to admit the male species is full of surprises, when they put their minds to it. Judging by your countenance of unutterable elation, I presume you are pleased?"

"Thrilled is more like it." Molly hugged herself and gazed at the ceiling. "Tom had roses delivered to my bedchamber, and you should have seen the blooms. There must have been two dozen. And he wrote me a poem."

"Roses and poetry in your bedchamber?" Alex rubbed her belly. "How remarkable."

"But that is not all." The nanny lifted her chin and grinned. "My dear Mr. Penniman gifted me a box of fine Belgian chocolates—the same brand you have delivered from London, and we enjoyed them in the gazebo, by moonlight."

"The very same?" Nagging suspicion nipped at Alex's heels, but she ignored the disconcerting sensation. "How fortunate for you."

"And dare I tell you of last week?" Molly averted her stare, and she blushed. "Never in my life had I imagined I would experience anything so grand."

"What happened?" Bile pooled in her throat, and Alex bit back the fast rising nausea. "I await your news with baited breath."

Hesitating, Molly bit her lip and twined her fingers. At last, she leaned near and cupped her palm to Alex's ear. In a quiet tone, the nursemaid divulged her news.

Raw and bitter anger surged through Alex's veins, and a shiver of dread coursed her spine. For the second time in her life, she suffered a mortal blow at Jason's hands, and never would she forgive him. But she would have her due, and he would suffer for giving her hope.

"Dearest Molly, I am so glad you found a good man, as they are a rare breed." Alex shimmied to the edge of the *chaise* and stood. "Now I am sorry to cut short our conversation, but I must speak with Captain Collingwood."

"Wait." With a pained visage, Molly jumped to her feet. "You will not tell Cap'n about the rosewater bath, will you? As I swear nothing untoward occurred in my chamber. Tom enlisted the aid of Miss Phipps, so he was not in attendance when I enjoyed his present."

"Calm yourself, friend." Alex forced a smile, even as she ached to tear her wayward spouse apart, limb from limb. "The matter I wish to discuss with my husband has nothing to do with you, I promise. And now I order you to seek out your Mr. Penniman and join him for lunch."

"Perhaps I could prepare his meal, to thank him for everything he has done for me." Molly curtseyed. "I shall meet you in the nursery, this afternoon."

"We can finish our needlework." With the strength of which she had not known she possessed, until that moment, Alex composed herself and strolled from the back parlor, down the hall, and into the foyer, where she located the butler. "Is Captain Collingwood in residence?"

"Yes, your ladyship." Phipps dipped his chin. "Cap'n is just returned from his ride and is in his study."

"Thank you." With head held high, Alex turned on her heel, as inside her something fractured.

At the double door entry, she had not bothered to knock. Riding a wave of high dudgeon, she stormed into Jason's domain and slammed the oak panel behind her. At that very second, her husband came alert.

"Hello, beautiful." The smile with which he had welcomed her faded, his expression sobered, and he shot from his chair and rounded the desk. "What is wrong? Are you ill? Is it the babes?"

Ire invested her muscles, gathered in her chest and found a convenient outlet in her hand. Summoning all her might, she slapped Jason across the face. "How dare you?"

"How dare I—what?" Rubbing his jaw, he retreated a step. "Explain yourself."

"Explain *yourself*, sir." As reality dawned, Alex shook her head, in denial. "How could you do it? Of all the things to take from a person, how could you steal a leap of faith?"

"Wait a minute." Jason scowled. "Wait one bloody minute. What are you talking about, as I am innocent?"

"You are the lowest of the low, luring me with pleasantries and overtures intended for someone else." Tears beckoned, and she cursed them, as she would not cry. "Well

I am no longer your fool, and you have toyed with my affection for the last time."

"What do you imply?" With fists on hips, Jason shifted his weight.

"Did you really expect to get away with your unscrupulous manipulations? Did you think I would not discover your deceit?" The babes kicked, and she sucked in a breath. "I am not some fresh-faced twit just out of the schoolroom."

"Enlighten me, Alex." He yanked his cravat. "As God is my witness, I am blameless."

"Liar." She bared her teeth.

Jason caught her, fast as lightning, in a half hug. Twining his fingers in the hair at the nape of her neck, he forced her to meet his stare. "I am a man of countless faults, but engaging in falsehoods is not one of them."

"I reference the roses, the poetry, the chocolates, and the bath." When he tightened his grip, she whimpered. "How could you do it? How could you resort to such vile tactics and steal the ideas of our stablemaster?"

"I beg your pardon?" He released her. "You believe I took cues from Tom?"

"I know you did, without doubt." And it killed her to admit it. "Have you no shame? You are without honor."

"Calm yourself, as you are mistaken." With a lethal glare, he folded his arms. "If I borrowed from anyone, I borrowed from you, as I know your tastes and predilections. I catered to your whims, and this is the thanks I get?"

"We both know you did more than that, and I fell for your ruse." And it galled Alex to recall she had almost given herself to him the previous night. "Once again, you have played me false, and you may go to the devil."

"With relish, my dear bride." Jason sketched a bow. "And I wish you the same."

"I am already there." Preparing to strike a blow, she squared her shoulders. "And I shall have you moved into a guestroom, as I will play your whore, no more."

"Worry not, my lady wife." To her unmitigated shock, her husband stomped to the door. Over his shoulder, he said, "This time, you have hurt me, and I refuse to spend another night where I am not wanted."

With that, he quit the study, leaving Alex standing stock-still, as she digested what had just happened. For several minutes, she lingered amid her captain's sanctuary, the diligent decoration of which she had invested with love. Nothing had escaped her touch, so in light of the heated argument, the furnishings and trimmings seemed to mock her.

"I beg your pardon, your ladyship." Mr. Penniman tarried in the entry. "I need to speak with Cap'n."

"He is indisposed." Composing herself, she leaned on the back of a chair. "May I be of assistance?"

"It is a personal matter." With a blush, Tom shuffled his feet. "But Cap'n is familiar with my situation."

"Do come in, and have a seat." She occupied Jason's place behind the impressive desk she had purchased for her husband.

"My lady, I wish to propose to Molly." The stablemaster scratched his chin. "My problem is I am not very good at romantic enterprises."

"I would not say that, as my nanny sings your praises." Alex catalogued the various demonstrations Jason had enacted.

"But those were Cap'n's ideas." Tom grinned. "Forgive my forwardness, but he is what most men refer to as done for, when it comes to your ladyship. To assume credit for his efforts would be dishonest."

Her ears rang, as the bells in a Wren steeple, and she sank in the leather, high-back chair. "So the roses, poetry, chocolates, and bath—"

"—Were at Captain Collingwood's direction, and he advanced me the money so I might woo Molly." The stablemaster compressed his lips. "Must admit I am a poor excuse for a lovesick hero. In the realm of amorous endeavors, I am a fraud. What I did for Miss Duckett was at Cap'n's suggestion. Beggin' your pardon, your ladyship, but are you all right? You are quite pale."

"Actually, I have never been better." While Alex regretted her actions, and she would apologize to Jason, what she had discovered in the process made her heart sing. "And we shall devise a plan for you to propose, so that Miss Duckett counts herself a most fortunate wife."

"Thank you, your ladyship." Tom cleared his throat. "I am in your debt, as well as Captain Collingwood's."

That makes two of us. Because it was her turn to set things right with her husband, and she would not fail. "Worry not, Mr. Penniman. We will catch your bride."

And with a little luck, Alex would, at last, snare her captain.

CHAPTER SEVENTEEN

"*Y*our ladyship, Captain Collingwood requests your presence in his study." Miss Phipps frowned, when she noted the untouched bowl of soup, which remained on the tray, along with the slice of bread, because Alex had no appetite. "Was the fare not to your liking, my lady?"

"I am sure it is fine." Alex closed the book she had not been reading, as she sulked in her sitting room. "But I am not hungry."

Two days, and as many painfully lonely nights, had passed since her row with Jason, and he had not spoken to her. Avoiding her at every turn, he showed no inclination to resolve their differences and allowed her no opportunity to make amends. Thrilled he had, at last, summoned her, she flew from the overstuffed chair.

"Will you help me change?" Alex tottered into the bedchamber and scrutinized her appearance. "I wish to wear the pale yellow morning dress, as Captain Colling-wood favors it. And would you rearrange my hair, as I would prefer a single curl draped at my neck."

"Of course, your ladyship." Gertie chuckled, as she retrieved the requested garment from the armoire. "Daresay Cap'n would enjoy your company, regardless of your attire, if I may be so bold."

Approximately fifteen minutes later, coiffed and gowned to perfection Alex descended the grand staircase. Riding a wave of renewed confidence, unlike any she had experienced since Plymouth, she squared her shoulders and marched into battle. When she entered the study, she was nonplussed to discover Jason, Molly, and Mr. Penniman.

"So glad you could join us." Although her husband smiled, the set of his jaw and the lines etched at the corners of his eyes belied the relaxed appearance he attempted to portray.

"Sorry it took me so long." When he escorted her to one of the chairs positioned before his desk, the muscles of his arm flexed beneath her palm. "But I do not move so fast, these days."

"I believe we guessed that." His tone and manner was curt, and her spirits sank. "So I shall stem the tide and cut to the chase. We have cause for celebration, as Tom and Molly are to wed."

"How wonderful." Was that not a positive sign? Alex peered at the happy couple, and she noted they held hands, as they perched on the daybed. "And I offer you both my sincerest congratulations."

"Thank you, your ladyship." Tom brought Molly's knuckles to his lips. "We are in your debt, as you have given us a home, an occupation, and wise counsel. And never could I have successfully wooed my bride, were it not for Cap'n's sage advice."

In that moment, Alex could have swallowed her tongue, as she had hoped to make her apologies before Jason realized she knew of her mistake. As Mr. Penniman had just let the cat out of the bag, she plotted and planned at a grievous disadvantage, given the pained glance Jason cast her, just then.

"Then we must mark the event with a suitable ceremony, which we shall celebrate, in the grand dining hall." And then a brilliant idea rocked her, and she just managed to stifle a euphoric shout. "And I would so love to host your wedding. When do you intend to marry?"

"Saturday, your ladyship." Molly all but bounced with enthusiasm. "Tom and I will not wait a minute longer."

"*This* Saturday?" As she pondered the requisite coordination, Alex gulped. "But that is so soon. And I cannot possibly have the banns posted—"

"We are simple country folk, my lady." Mr. Penniman smiled. "No one requires notice of our nuptials."

"And our parents can journey to Stratfield in a day." Profuse in love and adoration, the nanny gazed at her husband-to-be and smiled. "We have no reason to delay."

"If that is your wish, then we shall accommodate you," her captain declared. Standing to Alex's left, Jason rested his palm to the back of her neck. "We wish you every happiness."

"And I will send a directive to the vicar, posthaste." As Jason rubbed her nape, she shivered. "Molly, you and I must confer with Miss Phipps, regarding the number of guests, the floral selections, and the menu."

"Also, I offered Molly and Tom the gardener's cottage, as Helms prefers to bunk with the stable hands." Now Jason toyed with the flirty curl draped at her throat, and she knew, without doubt, she had garnered his special attention. "It seemed the logical choice and a perfect abode for our newlyweds."

"That is a marvelous idea." And then she ticked off a mental list to organize the events. "Molly, you and I should inspect the structure. We have little time, but Mr. Harper is a miracle worker, and we shall engage his services, today. And I shall accompany you into town, where we would purchase your gown."

"Your ladyship, you are too generous." Grasping Mr. Penniman's wrist, Molly jumped to her feet. "I should change my dress and fetch my coat. Come, Tom."

"Have the coach brought around front." Alex stood. "I will meet you in the foyer, in twenty minutes."

Alone with her despondent captain, Alex pondered her approach, even as she mulled her most ambitious stratagem, to date. When Jason retreated, she snapped to attention, grabbed his hand, and brought it to her bosom, and he swallowed hard.

"Wait." Then she cupped his cheek. "I owe you an apology—"

"I am busy, Alex." With a mighty grimace, which she felt all the way to her toes, he sighed.

"But you are never too busy for me." Slow and steady, Lady Alexandra Elizabeth Seymour Collingwood emerged from her shell, and she charged the field of her beautiful sailor, without fear or hesitation. Drawing him close, she held his stare, licked his lips, and then covered his mouth with hers. It was so good to taste her husband, again.

At first, Jason did not respond. He loomed as a statue, until she grazed his flesh with her teeth. All of a sudden, her randy seaman came alive and assumed control of their kiss. Gripping her bottom, he plundered her as fifty men, laving and suckling, taunting and tempting. How she had missed his bawdy, unpolished ravishment.

When at last they surfaced, he rested his forehead to

hers, closed his eyes, and frowned. "This time, you hurt me, Alex. And I understand your fear, more than you realize."

"My darling, I am so sorry we quarreled." Hugging him about his waist, she rubbed her nose to his. "And I do so regret that I doubted you, as I cherished every sweet gesture of your affection, which is why I responded so forcefully, when I thought you wooed me with Mr. Penniman's efforts. Will you return to our bed? Will you not resume your most treasured courtship?"

"You enter the final days of your pregnancy." Now he caressed her belly. "I had thought, perhaps, you might rest easier without me."

"Never, as you know I sleep best in your arms." To emphasize the depth of her regard, she squeezed him. "Please, Jason. If you require it, I would beg, on my knees, if you would help me to the floor. Come back to me, as I need you."

A war of will raged within him, and she ached to press her cause. Alternating between what she suspected was nothing more than feigned disinterest and tangible enthusiasm he furrowed his brow.

"All right." With a boyish, shy grin, he shrugged. "If that is your wish, then I will reinstall myself in our quarters, tonight."

Familiar hunger blossomed in the pit of her gut, and she longed to make love to her husband. But she would wait, as she had something remarkable reserved for her man. "You know it is near my usual nap time. I can postpone my journey into town, until later this afternoon, if you would care to partake of a brief respite from your work."

"You tempt me, beyond reason." To her dismay, he released her and sank into the high-back chair behind his desk. "Given your expensive restoration of our home, I must reorganize our finances. And now that we are tasked with an unforeseen wedding celebration, I must shuffle some funds."

"Are we in trouble?" Never had she spared a thought for money, as her brother possessed a seemingly endless supply of the necessary evil. "What of my dowry?"

"It is deposited for our children, and I would not spend it." He gave his attention to a large ledger. "But worry not, as we will survive. I have worked for everything I own, and I have yet to sink a ship."

"Why did you not tell me, as I could have offered Molly one of my old gowns, and we can improvise floral displays from our gardens." Alex perched before the desk. "The burden is not yours alone to carry. We are married, in sickness and in health. Do you not remember our vows?"

"But you made no oath. At our ceremony, you stood quiet." He calculated a sum and scribbled the total in the log. "Take Molly shopping for the frock and flowers, as we are not paupers. And everything will be fine, once we reap the rewards of our transatlantic timber deal with Everett, and the lease of my retail property in London is completed."

Jason could not have known it, but he had just struck upon her grand scheme, and so she took no offense to his insult, as his assertion was true. But Alex would no longer remain silent.

THE SUN SHONE amid an unblemished sky of pure cerulean, and dew-tipped blades of grass glittered as a blanket of countless diamonds, as the nanny and the stablemaster's wedding day dawned. In the master suite, Alex basked in the warm light, as she gazed out the mullioned window overlooking the back lawn.

While Jason had returned to their bed, and he held her every night, he had not permitted her to pleasure him, and she had realized how much she valued his happiness, as it inextricably intertwined with hers. An invisible but nonetheless powerful connection imprisoned them in palpable sadness, and she resolved to break free.

At the long mirror, she turned left and then right, examining every aspect of her reflection. A burgundy gown of sumptuous velvet encased her full figure, and her dark brown locks had been swept into a cascade of curls. Satisfied with the outcome of her efforts, she sat at her vanity and dabbed a few drops of her favorite French perfume, which her husband had proclaimed drove him well nigh insane, to her pulse points.

"Perfect." She winked at her image. "Jason Collingwood, tonight, you are mine."

As she trudged forth into battle, Alex felt like her old self, again, and she rejoiced. Her husband had described her as generous, and she could not argue his observation. No matter what the outcome, she would never lament her second pursuit of love. While her captain had not proclaimed his unequivocal devotion, she would make her declaration without fear, hesitation, or regret.

In the foyer, her prey, resplendent in his coat of Bath superfine, awaited their guests, and she assumed her place at his side. "Any sign of the vicar or the happy couple?"

"Mr. Avery is in the drawing room. Molly is in the back parlor, chewing her nails and pacing." Jason chuckled. "When I last spied Tom, he was revisiting his breakfast in one of the horse stalls."

"Then all we need is the parents of the bride and

groom." She clutched his arm, inclined her head, and batted her lashes. "And how handsome you look in your formalwear, Captain Collingwood. I never could resist you in such attire."

A red flush contrasted with his white cravat, and the charming blush spread to his cheeks. In that instant, Alex had scored a direct hit, and she marked her first victory. She would require several more, were she to succeed in her endeavor.

As if on cue, a traveling coach bobbed along the driveway and halted in the forecourt. Her husband escorted her to the landing, but he paused at the edge of the threshold.

"Dearest, while we have yet to settle our problems, I ask that we put aside our differences, for Tom and Molly." Jason frowned and shuffled his feet. "Please, Alex. I would not ruin their special day."

"It appears we are on the same page, sir." She could have taken offense to his insult, but she had more important things on her mind, so she forgave the slight as fast as he had uttered it. "And this is a momentous occasion, in more ways than one, and I would not spoil it for anything in the world."

"Thank you, darling." With a half-hearted smile, he gave his attention to their guests. "Mr. and Mrs. Duckett, Mr. and Mrs. Penniman, welcome to Stratfield Manor."

After quick introductions, the wedding party withdrew to the drawing room, which boasted vivid sprays of red roses mixed with autumn mums, where Molly reunited with her parents. Hugging the shadows, Alex yielded the spotlight to the nanny and focused on her seaman. From a vase, she drew a single red rose, broke the stem, and strolled to her husband.

"Allow me, most cherished Captain." Once she affixed the bud to his coat, she splayed her hands across his chest, and he rewarded her with a sharp intake of breath. "Perfection."

"Indeed?" With a countenance of confusion, he furrowed his brow. "Is it safe to assume I pass inspection?"

"I would not say that." She leaned near and whispered, "But I shall be too delighted to give you a thorough examination, tonight."

In an instant, she noticed the stillness investing his frame and the hunger burning in his gaze. He wanted her, as she wanted him. "My lady wife, I am most definitely at your service."

"Shall we begin the ceremony?" Mr. Avery, the local vicar, cleared his throat and opened the *Book of Common Prayer*. "Everyone, take your respective places."

Positioned, side-by-side, behind Molly and Tom, Jason and Alex stood as a united front, to witness the nanny and the stablemaster's union. Myriad sensations kissed her flesh, as she teetered on the precipice of a renewed leap of faith.

When Mr. Avery recited the first oath, she clutched Jason's hand, squeezed his fingers until he met her stare, and she mouthed, at the correct moment, *I do*.

And so Lady Alexandra Elizabeth Seymour Collingwood pledged her oath to her captain, some eight and a half weeks after her wedding, but better late than never. Slowly, excruciatingly slowly, Jason smiled and dipped his chin. At last, she declared in a small voice, "My heart will be your shelter, and my arms will be your home."

It was a commitment made in love, kept in faith, lived in hope, and always made new.

Tears of inexpressible joy welled, as Jason mirrored her

actions and made his affirmations, in time with Tom. When the vicar asked for the ring, Alex almost fainted, when her husband retrieved a stunning band, bearing a large sapphire fringed with diamonds, from his waistcoat pocket. As Mr. Avery officiated the nuptials, Jason slipped the precious bauble on her finger and winked.

"...I now pronounce you husband and wife." The vicar closed the book and adjusted his spectacles. "You may kiss the bride."

Without warning, her shameless sailor grabbed her about the waist, tipped back her head, and well nigh devoured her, in full view of their guests. A chorus of feminine giggles and male chuckles brought them up for air.

"Oh, dear. I do apologize." Alex bit her lip and glanced at the vicar. "Captain Collingwood and I quite enjoyed the celebration."

"No apologies necessary, your ladyship." Mr. Avery snickered. "One could argue you still qualify as newlyweds."

Together, the party crowded Tom and Molly to extended felicitations, and the bridegroom wiped his wife's tearstained cheeks.

"Shall we remove to the dining room?" Jason ushered the gathering into the hall but Alex stayed him. "We have much to celebrate."

"Indeed." Alex turned her husband to face her, and then she rubbed his crotch and could have shouted with pleasure when she found him hard as a rock. "As I have festivities planned for well into the night."

IN THE ELEGANT DINING ROOM, amid an assortment of hothouse blooms, and the finest table linens, china, and silverware, Jason popped the cork on a bottle of champagne, as he wrangled with the one-eyed pirate that had popped up in his breeches. Reminding himself to keep his coat buttoned, lest he scandalize the wedding party, he poured the bubbling liquid into crystal glasses. Although he had yet to partake of the intoxicating concoction, he was already drunk.

From the scent of his wife's perfume.

From the tantalizing view of her décolletage.

Had he mistaken Alex's intent, or had he read her true aim? From whichever angle he approached his conundrum, it appeared his tempting vixen, long absent, had made a stunning, most unexpected but prayed for return. And every time he had convinced himself he had imagined her bold behavior, she favored him with a heated stare that deuced near fired the cannon in his crotch.

When Molly's father toasted the bride and groom, none of which Jason heeded, because Alex had captured him, he availed himself of the chance to adjust himself, as he well nigh exploded. Seated to his immediate left, within striking distance, the source of his torment moved with the grace and ease of the confident woman who had claimed him that memorable night in the Richmond's ballroom, more than two years ago.

With a casual brush of her hand and a sultry, come-hither expression, she had branded him hers. Even now, after all that time, she owned him, body and soul. And she was his, by decree.

"Captain Collingwood, shall I serve dinner?" Phipps stood upright.

"Please, do so." Jason nodded once.

"May I serve you, darling?" Doe-eyed, Alex licked her lips.

"Oh, yes." Gritting his teeth, he swallowed a groan and clenched his gut, as he teetered on the verge of sweet release. Beneath the table, he crossed his legs.

"Would you favor some meat, as it is very tender and juicy?" And there was the smile that roused every inch of him to full alert. But he almost fell out of his chair, when she imparted, in a low tone, "Just like you."

"Alex, I—" Jason jumped, when she sashayed her slippered foot to his calf, and almost knocked over his champagne. Bloody hell, he would be hard until Christmas.

"Is something wrong, love?" She blinked, as would an innocent.

"Uh, no." In search of a distraction, he picked up his fork and plowed through his food, without bothering to taste the fare. When he had cleaned his plate, he summoned Phipps and portioned himself another robust helping, yet his hunger burgeoned beyond his control.

Then Jason chastised himself, in silence. Perhaps he had read too much into his wife's curious behavior. How long had he yearned to weigh anchor in her harbor? Given his none-too-successful courtship had failed to achieve the desired results, he reconsidered his conclusions. And that was his thought, as Alex leaned close, as if to impart a bit of private conversation, just as he had taken a gulp of champagne.

"I want you." And concealed by the expensive linens, she walked a naughty path with her fingers and stroked his erection. "And I intend to consummate our vows—tonight."

Jason choked violently, as there was no mistaking her statement. Pounding his fist to the table, he declared, "Bring on the dessert."

But the events could not have moved swift enough for Jason, and he simmered in a seemingly endless state of arousal, as Phipps opened another bottle of champagne. He cheered, as Molly and Tom cut the cake, Jason laughed, as the groom fought to conceal a nervous twitch, when he thanked his employers for hosting the wedding ceremony and feast.

The sun sank below the yardarm, and the lamps were lit, as the Ducketts regaled the guests with stories of the nanny's youthful adventures. In turn, the Penniman's shared tales of Tom's exploits, and Jason wanted to scream. But he found salvation in his pregnant ally, when she pushed from the table and stood.

"Please, do not feel you must end your celebrations on my account, but I must retire, by your leave." Alex hugged her belly. "I have little energy, these days. Phipps can show you to your traveling coach, when you are ready."

In unison, the partygoers composed a choral of understanding, compassion, and appreciation.

"Of course, you may be excused, sweetheart." Jason vacated his seat and strolled to her side. "Should I see you to our chamber?"

"That is not necessary." When he bent to kiss her forehead, she whispered, "Do not make me wait too long."

To his infinite thanks, Molly made her farewells, with a shy smile at her new husband, and the parents offered their congratulations. Propriety be damned, Jason all but ran them out of the house. At last, he adjourned to the study, with Tom, who appeared on the verge of swooning.

"I think you need a brandy." As it was customary for the bridegroom to grant his bride a deferment on their wedding night, Jason assumed his duty, with a benevolent spirit, and passed the lad a balloon of the amber liquid. "Here. It will fortify you and calm your nerves."

"I am not nervous, Cap'n." To Jason's surprise, the stablemaster downed the contents in a single gulp and then commenced a wicked coughing fit.

"Of course, not." Chuckling, he refilled the gadling's glass. "You are a pillar of strength."

"Thank you." Again, Tom emptied the balloon and then set it atop the desk.

"Better?" Jason bit his tongue to keep from laughing, aloud.

"Molly is a very gentle spirit, sir." The stablemaster paced. "I would not frighten her."

"I understand." He envisioned his feisty Alex and thanked whatever compassionate fate had bestowed upon him a women with a hunger to match his own.

"Cap'n, just how long is long enough?" The lad clenched and unclenched his fists.

"I would assert you have done the honorable by your new wife." Jason shook hands with the stablemaster. "Go to Molly, and I bid you a pleasant evening."

"And the same to you, sir." Tom turned, walked straight into a chair, and toppled to the floor. Just as fast, he leaped to his feet. "Right. Goodnight, Cap'n."

Oh, to be so young and green, again. Jason shook his head and clucked his tongue. Then he started, as he recalled his assignation with the woman of his dreams. With determination and desire burning in his veins, he ran to the door, set the oak panels wide, shot down the hall, and soared up the stairs, two at a time.

Sparing nary a glance at the gallery, he navigated the passageway to the master suite and entered the sitting room. All was quiet, when he opened the door to the inner chamber, and he was nonplussed to discover the bed empty.

"Blast, blast, blast." At the armoire, his wife fought a wicked battle with a diaphanous gown, which covered her head and shoulders. Wrenching hard, she swore a blue streak that made him proud, and he clamped his mouth shut, as her unintended performance was a comedic treasure not to be missed.

Naked from the waist down, she twisted and turned, and the cleft of her bare derriere held him spellbound, as he remembered the day he claimed her bottom. After stripping his coat, waistcoat, and cravat, while he enjoyed her impromptu show, he doffed his boots. When Alex teetered precariously, and he feared she might injure herself and the babes, he sprang into action.

With his hands on her hips, he steadied her. "Captain Jason Collingwood reporting for duty, my delectable wife."

CHAPTER EIGHTEEN

*W*restling with the garment that no longer accommodated her belly, Alex almost jumped out of her skin, when her husband steadied her. To her relief, he drew the tangled swath of silk from her head. "Oh, Jason. In the excitement of Molly and Tom's wedding plans, I forgot to purchase a new nightgown for our special occasion, and nothing fits me."

"That is all right, as I have always preferred you naked." With a gentle tug, he pulled her into his welcoming embrace and settled her arms about his waist. "And given the strength of my appetite, I would have destroyed anything you donned, so you saved us time and money, sweetheart."

"But I did so wish to be pretty for you tonight." She pouted. "As I shall finally be yours."

"Alex, you were mine from the moment I saw you." His hands were everywhere, at once, awakening her desire, setting her alight, and sweeping her into a decadent storm. "And you—pretty? Never, as nothing so simple or tame could ever encompass your inner fire, your breathtaking beauty, or your ineffably generous nature, which I grossly underestimated."

"Jason." She erupted as soon as their lips met. Licking and nibbling his tongue, she twined her fingers in his hair and thrilled to the passion of his attack.

Delicious heat poured through her veins, searing every muscle, and charging every nerve. A hint of derring-do, an old familiar feeling, traversed her spine and then spread, pervading every fiber of her existence. Invested with a strength of which she had not known she possessed, Alex ripped the lawn shirt from his body, skimmed his magnificent chest, and charted a course for seduction.

Where there had been fear, now there was confidence.

Where there had been hesitation, now there was certainty.

Where there had been indecision, now there was determination.

After unhooking his waistband, she drew the most elementally male aspect of his anatomy from his breeches and worked him, hard and rough, just as he liked it. Then she broke their kiss, bent, and took him into her mouth, and Jason lauded her efforts with a lusty groan.

Pumping and grinding his hips, he growled, and her jaw would be sore, in the morning, but she cared not, as she loved her captain. Then she shifted her attention, just as he reached about her, to wreak sweet havoc between her legs. As she kept rhythm with her fingers, she suckled and laved the soft pouch at the base of his length, and he hissed. Emboldened by the power she wielded, Alex charged his field.

Over and over, she pressed on him caresses intended to entice and arouse, just as he had taught her, back in Plymouth. But an undercurrent of contrition had tempered her enjoyment, in January, when she gifted Jason her bride's prize without the requisite license. But things were different, now, and what good was the official document that bound them for eternity, if it had not granted permission for her to behave improperly with her spouse?

Ravenous with hunger only her captain could satisfy, she stood upright. "Darling, I want you so much it hurts."

"Are you sure?" Gritting his teeth, he closed his eyes. "You are so wet for me, Alex. So tell me if this is what you want. I promise, if you have changed your mind, I will cease my attentions. I will not be happy, and I may not even be kind, but I will stop."

To wit she framed his face, bit his chin, and replied, "Like bloody hell you will."

In that instant, Jason all but tackled her. "I want you."

"Then take me." She scored her nails to the nape of his neck.

"Are you afraid?" He hunched, cupped her breasts, and plunged his tongue into her cleavage. When he grazed his teeth to a pert nipple, she cried out his name.

"I am a little scared." Alex gasped, when he sucked hard on her sensitive flesh. "What most frightens me is that it might not be possible to...for us...what I mean is, given my belly is so large, are you positive we can engage in your favorite activity?"

"Sweetheart, where there is a will, there is a way." Lifting his head, Jason chuckled. "And I am of a singular intent, so let us improvise in a manner that pleases us, both."

"Have you any ideas, in mind?" She peered at the bed and blanched. "As the usual position would not suit, in this circumstance."

"As a matter of fact, do you recall the time I took you at the kitchen table, in the cottage?" He arched a brow.

"Of course." Alex had an epiphany. "Fetch the Sheraton chair from our sitting room, as it is the perfect height."

"Yes, ma'am." He sketched a mock salute, as had the Jolly Roger, jutting proudly from its nest of blonde curls. In play, she placed a chaste kiss on the plum-shaped tip, and he narrowed his stare. "Woman, you make me tremble."

"Hurry back." With a giggle, she located the other item she required. Beneath her vanity rested a footstool, and she kicked it into the center of the room, just as her husband carried in the requested piece of furniture. "Set it here."

He glanced at the floor and then pinned her with a heated stare. "Alex, you are a genius."

"Now take off your breeches and make love to me." She gave him her back, stepped onto the stool, and bent forward, using the chair as a base, of sorts. "Please, Jason. I can wait no longer."

Biting her lip, she focused on the sliver of moonlight, which peeked through a separation in the drapes. The silvery ray seemed to shimmer in the air, and it cast a dagger-like silhouette, similar to the particular protuberance her husband prepared to deploy, on the carpet. So entranced by the mystical sight, she started when her captain settled his warm hands on her hips.

"Are you ready, love?" He caught the crest of her ear with his teeth, as he pressed his erection to the cleft of her bottom.

"*Yes.*" She dropped her head back, as he curled about her and nuzzled her neck.

"Spread your legs just a tad, angel." When she obeyed, he probed the pliant flesh at the apex of her thighs and then pushed forward, inch by glorious inch. Seated to the hilt, he held perfectly still and exhaled, and she moaned. "Are you in pain? Have I hurt you?"

"No." Had she any reservations, his concern for her welfare vanquished them. "Jason, I beg you—move."

Hugging her close, he splayed one hand over her belly, as his other played an arresting duet with the gem of her desire, in time with his thrusts. In a gentle slip and slide, he set a conservative cadence, marked by the audial slap of skin against skin, mixed with her pants and sighs and his guttural grunts, which drove her to the brink of euphoria.

Together, they soared, reaching as one entity for the succulent pinnacle of their consummation. Alex claimed her prize, first. With an ear-splitting scream, she shattered, as wave upon luxurious wave of pure pleasure cascaded over her. And just as she descended to reality, Jason gripped her derriere, gave vent to a primal bellow, and pulsed repeatedly.

Then, to her chagrin, tears flowed.

"Did I injure you, sweetheart?" He loosened his hold, but she stayed him.

"No." She pulled his arms tighter about her.

"Then why do you cry?" Jason pressed his cheek to hers.

"Because I have long dreamed of this day, and I can scarcely believe it has happened." In that instant, the naïve society maiden yielded to the woman, the wife, and the expectant mother Alex had become, and she wept, as she clutched his wrist and brought his knuckles to her lips. "At last, our vows are unimpeachable, and I am yours —irrefutably."

In the wee hours just before dawn, Jason stirred. Confusion had him shaking his head, as he discovered himself in the master suite, given he had spent a few recent nights in a guestroom. When he realized he curled up to his bride, his chest to her back, with their bodies joined, he thought he lingered in a most cherished dream.

Then the babes kicked beneath his palm, which he had splayed protectively over his wife's abdomen, at some point, as he had slept, and images from their multiple fiery couplings flooded his consciousness. As his children moved, Alex sniffed and shifted. Then she grasped his wrist, drew his hand to her mouth, and kissed his fingertips.

"I love you." With a sigh, she stilled, and her breath came in a steady rhythm, as she returned to slumber.

Her declaration, freely spoken, touched him more than he was willing to admit, to himself or anyone else, and he hugged her closer. Bent forward, with his flesh encased in hers, and his arms wrapped about her belly, swollen with the fruit of his seed, Jason had never felt more a man in his life. Yet he had struggled to utter the elementary phrase.

They were but three simple words, when voiced on their own. But articulated together, the proclamation expressed the single most important commitment known to humanity and possessed the power to reduce the most stalwart man into a blithering nincompoop. So he had practiced as an actor preparing to take the stage on Drury Lane.

In that moment, Jason rode a heady tide of emotion he could not explain, define, or control. "I love you, too."

And so it was done.

For the first time in his life, he declared himself to a woman, but she was not just anyone. She was his lady, his wife—his Alex. A tidal wave of sentiment trapped him somewhere between heaven and hell, and he pumped his hips, in search of distraction. Again and again, he found sanctuary in her honey harbor, until she reached behind and squeezed his arse.

"Did I hurt you, angel?" He halted.

"Oh, no." Then she skimmed his thigh and wiggled her bottom. "I am hungry."

"Shall I raid the kitchen?" Deuced rotten luck, as her needs took precedence over his. "I wager the staff remains abed, as the hour is early, but I can fetch something to satisfy you."

"Perhaps, later, I might want food." Once more, she shimmied. "Right now, my naughty captain, I crave you."

"Darling Alex, I am so glad I married you." So he gave her what she wanted, savored her feminine crescendo worthy of Handel, and found comfort in release.

"That was wonderful." Alex twined her fingers in his. "Do you suppose this is what some refer to as wedded bliss?"

"Could be true." With a chuckle, he nipped her shoulder. "As I feel mighty blissful, right now."

"Promise me something." She drew imaginary circles on his arm, as he held her.

"Anything, sweetheart." How Jason wished he could muster sufficient courage to declare himself when she was fully awake and alert.

"Promise me we will always be like this." She stretched her legs and then tucked them to his. "While I know we do not enjoy the same relationship as our married friends, and I am learning to settle for what we have, I pray you will always want me, in your bed."

"Alex, I hope this does not lessen your opinion of me, as a man, but I have had no other woman, since I met you." He understood too well what she had meant by *learning to settle*, and it irritated him. "I want you and none other, as long as we both shall live."

"Do you mean that?" She turned and peered at him. "Or do you say it because you think it is what I want to hear?"

"Do you doubt me?" Jason propped himself on an elbow. "Because I am deadly serious. No doxie, or otherwise, has docked between my sheets, from the moment we waltzed in the Richmond's ballroom, as you, alone, hold my interest."

"Really?" she asked, in a small voice, and he sensed underlying fear and trepidation.

"When I am aboard ship, and longing for home, yours is the face I conjure, as you are home, to me." No, Jason could not say the words she most wanted to hear, but he could describe what he felt for her. "When the enemy bears down, firing cannon shot in my wake, yours are the arms I imagine, as you are my strength. And when I am alone, and death nips at my heels, I invoke your glowing countenance, as you are life, to me."

"Never has anyone said anything so lovely to me." Alex cupped his cheek. "And I would have you know that I—" With a sharp intake of breath, she scrunched her face and clutched his hand.

"What is it, love?" He eased his length from her body and sat upright. "Are you all right?"

"I am not sure." Gasping for air, she sank her teeth into her clenched fist. "Jason, I want you to know that I—"

Now his wife cried out and wrenched hard, in a tangle of linens. In an effort to soothe her, he jumped from the four-poster, donned his robe, and ran to the opposite side of the bed. "Alex, what is wrong? Is it the babes?"

Coughing and wheezing, she hugged her belly. "I think—*oh*."

"Easy, angel." After fluffing her pillows and helping her into a more comfortable position, he trod to the side wall and yanked the bellpull.

As tears seeped from the corners of her eyes, his bride gritted her teeth, and he would have done anything to ease her suffering. "Jason, send for the doctor."

"HERE, DARLING." Jason draped one of his robes about her shoulders, and she slipped her arms into the sleeves. "Tom rode into town to fetch the physician, and they should be here, any minute. And Miss Phipps is preparing tea and a light breakfast."

"But I am feeling much better, and the pain has stopped." Alex giggled, as her husband fussed over her health and welfare, and she quite adored her excessively solicitous captain. "And I could eat your stallion, as I am starved after our night of debauchery."

"Sweetheart, this is no time for jokes." It was then she noted the perspiration beaded on his brow.

"Who is joking, as you exercised me, quite thoroughly?" She clucked her tongue. "But I am not complaining."

A knock at the door had her covering her mouth, just as Dr. Studly entered the chamber. "Mrs. Collingwood, how are you this morning?"

"Who in bloody hell are you?" Jason stormed into the path of the young, very handsome doctor.

"Dr. Robert Studly, at your service." The physician extended his hand. "You must be Mr. Collingwood—"

"*Captain* Collingwood, and how old are you?" With a

lethal scowl, Jason rested fists on hips. "How long have you been in practice?"

"I began my study of medicine at age eighteen, under my father's tutelage, completed my education at Guy's Hospital in Southwark, and I am thirty-three." Dr. Studly set his black bag on the bedside table and shrugged from his coat. "Now, if you would be so kind as to vacate the room, I shall wash, and then I will examine Mrs. Collingwood."

"I beg your pardon?" Brooding and beautiful, in his skintight breeches and flowing lawn shirt, her husband scoffed. "If you think I am leaving you alone, with my wife, then you—"

"Jason, stop it, this instant." Propped on a mountain of pillows, Alex opened the robe, so the physician could commence the checkup.

"Captain Collingwood, regardless of my youthful appearance, I assure you, I am a professional." At the basin, Dr. Studly rolled up his shirtsleeves, poured water into the bowl, and soaped his hands. "But if you insist on attending the appointment, then you must not interfere with my duties, as you would impede my ability to assess your wife's condition, as well as that of your children."

As Dr. Studly conducted a thorough evaluation, Jason huffed and puffed from the opposite side of the bed. At last, Alex reached for him and squeezed his fingers, but her husband frowned at the physician.

"It is false labor." Dr. Studly returned the tools of his trade to his bag. "What were you doing when the contractions began?"

Gulping, Alex glanced at Jason, and his eyes widened. Then he flinched and gazed at the ceiling. So much for her chivalrous knight.

"I lounged abed." Oh, how her cheeks burned, as salacious vignettes flashed in her brain. "As the captain and I enjoyed a relaxed morning."

"How peculiar." The physician scratched his chin. "False labor is usually brought about by overexertion, excitement, or a combination, thereof."

"Really?" Alex mustered a nervous laugh. "How odd."

"Did we—I mean, were the babes harmed?" Jason's face flushed. "And what of my wife? Is she injured?"

"I am happy to report her ladyship is in fine fettle." Dr. Studly wrinkled his nose, as he collected his bag and hat. "However, as she is very near her time, I recommend confining her ladyship to bed, Captain."

"What?" She sat upright, drew the covers over her belly, and nodded, as Jason adjusted a pillow. "For how long?"

"Until you give birth, my lady." The good doctor cast her an expression of sympathy.

"You can't be serious. Dr. Studly, please, is there not an easier way?" The nursery needed a final review, and Alex intended to make love to her husband, all afternoon. "You know not what you ask of me."

"Fret not, your ladyship." Dr. Studly checked his time-piece. "Given the length and magnitude of your false labor, I expect you will deliver at any moment."

"*Any moment*?" Jason leaped from the mattress, paled, and slumped against the footboard. "Are you leaving?"

"Calm yourself, Captain Collingwood. Childbirth can be a very tedious process, and the entire affair can take hours." At the door, the physician peered over his shoulder. "I promise, when you have need of my services, you will have ample opportunity to send your man, and I shall remain at the ready."

"Thank you, Dr. Studly." Alone with her sailor, she slipped free of the robe, tossed it to the floor, and licked her lips. "This is so unfair. Whatever shall I do, while locked in our room, as it is early, yet?"

"Well I know what you will not do, as I ought to be horsewhipped for waylaying you, last night—and in the wee hours, this morning." After retrieving the discarded garment, Jason attempted to clothe her. "What the deuce was I thinking?"

"I beg to differ, my lusty captain, as I loved every minute of it." She wriggled as he tried to drape the silk garment over her shoulders. "And do you regret consummating our vows?"

"Alex—"

"Jason." She mocked his sigh.

"I regret nothing, as I cannot resist you, when you are as accommodating as you were last night." At last, he relented and abandoned the robe. "And I have been trying to get under your skirts since we married."

"Jason Collingwood, I like the way you think." And her confidence soared, as she rested her palm to his flat belly and then she skimmed her hand lower, to squeeze a telltale bulge.

"Stop that." He leaped beyond reach, as if she had set fire to his breeches. Wagging a finger, her suddenly shy husband grimaced. "You heard what Dr. Studly said. We are not to excite you."

"Too late, as I burn for you." Biting her lip, she inclined her head. "Will you not climb between the sheets and suffer with me?"

"No." Utter panic invested his visage.

"All right." Alex threw back the blankets. "If you think I am going to sit here, alone, all day, you are mistaken. And if you refuse to entertain me, than I shall fend for myself."

"Stay in bed." Gritting his teeth, Jason stomped to the

edge of the mattress, grasped the end of the counterpane, and tucked it beneath her chin. "If you have need of me, you have only to ask. But I do not see what I can provide by way of amusement."

"Actually, I have a wonderful idea." And it was time to embark on her campaign to win his heart. "You may read to me. The book is on the bedside table."

"That sounds simple." Jason retrieved the requisite volume and flipped through the pages. "If you swear you will rest, for the remainder of the day."

"With your help, I should relax." And the contents might motivate him to make his declaration. "And I shall nap."

"Love sonnets?" He blanched. "Oh, Alex."

"You swore you would do it, for me." She folded her arms and thrust her chin. "Do you renege, sir?"

"But you said nothing about foppish sentiments written by overemotional parlor dandies, who are a bit too in touch with their feminine side, for my tastes." How she cherished his pout.

"Read—now." She narrowed her stare.

"Where did you leave off?" he inquired, with a glower.

"You may start at the beginning." And then she clamped her tongue against a giggle.

"Very well." Holding the leather-bound tome, he turned to the first page and groaned. "Your eyes are like limpid pools—you can't be serious."

"That does it." Alex scooted to the edge of the bed. "There are some entries I must note in the supply ledger, and—"

"Oh, all right." With a look that might have frightened her before their marriage, her husband stomped to her side of the four-poster, grasped her ankles, and eased her beneath the blankets. "Weigh your anchor, and I will read the damn romantic drivel."

Then he yanked off his boots and flung them none too gracefully to the floor. "May as well be comfortable if I am to endure such humiliating degradation."

"Humiliating degradation?" She snorted. "Are we not a tad dramatic?"

"Adequate to the occasion." The man was downright menacing. "Because you are the only woman who could ever coax me to enact something so ridiculous, and if you breathe one word of this to anyone, I will deny it to my death."

"Poor aggrieved darling." In that instant, Alex opened her heart and let it sing. "I shall be as silent as the grave."

"My sire is probably rolling over in his." Jason glared, but he fooled her not for a minute.

With a final mumbled protest, her captain embarked on a poetic oration that would have moved many of the fairer sex to tears, if only to make him stop. At first, he practically barked the sonnets, which she thought an original, if not amusing, interpretation.

However, with each subsequent verse, he gazed into her eyes, emphasized more sensuous text, interjected bits of ribald humor, and then moved to sit beside her, so he could claim a kiss at the end of each line. And Alex imagined that, years later, when she reminisced of her fledgling months of wedded life, the hour she passed that morning with Jason would prevail as her most cherished memory.

"Well, that was the last poem, my dear." He closed the book. "Have you another?"

"I do." She nuzzled his chest and sighed. "But right now, I would indulge in alternative recreation, if you retain your cooperative nature."

"What is next?" With a hearty chuckle, he kissed the crown of her head. "Shakespeare?"

"Perhaps, this evening." She retraced her earlier path, straight to his crotch. "As I am in the mood for your favorite activity."

"No, Alex." Jason covered her hand with his. "Dr. Studly said you are not to be excited."

"But I am, and it is your fault." She squeezed his fast rising erection. "As you have showered with me sonnets, and I want you."

"You asked me to read them." He groaned and flexed his hips.

"Yes, I know, and all that flowery language worked on my senses." He released her, and she unhooked his waistband. "Can we not enjoy the fruit of your labor?"

Jason dropped his head back on the pillow. "The doctor said—"

"Bother the doctor." She closed her fingers about his girth. "He is an old woman."

"Admit it." He hissed. "You are trying to kill me."

"With pleasure, darling." How well she knew the rhythm, to make him howl in delight. "Let me have you, just this once."

Exhaling audibly, he closed his eyes. "Do with me, as you wish."

It was an enthralling experience, brandishing something so elementally male, yet delicate and vulnerable as a ripe peach, in her clutch. "Have you ever given yourself into another woman's control?"

"Never have I granted license of my body to anyone— until I met you." Clenching his jaw, Jason thrust in time with her movements.

"What is so special about me?" She toyed with the drop of moisture that had seeped from the tip.

He pinned her with his stare. "I trust you."

Passion glimmered, and smug satisfaction rode in its wake. Emboldened by his statement, she licked her palm and resumed her naughty handiwork, and that sent her husband over the brink. With a startling roar, he jerked and exploded in an impressive display of virility. After a few seconds, he whistled in monotone, and Alex burst into laughter.

"You unman me, love, but that is no criticism." To wit Jason grinned and waggled his brows. "However, you forgot the towel, and I made a mess."

"Wait there. I will fetch a wet cloth and tend you, for a change." She shimmied and stepped to the floor. At the washstand, she picked up the pitcher, just as a rush of warmth flooded between her thighs and puddled on the carpet. "Oh, no."

"Good God, you have sprung a leak." Jason leaped from the bed and rushed to her side. "What happened?"

Leaning against him for support, she gasped. "My water broke."

He furrowed his brow. "Speak English, Alex."

"The babes." She hugged her belly. "They are coming."

CHAPTER NINETEEN

*O*h, the pain. Oh, the agony. Oh, the misery.

It was an unimaginable torture. Standing in the middle of the master suite, Jason grimaced, as his wife bent forward in the throes of another vicious contraction, moaned, and clutched his hand in a death grip. Though she, alone, bore the burden of delivering their babes into the world, he suffered her torment down to his toes—if he still had toes. At present, his legs had weakened to the point that he feared his limbs had been severed at the knees.

"*Bastard!*" Her delicate features contorted as proof of her distress, and Alex gritted her teeth and sucked in a breath. "You did this to me."

"I know, dearest." He tried to remain calm and reassuring, but he was deuced scared.

"This is all your fault." With a fist pressed to her mouth, she sank her teeth into the fleshy base of her thumb and panted as a thoroughbred that had just crossed the finish line. Only her race had just begun.

"Yes, darling." Jason patted her bottom. "I am entirely to blame."

"Sabrina was right, as this is not fair." Alex winced and emitted a soft sob. "The woman must bear the pregnancy and birthing, while you get your jollies and an heir."

"I am a double-damned heathen, sweetheart." He kissed her forehead and tamped his concerns. "Do you feel better?"

"Yes." Yet his wife looked worse in his estimation, but he knew not to tell her as much. "I think that one has passed."

"Are you sure this is right?" He glanced at Miss Phipps and then the huge four-poster. "I thought the whole process occurred in bed."

"The doctor will determine that, Cap'n. But her ladyship has quite a journey ahead of her." The housekeeper cast him a half-smile. "Trust me, it will be much easier for Lady Alex, and hasten the labor, if she remains upright. Help her walk, sir. Her ladyship must stay afoot."

All manner of weird scenarios flashed in his brain, and Jason blanched. What if his bride rushed her fences? Would his children drop to the floor, on their tender heads? And his wife's current position seemed to amplify her travails. Yet, as the man, his chief responsibility in such circumstances was to sit in his study and consume mass quantities of brandy, according to the edicts of polite society. But Jason was no damned nobleman, so he resolved to write his own rules.

"Where is the bloody doctor?" He soaked a cloth in cool water. "How long has Tom been gone?"

"He departed more than four hours ago, sir." Molly drew a wayward curl from Alex's face, as he wiped the perspiration from his bride's brow. "I expected their arrival, long before now. I know not what keeps them."

"Perhaps I should go after the eminent Dr. Studly." The

mere prospect of that young dandy touching Alex spiked Jason's temper.

"Do not leave me. Please, I beg you, do not leave me." With a vise-like clamp on his fingers, his wife wrenched him. "Jason, I am frightened."

"I am not going anywhere, love." In that instant, he had never felt so helpless, so utterly useless, in his life. So he slipped his arm about her shoulders and provided succor. "We will get through this, together."

A subtle flinch signaled an impending contraction. Alex tensed, clenched her jaw, thrust her chin, and the muscles flexed in her neck, in an ominous display of distress.

Jason wanted to cry.

"Make it stop." Panting, she scrunched her face. "I can take no more."

"Lean on me, darling." He cradled her head.

"Lean on you?" Alex snorted. "That is what got me here. Touch me again, come at me with the Jolly Roger at full salute, and I shall chop it off. I swear I will."

In light of the raucous outburst, Miss Phipps chuckled, and Molly averted her stare. And just as quick, Alex reversed course, clutched his arm, and rested against his chest. Hell, after what he had endured the past four hours, he considered moving into separate quarters. Given the brutality of the so-called miracle of life, he might never resume marital relations.

"Keep her ladyship walking, Cap'n." The housekeeper humphed and shuffled her feet. "Else it will be more difficult."

"As you wish." As Alex moaned and groaned, he led her on a tour about their bedchamber.

Around and around, they navigated the master suite, and with each successive revolution, he marked the path of the sun's rays across the carpet, until nothing remained but a sliver of gold on the horizon. At last, Dr. Studly strolled into the room.

"Good evening, Captain and Mrs. Collingwood." The physician placed his black bag at the foot of the four-poster, doffed his hat and coat, and rolled up his sleeves. "How does our expectant mother fare?"

Alex vented a woeful whimper.

"Where in bloody hell have you been?" The perfumed physician sparked Jason's ire. "My wife has languished for hours."

"Her water broke, this morning, after your earlier visit, Dr. Studly." Molly wrung her fingers. "And her contractions are quite close."

"Excellent." With unimpaired aplomb, the physician washed his hands and then prepared the tools of his trade. "Relax, Captain. There was an accident at the Miller farm, and I have been stitching wounds and setting broken bones, since before noon. Please, help her ladyship into bed, so I may check her progress."

In a flash, Jason scooped Alex into his arms and eased her to the mattress. "There's a girl."

"That will be all." Dr. Studly snatched a large towel from the side table and spread it atop the counterpane. "You may retire to your study, and I shall send for you, once the babes are born and bathed."

Jason—*no*." His terrified bride caught the folds of his cravat and well nigh choked him.

"Hush, darling." He loosened the neck cloth, swallowed hard, and shook his head. "As I already promised you, I am not going anywhere."

"Captain Collingwood, I must protest. The ladies may remain, as I require their assistance, but I must examine her ladyship." Dr. Studly arched a brow. "The birthing room is no place for a husband."

Alex blared.

"Then I suggest you adjust to the changing circumstance, because I am staying with my wife." Wild horses could not drag Jason from her side. He had disappointed her in so many ways, and he would not fail her now.

Alex wailed.

"Suit yourself, as I have no time to argue the point." The young doctor commenced his inspection and assessment. "But if you insist on lingering, then I would make use of you."

"Tell me what to do, and I am at your service." Of course, he knew not what that encompassed, but Jason had survived numerous battles in the heat of war, so childbirth could not have been that bad.

Alex shrieked.

"Get behind her ladyship, and cradle her body with yours. When I give the command for her to push, you must be unfailing in your support and encouragement." To Molly and Miss Phipps, Dr. Studly said, "Ladies, hold her legs. And if any of you feel faint or believe you are sick at your stomach, for heaven's sake, step away from the bed."

"I beg your pardon." Jason took offense to such characterization. "As I am a navy man, I am no stranger to blood or injuries. I assure you, I am no namby-pamby fop."

Alex screeched.

"So you say, Captain." Dr. Studly laughed. "But pain is an altogether different matter, when the suffering party is one we love. However, you may retire the field, without shame, if necessary."

Just then, his wife clawed at his arms and screamed, and Jason feared he might swoon. The ensuing hour passed in a haze of panic and frustration, as Alex emitted one gut-wrenching cry after another and shed a tidal wave of tears.

"Hold her steady, Captain." In the candlelight, beads of perspiration glistened on his brow, as the physician positioned himself between her legs. "All right, your ladyship. *Push*."

With a long, drawn out groan, his amazing bride tensed and gritted her teeth, and Jason whispered praise in her ear.

"I can see the babe." Dr. Studly grabbed another towel. "Push, my lady. Give it everything you can muster."

"Come on, love." Jason braced and willed his strength into her feminine frame. "You can do it, my brave Alex."

For a scarce second, time stood still, as she froze, with her mouth open in a silent scream. An eerie quiet fell over the bedchamber—until an unholy bellow rent the air.

Misty-eyed, Jason choked up, as his heir entered the world. And in true Collingwood fashion, his son let loose an impressive squall, as Miss Phipps scurried forward to claim him.

"He is beautiful, Alex." Jason peered at his incredible wife and discovered she had fainted.

"Good God, revive her." Dr. Studly tossed a bag of smelling salts at Jason. "Hurry. Your second child arrives, even now."

"But would it not be easier if she slept through it?" Jason retrieved the salts.

"Are you out of your mind?" The physician assumed his position. "*Do it, man*. Else your other babe will die."

At that point, Jason had not hesitated. As her eyelids fluttered, Alex moaned and reached for him.

"How is my baby?" She sucked in a breath.

"We have a fine son, sweetheart." He kissed her temple. "Now be strong, love. As we have one more on the way."

"I cannot do it." She wept. "I simply—" Her shrill wail reverberated throughout the master suite.

Blood stained the white towels, and Jason shuddered.

"All right." Dr. Studly dragged his shirtsleeve across his face. "Push, your ladyship."

And so the nightmare began again.

Instead of the thirteen hours Alex had already labored, things moved with amazing swiftness. His second son came into being much the same as the first, with a thunderous roar, and Molly took him into her care.

"Thank you, Alex." Jason gazed on his offspring with pride, then studied his wife and realized she had again swooned. Relief mixed with gratitude, yet he could not translate his emotions into words. "Should I wake her, Dr. Studly?"

"Not this time, as her work is done." The physician tended Alex. "Her ladyship is in excellent condition, so I shall examine the children and take my leave."

"I am in your debt, Dr. Studly." Jason focused on his bride. Damp brown ringlets hung limp about her brow and emphasized her pale skin and the dark circles beneath her eyes. But in that moment, Jason thought she had never looked lovelier. In her ear, he whispered, "I am so proud of you, darling. You have made me so happy."

"Cap'n, I would like to bathe her ladyship and change the linens. Molly guards the babes in the nursery, if you wish to visit them." Miss Phipps smiled. "And might I suggest you get some rest?"

"I will, Gertie." He claimed a kiss, before relinquishing his wife.

Rubbing the back of his neck, Jason strolled into the hall. At the door to the nursery, he met Dr. Studly.

"You have two strapping sons, Captain Collingwood."

The physician extended a hand, and they shared a vigorous shake. "Must take after their father."

"You are too kind." Jason chuckled.

"And they are identical, with one exception." Dr. Studly smiled. "But I wager her ladyship will be pleased."

Minutes later, as he cradled his sleeping baby boys, Jason understood the doctor's cryptic comment. Gerald and Gerard, named as his wife had decreed, were perfectly matched twins with a sole distinguishing feature—their hair. One babe boasted a shock of blonde, and the other sported a brunette thatch.

"I suppose we have both left our mark, Alex." With a son nestled in the crook of each arm, his body trembled with incomprehensible elation, and his heart burst with unfathomable joy, as Jason relaxed in a chair before the windows and wept.

"Must say you have healed at a remarkable pace, your ladyship." Dr. Studly gathered his black bag and hat. "You may resume marital relations, but take it slow, as you seem a bit warm."

"Thank you, doctor. And I assure you, I am quite well." Alex gave her back to Miss Phipps, who retied the laces of Alex's gown. "Will I require another examination?"

"As long as you follow my advice, I think not." At the door, he paused and smiled. "Captain Collingwood made an excellent midwife. Now, if you have no more questions, I shall check on the twins and be on my way, as it would be nice to dine with my wife."

"You have been so helpful." Alex smoothed her skirts.

"We appreciate everything you have done for us, Dr. Studly."

"That is my job, your ladyship." He plopped his hat atop his head and nodded once. "Good day."

With a bawdy little ditty playing in her brain, Alex walked to the armoire and set the doors wide. It took all of two seconds to decide on the gown she would wear for dinner. Holding the sumptuous garment to her chest, she turned and scrutinized her appearance in the long mirror.

To the casual observer, she wanted for nothing. She had two healthy, beautiful babies. She had the elegant manor of which she had dreamed. And Alex had more than she could have fathomed in a spouse—except the one thing she wanted most.

Her husband's declaration.

"Oh, my lady." Gertie pressed a hand to her throat. "What a lovely dress."

"Is it not?" She fitted the bodice to her breasts, as she had lost most of the excess weight from her pregnancy. The lone noticeable change in her figure was her ample bosom. "I wore this gown the night I met Captain Collingwood."

"Oh, I say." The housekeeper snickered. "Cap'n will fall over himself, when he gets a look at you, in that frock."

"Indeed, that is the plan." How she cherished the sweet memory, as she recalled his expression, the raw hunger, when they had locked gazes, so long ago. And she intended to resurrect that yearning—tonight. "Miss Phipps, will you help me?"

"Of course, your ladyship." Gertie fetched a matching pair of slippers. "What have you in mind?"

"Ring for a bath." Alex plotted her strategy. "Add some of my rosewater, as Jason favors it. And could you arrange my hair, as Molly and Tom are repainting their bedchamber in the cottage, and I would rather not delay their progress."

"I should be too delighted to assist you, my lady." The housekeeper winked. "Shall I air your dress for this evening?"

"What a marvelous idea." Sitting at her vanity, Alex gazed at her reflection in the oval mirror and almost cried. As she admired her image, she filled not with vanity or pride but with relief. It was as if she had just returned home from a long voyage and welcomed an old friend.

Behind her, the massive four-poster loomed not as a specter of doom but of hope for the future she desperately desired but had not permitted herself to covet, since Plymouth. In an instant, she invoked the vision of her husband, his handsome features marred by worry and fear, as he held her while she gave birth. She recalled his tender care, his words of praise, and his unwavering support—and then Jason had moved into a guestroom.

To her chagrin, he had not returned to their bed.

So for the next couple of hours, she put her altruistic scheme into action, as she washed, primped, coiffed, and garbed herself with the singular objective of catching her knight.

"Hold your breath, my lady." Miss Phipps yanked hard on the laces. "Just a tad more should do it."

"Oh, what we do for fashion." Alex hugged the corner post of the footboard and winced. "This had better work."

"There, now." Retreating a step, Gertie admired the results. "Cap'n will be at your command, my lady."

"I pray your are correct in your estimation." If Jason rejected her now, she knew not how she would react.

"Arnold will soon ring the dinner bell, so you should join Cap'n." The housekeeper collected the discarded clothing. "I will tidy the room, set out fresh towels, and turn down the sheets."

"Gertie, you are a priceless gem." Alex had done all she could. The rest was up to Jason.

And so she charged into the fray but drew up short as she descended the stairs. Summoning her expertise and cataloguing the skills useful in the pursuit of the male species, she halted, squared her shoulders, lifted her chin, and inhaled a deep, calming breath. A lady never rushed into a room, as a gust of wind. Rather, she glided as an elegant swan on a still pond.

Nervous excitement mixed with sweet anticipation bubbled beneath her flesh, as she sailed into the drawing room to await her husband. Standing near the hearth, she laughed, as she pondered the transformation of the time-worn house and grounds into a grand estate.

"Good evening, my lovely wife." Gorgeous, in a chocolate brown waistcoat, a navy coat, buckskin breeches, and polished Hessians, with the collar of his shirt opened, sans cravat, Jason smiled. "The dinner bell—"

The stillness of his frame, the fire in his blue eyes, and the slackening of his jaw attested to the fact that he had noted the significance of her attire.

"And a very good evening to you, my handsome husband." Alex lowered her chin, walked straight to her tongue-tied spouse, and splayed her hands to his chest. "How delicious you look. I should just as soon take a bite of you."

"What?" He blinked. "Uh—yes, I am fine. Shall we dine?"

"As you wish." As they navigated the hall, she squeezed his arm, and his muscles flexed. "I had my final appointment with Dr. Studly, today."

"Oh?" At the table, Jason held her chair, and her usual place setting to his left situated her within striking distance. "And what is the estimable physician's diagnosis?"

"I am free to continue my duties, as your wife." She pinned him with her stare, as she licked her lips. "All of them."

Just then, Phipps entered the dining room, carrying a large covered dish. "Shall I commence serving, your ladyship?"

"I will care for my bride, Arnold." Jason snatched the tongs and a plate. "You are dismissed."

"We are having braised beef, with carrots and potatoes, one of your favorite meals." Alex cast a coy smile at her captain. "Darling, I no longer eat for three."

He glanced at the mountainous amount of fare and frowned. But when she rubbed her foot to his calf, he jumped. "Bloody hell. I will take this portion and prepare another for you."

"There is no rush, although I am ravenously hungry." Then she reached under the table and caressed his crotch. "But not for food."

A telltale flush crept up his neck and spread, into his cheeks. "I initiated the search for tutors, for our boys."

"What?" She offered herself on the proverbial silver platter, and he changed the topic. "Jason, they are babies, and it is too soon to interview tutors."

"There is no time like the present." As he lifted his tankard of ale, his hand shook. "And I want the best of everything for Gerald and Gerard."

Over the next hour, her husband detailed his future plans for the twins, and Alex noted a serious deficiency. He made no mention of her. But she remained undaunted, as she clutched his hand and drew flirty circles in his palm.

When she signaled for the final course, a decadent cherry compote, which she had intended to feed her uncharacteristically shy spouse while seated in his lap, Jason pushed from the table and stood.

"I will pass on dessert." He tossed his napkin on his plate, stretched, and then bent to kiss her forehead. "If you need me, I will be in the study, as I have much work to complete."

It took several minutes for Alex to register what had just happened and that she, alone, occupied the dining room. Her husband wanted her, of that she was certain. Yet he had rebuffed her advances. When she leaped from her chair, the floor seemed to pitch and roll beneath her feet, and she swayed.

"Are you unwell, your ladyship?" Phipps steadied her. "Shall I summon Cap'n?"

"No." She smoothed her skirt. "I am fine."

Then she turned on a heel and marched into her erstwhile fervent suitor's private domain. When she stormed into the study, she found Jason at his desk.

"Alex?" He returned his pen to the inkstand. "Is there something—"

"Why do you avoid me?" She folded her arms, as she could take no more. "Why do you refuse to share our bed?"

IT WAS A CURIOUS QUESTION, for which Jason had no answer.

Staring at his hands, he clenched his fists to conceal his trembling. What could he tell his wife? Would she laud the fact that her velvet gown reminded him of the blood that had stained the linens, when she birthed their sons? Would she dance a jig, were he to apprise her that nightmares had plagued his slumber, as he had relived her suffering, again and again, since Gerald and Gerard entered the world? Or would Alex mock his fear?

"I am not avoiding you." Jason sighed. "I am protecting you."

"From what?" With her brow a mass of furrows, she neared. "You make no sense."

"I guard you from myself." Resting his elbows to the blotter, he cradled his head. "As I cannot bear to lose you."

"Do you mean that?" his wife inquired, in a small voice.

"Of course." Jason lifted his chin and peered at her. "Every night, I see you writhing in agony, and I will not risk another pregnancy, after what you endured with our sons."

"But I am recovered, and the process, though painful, is natural." She rounded the desk, pushed him back in his chair, and slid to his lap. Framing his face, she kissed him. "And I want more children, so your position is unacceptable."

"While I am glad you have healed, I may never forget what you braved." In that instant, he clung to her. "What would I do without my beautiful Alex?"

Without warning, his wife grabbed his hair, wrenched hard, emitted something between a sob and a sigh, and came at him with the force of a brigade. At first, he tried to resist the temptation she presented, but when his bride shifted and situated her knees to either side of his thighs, he dug through the seemingly endless folds of heavy velvet in search of her bare bottom.

As their tongues twined, she moaned, and he deuced near shot his seed in his breeches. But when Alex rocked her hips, something inside Jason snapped.

"I want you." She bit his lip and ground against his

stony erection. "And you want me, so do not dare claim otherwise."

"Not here." He slipped a finger into her bodice and teased a pert nipple. "I would take you in our bed, as I prefer you naked and spread for my delectation, and I would lick every part of you."

"Promises, promises." With a charming giggle, that again brought him to the brink of sweet release, she stood. "I shall retire to our suite, where I will prepare myself for the much anticipated assault and await your company with baited breath. Do not make me linger too long, my naughty sailor."

"Madame, I am your most devoted servant." When she bent and squeezed his Jolly Roger, which had prepared a steely, one-gun salute, he enjoyed a spectacular view of her ample décolletage. "You have twenty minutes."

"My dear Captain, I am ready for you." She trailed her little pink tongue along his jawline, and he clenched his gut. Then she all ran from the study, and he could not help but laugh.

"Collingwood, you are in trouble." Dropping his head back, he collapsed in his chair and gazed at the ceiling. Huffing a breath, he peered at the telltale bulge in his crotch and snorted. "This is all your fault, as you are but moulding clay in her hands."

After pouring a brandy, Jason walked to the window and studied the night sky. When the mantel clock signaled the hour, he downed the contents of his glass and set it on the desk.

Candlestick in his grasp, he exited his sanctuary, turned right in the hall, almost skipped through the foyer, and ascended the stairs. Instead of steering straight for the master suite and Alex's arms, he veered in the opposite direction to check on his sons.

In the nursery, his heirs slept. As always pride surged in his chest when he looked on his boys and imagined the adventures they would share. With care, he tiptoed—yes, he bloody tiptoed from the chamber.

At last, he strolled into the sitting room and set the bolt on the doors, as he would brook no interruptions when he made love to his wife. To his surprise, the inner sanctum was dark and quiet.

Holding the candle high, he was nonplussed to discover the bed empty. A soft sniffle snared his trained ear, and he turned. "Alex, are you there?"

"Jason, help me." It was then he noticed the shadowy slumped form on the floor, near the armoire, and a chill of terror shook his frame.

"What is it, darling?" After depositing the candlestick on her vanity, he knelt at her side and drew her into his arms. "What happened?"

"The pain is unbearable." When he lifted her, she whimpered and clung to him as a frightened child. "Send for Dr. Studly, as I am gravely ill."

CHAPTER TWENTY

*a*lex burned, but hers was not the heat of unchecked passion. She ached, but her discomfit had nothing to do with unfulfilled desire.

Settled in the impressive four-poster in the master suite, she closed her eyes and clenched her teeth against the excruciating pain in her breasts. Intense fever had reduced her to a violent, shivering mess, but she tried to be brave, even as she sobbed.

"I dispatched Tom to fetch Dr. Studly." Jason draped another blanket over her. "How do you feel, love?"

"I hate to bother him, at this hour, but I feel terrible." She shook uncontrollably. "And I am frightened."

"How can I make it better?" Jason reclined beside her. "Tell me what to do, and I will do it, sweetheart."

"I know not. Oh, Jason." Alex possessed only so much courage, as the damn broke, and she burst into tears.

"Hold hard, darling." Counterpane and all, he scooped her into his arms. "You must be strong, as the doctor will be here, any second."

"But I am so tired." She buried her face in his chest and cried. "It hurts."

Just then, Dr. Studly entered the chamber. "Captain and Mrs. Collingwood. I understand her ladyship is ill?"

"Thank you, for coming so soon." Ashamed of her appearance, she dried her cheeks on the sleeve of her night-gown and explained her symptoms. "I know not what is wrong, Dr. Studly."

The physician sat at the edge of the bed and drew down the covers. "Captain Collingwood, if you would wait in—"

"I am not leaving." Jason scowled.

"Why am I not surprised?" The doctor rolled his eyes. "Then if you intend to remain, do not interfere, as I must conduct a thorough examination of her ladyship. Now, show me where your ailment persists."

Wincing, Alex cupped her breasts. "Here."

"I beg your pardon, my lady, but I must assess your condition." He pressed his palm to one tender mound and then the other, and she flinched. "Just as I suspected."

"What is it, Dr. Studly?" Jason swallowed hard.

The physician lowered his chin. "My diagnosis is milk fever."

"Is it fatal?" Jason clutched her hand.

"No, Captain." Dr. Studly compressed his lips and shook his head. "But it can be quite uncomfortable."

"Is it treatable?" Never had she experienced anything so horrible.

"Yes." The doctor shrugged into his coat and claimed his bag. "Although the remedy resides not in a bottle."

"I do not understand." Jason rubbed the back of his neck and narrowed his stare. "Then how can you cure her?"

"The treatment is simple but just as unpleasant, if not

more so, as the malady." Snatching his hat from the bedside table, Dr. Studly frowned. "You must nurse, your ladyship."

"What?" She gulped, as the mere thought struck terror in her chest.

"I am aware it does not sound agreeable, given the burning agony, but you must persevere. Feeding the babes will ease the symptoms, and the fever will pass as swiftly as it began." After pulling on his gloves, Dr. Studly dipped his chin. "I shall take my leave, but I will visit you, in the morning, to monitor your health."

"Miss Phipps, show the doctor to the door, and have Molly bring our sons, at once." To her relief, Jason remained rooted to her side.

"Yes, Cap'n." Gertie bowed. "This way, please."

"Bloody hell, Alex." And then her captain's calm façade broke, as he bent and bestowed upon her a kiss that ignited her skin in an altogether more enjoyable fashion. "I thought you were going to die, and I would never have the chance to tell you that I can't live without you. I would sooner lose my heart, for you are far more precious. And I need you to know how much I love you."

"Do you really mean it?" Was it possible? Had she hallucinated his declaration, in her agony? Had she known a miserable illness would have provoked his proclamation, she would have feigned a fever. "Do you love me, as I dearly love you?"

"Of course, as never have I uttered those words to any woman, because you are my only lady." He tucked a wayward curl behind her ear. "I have loved you from the night we met, in full view of the *ton*, in the Richmond's ballroom. You won me, right then and there."

"Why did you not state as much?" Thrilled but in immeasurable distress, Alex snuggled close to him. "Have you any idea how much torment you might have spared us, had you only said so?"

"To my undying shame, I lacked the courage to apprise you of the truth, and I assumed you knew, to some extent, as I purchased this property for the expressed purpose of providing a home for our family." Jason wrinkled his nose and then grinned. "I even wrote your friends for advice. But the flowers, rosewater baths, and poetry were my ideas."

She giggled, and searing pain had her gasping. "I believe I knew your poetry was an original production, and I treasure it, so you must compose more."

Molly and Miss Phipps arrived, each bearing a babe.

"I apologize for the delay, but Gerard had soiled himself, so I had to change his towel." With an expression of sympathy, the nanny laid the youngest boy at Alex's left.

Jason fluffed the pillows and unbuttoned the front of her nightgown. "Shall I situate Gerald to your right?"

"Yes." When Alex sat upright, the discomfort increased twofold, and she doubled over and moaned.

"I will convey my sons to the nursery." Her husband supported the babe. "You are dismissed."

Two greedy mouths clamped onto her nipples, and Alex feared she might swoon from the sheer torture. "*Jason.*"

"Give me something to do for you, as I can't stand by idly, while you suffer." He untied his cravat, stripped the yard length of linen from his neck, and used the cloth to dry the perspiration on her brow. "It is the least I can do, given I am to blame for your troubles. The birthing and milk fever —everything is my fault. I never should have made love to you."

Through the miasma of anguish, she deciphered his comment, and it dawned on her why he had moved to the guestroom. It was not because of indifference. Rather, he had, by some misplaced sense of responsibility, assumed culpability for what was nothing more than the twists and turns of life.

"Had you not taken my bride's prize, I never would have forgiven you." She panted, as her sons fed. "And mine is a labor of love, as I have longed to give you an heir. My darling, I would not have missed this for the world, so I thank you, for everything you have given me."

"Dearest and loveliest Alex." Again, Jason kissed her. "You are amazing. Have I told you how much I love you?"

"Not in detail." As another wave of torment wracked her body, she sobbed. "But there is something you can do to ease my current burden."

"Name it, sweetheart." He nuzzled her temple.

"You could climb beneath the covers and hold me, as I always rest better in your arms. And you give me strength." She bit her lip. "But take off your clothes, as I prefer you naked."

"Yes, ma'am." In mere seconds, Jason stripped, and it was quite a show, and then he slipped between the sheets. Clenching her jaw, she jostled, when he moved her to recline against him, and he gave her a gentle hug. "Better?"

"Yes." With a sigh, she relaxed and closed her eyes. "Tell me, again."

"I love you." With a husky chuckle, he nibbled the crest of her ear. "I love you." He kissed her neck. "I love you, Alex."

A FORTNIGHT HAD PASSED since Alex had wrangled with the dreaded milk fever, and although she had fully recuperated, her husband still suffered from uncharacteristic and unwelcome shyness, in relation to their marital bed. Although Jason held her every night, and he made his declaration, time and again, he had not made love to her, citing concern for her welfare. And she had reached the end of her tether.

Studying her reflection in the long mirror, she admired the parure of sapphires and diamonds, which matched her wedding ring, that Jason had gifted her yesterday evening, at dinner. Donning a new red velvet coat, she buttoned the outerwear to her throat and marched into battle, as it was past due to thank her temperamental spouse.

In the foyer, she almost bumped into Phipps.

"Your ladyship, Cap'n requests your presence in the study." The butler bowed.

"Thank you, Phipps." She nodded once. "And hold the dinner bell an additional hour."

At the door to her husband's domain, she smoothed her palms over the curves of her hips and rolled her shoulders. Then she knocked and entered the fray.

As soon as their gazes met, Jason's expression warmed. "There is my beautiful wife."

"You wished to see me?" Nervous excitement blossomed in the pit of her belly.

"Actually, I requested the honor of your company, kitten." Her brother jumped from the daybed and spread wide his arms. "Little sister, I have missed you."

"*Damian!*" In a flash, she launched herself at her elder sibling, and he caught her in a bear of a hug. Then she burst into tears. "I am so sorry we quarreled. It was all my fault."

"No." He cradled her head and rocked, as he had when she was but a young girl. "I am entirely to blame, as I should have sought an alternative solution, before forcing you into marriage. Can you ever forgive me?"

"There is nothing to forgive, as I have never been happier, brother." It was then she noted the lines of strain etched at the corners of his eyes, as well as his gaunt appearance. "Oh, Damian. I love Jason, and he loves me. And our boys are beautiful. Have you seen them?"

"Not yet, as I only just arrived, after Collingwood sent a directive informing me of the new additions to our family and inviting me for a weekend visit." Setting her on her feet, he assessed her attire. "But you wear a coat. Are you going somewhere? Have I interrupted your schedule?"

"Not in the least, as I had thought to take a bit of exercise." And now was the perfect opportunity to enact her invasion of one reticent sea captain, as she escorted Damian into the hall. "Have Phipps show you to the nursery, so you may meet your nephews."

"Do you always indulge in physical activity while sporting a tiara? Some things never change." Damian turned but reversed course and caught her in a rough, haphazard embrace. "You know not what it does for me to see you so well. I feared I had destroyed our close bond."

"Never, as you are my first champion, and no one will ever supplant you, brother." She winked, and he grinned. "Now go introduce my sons to their favorite uncle, and linger as long as you wish."

Returning to the study, Alex gave her attention to her bashful spouse, as he arched a brow and snorted. "Just where do you intend to walk, without benefit of shoes?"

"I said nothing about walking, my oh-so-dashing husband." She glanced at the floor and wiggled her toes. Then she set the bolt. "I intend to partake of your favorite activity, which you have neglected, of late. But I shall rectify that problem."

"I beg your pardon?" Jason blinked.

Without fear or hesitation, she unbuttoned the coat and dropped it to the floor. Naked but for the expensive collection of matching jewelry, she held her head high. "How do you like my gems?"

NEVER HAD Jason looked upon anything so stunning, and the fancy baubles were nice, too. Sagging against his desk, he plopped his bottom along the edge, swallowed hard, and remained silent, as words failed him.

"All right." To his unmitigated horror, and fast faltering self-control, Alex charged his field, grasped the lapels of his coat, perched on tiptoes, and covered his mouth with hers.

In that instant, something inside him fractured, and he pounced. How they made it to the daybed, he neither knew nor cared, but he bothered not to remove his clothes. Instead, he unhooked his breeches, freed his length, and drove into her, hard and quick.

And Alex lauded every minute of his lascivious attack with a lusty chorus of pants and sighs, as took her on her back, on her knees, and against the wall, while the display case rattled in rhythm with his thrusts. Later, she collapsed atop him.

"Your tiara sits askew, love." As he adjusted the over-priced crown, he suckled her lower lip.

"Well I secured it with pins, but you knocked them loose." She nibbled playfully on his tongue, and his Jolly Roger roused. "But I am not complaining, as I do so adore your particular brand of ravishment, Captain of my heart."

The unique endearment, so long absent from her vocabulary, struck him as a vicious punch, and he flinched. Then, to his complete and utter embarrassment, tears welled, and he averted his stare in an attempt to conceal his reaction.

"Jason, what is wrong?" His bride framed his face.

"Am I still the captain of your heart, as you have not called me thus, since Plymouth. And I live to hear you say it." Twining his fingers in the hair at the nape of her neck, he held her in his firm embrace. "Do you understand, Alex? I *live* for it."

"Oh, Jason." She bestowed upon him an inexpressibly tender kiss. "Never doubt my love for you, as you have been, are now, and always will be the captain of my heart. But I had feared the pet name might make you uncomfortable, given I assumed you shared not my devotion, so I had refrained from addressing you, as such."

"How I do love you, and I should have apprised you of that fact, much sooner. And while neither of us is without fault, I believe you and I are prefect for each other." He rubbed his nose to hers. "Now will you do something for me?"

"Anything, darling." Once before, she had made that offer, and he had squandered it. Not so, anymore.

"Find another physician." Jason frowned. "Perhaps, one about twenty years older than I, with a gotch-gut and a wart on his nose, as I cannot tolerate Dr. Studly putting his hands on your luscious curves."

"Jason Collingwood." Alex giggled, and how he cherished that sound. "The man is a professional. Are you truly jealous?"

"Christ, yes." He blanched, as he recalled the young doctor, during childbirth, situated far too close to Jason's personal playground.

"Never have I heard anything so ridiculous, because I love you. And he is the only medical practitioner, for miles." Then she adopted a slow, sensual smile, which set his blood boiling. "So how might I allay your concerns, as you are the captain of my heart, body, and soul?"

Hers was a tempting proposition, and he gave it due consideration. Then a brilliant idea formed in his passion-clouded brain. "Do you remember that rainy afternoon we passed in Plymouth?"

"On the sofa?" With a wicked shimmy, she flexed her hips, enveloping his flesh deep within hers. "When I took you?"

"Ride me, like you did then, as there is nothing so spectacular." Crossing his arms behind his head, he relaxed on the daybed. Just as fast, he scowled. "Damn. I should have told Phipps to hold the dinner bell an extra thirty minutes."

"Worry not, my naughty sailor." Alex commenced the decadent slip and slide. "As I informed Arnold we would dine an hour late, so we have plenty of time."

To wit Jason burst into laughter. "Woman, I am so glad I married you."

EPILOGUE

March, 1814

After defeats by Napoleon at Lützen and Bautzen, the Prussian-Russian alliance had been bolstered by Wellington's advance on the Pyrenees, and Austria's subsequent decision to re-enter the war. When Wellington crossed the Bidassoa into France, Napoleon's defenses along the line of Nivelle were broken. As a result, British forces were in dire need of replenishment for a final assault on Paris, and the infamous Nautionnier Knights descended of the Templars had been ordered into the breach.

It was a lazy Saturday morning, as the Brethren wives, save a heavily pregnant Sabrina, gathered at Caroline's Mayfair mansion. With baited breath the women awaited news from the watch in the North Forelands, which always provided fair warning of ships in the Thames Estuary and an impending, much prayed for arrival. Tasked with a six-week mission, the men had departed England's shores in a flurry of activity, amid the joyous news that Caroline and Rebecca expected additions to their extended family, yet there had been no time for celebrations, as duty summoned their husbands into action.

"How fares Brie?" Alex swiped a second scone.

"Green as a toad." Caroline snickered and shook her head. "Elaine keeps her company, today."

"And Everett?" Rebecca inquired.

"I would have thought he had become accustomed to the morning malaise, when Sabrina carried Edward, but the poor man is a wreck." Caroline rolled her eyes and giggled. "Husbands are such funny creatures. Once again, when I informed Trevor we look forward to our third child, he wept like a babe."

"So did Dirk, when I delivered the news of our second blessing." Rebecca hugged her slightly protruding belly and smiled. "But it warms my heart that he is thus affected, and I do so long to give him a son."

The room grew quiet, as a wicked March storm raged beyond the walls, and the wind thrummed and howled.

"What a nasty tempest." Alex gazed out the window, as rain pelted the glass. "Can't imagine how Cara manages aboard ship, given she is in her eighth month."

"She would not allow Lance to sail without her, and he was just as reluctant to leave her." Caroline snorted. "And Trevor told me Lance cried, in the middle of White's, when it dawned on him that Cara was with child."

In unison, the women sighed.

"Alex, you never said, how did Jason respond when he returned home and discovered your condition?" And then Caroline frowned. "If it pains you to remember, I apologize, and you need say nothing more."

"Oh, it is blood under the bridge." Alex recalled that tumultuous scene in Damian's library at Penhurst Castle. "Jason paled, and I feared he might vomit."

"How unfortunate." Caroline glanced at Rebecca. "I should not have inquired."

"Really, sister." Alex clutched Caroline's hand and squeezed her fingers. "My captain cradled me in his arms, as I birthed our sons, and he loves me. What more could I want?"

"So you are happy?" Rebecca perched on the edge of her seat. "We have been so worried for you."

"My friends, your concern is misplaced, as Jason is truly the captain of my heart." Alex revisited the morning of Jason's departure, and her sailor's bawdy behavior, and the burn of a blush teased her cheeks. "Never have I—"

A knock at the door interrupted the conversation.

"I beg your pardon, your ladyship." The butler bowed. "A missive is just arrived by special messenger, and I thought you would want to read it, posthaste."

"Is it from the Forelands watch?" Rebecca jumped to her feet, and Caroline grabbed the note from the salver. "Hurry and open it."

"It is from Deptford." Caroline furrowed her brow and then shrieked. "Bloody hell, our men have docked."

A wave of panic struck the elegant back parlor, as Alex toppled her plate from her lap, and Rebecca almost tripped over the table.

"I must away, as Dirk is, no doubt, en route to our home." Rebecca all but ran for the door. "Take care, ladies. And enjoy the ride."

"Oh, dear." Alex kissed Caroline's cheek. "In the time it took the messenger to reach the city, Jason will have started his journey, too. I must prepare myself."

"You will understand if I do not see you out," Caroline replied, as they scrambled into the hall. "As Trevor will want—well, you know what our husbands want."

"I do, indeed." Alex wasted no energy in donning her coat and hurried out the front portal, where her coach parked. To the driver she shouted, "Make haste, make haste."

After a short but white-knuckled trip through the streets of London, she flew into the Collingwood town residence.

The butler stood in the foyer. "There is an urgent communication for you—"

"Yes, I know, Haynes. Captain Collingwood is returned, and we may expect him at any minute." As she soared up the stairs, she hollered over her shoulder, "Send my lady's maid, immediately."

In the bedchamber she shared with Jason, Alex kicked off her slippers and tugged at her laces.

"My lady, let me help you." Lily rushed into the room.

"No, as I am almost free." Alex shimmied out of her morning dress. "Fetch the red velvet gown, and hurry, as we have not a second to spare.

It had taken months, but Alex had worked hard to regain her figure, until she could wear the very dress that had tempted her captain, more than two years ago, in the Richmond's ballroom, without the painful lacing. At last, garbed and coiffed to perfection, Alex assessed her appearance in the long mirror and smiled.

"Your ladyship, you look beautiful." Lily curtseyed. "Cap'n will be beside himself. Will that be all, ma'am?"

"Yes." Oh, her lusty captain would be a vast deal more than beside himself. He would be inside her, over her, atop her, behind her, and beneath her. Alex strolled into the sitting room. "As usual, I would like a light repast and a hot bath, approximately three hours after the captain arrives."

As she considered the logistics of Jason's reception, Alex laughed. On normal occasions, when she met her husband at the dock, he pounced as soon as they entered their coach and lowered the shades, so his attack was somewhat tempered, by the time they reached their bed. As the situation presented unique circumstances, she knew not what anticipate.

"If you will tidy my things, and turn down the covers, you may take the rest of the afternoon off." With that, Alex inhaled a deep, calming breath and glided along the hall. As she stood at the landing, Jason charged into the foyer.

Remaining stock-still, with his gaze locked on hers, her husband handed his coat, hat, gloves, and rucksack to Haynes. Then, without a word, he bounded in her direction, and she set course for him.

With her arms outstretched, she welcomed him. "Captain of my heart, how I missed—"

They collided midway up the grand staircase, and he covered her mouth with his, but Jason retraced her path, and carried her to the gallery. Pinning her against the wall, he bent and buried his face in her bosom, and her knees buckled.

"I remember that dress and the sumptuous body it conceals." He nipped her chin, as he grabbed her derriere and pressed her into his erection. When her husband was aroused, he employed every inch of his hearty frame to entice and seduce. "But if you wish to keep the frock in one piece, you will remove it, as you have ten minutes to fortify yourself, my delectable wife. First, I will visit our sons, and then I am coming for you, in more ways than one. I want you naked and in our bed, else I will not be responsible for my conduct and the destruction of your attire."

"Your wish is my command, Captain of my heart." She trailed her tongue along his jaw, and then she caressed the ridge of his stout cannon. "And I ache to kiss you, right here."

"Bloody hell, Alex." He growled. "Woman, I am about to spill my seed in my breeches, so I rescind my previous offer, which is far too generous. You may have five minutes. Go—now." Then he turned and sprinted to the nursery.

"Hurry, Lily." When Alex re-entered her bedchamber, she kicked off her slippers, in a comical sense of *déjà vu*, and the lady's maid started. "Unlace me, as Captain Collingwood is in residence, and I have no time to spare."

While the maid loosened the gown, Alex pulled the pins from her hair. After stepping from the dress, she bent, unhooked her garters, and rolled down her stockings. Wearing only her chemise, she grabbed a brush and smoothed her wayward locks.

"You are dismissed, Lily." Alex perched on the mattress. "Enjoy your day."

With a vivid blush, the maid curtseyed. "You, too, your ladyship."

Alone, Alex drew the slip over her head and flung it to the floor. Naked, she crawled to the middle of the expansive four-poster, fluffed the pillows, reclined on her side, and draped her hair over her shoulder.

Like a man on a mission, Jason barged into the room, met her stare, licked his lips, and smiled. As he neared, he doffed his cravat, coat, and waistcoat, but nothing else. Instead, he unfastened his collar, unhooked his breeches, and worked his length, and she ignited. Then, without warning, he grasped her ankles, dragged her to the end of the mattress, bent, and entered her in one powerful thrust.

And so the voluptuous assault commenced.

For the next three hours, Jason took Alex against the wall, on the floor, against the corner post of the footboard, bent over the washstand, in the bed, on the two-seater bench, atop the table, and in the overstuffed chair in the sitting room.

Later, they lounged in a much deserved, soothing hot bath.

Sitting between his legs, she rested her head to his chest and sighed, as he toyed with her nipple.

"I missed you." He pressed his lips to her temple.

"Really?" She squeezed his thighs. "I had not noticed."

"I wager you will, tonight, when I return from the debriefing." He caught the crest of her ear with his teeth. "As I shall make love to you, until dawn."

"Only until then?" She sniffed. "My captain can do better."

"What a demanding little thing I have married." He lifted her into his lap. "But I would have you no other way, love."

"Then consider that my welcome home gift to you." She shifted, found the perfect angle, and joined their bodies.

"That reminds me, I have my customary offering to your incomparable beauty." Leaning over the edge of the tub, he retrieved his rucksack, which rested on the floor, and drew a curious object from the bag. "For my bride, as I was at sea for our first such special occasion, as husband and wife."

"How remarkable." The octagonal-shaped box, made of mahogany, reminded her of their private apartment at Stratfield Manor. But the contents quite took her breath away. Clusters of colorful flowers filled the container, and a pink heart rested at the center, holding three delicate blooms. An outer circle boasted the phrase: *Forget me not when far away.* "Why, the flowers are comprised of tiny sea shells. Never have I seen anything like it."

"Then you are pleased?" Jason inquired, in an earnest tone.

"I love it—and you." True to his promise, her nautionnier knight never forgot her. Whenever he returned to England's shores, he always arrived with an expression of devotion. She peered over her shoulder and then kissed him. "Captain of my heart."

"How I live for that." He rocked his hips, she clenched her muscles, and he hissed, as he initiated the delicate dance. "And I would have been surprised were you familiar with such artwork, as it is a sailor's valentine. The tars make them for their sweethearts. When I first commissioned in the navy, I knew not where I belonged. As I was lowborn, I had nothing in common with the pedigreed midshipmen, but neither did I blend with the noncommissioned hands. An old kitchen mate taught me the craft, but I always threw them in the trash, as I had no sweetheart, so you are the lone recipient of my handiwork."

"Darling, I treasure it." She tilted, assumed control of the mating ritual, and he tensed beneath her. "But what is the significance of the three flowers, within the heart?"

"There is one for each of my loves." He quickened his pace, and the water sloshed. "You and our sons."

"Perhaps we should save this for our children, as it is the appropriate number, and you can make another one, just for me, on your next journey." She bit her lip and allowed the words to penetrate his thoughts.

"But we only have two—"

Alex knew the precise instant Jason realized the significance of her statement, as he stilled, and his countenance sobered. Then, to her unutterable amazement, he bowed his head and closed his eyes.

"Oh, no." With great care, she deposited the unique

valentine on the floor, twisted in his lap, and framed his face. "Jason, please. Do not cry, as this is most wonderful news."

"Sorry, darling. I missed this moment, with our first babes, and I fear you have turned me into a milksop." He chuckled, as a tear trailed his cheek. "So we have another Collingwood in the making?"

"That is all right, as I wept, too, when Dr. Handley made the confirmation." Now he favored her with an inexpressibly tender kiss, which he abruptly ceased, to her dismay.

"Sweetheart, while I adore my heirs, I would set the world at your feet, if you give me a daughter just like you." He hugged her tight. "My gorgeous wife, I am so glad I married you."

"But you have already given me the world." She nuzzled his neck. "And all I want is you."

Then, to her shock and confusion, he wrenched hard and held her at arm's length.

"Bloody hell, Alex, you should have told me of your pregnancy, given I just waylaid you, as a randy barbarian." Then Jason winced and raked his fingers through his hair. "And when I think of how I handled you, when I bent you over the washstand and took your bottom, I was deuced rough." Then he groaned. "And we broke the damned chair —really, you should have said something."

"What, and have you temper your delicious assault?" She glanced at the crumpled piece of furniture, which sat askew, with a broken leg and a splintered armrest dangling, and giggled. "Not a chance, and I can purchase another chair. But I shall never forget your genius maneuver, involving that new two-seater bench. Just thinking of it gives me shivers, and I can't wait to use it, again."

"I have a confession to make, as I cannot, in good

conscience, take credit for that gem of brilliance." He frowned and cupped her cheek. "Dirk gave me the idea, but I never should have employed that tactic, given your delicate state. Did I hurt you, angel?"

"No, as I enjoyed every minute of your naughty invasion." Now she rotated fully, bringing them chest-to-chest. Dropping her knees to either side of his thighs, she rocked, and he grabbed her derriere. With a shriek of elation, she rode her man hell-bent for leather to a fiery finish, as water splashed the carpet.

When she, at last, collapsed in Jason's embrace, he lifted her from the bath. With a towel, he dried her, as though she were a priceless treasure, and carried her to bed. As soon as her head hit the pillow, Alex dozed. Fanciful visions and whimsical vignettes invested her dreams, weaving a cherished future, which once had persisted only in the realm of fantasy. Minutes later, she roused, when Jason kissed her.

"Rest, my darling wife, as you need to recover." Garbed in gentleman's attire, he reached beneath the covers to caress her flat belly as he rubbed his nose to hers. "When I return from the debriefing, we will dine in our sitting room, whereupon I shall feed you every morsel, as you lounge in my lap, and then I intend to make love to you, gently, all night."

"We shall see about that, the gently part, I mean." She twined her fingers in the hair at the nape of his neck and pulled him close for another kiss. "And is that a promise?"

"You may depend upon it." Then he drew her lip into his mouth and suckled her tender flesh. "I love you, Alex."

On her bedside table, he had placed the precious sailor's valentine beside the miniature replica of the *Intrepid*, which he had given her at Stratfield Manor, and the journal in which she kept her collection of his original, ribald poetry.

Never had she journeyed without the irreplaceable keep-sakes. Countless times, during their unconventional courtship, she had envisioned such tender scenarios, and at last, Alex had won the much-desired prize. Cupping his cheek, she smiled. "And I love you, Captain of my heart."

ABOUT BARBARA DEVLIN

A proud Latina, USA Today bestselling author Barbara Devlin was born a storyteller, but it was a weeklong vacation to Bethany Beach, Delaware that forever changed her life. The little house her parents rented had a collection of books by Kathleen Woodiwiss, which exposed Barbara to the world of romance, and *Shanna* remains a personal favorite.

Barbara writes heartfelt historical romances that feature not so perfect heroes who may know how to seduce a woman but know nothing of marriage. And she prefers feisty but smart heroines who sometimes save the hero before they find their happily ever after.

Barbara is a disabled-in-the-line-of-duty retired police officer, and she earned an MA in English and continued a course of study for a Doctorate in Literature and Rhetoric. She happily considered herself an exceedingly eccentric English professor, until success in Indie publishing lured her into writing, full-time, featuring her fictional knighthood, the Brethren of the Coast.

Connect with Barbara Devlin at BarbaraDevlin.com, where you can sign up for her newsletter, The Knightly News.

ALSO BY BARBARA DEVLIN

BRETHREN OF THE COAST

Loving Lieutenant Douglas

Enter the Brethren

My Lady, the Spy

The Most Unlikely Lady

One-Knight Stand

Captain of Her Heart

The Lucky One

Love with an Improper Stranger

To Catch a Fallen Spy

Hold Me, Thrill Me, Kiss Me

The Duke Wears Nada

A Very Brethren Christmas

Owner of a Lonely Heart

BRETHREN ORIGINS

Arucard

Demetrius

Aristide

Morgan

Geoffrey

PIRATES OF THE COAST

The Black Morass

The Iron Corsair

The Buccaneer

The Stablemaster's Daughter

The Marooner

Once Upon a Christmas Knight

The Reaper

WORLD OF DE WOLFE PACK

Lone Wolfe

The Big Bad De Wolfe

Tall, Dark & De Wolfe

MAGICK TRILOGY

Magick, Straight Up

A Taste of Magick

Magick in the Air

PIRATES OF BRITANNIA

The Blood Reaver

THE MAD MATCHMAKING MEN OF WATERLOO

The Accidental Duke

The Accidental Groom